FINAL ACTS

FINAL ACTS

THEATRICAL MYSTERIES

Edited and Introduced by
Martin Edwards

Poisoned Pen
PRESS

Contents

Introduction

Crime writers utilise an extraordinarily wide range of backgrounds for their stories, but the stage is one of the most popular of them all. Stories set in—or connected with—the theatre, concert halls, or similar venues have entertained readers since the nineteenth century, and there is no sign of this changing. One of the main strengths of Janice Hallett's recent bestseller *The Appeal*, for instance, is that the story revolves around the members of a local amateur dramatic group who are involved with a production of Arthur Miller's *All My Sons*.

It's interesting to speculate why the stage exerts such an appeal for mystery writers. A minority of crime authors are themselves enthusiastic actors; this tradition goes back to the days of Wilkie Collins and Charles Dickens, who were keen amateur performers on the stage, and encompasses a wide range of twentieth-century crime novelists. They include Dulcie Gray (who played Miss Marple on the stage and whose own titles included *Epitaph for a Dead Actor* in 1960 and

Understudy to Murder in 1972) and the less celebrated Fiona Sinclair, whose tragic early death in 1961 deprived crime fiction of an emerging talent. Alex Atkinson was an actor whose solitary venture into mystery fiction, *Exit Charlie*, was published in 1955 and remains a good read. V. C. Clinton-Baddeley was a playwright as well as an actor who turned to writing traditional detective novels late in life; his final mystery, *To Study a Long Silence*, posthumously published in 1972, takes its title from John Webster and makes good use of his knowledge of the performing arts.

Simon Brett, a former president of Oxford University Dramatic Society, proceeded to achieve sustained success as a playwright and as a prolific author, not least of the wonderfully entertaining Charles Paris series, which includes such witty titles as *Cast, in Order of Disappearance* (1975) and *Not Dead, Only Resting* (1984). The contemporary American popular singer and composer Rupert Holmes, whose CV includes a superb murder mystery musical *about* a musical, *Curtains*, makes effective use of his understanding of the world of showbiz in his novel *Where the Truth Lies*, which was filmed by Atom Egoyan in 2005.

Ngaio Marsh was an accomplished exponent of detective fiction in the Golden Age vein, but there is no doubt that the first love of Roderick Alleyn's creator was the theatre, a field in which she achieved distinction. Her intimate knowledge of the theatre enabled her to use the world of the stage convincingly in several of Alleyn's cases, including *Opening Night* and *Vintage Murder*, which is set in her native New Zealand.

Josephine Tey is the pen-name by which another "Queen of Crime," Elizabeth MacKintosh, is today best remembered, not least in the form of an English Heritage blue plaque installed in 2022 on the building, which had housed the Mackintosh family fruit shop in Inverness. But she first came to prominence writing under the pseudonym Gordon Daviot, whose 1932 play *Richard of Bordeaux* ran for over a year in the West End and made a star of John Gielgud. Her love of the theatre spills over into some of her detective fiction; in her debut mystery, *The Man in the Queue*, the queue in question is outside a theatre, while an actress is drowned in *A Shilling for Candles*, a story which benefits from her inside knowledge of the theatrical world.

The most commercially successful female playwright in history is none other than Agatha Christie. Murder mystery plays constitute a subject in themselves (explored in depth by Amnon Kabatchnik in a series of massive and highly informative tomes, *Blood on the Stage*) and Christie's *The Mousetrap* is legendary for its longevity, while *Witness for the Prosecution* is a superb courtroom drama. *Three-Act Tragedy* is a Hercule Poirot novel that weaves the theatrical into the storyline with breathtaking ingenuity; to say much more would be a spoiler, but the book is an underestimated example of her mastery of her craft. There is also an important theatrical component in another of Poirot's cases, *Lord Edgware Dies*.

Shakespearean references abound in the Christie canon and in crime fiction generally. Clifford Witting's *Measure for Murder*, for instance, is set around an am dram version of *Measure for Measure*, while there are no prizes for guessing the title of the play which is the subject of a school production in Michael Gilbert's excellent crime novel *The Night of the Twelfth*.

Many writers have taken advantage of the fact that the theatre and the concert hall offer marvellous opportunities for a dramatic murder; the same is, of course, true in film and television, as with Alfred Hitchcock's two versions of *The Man Who Knew Too Much*. The opportunities are not only endless, but also infinitely varied. Take, for instance, two American crime novels which appeared close together in time (1929 and 1931) but which could hardly be more different in terms of content and style. Ellery Queen's debut whodunit, *The Roman Hat Mystery*, is a cerebral puzzle concerning the death of a lawyer who is a member of a theatre audience. Raoul Whitfield's *Death in a Bowl* concerns the killing of maestro Hans Reiner at the Hollywood Bowl, which gives rise to another case for Ben Jardinn, a tough Los Angeles detective. The novel is a minor classic of the hardboiled sub-genre and a world away from the good-natured gentility of Sebastian Farr's *Death on the Down Beat* and Cyril Hare's *When the Wind Blows*, both of which see murder committed at a concert.

Actors regularly pop up as characters in murder mysteries, no doubt because their chameleon skills are very useful in stories in which imposture and identity switches form a key ingredient. Occasionally they operate as amateur detectives; Charles Paris is one prominent example, while Anne Morice's Tessa Crichton, although less well-known, enjoyed a lengthy career as a sleuth. In Ruth Rendell's best-selling series about the Sussex cop Reg Wexford, a key presence in the supporting cast is his daughter Sheila, a successful actress who plays a significant part in several of the novels.

Short stories set in the world of the stage are not quite as plentiful, but in this anthology I have endeavoured to provide a mix of mysteries featuring famous crime writers and also those who are long-forgotten. I'm grateful to Nigel Moss, Jamie Sturgeon, and John Cooper for their suggestions and advice and also to everyone at the British Library who helped to bring this collection to life.

Martin Edwards
www.martinedwardsbooks.com

A Note from the Publisher

The original novels and short stories reprinted in the British Library Crime Classics series were written and published in a period ranging, for the most part, from the 1890s to the 1960s. There are many elements of these stories which continue to entertain modern readers; however, in some cases there are also uses of language, instances of stereotyping, and some attitudes expressed by narrators or characters which may not be endorsed by the publishing standards of today. We acknowledge that some elements in the works selected for reprinting may make uncomfortable reading for some of our audience. With this series British Library Publishing and Poisoned Pen Press aim to offer a new readership a chance to read some of the rare books of the British Library's collections in an affordable paperback format, to enjoy their merits, and to look back into the world of the twentieth century as portrayed by its writers. It is not possible to separate these stories from the history of their writing and, as such, the following stories are presented as they were originally published with the inclusion of minor edits made for consistency of style and sense, and with pejorative terms of an extremely offensive nature partly obscured. We welcome feedback from our readers.

The Affair at the Novelty Theatre

Baroness Orczy

Baroness Orczy (1865–1947) was a native of Hungary whose family moved to Britain whilst she was a teenager. Her full name was Emma Magdolna Rozália Mária Jozefa Borbála Orczy de Orc, although her friends called her Emmuska. She married the son of an English clergyman in 1894, and nine years later the couple collaborated on a play, *The Scarlet Pimpernel*, based on one of her historical short stories. The hero was Sir Percy Blakeney, who helped French aristocrats to escape the wrath of the revolutionaries. The play enjoyed great success on the West End, running for four years. A long sequence of novels featuring the Pimpernel followed, making Orczy so rich that she left English shores for Monte Carlo. Her other work for the theatre included a play, *Beau Brocade*, based on a novel of the same name.

Her most intriguing sleuth was "The Old Man in the Corner," who features in "The Affair at the Novelty Theatre." The story first appeared in the *Royal Magazine* and was subsequently edited and included in the collection *The Case of*

Miss Elliott (1905) from which the following text has been sourced. In the twenty-first century, Rachel Laurence and Sandra Hunt adapted Orczy's short stories about a female detective for the stage, touring *Lady Molly of Scotland Yard* around England to considerable acclaim.

———

"TALKING OF MYSTERIES," SAID THE MAN IN THE CORNER, rather irrelevantly, for he had not opened his mouth since he sat down and ordered his lunch, "talking of mysteries, it is always a puzzle to me how few thefts are committed in the dressing-rooms of fashionable actresses during a performance."

"There have been one or two," I suggested, "but nothing of any value was stolen."

"Yet you remember that affair at the Novelty Theatre a year or two ago, don't you?" he added. "It created a great deal of sensation at the time. You see, Miss Phyllis Morgan was, and still is, a very fashionable and popular actress, and her pearls are quite amongst the wonders of the world. She herself valued them at £10,000, and several experts who remember the pearls quite concur with that valuation.

"During the period of her short tenancy of the Novelty Theatre last season, she entrusted those beautiful pearls to Mr. Kidd, the well-known Bond Street jeweller, to be re-strung. There were seven rows of perfectly matched pearls, held together by a small diamond clasp of 'art-nouveau' design.

"Kidd and Co. are, as you know, a very eminent and old-established firm of jewellers. Mr. Thomas Kidd, its present sole representative, was some time president of the London Chamber of Commerce, and a man whose integrity has always been held to be above suspicion. His clerks, salesmen, and book-keeper had all been in his employ for years, and most of the work was executed on the premises.

"In the case of Miss Phyllis Morgan's valuable pearls, they were re-strung and re-set in the back shop by Mr. Kidd's most valued and most trusted workman, a man named James Rumford, who is justly considered to be one of the cleverest craftsmen here in England.

"When the pearls were ready, Mr. Kidd himself took them down to the theatre, and delivered them into Miss Morgan's own hands.

"It appears that the worthy jeweller was extremely fond of the theatre; but, like so many persons in affluent circumstances, he was also very fond of getting a free seat when he could.

"All along he had made up his mind to take the pearls down to the Novelty Theatre one night, and to see Miss Morgan for a moment before the performance; she would then, he hoped, place a stall at his disposal.

"His previsions were correct. Miss Morgan received the pearls, and Mr. Kidd was on that celebrated night accommodated with a seat in the stalls.

"I don't know if you remember all the circumstances connected with that case, but, to make my point clear, I must remind you of one or two of the most salient details.

"In the drama in which Miss Phyllis Morgan was acting at the time, there is a brilliant masked ball scene which is the crux of the whole play; it occurs in the second act, and Miss Phyllis Morgan, as the hapless heroine dressed in the shabbiest of clothes, appears in the midst of a gay and giddy throng; she apostrophises all and sundry there, including the villain, and has a magnificent scene which always brings down the house, and nightly adds to her histrionic laurels.

"For this scene a large number of supers are engaged, and in order to further swell the crowd, practically all the available stage hands have to 'walk on' dressed in various coloured dominoes, and all wearing masks.

"You have, of course, heard the name of Mr. Howard Dennis in connection with this extraordinary mystery. He is what is usually called 'a young man about town,' and was one of Miss Phyllis Morgan's most favoured admirers. As a matter of fact, he was generally understood to be the popular actress's *fiancée*, and as such, had of course the *entrée* of the Novelty Theatre.

"Like many another idle young men about town, Mr. Howard Dennis was stage-mad, and one of his greatest delights was to don nightly a mask and a blue domino, and to 'walk on' in the second act, not so much in order to gratify his love for the stage, as to watch Miss Phyllis Morgan in her great scene, and to be present, close by her, when she received her usual salvo of enthusiastic applause from a delighted public.

"On this eventful night—it was on 20th July last—the second act was in full swing; the supers, the stage hands, and all the principals were on the scene, the back of the stage was practically deserted. The beautiful pearls, fresh from the hands of Mr. Kidd, were in Miss Morgan's dressing-room, as she meant to wear them in the last act.

"Of course, since that memorable affair, many people have talked of the foolhardiness of leaving such valuable jewellery in the sole charge of a young girl—Miss Morgan's dresser—who acted with unpardonable folly and careless-ness, but you must remember that this part of the theatre is only accessible through the stage door, where sits enthroned that uncorruptible dragon, the stage door-keeper.

"No one can get at it from the front, and the dressing-rooms for the supers and lesser members of the company are on the opposite side of the stage to that reserved for Miss Morgan and one or two of the principals.

"It was just a quarter to ten, and the curtain was about to be rung down, when George Finch, the stage door-keeper, rushed excitedly into the wings; he was terribly upset, and was wildly clutching his coat, beneath which he evidently held something concealed.

"In response to the rapidly-whispered queries of the one or two stage hands that stood about, Finch only shook his head excitedly. He seemed scarcely able to control his impatience, during the close of the act, and the subsequent prolonged applause.

"When at last Miss Morgan, flushed with her triumph, came off the stage, Finch made a sudden rush for her.

"'Oh, Madam!' he gasped excitedly, 'it might have been such an awful misfortune! The rascal! I nearly got him, though! but he escaped—fortunately it is safe—I have got it—!'

"It was some time before Miss Morgan understood what in the world the otherwise sober stage door-keeper was driving at. Every one who heard him certainly thought that he had been drinking. But the next moment from under his coat he pulled out, with another ejaculation of excitement, the magnificent pearl necklace which Miss Morgan had thought safely put away in her dressing-room.

"'What in the world does all this mean?' asked Mr. Howard Dennis, who, as usual, was escorting his *fiancée*. 'Finch, what are you doing with Madam's necklace?'

"Miss Phyllis Morgan herself was too bewildered to question Finch; she gazed at him, then at her necklace, in speechless astonishment.

"'Well, you see, Madam, it was this way,' Finch managed to explain at last, as with awestruck reverence he finally deposited the precious necklace in the actress's hands. 'As you know, Madam, it is a very hot night. I had seen every one into the theatre and counted in the supers; there was nothing much for me to do, and I got rather tired and very thirsty. I seed a man loafing close to the door, and I ask him to fetch me a pint of beer from round the corner, and I give him some coppers; I had noticed him loafing round before, and it was so hot I didn't think I was doin' no harm.'

"'No, no,' said Miss Morgan impatiently. 'Well!'

"'Well,' continued Finch, 'the man, he brought me the beer, and I had some of it—and—and—afterwards, I don't quite know how it happened—it was the heat, perhaps—but—I was sitting in my box, and I suppose I must have dropped asleep. I just remember hearing the ring up for the second act, and the call-boy calling you, Madam, then there's a sort of a blank in my mind. All of a sudden I seemed to wake with the feeling that there was something wrong somehow. In a moment I jumped up, and I tell you I was wide awake then, and I saw a man sneaking down the passage, past my box, towards the door. I challenged him, and he tried to dart past me, but I was too quick for him, and got him by the tails of his coat, for I saw at once that he was carrying something, and I had recognised the loafer who brought me the beer. I shouted for help, but there's never anybody about in this back street, and the loafer, he struggled like old Harry, and sure enough he managed to get free from me and away before I could stop him, but in his fright the rascal dropped his booty, for which Heaven be praised! and it was your pearls, Madam. Oh, my! but I did have a tussle,' concluded the worthy door-keeper, mopping his forehead, 'and I do hope, Madam, the scoundrel didn't take nothing else.'

"That was the story," continued the man in the corner, "which George Finch had to tell, and which he subsequently repeated without the slightest deviation. Miss Phyllis Morgan, with the light-heartedness peculiar to ladies of her profession, took the matter very quietly; all she said at the time was that she had nothing else of value in her dressing-room, but that Miss Knight—the dresser—deserved a scolding for leaving the room unprotected.

"'All's well that ends well,' she said gaily, as she finally went into her dressing-room, carrying the pearls in her hand.

"It appears that the moment she opened the door, she found Miss Knight sitting in the room, in a deluge of tears. The girl had overheard George Finch telling his story, and was terribly upset at her own carelessness.

"In answer to Miss Morgan's questions, she admitted that she had gone into the wings, and lingered there to watch the great actress's beautiful performance. She thought no one could possibly get to the dressing-room, as nearly all hands were on the stage at the time, and of course George Finch was guarding the door.

"However, as there really had been no harm done, beyond a wholesome fright to everybody concerned, Miss Morgan readily forgave the girl and proceeded with her change of attire for the next act. Incidentally she noticed a bunch of roses, which were placed on her dressing-table, and asked Knight who had put them there.

"'Mr. Dennis brought them,' replied the girl.

"Miss Morgan looked pleased, blushed, and dismissing the whole matter from her mind, she proceeded with her toilette for the next act, in which, the hapless heroine having come into her own again, she was able to wear her beautiful pearls around her neck.

"George Finch, however, took some time to recover himself; his indignation was only equalled by his volubility. When his excitement had somewhat subsided, he took the precaution of saving the few drops of beer which had remained at the bottom of the mug, brought to him by the loafer. This was subsequently shown to a chemist in the neighbourhood, who, without a moment's hesitation, pronounced the beer to contain an appreciable quantity of chloral."

———

"The whole matter, as you may imagine, did not affect Miss Morgan's spirits that night," continued the man in the corner, after a slight pause.

"'All's well that ends well,' she had said gaily, since almost by a miracle, her pearls were once more safely round her neck.

"But the next day brought the rude awakening. Something had indeed happened which made the affair at the Novelty Theatre, what it has ever since remained, a curious and unexplainable mystery.

"The following morning Miss Phyllis Morgan decided that it was foolhardy to leave valuable property about in her dressing-room, when, for stage purposes, imitation jewellery did just as well. She therefore determined to place her pearls in the bank until the termination of her London season.

"The moment, however, that, in broad daylight, she once more handled the necklace, she instinctively felt that there was something wrong with it. She examined it eagerly and closely, and, hardly daring to face her sudden terrible suspicions, she rushed round to the nearest jeweller, and begged him to examine the pearls.

"The examination did not take many moments: the jeweller at once pronounced the pearls to be false. There could be no doubt about it; the necklace was a perfect imitation of the original, even the clasp was an exact copy. Half-hysterical with rage and anxiety, Miss Morgan at once drove to Bond Street, and asked to see Mr. Kidd.

"Well, you may easily imagine the stormy interview that took place. Miss Phyllis Morgan, in no measured language, boldly accused Mr. Thomas Kidd, late president of the London Chamber of Commerce, of having substituted false pearls for her own priceless ones.

"The worthy jeweller, at first completely taken by surprise, examined the necklace, and was horrified to see that Miss Morgan's statements were, alas! too true. Mr. Kidd was indeed in a terribly awkward position.

"The evening before, after business hours, he had taken the necklace home with him. Before starting for the theatre, he had examined it to see that it was quite in order. He had then, with his own hands, and in the presence of his wife, placed it in its case, and driven straight to the Novelty, where he finally gave it over to Miss Morgan herself.

"To all this he swore most positively; moreover, all his *employés* and workmen could swear that they had last seen the necklace just after closing time at the shop, when Mr. Kidd walked off towards Piccadilly, with the precious article in the inner pocket of his coat.

"One point certainly was curious, and undoubtedly helped to deepen the mystery which to this day clings to the affair at the Novelty Theatre.

"When Mr. Kidd handed the packet containing the necklace to Miss Morgan, she was too busy to open it at once. She only spoke to Mr. Kidd through her dressing-room door, and never opened the packet till nearly an hour later, after she was dressed ready for the second act; the packet at that time had been untouched, and was wrapped up just as she had had it from Mr. Kidd's own hands. She undid the packet, and handled the pearls; certainly, by the artificial light she could see nothing wrong with the necklace.

"Poor Mr. Kidd was nearly distracted with the horror of his position. Thirty years of an honest reputation suddenly tarnished with this awful suspicion—for he realised at once that Miss Morgan refused to believe his statements; in fact, she openly said that she would—unless immediate compensation was made to her—place the matter at once in the hands of the police.

"From the stormy interview in Bond Street, the irate actress drove at once to Scotland Yard; but the old-established firm of Kidd and Co. was not destined to remain under any cloud that threatened its integrity.

"Mr. Kidd at once called upon his solicitor, with the result that an offer was made to Miss Morgan, whereby the jeweller would deposit the full value of the original necklace, *i.e.* £10,000, in the hands of Messrs Bentley and Co., bankers, that sum to be held by them for a whole year, at the end of which time, if the perpetrator of the fraud had not been discovered, the money was to be handed over to Miss Morgan in its entirety.

"Nothing could have been more fair, more equitable, or more just, but at the same time nothing could have been more mysterious.

"As Mr. Kidd swore that he had placed the real pearls in Miss Morgan's hands, and was ready to back his oath by the sum of £10,000, no more suspicion could possibly attach to him. When the announcement of his generous offer appeared in the papers, the entire public approved and exonerated him, and then turned to wonder who the perpetrator of the daring fraud had been.

"How came a valueless necklace in exact imitation of the original one to be in Miss Morgan's dressing-room? Where were the real pearls? Clearly the loafer who had drugged the stage door-keeper, and sneaked into the theatre to steal a necklace, was not aware that he was risking several years' hard labour for the sake of a worthless trifle. He had been one of the many dupes of this extraordinary adventure.

"Macpherson, one of the most able men on the detective staff, had, indeed, his work cut out. The police were extremely reticent, but, in spite of this, one or two facts gradually found their way into the papers, and aroused public interest and curiosity to its highest pitch.

"What had transpired was this:

"Clara Knight, the dresser, had been very rigorously

cross-questioned, and, from her many statements, the following seemed quite positive.

"After the curtain had rung up for the second act, and Miss Morgan had left her dressing-room, Knight had waited about for some time, and had even, it appears, handled and admired the necklace. Then, unfortunately, she was seized with the burning desire of seeing the famous scene from the wings. She thought that the place was quite safe, and that George Finch was as usual at his post.

"'I was going along the short passage that leads to the wings,' she exclaimed to the detectives, 'when I became aware of some one moving some distance behind me. I turned and saw a blue domino about to enter Miss Morgan's dressing-room.

"'I thought nothing of that,' continued the girl, 'as we all know that Mr. Dennis is engaged to Miss Morgan. He is very fond of "walking on" in the ball-room scene, and he always wears a blue domino when he does; so I was not at all alarmed. He had his mask on as usual, and he was carrying a bunch of roses. When he saw me at the other end of the passage, he waved his hand to me and pointed to the flowers. I nodded to him, and then he went into the room.'

"These statements, as you may imagine, created a great deal of sensation; so much so, in fact, that Mr. Kidd, with his £10,000 and his reputation in mind, moved heaven and earth to bring about the prosecution of Mr. Dennis for theft and fraud.

"The papers were full of it, for Mr. Howard Dennis was well known in fashionable London society. His answer to these curious statements was looked forward to eagerly; when it came it satisfied no one and puzzled everybody.

"'Miss Knight was mistaken,' he said most emphatically, 'I did not bring any roses for Miss Morgan that night. It was not I that she saw in a blue domino by the door, as I was on the stage before the curtain was rung up for the second act, and never left it until the close.'

"This part of Howard Dennis's statement was a little difficult to substantiate. No one on the stage could swear positively whether he was 'on' early in the act or not, although, mind you, Macpherson had ascertained that in the whole crowd of supers on the stage, he was the only one who wore a blue domino.

"Mr. Kidd was very active in the matter, but Miss Morgan flatly refused to believe in her *fiancée's* guilt. The worthy jeweller maintained that Mr. Howard Dennis was the only person who knew the celebrated pearls and their quaint clasp well enough to have a facsimile made of them, and that when Miss Knight saw him enter the dressing-room, he actually substituted the false necklace for the real one; whilst the loafer who drugged George Finch's beer was—as every one supposed—only a dupe.

"Things had reached a very acute and painful stage, when one more detail found its way into the papers, which, whilst entirely clearing Mr. Howard Dennis's character, has helped to make the whole affair a hopeless mystery.

"Whilst questioning George Finch, Macpherson had ascertained that the stage door-keeper had seen Mr. Dennis enter the theatre some time before the beginning of the celebrated second act. He stopped to speak to George Finch for a moment or two, and the latter could swear positively that Mr. Dennis was not carrying any roses then.

"On the other hand a flower-girl, who was selling roses in the neighbourhood of the Novelty Theatre late that memorable night, remembers selling some roses to a shabbily-dressed man, who looked like a labourer out of work. When Mr. Dennis was pointed out to her she swore positively that it was not he.

"'The man looked like a labourer,' she explained. 'I took particular note of him, as I remember thinking that he didn't look much as if he could afford to buy roses.'

"Now you see," concluded the man in the corner excitedly, "where the hitch lies. There is absolutely no doubt, judging from the evidence of George Finch and of the flower-girl, that the loafer had provided himself with the roses, and had somehow or other managed to get hold of a blue domino, for the purpose of committing the theft. His giving drugged beer to Finch, moreover, proved his guilt beyond a doubt.

"But here the mystery becomes hopeless," he added with a chuckle, "for the loafer dropped the booty which he had stolen—that booty was the false necklace, and it has remained an impenetrable mystery to this day as to who made the substitution and when.

"A whole year has elapsed since then, but the real necklace has never been traced or found; so Mr. Kidd has paid, with absolute quixotic chivalry, the sum of £10,000 to Miss Morgan, and thus he has completely cleared the firm of Kidd and Co. of any suspicion as to its integrity."

———

"But then, what in the world is the explanation of it all?" I asked bewildered, as the funny creature paused in his narrative and seemed absorbed in the contemplation of a beautiful knot he had just completed in his bit of string.

"The explanation is so simple," he replied, "for it is obvious, is it not, that only four people could possibly have committed the fraud?"

"Who are they?" I asked.

"Well," he said, whilst his bony fingers began to fidget with that eternal piece of string, "there is, of course, old Mr. Kidd; but as the worthy jeweller has paid £10,000 to prove that he did not steal the real necklace and substitute a false one in its stead, we must assume that he was guiltless. Then, secondly, there is Mr. Howard Dennis."

"Well, yes," I said, "what about him?"

"There were several points in his favour," he rejoined, marking each point with a fresh and most complicated knot; "it was not he who bought the roses, therefore it was not he who, clad in a blue domino, entered Miss Morgan's dressing-room directly after Knight left it.

"And mark the force of this point," he added excitedly.

"Just before the curtain rang up for the second act, Miss Morgan had been in her room, and had then undone the packet, which, in her own words, was just as she had received it from Mr. Kidd's hands.

"After that Miss Knight remained in charge, and a mere ten seconds after she left the room she saw the blue domino carrying the roses at the door.

"The flower-girl's story and that of George Finch have proved that the blue domino could not have been Mr. Dennis, but it was the loafer who eventually stole the false necklace.

"If you bear all this in mind you will realise that there was no time in those ten seconds for Mr. Dennis to have made the substitution *before* the theft was committed. It stands to reason that he could not have done it afterwards.

"Then, again, many people suspected Miss Knight, the dresser; but this supposition we may easily dismiss. An uneducated, stupid girl, not three-and-twenty, could not possibly have planned so clever a substitution. An imitation necklace of that particular calibre and made to order would cost far more money than a poor theatrical dresser could ever afford: let alone the risks of ordering such an ornament to be made.

"No," said the funny creature, with comic emphasis, "there is but one theory possible, which is my own."

"And that is?" I asked eagerly.

"The workman, Rumford, of course," he responded triumphantly. "Why! it jumps to the eyes, as our French friends would tell us. Who, other than he, could have the opportunity of making an exact copy of the necklace which had been entrusted to his firm?

"Being in the trade he could easily obtain the false stones without exciting any undue suspicion; being a skilled craftsman, he could easily make the clasp, and string the pearls in exact imitation of the original: he could do this secretly in his own home and without the slightest risk.

"Then the plan, though extremely simple, was very cleverly thought out. Disguised as the loafer—"

"The loafer!" I exclaimed.

"Why, yes! the loafer," he replied quietly, "disguised as the loafer, he hung round the stage door of the Novelty after business hours, until he had collected the bits of gossip and information he wanted; thus he learnt that Mr. Howard Dennis was Miss Morgan's accredited *fiancée*; that he, like everybody else who was available, 'walked on' in the second act; and that during that time the back of the stage was practically deserted.

"No doubt he knew all along that Mr. Kidd meant to take the pearls down to the theatre himself that night, and it was quite easy to ascertain that Miss Morgan—as the hapless heroine—wore no jewellery in the second act, and that Mr. Howard Dennis invariably wore a blue domino.

"Some people might incline to the belief that Miss Knight was a paid accomplice, that she left the dressing-room unprotected on purpose, and that her story of the blue domino and the roses was prearranged between herself and Rumford, but that is not my opinion.

"I think that the scoundrel was far too clever to need any accomplice, and too shrewd to put himself thereby at the mercy of a girl like Knight.

"Rumford, I find, is a married man: this to me explains the blue domino, which the police were never able to trace to any business place, where it might have been bought or hired. Like the necklace itself, it was 'homemade.'

"Having got his properties and his plans ready, Rumford then set to work. You must remember that a stage doorkeeper is never above accepting a glass of beer from a friendly acquaintance; and, no doubt, if George Finch had not asked the loafer to bring him a glass, the latter would have offered him one. To drug the beer was simple enough; then Rumford went to buy the roses, and, I should say, met his wife somewhere round the corner, who handed him the blue domino and the mask; all this was done in order to completely puzzle the police subsequently, and also in order to throw suspicion, if possible, upon young Dennis.

"As soon as the drug took effect upon George Finch, Rumford slipped into the theatre. To slip a mask and domino on and off is, as you know, a matter of a few seconds. Probably his intention had been—if he found Knight in the room—to knock her down if she attempted to raise an alarm; but here fortune favoured him. Knight saw him from a distance, and mistook him easily for Mr. Dennis.

"After the theft of the real necklace, Rumford sneaked out of the theatre. And here you see how clever was the scoundrel's plan: if he had merely substituted one necklace for another there would have been no doubt whatever that the loafer—whoever he was—was the culprit—the drugged beer would have been quite sufficient proof for that. The hue and cry would have been after the loafer, and, who knows? there might have been some one or something which might have identified that loafer with himself.

"He must have bought the shabby clothes somewhere, he certainly bought the roses from a flower-girl; anyhow, there were a hundred and one little risks and contingencies which might have brought the theft home to him.

"But mark what happens: he steals the real necklace, and keeps the false one in his hand, intending to drop it sooner or later, and thus sent the police entirely on the wrong scent. As the loafer, he was supposed to have stolen the false necklace, then dropped it whilst struggling with George Finch. The result is that no one has troubled about the loafer; no one thought that he had anything to do with the substitution, which was the main point at issue, and no very great effort has ever been made to find that mysterious loafer.

"It never occurred to any one that the fraud and the theft were committed by one and the same person, and that that person could be none other than James Rumford."

1917

The Affair at the Semiramis Hotel

A. E. W. Mason

If anyone deserves to be described as a Renaissance Man, surely it is Alfred Edward Woodley Mason (1865–1948). Mason was, amongst other things, a novelist, playwright, biographer, mountaineer, traveller, a Member of Parliament— and even a spy. Although he was offered a knighthood, he turned it down. He was educated at Dulwich College and Cambridge and then became an actor with the Compton Comedy Company. Before long he was writing plays, while his first novel appeared in 1895; this was *A Romance of Wastdale*, which—like much of his output—was subsequently filmed. His work for the stage includes *The Witness for the Defence*, premiered in London in 1911; he adapted the play into a novel, which was filmed in 1919.

In the field of crime fiction, he made a considerable impression, despite being far from prolific. Above all he is remembered as the creator of Inspector Hanaud, who first appeared in *At the Villa Rose* in 1910. Hanaud eventually returned in "The Affair at the Semiramis Hotel," which was published in a magazine called *The Story-Teller* in March 1917 before being collected in *The Four Corners of the World*; in the USA, it appeared as a stand-alone novella. Mason originally intended to develop the plot into a screenplay called *The Carnival Ball*, but when that project proved abortive, he adapted the material into this story. Four more Hanaud novels appeared at intervals, the final title being *The House in Lordship Lane* (1946).

———

MR. RICARDO, WHEN THE EXCITEMENTS OF THE VILLA ROSE were done with, returned to Grosvenor Square and resumed the busy, unnecessary life of an amateur. But the studios had lost their savour, artists their attractiveness, and even the Russian opera seemed a trifle flat. Life was altogether a disappointment; Fate, like an actress at a restaurant, had taken the wooden pestle in her hand and stirred all the sparkle out of the champagne; Mr. Ricardo languished—until one unforgettable morning.

He was sitting disconsolately at his breakfast-table when the door was burst open and a square, stout man, with the blue, shaven face of a French comedian, flung himself into the room. Ricardo sprang towards the new-comer with a cry of delight.

"My dear Hanaud!"

He seized his visitor by the arm, feeling it to make sure that here, in flesh and blood, stood the man who had introduced him to the acutest sensations of his life. He turned towards his butler, who was still bleating expostulations in the doorway at the unceremonious irruption of the French detective.

"Another place, Burton, at once," he cried, and as soon as he and Hanaud were alone: "What good wind blows you to London?"

"Business, my friend. The disappearance of bullion somewhere on the line between Paris and London. But it is finished. Yes, I take a holiday."

A light had suddenly flashed in Mr. Ricardo's eyes, and was now no less suddenly extinguished. Hanaud paid no attention whatever to his friend's disappointment. He pounced upon a piece of silver which adorned the tablecloth and took it over to the window.

"Everything is as it should be, my friend," he exclaimed, with a grin. "Grosvenor Square, *The Times* open at the money column, and a false antique upon the table. Thus I have dreamed of you. All Mr. Ricardo is in that sentence."

Ricardo laughed nervously. Recollection made him wary of Hanaud's sarcasms. He was shy even to protest the genuineness of his silver. But, indeed, he had not the time. For the door opened again and once more the butler appeared. On this occasion, however, he was alone.

"Mr. Calladine would like to speak to you, sir," he said.

"Calladine!" cried Ricardo in an extreme surprise. "That is the most extraordinary thing." He looked at the clock upon his mantelpiece. It was barely half-past eight. "At this hour, too?"

"Mr. Calladine is still wearing evening dress," the butler remarked.

Ricardo started in his chair. He began to dream of possibilities; and here was Hanaud miraculously at his side.

"Where is Mr. Calladine?" he asked.

"I have shown him into the library."

"Good," said Mr. Ricardo. "I will come to him."

But he was in no hurry. He sat and let his thoughts play with this incident of Calladine's early visit.

"It is very odd," he said. "I have not seen Calladine for months—no, nor has anyone. Yet, a little while ago, no one was more often seen."

He fell apparently into a muse, but he was merely seeking to provoke Hanaud's curiosity. In this attempt, however, he failed. Hanaud continued placidly to eat his breakfast, so that Mr. Ricardo was compelled to volunteer the story which he was burning to tell.

"Drink your coffee, Hanaud, and you shall hear about Calladine."

Hanaud grunted with resignation, and Mr. Ricardo flowed on:

"Calladine was one of England's young men. Everybody said so. He was going to do very wonderful things as soon as he had made up his mind exactly what sort of wonderful things he was going to do. Meanwhile, you met him in Scotland, at Newmarket, at Ascot, at Cowes, in the box of some great lady at the Opera—not before half-past ten in the evening *there*—in any fine house where the candles that night happened to be lit. He went everywhere, and then a day came and he went nowhere. There was no scandal, no trouble, not a whisper against his good name. He simply vanished. For a little while a few people asked: 'What has become of Calladine?' But there never was any answer, and London has no time for unanswered questions. Other promising young men dined in his place. Calladine had joined the huge legion of the Come-to-nothings. No one even seemed to pass him in the street.

Now unexpectedly, at half-past eight in the morning, and in evening dress, he calls upon me. 'Why?' I ask myself."

Mr. Ricardo sank once more into a reverie. Hanaud watched him with a broadening smile of pure enjoyment.

"And in time, I suppose," he remarked casually, "you will perhaps ask him?"

Mr. Ricardo sprang out of his pose to his feet.

"Before I discuss serious things with an acquaintance," he said with a scathing dignity, "I make it a rule to revive my impressions of his personality. The cigarettes are in the crystal box."

"They would be," said Hanaud, unabashed, as Ricardo stalked from the room. But in five minutes Mr. Ricardo came running back, all his composure gone.

"It is the greatest good fortune that you, my friend, should have chosen this morning to visit me," he cried, and Hanaud nodded with a little grimace of resignation.

"There goes my holiday. You shall command me now and always. I will make the acquaintance of your young friend."

He rose up and followed Ricardo into his study where a young man was nervously pacing the floor.

"Mr. Calladine," said Ricardo, "this is Mr. Hanaud."

The young man turned eagerly. He was tall, with a noticeable elegance and distinction, and the face which he showed to Hanaud was, in spite of its agitation, remarkably handsome.

"I am very glad," he said. "You are not an official of this country. You can advise—without yourself taking action, if you'll be so good."

Hanaud frowned. He bent his eyes uncompromisingly upon Calladine.

"What does that mean?" he asked, with a note of sternness in his voice.

"It means, that I must tell someone," Calladine burst out in quivering tones, "that I don't know what to do. I am in a difficulty too big for me. That's the truth."

Hanaud looked at the young man keenly. It seemed to Ricardo that he took in every excited gesture, every twitching feature in one comprehensive glance. Then he said in a friendlier voice:

"Sit down and tell me"—and he himself drew up a chair to the table.

"I was at the Semiramis last night," said Calladine, naming one of the great hotels upon the Embankment. "There was a fancy-dress ball."

All this happened, by the way, in those far-off days before the war—nearly, in fact, three years ago today—when London, flinging aside its reticence, its shy self-consciousness, had become a city of carnivals and masquerades, rivalling its neighbours on the Continent in the spirit of its gaiety, and exceeding them by its stupendous luxury. "I went by the merest chance. My rooms are in the Adelphi Terrace."

"There!" cried Mr. Ricardo in surprise, and Hanaud lifted a hand to check his interruptions.

"Yes," continued Calladine. "The night was warm, the music floated through my open windows and stirred old memories. I happened to have a ticket. I went."

Calladine drew up a chair opposite to Hanaud, and seating himself, told, with many nervous starts and in troubled tones, a story which, to Mr. Ricardo's thinking, was as fabulous as any out of the *Arabian Nights*.

"I had a ticket," he began, "but no domino. I was consequently stopped by an attendant in the lounge at the top of the staircase leading down to the ball-room.

"'You can hire a domino in the cloak-room, Mr. Calladine,' he said to me. I had already begun to regret the impulse which had brought me, and I welcomed the excuse with which the absence of a costume provided me. I was, indeed, turning back to the door, when a girl who had at that moment run down from the stairs of the hotel into the lounge, cried gaily: 'That's not necessary'; and at the same moment she flung to me a long scarlet cloak which she had been wearing over her own dress. She was young, fair, rather tall, slim, and very pretty; her hair was drawn back from her face with a ribbon, and rippled down her shoulders in heavy curls; and she was dressed in a satin coat and knee-breeches of pale green and gold, with a white waistcoat and silk stockings and scarlet heels to her satin shoes. She was as straight-limbed as a boy, and exquisite like a figure in Dresden china. I caught the cloak and turned to thank her. But she did not wait. With a laugh she ran down the stairs, a supple and shining figure, and was lost in the throng at the doorway of the ball-room. I was stirred by the prospect of an adventure. I ran down after her. She was standing just inside the room alone, and she was gazing at the scene with parted lips and dancing eyes. She laughed again as she saw the cloak about my shoulders, a delicious gurgle of amusement, and I said to her:

"'May I dance with you?'

"'Oh, do!' she cried, with a little jump, and clasping her hands. She was of a high and joyous spirit and not difficult in the matter of an introduction. 'This gentleman will do very well to present us,' she said, leading me in front of a bust of the God Pan, which stood in a niche of the wall. 'I am, as you see, straight out of an opera. My name is Celymène or anything with an eighteenth century sound to it. You are—what you will. For this evening we are friends.'

"'And for tomorrow?' I asked.

"'I will tell you about that later on,' she replied, and she began to dance with a light step and a passion in her dancing which earned me many an envious glance from the other men. I was in luck, for Celymène knew no one, and though, of course, I saw the faces of a great many people whom I remembered, I kept them all at a distance. We had been dancing for about half an hour when the first queerish thing happened. She stopped suddenly in the midst of a sentence with a little gasp. I spoke to her, but she did not hear. She was gazing past me, her eyes wide open, and such a rapt look upon her face as I had never seen. She was lost in a miraculous vision. I followed the direction of her eyes and, to my astonishment, I saw nothing more than a stout, short, middle-aged woman, egregiously over-dressed as Marie Antoinette.

"'So you do know someone here?' I said, and I had to repeat the words sharply before my friend withdrew her eyes. But even then she was not aware of me. It was as if a voice had spoken to her whilst she was asleep and had disturbed, but not wakened her. Then she came to—there's really no other word I can think of which describes her at that moment—she came to with a deep sigh.

"'No,' she answered. 'She is a Mrs. Blumenstein from Chicago, a widow with ambitions and a great deal of money. But I don't know her.'

"'Yet you know all about her,' I remarked.

"'She crossed in the same boat with me,' Celymène replied. 'Did I tell you that I landed at Liverpool this morning? She is staying at the Semiramis too. Oh, let us dance!'

"She twitched my sleeve impatiently, and danced with a kind of violence and wildness as if she wished to banish some sinister thought. And she did undoubtedly banish it. We supped together and grew confidential, as under such conditions people will. She told me her real name. It was Joan Carew.

"'I have come over to get an engagement if I can at Covent Garden. I am supposed to sing all right. But I don't know anyone. I have been brought up in Italy.'

"'You have some letters of introduction, I suppose?' I asked.

"'Oh, yes. One from my teacher in Milan. One from an American manager.'

"In my turn I told her my name and where I lived, and I gave her my card. I thought, you see, that since I used to know a good many operatic people, I might be able to help her.

"'Thank you,' she said, and at that moment Mrs. Blumenstein, followed by a party, chiefly those lapdog young men who always seem to gather about that kind of person, came into the supper-room and took a table close to us. There was at once an end of all confidences—indeed, of all conversation. Joan Carew lost all the lightness of her spirit; she talked at random, and her eyes were drawn again and again to the grotesque slander on Marie Antoinette. Finally I became annoyed.

"'Shall we go?' I suggested impatiently, and to my surprise she whispered passionately:

"'Yes. Please! Let us go.'

"Her voice was actually shaking, her small hands clenched. We went back to the ball-room, but Joan Carew did not recover her gaiety, and halfway through a dance, when we were near to the door, she stopped abruptly—extraordinarily abruptly.

"'I shall go,' she said abruptly. 'I am tired. I have grown dull.'

"I protested, but she made a little grimace.

"'You'll hate me in half an hour. Let's be wise and stop now whilst we are friends,' she said, and as I removed the domino from my shoulders she stooped very quickly. It seemed to me that she picked up something which had lain hidden beneath the sole of her slipper. She certainly moved her foot, and I certainly saw something small and bright flash in the palm of her glove as she raised herself again. But I imagined merely that it was some object which she had dropped.

"'Yes, we'll go,' she said, and we went up the stairs into the lobby. Undoubtedly all the sparkle had gone out of our adventure. I recognised her wisdom.

"'But I shall meet you again?' I asked.

"'Yes. I have your address. I'll write and fix a time when you will be sure to find me in. Good-night, and a thousand thanks. I should have been bored to tears if you hadn't come without a domino.'

"She was speaking lightly as she held out her hand, but her grip tightened a little and—clung. Her eyes darkened and grew troubled, her mouth trembled. The shadow of a great trouble had suddenly closed about her. She shivered.

"'I am half inclined to ask you to stay, however dull I am; and dance with me till daylight—the safe daylight,' she said.

"It was an extraordinary phrase for her to use, and it moved me.

"'Let us go back then!' I urged. She gave me an impression suddenly of someone quite forlorn. But Joan Carew recovered her courage. 'No, no,' she answered quickly. She snatched her hand away and ran lightly up the staircase, turning at the corner to wave her hand and smile. It was then half-past one in the morning."

So far Calladine had spoken without an interruption. Mr. Ricardo, it is true, was bursting to break in with the most important questions, but a salutary fear of Hanaud restrained him. Now, however, he had an opportunity, for Calladine paused.

"Half-past one," he said sagely. "Ah!"

"And when did you go home?" Hanaud asked of Calladine.

"True," said Mr. Ricardo. "It is of the greatest consequence."

Calladine was not sure. His partner had left behind her the strangest medley of sensations in his breast. He was puzzled, haunted, and charmed. He had to think about her; he was a trifle uplifted; sleep was impossible. He wandered for a while about the ball-room. Then he walked to his chambers along the echoing streets and sat at his window; and some time afterwards the hoot of a motor-horn broke the silence and a car stopped and whirred in the street below. A moment later his bell rang.

He ran down the stairs in a queer excitement, unlocked the street door and opened it. Joan Carew, still in her masquerade dress with her scarlet cloak about her shoulders, slipped through the opening.

"Shut the door," she whispered, drawing herself apart in a corner.

"Your cab?" asked Calladine.

"It has gone."

Calladine latched the door. Above, in the well of the stairs, the light spread out from the open door of his flat. Down here all was dark. He could just see the glimmer of her white face, the glitter of her dress, but she drew her breath like one who has run far. They mounted the stairs cautiously. He did not say a word until they were both safely in his parlour; and even then it was in a low voice.

"What has happened?"

"You remember the woman I stared at? You didn't know why I stared, but any girl would have understood. She was wearing the loveliest pearls I ever saw in my life."

Joan was standing by the edge of the table. She was tracing with her finger a pattern on the cloth as she spoke. Calladine started with a horrible presentiment.

"Yes," she said. "I worship pearls. I always have done. For one thing, they improve on me. I haven't got any, of course. I have no money. But friends of mine who do own pearls have sometimes given theirs to me to wear when they were going sick, and they have always got back their lustre. I think that has had a little to do with my love of them. Oh, I have always longed for them—just a little string. Sometimes I have felt that I would have given my soul for them."

She was speaking in a dull, monotonous voice. But Calladine recalled the ecstasy which had shone in her face when her eyes first had fallen on the pearls, the longing which had swept her quite into another world, the passion with which she had danced to throw the obsession off.

"And I never noticed them at all," he said.

"Yet they were wonderful. The colour! The lustre! All the evening they tempted me. I was furious that a fat, coarse creature like that should have such exquisite things. Oh, I was mad."

She covered her face suddenly with her hands and swayed. Calladine sprang towards her. But she held out her hand.

"No, I am all right." And though he asked her to sit down she would not. "You remember when I stopped dancing suddenly?"

"Yes. You had something hidden under your foot?"

The girl nodded.

"Her key!" And under his breath Calladine uttered a startled cry.

For the first time since she had entered the room Joan Carew raised her head and looked at him. Her eyes were full of terror, and with the terror was mixed an incredulity as though she could not possibly believe that that had happened which she knew had happened.

"A little Yale key," the girl continued. "I saw Mrs. Blumenstein looking on the floor for something, and then I saw it shining on the very spot. Mrs. Blumenstein's suite was on the same floor as mine, and her maid slept above. All the maids do. I knew that. Oh, it seemed to me as if I had sold my soul and was being paid."

Now Calladine understood what she had meant by her strange phrase—"the safe daylight."

"I went up to my little suite," Joan Carew continued. "I sat there with the key burning through my glove until I had given her time enough to fall asleep"—and though she hesitated before she spoke the words, she did speak them, not looking at Calladine, and with a shudder of remorse making her confession complete. "Then I crept out. The corridor was dimly lit. Far away below the music was throbbing. Up here it was as silent as the grave. I opened the door—her door. I found myself in a lobby. Her rooms, though bigger, were arranged like mine. I slipped in and closed the door behind me. I listened in the darkness. I couldn't hear a sound. I crept forward to the door in front of me. I stood with my fingers on the handle and my heart beating fast enough to choke me. I had still time to turn back. But I couldn't. There were those pearls in front of my eyes, lustrous and wonderful. I opened the door gently an inch or so—and then—it all happened in a second."

Joan Carew faltered. The night was too near to her, its memory too poignant with terror. She shut her eyes tightly and cowered down in a chair. With the movement her cloak slipped from her shoulders and dropped on to the ground. Calladine leaned forward with an exclamation of horror; Joan Carew started up.

"What is it?" she asked.

"Nothing. Go on."

"I found myself inside the room with the door shut behind me. I had shut it myself in a spasm of terror. And I dared not turn round to open it. I was helpless."

"What do you mean? She was awake?"

Joan Carew shook her head.

"There were others in the room before me, and on the same errand—men!"

Calladine drew back, his eyes searching the girl's face.

"Yes?" he said slowly.

"I didn't see them at first. I didn't hear them. The room was quite dark except for one jet of fierce white light which beat upon the door of a safe. And as I shut the door the jet moved swiftly and the light reached me and stopped. I was blinded. I stood in the full glare of it, drawn up against the panels of the door, shivering, sick with fear. Then I heard a quiet laugh, and someone moved softly towards me. Oh, it was terrible! I recovered the use of my limbs; in a panic I turned to the door, but I was too late. Whilst I fumbled with the handle I was seized; a hand covered my mouth. I was lifted to the centre of the room. The jet went out, the electric lights were turned on. There were two men dressed as apaches in velvet trousers and red scarves, like a hundred others in the ball-room below, and both were masked. I struggled furiously; but, of course, I was like a child in their grasp. 'Tie her legs,' the man whispered who was holding me; 'she's making too much noise.' I kicked and fought, but the other man stooped and tied my ankles, and I fainted."

Calladine nodded his head.

"Yes?" he said.

"When I came to, the lights were still burning, the door of the safe was open, the room empty; I had been flung on to a couch at the foot of the bed. I was lying there quite free."

"Was the safe empty?" asked Calladine suddenly.

"I didn't look," she answered. "Oh!"—and she covered her face spasmodically with her hands. "I looked at the bed. Someone was lying there—under a sheet and quite still. There was a clock ticking in the room; it was the only sound. I was terrified. I was going mad with fear. If I didn't get out of the room at once I felt that I should go mad, that I should scream and bring every one to find me alone with—what was under the sheet in the bed. I ran to the door and looked out through a slit into the corridor. It was still quite empty, and below the music still throbbed in the ball-room. I crept down the stairs, meeting no one until I reached the hall. I looked into the ball-room as if I was searching for someone. I stayed long enough to show myself. Then I got a cab and came to you."

A short silence followed. Joan Carew looked at her companion in appeal. "You are the only one I could come to," she added. "I know no one else."

Calladine sat watching the girl in silence. Then he asked, and his voice was hard:

"And is that all you have to tell me?"

"Yes."

"You are quite sure?"

Joan Carew looked at him perplexed by the urgency of his question. She reflected for a moment or two.

"Quite."

Calladine rose to his feet and stood beside her.

"Then how do you come to be wearing this?" he asked, and he lifted a chain of platinum and diamonds which she was wearing about her shoulders. "You weren't wearing it when you danced with me."

Joan Carew stared at the chain.

"No. It's not mine. I have never seen it before." Then a light came into her eyes. "The two men—they must have thrown it over my head when I was on the couch—before they went." She looked at it more closely. "That's it. The chain's not very valuable. They could spare it, and—it would accuse me—of what they did."

"Yes, that's very good reasoning," said Calladine coldly.

Joan Carew looked quickly up into his face.

"Oh, you don't believe me," she cried. "You think—oh, it's impossible." And, holding him by the edge of his coat, she burst into a storm of passionate denials.

"But you went to steal, you know," he said gently, and she answered him at once:

"Yes, I did, but not this." And she held up the necklace. "Should I have stolen this, should I have come to you wearing it, if I had stolen the pearls, if I had"—and she stopped—"if my story were not true?"

Calladine weighed her argument, and it affected him.

"No, I think you wouldn't," he said frankly.

Most crimes, no doubt, were brought home because the criminal had made some incomprehensibly stupid mistake; incomprehensibly stupid, that is, by the standards of normal life. Nevertheless, Calladine was inclined to believe her. He looked at her. That she should have murdered was absurd. Moreover, she was not making a parade of remorse, she was not playing the unctuous penitent; she had yielded to a temptation, had got herself into desperate straits, and was at her wits' ends how to escape from them. She was frank about herself.

Calladine looked at the clock. It was nearly five o'clock in the morning, and though the music could still be heard from the ball-room in the Semiramis, the night had begun to wane upon the river.

"You must go back," he said. "I'll walk with you."

They crept silently down the stairs and into the street. It was only a step to the Semiramis. They met no one until they reached the Strand. There many, like Joan Carew in masquerade, were standing about, or walking hither and thither in search of carriages and cabs. The whole street was in a bustle, what with drivers shouting and people coming away.

"You can slip in unnoticed," said Calladine as he looked into the thronged courtyard. "I'll telephone to you in the morning."

"You will?" she cried eagerly, clinging for a moment to his arm.

"Yes, for certain," he replied. "Wait in until you hear from me. I'll think it over. I'll do what I can."

"Thank you," she said fervently.

He watched her scarlet cloak flitting here and there in the crowd until it vanished through the doorway. Then, for the second time, he walked back to his chambers, while the morning crept up the river from the sea.

———

This was the story which Calladine told in Mr. Ricardo's library. Mr. Ricardo heard it out with varying emotions. He began with a thrill of expectation like a man on a dark threshold of great excitements. The setting of the story appealed to him, too, by a sort of brilliant bizarrerie which he found in it. But, as it went on, he grew puzzled and a trifle disheartened. There were flaws and chinks; he began to bubble with unspoken criticisms, with swift and clever thrusts which he dared not deliver. He looked upon the young man with disfavour, as upon one who had half opened a door upon a theatre of great promise and shown him a spectacle not up to the mark.

Hanaud, on the other hand, listened imperturbably, without an expression upon his face, until the end. Then he pointed a finger at Calladine and asked him what to Ricardo's mind was a most irrelevant question.

"You got back to your rooms, then, before five, Mr. Calladine, and it is now nine o'clock less a few minutes."

"Yes."

"Yet you have not changed your clothes. Explain to me that. What did you do between five and half-past eight?"

Calladine looked down at his rumpled shirt front.

"Upon my word, I never thought of it," he cried. "I was worried out of my mind. I couldn't decide what to do. Finally, I determined to talk to Mr. Ricardo, and after I had come to that conclusion I just waited impatiently until I could come round with decency."

Hanaud rose from his chair. His manner was grave, but conveyed no single hint of an opinion. He turned to Ricardo.

"Let us go round to your young friend's rooms in the Adelphi," he said; and the three men drove thither at once.

———

Calladine lodged in a corner house and upon the first floor. His rooms, large and square and lofty, with Adams mantelpieces and a delicate tracery upon the ceilings, breathed the grace of the eighteenth century. Broad high windows, embrasured in thick walls, overlooked the river and took in all the sunshine and the air which the river had to give. And they were furnished fittingly. When the three men entered the parlour, Mr. Ricardo was astounded. He had expected the untidy litter of a man run to seed, the neglect and the dust of the recluse. But the room was as clean as the deck of a yacht; an Aubusson carpet made the floor luxurious underfoot; a few coloured prints of real value decorated the walls; and the mahogany furniture was polished so that a lady could have used it as a mirror. There was even by the newspapers upon the round table a china bowl full of fresh red roses. If Calladine had turned hermit, he was a hermit of an unusually fastidious type. Indeed, as he stood with his two companions in his dishevelled dress he seemed quite out of keeping with his rooms.

"So you live here, Mr. Calladine?" said Hanaud, taking off his hat and laying it down.

"Yes."

"With your servants, of course?"

"They come in during the day," said Calladine, and Hanaud looked at him curiously.

"Do you mean that you sleep here alone?"

"Yes."

"But your valet?"

"I don't keep a valet," said Calladine; and again the curious look came into Hanaud's eyes.

"Yet," he suggested gently, "there are rooms enough in your set of chambers to house a family."

Calladine coloured and shifted uncomfortably from one foot to the other.

"I prefer at night not to be disturbed," he said, stumbling a little over the words. "I mean, I have a liking for quiet."

Gabriel Hanaud nodded his head with sympathy.

"Yes, yes. And it is a difficult thing to get—as difficult as my holiday," he said ruefully, with a smile for Mr. Ricardo. "However"—he turned towards Calladine—"no doubt, now that you are at home, you would like a bath and a change of clothes. And when you are dressed, perhaps you will telephone to the Semiramis and ask Miss Carew to come round here. Meanwhile, we will read your newspapers and smoke your cigarettes."

Hanaud shut the door upon Calladine, but he turned neither to the papers nor the cigarettes. He crossed the room to Mr. Ricardo, who, seated at the open window, was plunged deep in reflections.

"You have an idea, my friend," cried Hanaud. "It demands to express itself. That sees itself in your face. Let me hear it, I pray."

Mr. Ricardo started out of an absorption which was altogether assumed.

"I was thinking," he said, with a faraway smile, "that you might disappear in the forests of Africa, and at once everyone would be very busy about your disappearance. You might leave your village in Leicestershire and live in the fogs of Glasgow, and within a week the whole village would know your postal address. But London—what a city! How different! How indifferent! Turn out of St. James's into the Adelphi Terrace and not a soul will say to you: 'Dr. Livingstone, I presume?'"

"But why should they," asked Hanaud, "if your name isn't Dr. Livingstone?"

Mr. Ricardo smiled indulgently.

"Scoffer!" he said. "You understand me very well," and he sought to turn the tables on his companion. "And you—does this room suggest nothing to you? Have you no ideas?" But he knew very well that Hanaud had. Ever since Hanaud had crossed the threshold he had been like a man stimulated by a drug. His eyes were bright and active, his body alert.

"Yes," he said, "I have."

He was standing now by Ricardo's side with his hands in his pockets, looking out at the trees on the Embankment and the barges swinging down the river.

"You are thinking of the strange scene which took place in this room such a very few hours ago," said Ricardo. "The girl in her masquerade dress making her confession with the stolen chain about her throat—"

Hanaud looked backwards carelessly. "No, I wasn't giving it a thought," he said, and in a moment or two he began to walk about the room with that curiously light step which Ricardo was never able to reconcile with his cumbersome figure. With the heaviness of a bear he still padded. He went from corner to corner, opened a cupboard here, a drawer of the bureau there, and—stooped suddenly. He stood erect again with a small box of morocco leather in his hand. His body from head to foot seemed to Ricardo to be expressing the question, "Have I found it?" He pressed a spring and the lid of the box flew open. Hanaud emptied its contents into the palm of his hand. There were two or three sticks of sealing-wax and a seal. With a shrug of the shoulders he replaced them and shut the box.

"You are looking for something," Ricardo announced with sagacity.

"I am," replied Hanaud; and it seemed that in a second or two he found it. Yet—yet—he found it with his hands in his pockets, if he had found it. Mr. Ricardo saw him stop in that attitude in front of the mantelshelf, and heard him utter a long, low whistle. Upon the mantelshelf some photographs were arranged, a box of cigars stood at one end, a book or two lay between some delicate ornaments of china, and a small engraving in a thin gilt frame was propped at the back against the wall. Ricardo surveyed the shelf from his seat in the window, but he could not imagine which it was of these objects that so drew and held Hanaud's eyes.

Hanaud, however, stepped forward. He looked into a vase and turned it upside down. Then he removed the lid of a porcelain cup, and from the very look of his great shoulders Ricardo knew that he had discovered what he sought. He was holding something in his hands, turning it over, examining it. When he was satisfied he moved swiftly to the door and opened it cautiously. Both men could hear the splashing of water in a bath. Hanaud closed the door again with a nod of contentment and crossed once more to the window.

"Yes, it is all very strange and curious," he said, "and I do not regret that you dragged me into the affair. You were quite right, my friend, this morning. It is the personality of your young Mr. Calladine which is the interesting thing. For instance, here we are in London in the early summer. The trees out, freshly green, lilac and flowers in the gardens, and I don't know what tingle of hope and expectation in the sunlight and the air. I am middle-aged—yet there's a riot in my blood, a recapture of youth, a belief that just round the corner, beyond the reach of my eyes, wonders wait for me. Don't you, too, feel something like that? Well, then—" and he heaved his shoulders in astonishment.

"Can you understand a young man with money, with fastidious tastes, good-looking, hiding himself in a corner at such a time—except for some overpowering reason? No. Nor can I. There is another thing—I put a question or two to Calladine."

"Yes," said Ricardo.

"He has no servants here at night. He is quite alone and—here is what I find interesting—he has no valet. That seems a small thing to you?" Hanaud asked at a movement from Ricardo. "Well, it is no doubt a trifle, but it's a significant trifle in the case of a young rich man. It is generally a sign that there is something strange, perhaps even something sinister, in his life. Mr. Calladine, some months ago, turned out of St. James's into the Adelphi. Can you tell me why?"

"No," replied Mr. Ricardo. "Can you?"

Hanaud stretched out a hand. In his open palm lay a small round hairy bulb about the size of a big button and of a colour between green and brown.

"Look!" he said. "What is that?"

Mr. Ricardo took the bulb wonderingly.

"It looks to me like the fruit of some kind of cactus."

Hanaud nodded.

"It is. You will see some pots of it in the hot-houses of any really good botanical gardens. Kew has them, I have no doubt. Paris certainly has. They are labelled. 'Anhalonium Luinii.' But amongst the Indians of Yucatan the plant has a simpler name."

"What name?" asked Ricardo.

"Mescal."

Mr. Ricardo repeated the name. It conveyed nothing to him whatever.

"There are a good many bulbs just like that in the cup upon the mantelshelf," said Hanaud.

Ricardo looked quickly up.

"Why?" he asked.

"Mescal is a drug."

Ricardo started.

"Yes, you are beginning to understand now," Hanaud continued, "why your young friend Calladine turned out of St. James's into the Adelphi Terrace."

Ricardo turned the little bulb over in his fingers.

"You make a decoction of it, I suppose?" he said.

"Or you can use it as the Indians do in Yucatan," replied Hanaud. "Mescal enters into their religious ceremonies. They sit at night in a circle about a fire built in the forest and chew it, whilst one of their number beats perpetually upon a drum."

Hanaud looked round the room and took notes of its luxurious carpet, its delicate appointments. Outside the window there was a thunder in the streets, a clamour of voices. Boats went swiftly down the river on the ebb. Beyond the mass of the Semiramis rose the great grey-white dome of St. Paul's. Opposite, upon the Southwark bank, the giant sky-signs, the big Highlander drinking whisky, and the rest of them waited, gaunt skeletons, for the night to dress them in fire and give them life. Below, the trees in the gardens rustled and waved. In the air were the uplift and the sparkle of the young summer.

"It's a long way from the forests of Yucatan to the Adelphi Terrace of London," said Hanaud. "Yet here, I think, in these rooms, when the servants are all gone and the house is very quiet, there is a little corner of wild Mexico."

A look of pity came into Mr. Ricardo's face. He had seen

more than one young man of great promise slacken his hold and let go, just for this reason. Calladine, it seemed, was another.

"It's like bhang and kieff and the rest of the devilish things, I suppose," he said, indignantly tossing the button upon the table.

Hanaud picked it up.

"No," he replied. "It's not quite like any other drug. It has a quality of its own which just now is of particular importance to you and me. Yes, my friend"—and he nodded his head very seriously—"we must watch that we do not make the big fools of ourselves in this affair."

"There," Mr. Ricardo agreed with an ineffable air of wisdom, "I am entirely with you."

"Now, why?" Hanaud asked. Mr. Ricardo was at a loss for a reason, but Hanaud did not wait. "I will tell you. Mescal intoxicates, yes—but it does more—it gives to the man who eats of it colour-dreams."

"Colour-dreams?" Mr. Ricardo repeated in a wondering voice.

"Yes, strange heated dreams, in which violent things happen vividly amongst bright colours. Colour is the gift of this little prosaic brown button." He spun the bulb in the air like a coin, and catching it again, took it over to the mantelpiece and dropped it into the porcelain cup.

"Are you sure of this?" Ricardo cried excitedly, and Hanaud raised his hand in warning. He went to the door, opened it for an inch or so, and closed it again.

"I am quite sure," he returned. "I have for a friend a very learned chemist in the Collège de France. He is one of those enthusiasts who must experiment upon themselves. He tried this drug."

"Yes," Ricardo said in a quieter voice. "And what did he see?"

"He had a vision of a wonderful garden bathed in sunlight, an old garden of gorgeous flowers, and emerald lawns, ponds with golden lilies and thick yew hedges—a garden where peacocks stepped indolently and groups of gay people fantastically dressed quarrelled and fought with swords. That is what he saw. And he saw it so vividly that when the vapours of the drug passed from his brain and he waked, he seemed to be coming out of the real world into a world of shifting illusions."

Hanaud's strong, quiet voice stopped, and for a while there was a complete silence in the room. Neither of the two men stirred so much as a finger. Mr. Ricardo once more was conscious of the thrill of strange sensations. He looked round the room. He could hardly believe that a room which had been—nay, was—the home and shrine of mysteries in the dark hours could wear so bright and innocent a freshness in the sunlight of the morning. There should be something sinister which leaped to the eyes as you crossed the threshold.

"Out of the real world," Mr. Ricardo quoted. "I begin to see."

"Yes, you begin to see, my friend, that we must be very careful not to make the big fools of ourselves. My friend of the Collège de France saw a garden. But had he been sitting alone in the window-seat where you are, listening through a summer night to the music of the masquerade at the Semiramis, might he not have seen the ball-room, the dancers, the scarlet cloak, and the rest of this story?"

"You mean," cried Ricardo, now fairly startled, "that Calladine came to us with the fumes of mescal still working in his brain, that the false world was the real one still for him."

"I do not know," said Hanaud. "At present I only put questions. I ask them of you. I wish to hear how they sound. Let us reason this problem out. Calladine, let us say, takes a great deal more of the drug than my professor. It will have on him a more powerful effect while it lasts, and it will last longer. Fancy dress balls are familiar things to Calladine. The music floating from the Semiramis will revive old memories. He sits here, the pageant takes shape before him, he sees himself taking his part in it. Oh, he is happier here sitting quietly in his window-seat than if he was really at the Semiramis. For he is there more intensely, more vividly, more really, than if he had actually descended this staircase. He lives his story through, the story of a heated brain, the scene of it changes in the way dreams have, it becomes tragic and sinister, it oppresses him with horror, and in the morning, so possessed by it that he does not think to change his clothes, he is knocking at your door."

Mr. Ricardo raised his eyebrows and moved.

"Ah! You see a flaw in my argument," said Hanaud. But Mr. Ricardo was wary. Too often in other days he had been leaped upon and trounced for a careless remark.

"Let me hear the end of your argument," he said. "There was, then, to your thinking no temptation of jewels, no theft, no murder, in a word no Celymène? She was born of recollections and the music of the Semiramis."

"No," cried Hanaud. "Come with me, my friend. I am not so sure that there was no Celymène."

With a smile upon his face, Hanaud led the way across the room. He had the dramatic instinct, and rejoiced in it. He was going to produce a surprise for his companion and, savouring the moment in advance, he managed his effects. He walked towards the mantelpiece and stopped a few paces away from it.

"Look!"

Mr. Ricardo looked and saw a broad Adams mantelpiece. He turned a bewildered face to his friend.

"You see nothing?" Hanaud asked.

"Nothing!"

"Look again! I am not sure—but is it not that Celymène is posing before you?"

Mr. Ricardo looked again. There was nothing to fix his eyes. He saw a book or two, a cup, a vase or two, and nothing else really except a very pretty and apparently valuable piece of—and suddenly Mr. Ricardo understood. Straight in front of him, in the very centre of the mantelpiece, a figure in painted china was leaning against a china stile. It was the figure of a perfectly impossible courtier, feminine and exquisite as could be, and apparelled also even to the scarlet heels exactly as Calladine had described Joan Carew.

Hanaud chuckled with satisfaction when he saw the expression upon Mr. Ricardo's face.

"Ah, you understand," he said. "Do you dream, my friend? At times—yes, like the rest of us. Then recollect your dreams? Things, people, which you have seen perhaps that day, perhaps months ago, pop in and out of them without making themselves prayed for. You cannot understand why. Yet sometimes they cut their strange capers there logically too, through subtle associations which the dreamer, once awake, does not apprehend. Thus, our friend here sits in the window, intoxicated by his drug, the music plays in the Semiramis, the curtain goes up in the heated theatre of his brain. He sees himself step upon the stage, and who else meets him but the china figure from his mantelpiece?"

Mr. Ricardo for a moment was all enthusiasm. Then his doubt returned to him.

"What you say, my dear Hanaud, is very ingenious. The figure upon the mantelpiece is also extremely convincing. And I should be absolutely convinced but for one thing."

"Yes?" said Hanaud, watching his friend closely.

"I am—I may say it, I think—a man of the world. And I ask myself"—Mr. Ricardo never could ask himself anything without assuming a manner of extreme pomposity—"I ask myself, whether a young man who has given up his social ties, who has become a hermit, and still more, who has become the slave of a drug, would retain that scrupulous carefulness of his body which is indicated by dressing for dinner when alone?"

Hanaud struck the table with the palm of his hand and sat down in a chair.

"Yes. That is the weak point in my theory. You have hit it. I knew it was there—that weak point, and I wondered whether you would seize it. Yes, the consumers of drugs are careless, untidy—even unclean as a rule. But not always. We must be careful. We must wait."

"For what?" asked Ricardo, beaming with pride.

"For the answer to a telephone message," replied Hanaud, with a nod towards the door.

Both men waited impatiently until Calladine came into the

room. He wore now a suit of blue serge, he had a clearer eye, his skin a healthier look; he was altogether a more reputable person. But he was plainly very ill at ease. He offered his visitors cigarettes, he proposed refreshments, he avoided entirely and awkwardly the object of their visit. Hanaud smiled. His theory was working out. Sobered by his bath, Calladine had realised the foolishness of which he had been guilty.

"You telephoned to the Semiramis, of course?" said Hanaud cheerfully.

Calladine grew red.

"Yes," he stammered.

"Yet I did not hear that volume of 'Hallos' which precedes telephonic connection in your country of leisure," Hanaud continued.

"I telephoned from my bedroom. You would not hear anything in this room."

"Yes, yes; the walls of these old houses are solid." Hanaud was playing with his victim. "And when may we expect Miss Carew?"

"I can't say," replied Calladine. "It's very strange. She is not in the hotel. I am afraid that she has gone away, fled."

Mr. Ricardo and Hanaud exchanged a look. They were both satisfied now. There was no word of truth in Calladine's story.

"Then there is no reason for us to wait," said Hanaud. "I shall have my holiday after all." And while he was yet speaking the voice of a newsboy calling out the first edition of an evening paper became distantly audible. Hanaud broke off his farewell. For a moment he listened, with his head bent. Then the voice was heard again, confused, indistinct;

Hanaud picked up his hat and cane, and without another word to Calladine, raced down the stairs. Mr. Ricardo followed him, but when he reached the pavement, Hanaud was half down the little street. At the corner, however, he stopped, and Ricardo joined him, coughing and out of breath.

"What's the matter?" he gasped.

"Listen," said Hanaud.

At the bottom of Duke Street, by Charing Cross Station, the newsboy was shouting his wares. Both men listened, and now the words came to them mis-pronounced but decipherable.

"Mysterious crime at the Semiramis Hotel."

Ricardo stared at his companion.

"You were wrong then," he cried. "Calladine's story was true."

For once in a way Hanaud was quite disconcerted.

"I don't know yet," he said. "We will buy a paper."

But before he could move a step, a taxi-cab turned into the Adelphi from the Strand, and wheeling in front of their faces, stopped at Calladine's door. From the cab a girl descended.

"Let us go back," said Hanaud.

———

Mr. Ricardo could no longer complain. It was half-past eight when Calladine had first disturbed the formalities of his house in Grosvenor Square. It was barely ten now, and during that short time he had been flung from surprise to surprise, he had looked underground on a morning of fresh summer, and had been thrilled by the contrast between the queer sinister life below and within and the open call to joy of the green world above. He had passed from incredulity to belief, from belief to incredulity, and when at last incredulity was firmly established, and the story to which he had listened proved the emanation of a drugged and heated brain, lo! the facts buffeted him in the face, and the story was shown to be true.

"I am alive once more," Mr. Ricardo thought as he turned back with Hanaud, and in his excitement he cried his thought aloud.

"Are you?" said Hanaud. "And what is life without a newspaper? If you will buy one from that remarkably raucous boy at the bottom of the street I will keep an eye upon Calladine's house till you come back."

Mr. Ricardo sped down to Charing Cross and brought back a copy of the fourth edition of the *Star*. He handed it to Hanaud, who stared at it doubtfully, folded as it was.

"Shall we see what it says?" Ricardo asked impatiently.

"By no means," Hanaud answered, waking from his reverie and tucking briskly away the paper into the tail pocket of his coat. "We will hear what Miss Joan Carew has to say, with our minds undisturbed by any discoveries. I was wondering about something totally different."

"Yes?" Mr. Ricardo encouraged him. "What was it?"

"I was wondering, since it is only ten o'clock, at what hour the first editions of the evening papers appear."

"It is a question," Mr. Ricardo replied sententiously, "which the greatest minds have failed to answer."

And they walked along the street to the house. The front door stood open during the day like the front door of any other house which is let off in sets of rooms. Hanaud and

Ricardo went up the staircase and rang the bell of Calladine's door. A middle-aged woman opened it.

"Mr. Calladine is in?" said Hanaud.

"I will ask," replied the woman. "What name shall I say?"

"It does not matter. I will go straight in," said Hanaud quietly. "I was here with my friend but a minute ago."

He went straight forward and into Calladine's parlour. Mr. Ricardo looked over his shoulder as he opened the door and saw a girl turn to them suddenly a white face of terror, and flinch as though already she felt the hand of a constable upon her shoulder. Calladine, on the other hand, uttered a cry of relief.

"These are my friends," he exclaimed to the girl, "the friends of whom I spoke to you"; and to Hanaud he said: "This is Miss Carew."

Hanaud bowed.

"You shall tell me your story, mademoiselle," he said very gently, and a little colour returned to the girl's cheeks, a little courage revived in her.

"But you have heard it," she answered.

"Not from you," said Hanaud.

So for a second time in that room she told the history of that night. Only this time the sunlight was warm upon the world, the comfortable sounds of life's routine were borne through the windows, and the girl herself wore the inconspicuous blue serge of a thousand other girls afoot that morning. These trifles of circumstance took the edge of sheer horror off her narrative, so that, to tell the truth, Mr. Ricardo was a trifle disappointed. He wanted a crescendo motive in his music, whereas it had begun at its fortissimo. Hanaud, however, was the perfect listener. He listened without stirring and with most compassionate eyes, so that Joan Carew spoke only to him, and to him, each moment that passed, with greater confidence. The life and sparkle of her had gone altogether. There was nothing in her manner now to suggest the waywardness, the gay irresponsibility, the radiance, which had attracted Calladine the night before. She was just a very young and very pretty girl, telling in a low and remorseful voice of the tragic dilemma to which she had brought herself. Of Celymène all that remained was something exquisite and fragile in her beauty, in the slimness of her figure, in her daintiness of hand and foot—something almost of the hot-house. But the story she told was, detail for detail, the same which Calladine had already related.

"Thank you," said Hanaud when she had done. "Now I must ask you two questions."

"I will answer them."

Mr. Ricardo sat up. He began to think of a third question which he might put himself, something uncommonly subtle and searching, which Hanaud would never have thought of. But Hanaud put his questions, and Ricardo almost jumped out of his chair.

"You will forgive me, Miss Carew. But have you ever stolen before?"

Joan Carew turned upon Hanaud with spirit. Then a change swept over her face.

"You have a right to ask," she answered. "Never." She looked into his eyes as she answered. Hanaud did not move. He sat with a hand upon each knee and led to his second question.

"Early this morning, when you left this room, you told

Mr. Calladine that you would wait at the Semiramis until he telephoned to you?"

"Yes."

"Yet when he telephoned, you had gone out?"

"Yes."

"Why?"

"I will tell you," said Joan Carew. "I could not bear to keep the little diamond chain in my room."

For a moment even Hanaud was surprised. He had lost sight of that complication. Now he leaned forward anxiously; indeed, with a greater anxiety than he had yet shown in all this affair.

"I was terrified," continued Joan Carew. "I kept think-ing: 'They must have found out by now. They will search everywhere.' I didn't reason. I lay in bed expecting to hear every moment a loud knocking on the door. Besides—the chain itself being there in my bedroom—her chain—the dead woman's chain—no, I couldn't endure it. I felt as if I had stolen it. Then my maid brought in my tea."

"You had locked it away?" cried Hanaud.

"Yes. My maid did not see it."

Joan Carew explained how she had risen, dressed, wrapped the chain in a pad of cotton-wool, and enclosed it in an enve-lope. The envelope had not the stamp of the hotel upon it. It was a rather large envelope, one of a packet which she had bought in a crowded shop in Oxford Street on her way from Euston to the Semiramis. She had bought the envelopes of that particular size in order that when she sent her letter of introduction to the Director of the Opera at Covent Garden she might enclose with it a photograph.

"And to whom did you send it?" asked Mr. Ricardo.

"To Mrs. Blumenstein at the Semiramis. I printed the address carefully. Then I went out and posted it."

"Where?" Hanaud inquired.

"In the big letter-box of the Post Office at the corner of Trafalgar Square."

Hanaud looked at the girl sharply.

"You had your wits about you, I see," he said.

"What if the envelope gets lost?" said Ricardo.

Hanaud laughed grimly.

"If one envelope is delivered at its address in London today, it will be that one," he said. "The news of the crime is published, you see," and he swung round to Joan.

"Did you know that, Miss Carew?"

"No," she answered in an awe-stricken voice.

"Well, then, it is. Let us see what the special investigator has to say about it." And Hanaud, with a deliberation which Mr. Ricardo found quite excruciating, spread out the newspaper on the table in front of him.

———

There was only one new fact in the couple of columns devoted to the mystery. Mrs. Blumenstein had died from chloroform poisoning. She was of a stout habit, and the thieves were not skilled in the administration of the anaesthetic.

"It's murder none the less," said Hanaud, and he gazed straight at Joan, asking her by the direct summons of his eyes what she was going to do.

"I must tell my story to the police," she replied painfully

and slowly. But she did not hesitate; she was announcing a meditated plan.

Hanaud neither agreed nor differed. His face was blank, and when he spoke there was no cordiality in his voice. "Well," he asked, "and what is it that you have to say to the police, miss? That you went into the room to steal, and that you were attacked by two strangers, dressed as apaches, and masked? That is all?"

"Yes."

"And how many men at the Semiramis ball were dressed as apaches and wore masks? Come! Make a guess. A hundred at the least?"

"I should think so."

"Then what will your confession do beyond—I quote your English idiom—putting you in the coach?"

Mr. Ricardo now smiled with relief. Hanaud was taking a definite line. His knowledge of idiomatic English might be incomplete, but his heart was in the right place. The girl traced a vague pattern on the tablecloth with her fingers.

"Yet I think I must tell the police," she repeated, looking up and dropping her eyes again. Mr. Ricardo noticed that her eyelashes were very long. For the first time Hanaud's face relaxed.

"And I think you are quite right," he cried heartily, to Mr. Ricardo's surprise. "Tell them the truth before they suspect it, and they will help you out of the affair if they can. Not a doubt of it. Come, I will go with you myself to Scotland Yard."

"Thank you," said Joan, and the pair drove away in a cab together.

Hanaud returned to Grosvenor Square alone and lunched with Ricardo.

"It was all right," he said. "The police were very kind. Miss Joan Carew told her story to them as she had told it to us. Fortunately, the envelope with the aluminium chain had already been delivered, and was in their hands. They were much mystified about it, but Miss Joan's story gave them a reasonable explanation. I think they are inclined to believe her; and, if she is speaking the truth, they will keep her out of the witness-box if they can."

"She is to stay here in London, then?" asked Ricardo.

"Oh, yes; she is not to go. She will present her letters at the Opera House and secure an engagement, if she can. The criminals might be lulled thereby into a belief that the girl had kept the whole strange incident to herself, and that there was nowhere even a knowledge of the disguise which they had used." Hanaud spoke as carelessly as if the matter was not very important; and Ricardo, with an unusual flash of shrewdness, said:

"It is clear, my friend, that you do not think those two men will ever be caught at all."

Hanaud shrugged his shoulders.

"There is always a chance. But, listen. There is a room with a hundred guns, one of which is loaded. Outside the room there are a hundred pigeons, one of which is white. You are taken into the room blindfolded. You choose the loaded gun, and you shoot the one white pigeon. That is the value of the chance."

"But," exclaimed Ricardo, "those pearls were of great value, and I have heard at a trial expert evidence given by pearl merchants. All agree that the pearls of great value are known; so, when they come upon the market—"

"That is true," Hanaud interrupted imperturbably. "But how are they known?"

"By their weight," said Mr. Ricardo.

"Exactly," replied Hanaud. "But did you not also hear at this trial of yours that pearls can be peeled like an onion? No? It is true. Remove a skin, two skins, the weight is altered, the pearl is a trifle smaller. It has lost a little of its value, yes—but you can no longer identify it as the so-and-so pearl which belonged to this or that sultan, was stolen by the vizier, bought by Messrs. Lustre and Steinopolis, of Hatton Garden, and subsequently sold to the wealthy Mrs. Blumenstein. No, your pearl has vanished altogether. There is a new pearl which can be traded." He looked at Ricardo. "Who shall say that those pearls are not already in one of the queer little back streets of Amsterdam, undergoing their transformation?"

Mr. Ricardo was not persuaded because he would not be. "I have some experience in these matters," he said loftily to Hanaud. "I am sure that we shall lay our hands upon the criminals. We have never failed."

Hanaud grinned from ear to ear. The only experience which Mr. Ricardo had ever had was gained on the shores of Geneva and at Aix under Hanaud's tuition. But Hanaud did not argue, and there the matter rested.

The days flew by. It was London's play-time. The green and gold of early summer deepened and darkened; wondrous warm nights under England's pale blue sky, when the streets rang with the joyous feet of youth, led in clear dawns and lovely glowing days. Hanaud made acquaintance with the wooded reaches of the Thames; Joan Carew sang "Louise" at Covent Garden with notable success; and the affair of the Semiramis Hotel, in the minds of the few who remembered it, was already added to the long list of unfathomed mysteries.

But towards the end of May there occurred a startling development. Joan Carew wrote to Mr. Ricardo that she would call upon him in the afternoon, and she begged him to secure the presence of Hanaud. She came as the clock struck; she was pale and agitated; and in the room where Calladine had first told the story of her visit she told another story which, to Mr. Ricardo's thinking, was yet more strange and—yes—yet more suspicious.

"It has been going on for some time," she began. "I thought of coming to you at once. Then I wondered whether, if I waited—oh, you'll never believe me!"

"Let us hear!" said Hanaud patiently.

"I began to dream of that room, the two men disguised and masked, the still figure in the bed. Night after night! I was terrified to go to sleep. I felt the hand upon my mouth. I used to catch myself falling asleep, and walk about the room with all the lights up to keep myself awake."

"But you couldn't," said Hanaud with a smile. "Only the old can do that."

"No, I couldn't," she admitted; "and—oh, my nights were horrible until"—she paused and looked at her companions doubtfully—"until one night the mask slipped."

"What—?" cried Hanaud, and a note of sternness rang suddenly in his voice. "What are you saying?"

With a desperate rush of words, and the colour staining her forehead and cheeks, Joan Carew continued:

"It is true. The mask slipped on the face of one of the

men—of the man who held me. Only a little way; it just left his forehead visible—no more."

"Well?" asked Hanaud, and Mr. Ricardo leaned forward, swaying between the austerity of criticism and the desire to believe so thrilling a revelation.

"I waked up," the girl continued, "in the darkness, and for a moment the whole scene remained vividly with me—for just long enough for me to fix clearly in my mind the figure of the apache with the white forehead showing above the mask."

"When was that?" asked Ricardo.

"A fortnight ago."

"Why didn't you come with your story then?"

"I waited," said Joan. "What I had to tell wasn't yet helpful. I thought that another night the mask might slip lower still. Besides, I—it is difficult to describe just what I felt. I felt it important just to keep that photograph in my mind, not to think about it, not to talk about it, not even to look at it too often lest I should begin to imagine the rest of the face and find something familiar in the man's carriage and shape when there was nothing really familiar to me at all. Do you understand that?" she asked, with her eyes fixed in appeal on Hanaud's face.

"Yes," replied Hanaud. "I follow your thought."

"I thought there was a chance now—the strangest chance—that the truth might be reached. I did not wish to spoil it," and she turned eagerly to Ricardo, as if, having persuaded Hanaud, she would now turn her batteries on his companion. "My whole point of view was changed. I was no longer afraid of falling asleep lest I should dream. I wished to dream, but—"

"But you could not," suggested Hanaud.

"No, that is the truth," replied Joan Carew. "Whereas before I was anxious to keep awake and yet must sleep from sheer fatigue, now that I tried consciously to put myself to sleep I remained awake all through the night, and only towards morning, when the light was coming through the blinds, dropped off into a heavy, dreamless slumber."

Hanaud nodded.

"It is a very perverse world, Miss Carew, and things go by contraries."

Ricardo listened for some note of irony in Hanaud's voice, some look of disbelief in his face. But there was neither the one nor the other. Hanaud was listening patiently.

"Then came my rehearsals," Joan Carew continued, "and that wonderful opera drove everything else out of my head. I had such a chance, if only I could make use of it. When I went to bed now, I went with that haunting music in my ears—the call of Paris—oh, you must remember it. But can you realise what it must mean to a girl who is going to sing it for the first time in Covent Garden?"

Mr. Ricardo saw his opportunity. He, the connoisseur, to whom the psychology of the green room was as an open book, could answer that question.

"It is true, my friend," he informed Hanaud with quiet authority. "The great march of events leaves the artist cold. He lives aloof. While the tumbrils thunder in the streets he adds a delicate tint to the picture he is engaged upon or recalls his triumph in his last great part."

"Thank you," said Hanaud gravely. "And now Miss Carew may perhaps resume her story."

"It was the very night of my début," she continued. "I had supper with some friends. A great artist, Carmen Valeri,"—and as Joan Carew uttered the name, almost imperceptibly Hanaud started—"honoured me also with her presence. I went home excited, and that night I dreamed again."

"Yes?"

"This time the chin, the lips, the eyes were visible. There was only a black strip across the middle of the face. And I thought—nay, I was sure—that if that strip vanished I should know the man."

"And it did vanish?"

"Three nights afterwards."

"And you did know the man?"

The girl's face became troubled. She frowned.

"I knew the face, that was all," she answered. "I was disappointed. I had never spoken to the man. I am sure of that still. But somewhere I have seen him."

"You don't even remember when?" asked Hanaud.

"No." Joan Carew reflected for a moment with her eyes upon the carpet, and then flung up her head with a gesture of despair. "No. I try all the time to remember. But it is no good."

Mr. Ricardo could not restrain a movement of indignation. He was being played with. The girl with her fantastic story had worked him up to a real pitch of excitement only to make a fool of him. All his earlier suspicions flowed back into his mind. What if, after all, she was implicated in the murder and the theft? What if, with a perverse cunning, she had told Hanaud and himself just enough of what she knew, just enough of the truth, to persuade them to protect her? What if her frank confession of her own overpowering impulse to steal the necklace was nothing more than a subtle appeal to the sentimental pity of men, an appeal based upon a wider knowledge of men's weaknesses than a girl of nineteen or twenty ought to have? Mr. Ricardo cleared his throat and sat forward in his chair. He was girding himself for a singularly searching interrogatory when Hanaud asked the most irrelevant of questions:

"How did you pass the evening of that night when you first dreamed complete the face of your assailant?"

Joan Carew reflected. Then her face cleared.

"I know," she exclaimed. "I was at the opera."

"And what was being given?"

"*The Jewels of the Madonna.*"

Hanaud nodded his head. To Ricardo it seemed that he had expected precisely that answer.

"Now," he continued, "you are sure that you have seen this man?"

"Yes."

"Very well," said Hanaud. "There is a game you play at children's parties—is there not?—animal, vegetable, or mineral, and always you get the answer. Let us play that game for a few minutes, you and I."

Joan Carew drew up her chair to the table and sat with her chin propped upon her hands and her eyes fixed on Hanaud's face. As he put each question she pondered on it and answered. If she answered doubtfully he pressed it.

"You crossed on the *Lucania* from New York?"

"Yes."

"Picture to yourself the dining-room, the tables. You have the picture quite clear?"

"Yes."

"Was it at breakfast that you saw him?"

"No."

"At luncheon?"

"No."

"At dinner?"

She paused for a moment, summoning before her eyes the travellers at the tables.

"No."

"Not in the dining-room at all, then?"

"No."

"In the library, when you were writing letters, did you not one day lift your head and see him?"

"No."

"On the promenade deck? Did he pass you when you sat in your deck-chair, or did you pass him when he sat in his chair?"

"No."

Step by step Hanaud took her back to New York to her hotel, to journeys in the train. Then he carried her to Milan where she had studied. It was extraordinary to Ricardo to realise how much Hanaud knew of the curriculum of a student aspiring to grand opera. From Milan he brought her again to New York, and at the last, with a start of joy, she cried: "Yes, it was there."

Hanaud took his handkerchief from his pocket and wiped his forehead.

"Ouf!" he grunted. "To concentrate the mind on a day like this, it makes one hot, I can tell you. Now, Miss Carew, let us hear."

It was at a concert at the house of a Mrs. Starlingshield in

Fifth Avenue and in the afternoon. Joan Carew sang. She was a stranger to New York and very nervous. She saw nothing but a mist of faces whilst she sang, but when she had finished the mist cleared, and as she left the improvised stage she saw the man. He was standing against the wall in a line of men. There was no particular reason why her eyes should single him out, except that he was paying no attention to her singing, and, indeed, she forgot him altogether afterwards.

"I just happened to see him clearly and distinctly," she said. "He was tall, clean-shaven, rather dark, not particularly young—thirty-five or so, I should say—a man with a heavy face and beginning to grow stout. He moved away whilst I was bowing to the audience, and I noticed him afterwards walking about, talking to people."

"Do you remember to whom?"

"No."

"Did he notice you, do you think?"

"I am sure he didn't," the girl replied emphatically. "He never looked at the stage where I was singing, and he never looked towards me afterwards."

She gave, so far as she could remember, the names of such guests and singers as she knew at that party. "And that is all," she said.

"Thank you," said Hanaud. "It is perhaps a good deal. But it is perhaps nothing at all."

"You will let me hear from you?" she cried, as she rose to her feet.

"Miss Carew, I am at your service," he returned. She gave him her hand timidly and he took it cordially. For Mr. Ricardo she had merely a bow, a bow which recognised that he distrusted her and that she had no right to be offended. Then she went, and Hanaud smiled across the table at Ricardo.

"Yes," he said, "all that you are thinking is true enough. A man who slips out of society to indulge a passion for a drug in greater peace, a girl who, on her own confession, tried to steal, and, to crown all, this fantastic story. It is natural to disbelieve every word of it. But we disbelieved before, when we left Calladine's lodging in the Adelphi, and we were wrong. Let us be warned."

"You have an idea?" exclaimed Ricardo.

"Perhaps!" said Hanaud. And he looked down the theatre column of *The Times*. "Let us distract ourselves by going to the theatre."

"You are the most irritating man!" Mr. Ricardo broke out impulsively. "If I had to paint your portrait, I should paint you with your finger against the side of your nose, saying mysteriously: '*I* know,' when you know nothing at all."

Hanaud made a schoolboy's grimace. "We will go and sit in your box at the opera tonight," he said, "and you shall explain to me all through the beautiful music the theory of the tonic sol-fa."

They reached Covent Garden before the curtain rose. Mr. Ricardo's box was on the lowest tier and next to the omnibus box.

"We are near the stage," said Hanaud, as he took his seat in the corner and so arranged the curtain that he could see and yet was hidden from view. "I like that."

The theatre was full; stalls and boxes shimmered with jewels and satin, and all that was famous that season for beauty and distinction had made its tryst there that night.

"Yes, this is wonderful," said Hanaud. "What opera do they play?" He glanced at his programme and cried, with a little start of surprise: "We are in luck. It is *The Jewels of the Madonna.*"

"Do you believe in omens?" Mr. Ricardo asked coldly. He had not yet recovered from his rebuff of the afternoon.

"No, but I believe that Carmen Valeri is at her best in this part," said Hanaud.

Mr. Ricardo belonged to that body of critics which must needs spoil your enjoyment by comparisons and recollections of other great artists. He was at a disadvantage certainly tonight, for the opera was new. But he did his best. He imagined others in the part, and when the great scene came at the end of the second act, and Carmen Valeri, on obtaining from her lover the jewels stolen from the sacred image, gave such a display of passion as fairly enthralled that audience, Mr. Ricardo sighed quietly and patiently.

"How Calvé would have brought out the psychological value of that scene!" he murmured; and he was quite vexed with Hanaud, who sat with his opera glasses held to his eyes, and every sense apparently concentrated on the stage. The curtains rose and rose again when the act was concluded, and still Hanaud sat motionless as the Sphinx, staring through his glasses.

"That is all," said Ricardo when the curtains fell for the fifth time.

"They will come out," said Hanaud. "Wait!" And from between the curtains Carmen Valeri was led out into the full glare of the footlights with the panoply of jewels flashing on her breast. Then at last Hanaud put down his glasses and turned to Ricardo with a look of exultation and genuine delight upon his face which filled that season-worn dilettante with envy.

"What a night!" said Hanaud. "What a wonderful night!" And he applauded until he split his gloves. At the end of the opera he cried: "We will go and take supper at the Semiramis. Yes, my friend, we will finish our evening like gallant gentlemen. Come! Let us not think of the morning." And boisterously he slapped Ricardo in the small of the back.

In spite of his boast, however, Hanaud hardly touched his supper, and he played with, rather than drank, his brandy and soda. He had a little table to which he was accustomed beside a glass screen in the depths of the room, and he sat with his back to the wall watching the groups which poured in. Suddenly his face lighted up.

"Here is Carmen Valeri!" he cried. "Once more we are in luck. Is it not that she is beautiful?"

Mr. Ricardo turned languidly about in his chair and put up his eyeglass.

"So, so," he said.

"Ah!" returned Hanaud. "Then her companion will interest you still more. For he is the man who murdered Mrs. Blumenstein."

Mr. Ricardo jumped so that his eyeglass fell down and tinkled on its cord against the buttons of his waistcoat.

"What!" he exclaimed. "It's impossible!" He looked again. "Certainly the man fits Joan Carew's description. But—" He turned back to Hanaud utterly astounded. And as he looked at the Frenchman all his earlier recollections of him, of his swift deductions, of the subtle imagination which his heavy body so well concealed, crowded in upon Ricardo and convinced him.

"How long have you known?" he asked in a whisper of awe.

"Since ten o'clock tonight."

"But you will have to find the necklace before you can prove it."

"The necklace!" said Hanaud carelessly. "That is already found."

Mr. Ricardo had been longing for a thrill. He had it now. He felt it in his very spine.

"It's found?" he said in a startled whisper.

"Yes."

Ricardo turned again, with as much indifference as he could assume, towards the couple who were settling down at their table, the man with a surly indifference, Carmen Valeri with the radiance of a woman who has just achieved a triumph and is now free to enjoy the fruits of it. Confusedly, recollections returned to Ricardo of questions put that afternoon by Hanaud to Joan Carew—subtle questions into which the name of Carmen Valeri was continually entering. She was a woman of thirty, certainly beautiful, with a clear, pale face and eyes like the night.

"Then she is implicated too!" he said. What a change for her, he thought, from the stage of Covent Garden to the felon's cell, from the gay supper-room of the Semiramis, with its bright frocks and its babel of laughter, to the silence and the ignominious garb of the workrooms in Aylesbury Prison!

"She!" exclaimed Hanaud; and in his passion for the contrasts of drama Ricardo was almost disappointed. "She has nothing whatever to do with it. She knows nothing. André Favart there—yes. But Carmen Valeri! She's as stupid as an owl, and loves him beyond words. Do you want to know how stupid she is? You shall know. I asked Mr. Clements, the director of the opera house, to take supper with us, and here he is."

Hanaud stood up and shook hands with the director. He was of the world of business rather than of art, and long experience of the ways of tenors and prima-donnas had given him a good-humoured cynicism.

"They are spoilt children, all tantrums and vanity," he said, "and they would ruin you to keep a rival out of the theatre."

He told them anecdote upon anecdote.

"And Carmen Valeri," Hanaud asked in a pause; "is she troublesome this season?"

"Has been," replied Clements dryly. "At present she is playing at being good. But she gave me a turn some weeks ago." He turned to Ricardo. "Superstition's her trouble, and André Favart knows it. She left him behind in America this spring."

"America!" suddenly cried Ricardo; so suddenly that Clements looked at him in surprise.

"She was singing in New York, of course, during the winter," he returned. "Well, she left him behind, and I was shaking hands with myself when he began to deal the cards over there. She came to me in a panic. She had just had a cable. She couldn't sing on Friday night. There was a black knave next to the nine of diamonds. She wouldn't sing for worlds. And it was the first night of *The Jewels of the Madonna*! Imagine the fix I was in!"

"What did you do?" asked Ricardo.

"The only thing there was to do," replied Clements with a shrug of the shoulders. "I cabled Favart some money and he dealt the cards again. She came to me beaming. Oh, she had been so distressed to put me in the cart! But what could she do? Now there was a red queen next to the ace of hearts, so she could sing without a scruple so long, of course, as she didn't pass a funeral on the way down to the opera house. Luckily she didn't. But my money brought Favart over here, and now I'm living on a volcano. For he's the greatest scoundrel unhung. He never has a farthing, however much she gives him; he's a blackmailer, he's a swindler, he has no manners and no graces, he looks like a butcher and treats her as if she were dirt, he never goes near the Opera except when she is singing in this part, and she worships the ground he walks on. Well, I suppose it's time to go."

The lights had been turned off, the great room was emptying. Mr. Ricardo and his friends rose to go, but at the door Hanaud detained Mr. Clements, and they talked together alone for some little while, greatly to Mr. Ricardo's annoyance. Hanaud's good humour, however, when he rejoined his friend, was enough for two.

"I apologise, my friend, with my hand on my heart. But it was for your sake that I stayed behind. You have a meretricious taste for melodrama which I deeply deplore, but which I mean to gratify. I ought to leave for Paris tomorrow, but I shall not. I shall stay until Thursday." And he skipped upon the pavement as they walked home to Grosvenor Square.

Mr. Ricardo bubbled with questions, but he knew his man. He would get no answer to any one of them tonight. So he worked out the problem for himself as he lay awake in his bed, and he came down to breakfast next morning fatigued but triumphant. Hanaud was already chipping off the top of his egg at the table.

"So I see you have found it all out, my friend," he said.

"Not all," replied Ricardo modestly, "and you will not mind, I am sure, if I follow the usual custom and wish you a good morning."

"Not at all," said Hanaud. "I am all for good manners myself."

He dipped his spoon into his egg.

"But I am longing to hear the line of your reasoning."

Mr. Ricardo did not need much pressing.

"Joan Carew saw André Favart at Mrs. Starlingshield's party, and saw him with Carmen Valeri. For Carmen Valeri was there. I remember that you asked Joan for the names of the artists who sang, and Carmen Valeri was amongst them."

Hanaud nodded his head.

"Exactly."

"No doubt Joan Carew noticed Carmen Valeri particularly, and so took unconsciously into her mind an impression of the man who was with her, André Favart—of his build, of his walk, of his type."

Again Hanaud agreed.

"She forgets the man altogether, but the picture remains latent in her mind—an undeveloped film."

Hanaud looked up in surprise, and the surprise flattered Mr. Ricardo. Not for nothing had he tossed about in his bed for the greater part of the night.

"Then came the tragic night at the Semiramis. She does not consciously recognise her assailant, but she dreams the scene again and again, and by a process of unconscious cerebration the figure of the man becomes familiar. Finally she makes her début, is entertained at supper afterwards, and meets once more Carmen Valeri."

"Yes, for the first time since Mrs. Starling's party," interjected Hanaud.

"She dreams again, she remembers asleep more than she remembers when awake. The presence of Carmen Valeri at her supper-party has its effect. By a process of association, she recalls Favart, and the mask slips on the face of her assailant. Some days later she goes to the Opera. She hears Carmen Valeri sing in *The Jewels of the Madonna*. No doubt the passion of her acting, which I am more prepared to acknowledge this morning than I was last night, affects Joan Carew powerfully, emotionally. She goes to bed with her head full of Carmen Valeri, and she dreams not of Carmen Valeri, but of the man who is unconsciously associated with Carmen Valeri in her thoughts. The mask vanishes altogether. She sees her assailant now, has his portrait limned in her mind, would know him if she met him in the street, though she does not know by what means she identified him."

"Yes," said Hanaud. "It is curious the brain working while the body sleeps, the dream revealing what thought cannot recall."

Mr. Ricardo was delighted. He was taken seriously.

"But of course," he said, "I could not have worked the problem out but for you. You knew of André Favart and the kind of man he was."

Hanaud laughed.

"Yes. That is always my one little advantage. I know all the cosmopolitan blackguards of Europe." His laughter ceased suddenly, and he brought his clenched fist heavily down upon the table. "Here is one of them who will be very well out of the world, my friend," he said very quietly, but there was a look of force in his face and a hard light in his eyes, which made Mr. Ricardo shiver.

For a few moments there was silence. Then Ricardo asked: "But have you evidence enough?"

"Yes."

"Your two chief witnesses, Calladine and Joan Carew— you said it yourself—there are facts to discredit them. Will they be believed?"

"But they won't appear in the case at all," Hanaud said. "Wait, wait!" and once more he smiled. "By the way, what is the number of Calladine's house?"

Ricardo gave it, and Hanaud therefore wrote a letter. "It is all for your sake, my friend," he said with a chuckle.

"Nonsense," said Ricardo. "You have the spirit of the theatre in your bones."

"Well, I shall not deny it," said Hanaud, and he sent out the letter to the nearest pillar-box.

Mr. Ricardo waited in a fever of impatience until Thursday came. At breakfast Hanaud would talk of nothing but the news of the day. At luncheon he was no better. The affair of the Semiramis Hotel seemed a thousand miles from any of his thoughts. But at five o'clock he said as he drank his tea:

"You know, of course, that we go to the opera tonight?"

"Yes? Do we?"

"Yes. Your young friend Calladine, by the way, will join us in your box."

"That is very kind of him, I am sure," said Mr. Ricardo.

The two men arrived before the rising of the curtain, and in the crowded lobby a stranger spoke a few words to Hanaud, but what he said Ricardo could not hear. They took their seats in the box, and Hanaud looked at his programme.

"Ah! It is '*Il Ballo de Maschera*' tonight. We always seem to hit upon something appropriate, don't we?"

Then he raised his eyebrows.

"Oh-o! Do you see that our pretty young friend, Joan Carew, is singing in the rôle of the page? It is a showy part. There is a particular melody with a long-sustained trill in it, as far as I remember."

Mr. Ricardo was not deceived by Hanaud's apparent ignorance of the opera to be given that night and of the part Joan Carew was to take. He was, therefore, not surprised when Hanaud added:

"By the way, I should let Calladine find it all out for himself."

Mr. Ricardo nodded sagely.

"Yes. That is wise. I had thought of it myself." But he had done nothing of the kind. He was only aware that the elaborate stage-management in which Hanaud delighted was working out to the desired climax, whatever that climax might be. Calladine entered the box a few minutes later and shook hands with them awkwardly.

"It was kind of you to invite me," he said and, very ill at ease, he took a seat between them and concentrated his attention on the house as it filled up.

"There's the overture," said Hanaud. The curtains divided and were festooned on either side of the stage. The singers came on in their turn; the page appeared to a burst of delicate applause (Joan Carew had made a small name for herself that season), and with a stifled cry Calladine shot back in the box as if he had been struck. Even then Mr. Ricardo did not understand. He only realised that Joan Carew was looking extraordinarily trim and smart in her boy's dress. He had to look from his programme to the stage and back again several times before the reason of Calladine's exclamation dawned on him. When it did, he was horrified. Hanaud, in his craving for dramatic effects, must have lost his head altogether. Joan Carew was wearing, from the ribbon in her hair to the scarlet heels of her buckled satin shoes, the same dress which she had worn on the tragic night at the Semiramis Hotel. He leaned forward in his agitation to Hanaud.

"You must be mad. Suppose Favart is in the theatre and sees her. He'll be over on the Continent by one in the morning."

"No, he won't," replied Hanaud. "For one thing, he never comes to Covent Garden unless one opera, with Carmen Valeri in the chief part, is being played, as you heard the other night at supper. For a second thing, he isn't in the house. I know where he is. He is gambling in Dean Street, Soho. For a third thing, my friend, he couldn't leave by the nine o'clock train for the Continent if he wanted to. Arrangements have been made. For a fourth thing, he wouldn't wish to. He has really remarkable reasons for desiring to stay in London. But he will come to the theatre later. Clements will send him an urgent message, with the result that he will go straight to Clements' office. Meanwhile, we can enjoy ourselves, eh?"

Never was the difference between the amateur dilettante and the genuine professional more clearly exhibited than by the behaviour of the two men during the rest of the performance. Mr. Ricardo might have been sitting on a coal fire from his jumps and twistings; Hanaud stolidly enjoyed the music, and when Joan Carew sang her famous solo his hands clamoured for an encore louder than anyone's in the boxes. Certainly, whether excitement was keeping her up or no, Joan Carew had never sung better in her life. Her voice was clear and fresh as a bird's—a bird with a soul inspiring its song. Even Calladine drew his chair forward again and sat with his eyes fixed upon the stage and quite carried out of himself. He drew a deep breath at the end.

"She is wonderful," he said, like a man waking up.

"She is very good," replied Mr. Ricardo, correcting Calladine's transports.

"We will go round to the back of the stage," said Hanaud.

They passed through the iron door and across the stage to a long corridor with a row of doors on one side. There were two or three men standing about in evening dress, as if waiting for friends in the dressing-rooms. At the third door Hanaud stopped and knocked. The door was opened by Joan Carew, still dressed in her green and gold. Her face was troubled, her eyes afraid.

"Courage, little one," said Hanaud, and he slipped past her into the room. "It is as well that my ugly, familiar face should not be seen too soon."

The door closed and one of the strangers loitered along the corridor and spoke to a call-boy. The call-boy ran off. For five minutes more Mr. Ricardo waited with a beating heart. He had the joy of a man in the centre of things. All those people driving homewards in their motor-cars along the Strand— how he pitied them! Then, at the end of the corridor, he saw Clements and André Favart. They approached, discussing the possibility of Carmen Valeri's appearance in London opera during the next season.

"We have to look ahead, my dear friend," said Clements, "and though I should be extremely sorry—"

At that moment they were exactly opposite Joan Carew's door. It opened, she came out; with a nervous movement she shut the door behind her. At the sound, André Favart turned, and he saw drawn up against the panels of the door, with a look of terror in her face, the same gay figure which had interrupted him in Mrs. Blumenstein's bedroom. There was no need for Joan to act. In the presence of this man her fear was as real as it had been on the night of the Semiramis ball. She trembled from head to foot. Her eyes closed; she seemed about to swoon.

Favart stared and uttered an oath. His face turned white; he staggered back as if he had seen a ghost. Then he made a wild dash along the corridor, and was seized and held by two of the men in evening dress. Favart recovered his wits. He ceased to struggle.

"What does this outrage mean?" he asked, and one of the men drew a warrant and notebook from his pocket.

"You are arrested for the murder of Mrs. Blumenstein in the Semiramis Hotel," he said, "and I have to warn you that anything you may say will be taken down and may be used in evidence against you."

"Preposterous!" exclaimed Favart. "There's a mistake. We will go along to the police and put it right. Where's your evidence against me?"

Hanaud stepped out of the doorway of the dressing-room.

"In the property-room of the theatre," he said.

At the sight of him, Favart uttered a violent cry of rage. "You are here, too, are you?" he screamed, and he sprang at Hanaud's throat. Hanaud stepped lightly aside. Favart was borne down to the ground, and when he stood up again, the handcuffs were on his wrists.

Favart was led away, and Hanaud turned to Mr. Ricardo and Clements.

"Let us go to the property-room," he said. They passed along the corridor, and Ricardo noticed that Calladine was no longer with them. He turned and saw him standing outside Joan Carew's dressing-room.

"He would like to come, of course," said Ricardo.

"Would he?" asked Hanaud. "Then why doesn't he? He's quite grown up, you know," and he slipped his arm through Ricardo's and led him back across the stage. In the property-room, there was already a detective in plain clothes. Mr. Ricardo had still not as yet guessed the truth.

"What is it you really want, sir?" the property-master asked of the director.

"Only the jewels of the Madonna," Hanaud answered.

The property-master unlocked a cupboard and took from it the sparkling cuirass. Hanaud pointed to it, and there, lost amongst the huge glittering stones of paste and false pearls, Mrs. Blumenstein's necklace was entwined.

"Then that is why Favart came always to Covent Garden when *The Jewels of the Madonna* was being performed!" exclaimed Ricardo.

Hanaud nodded:

"He came to watch over his treasure."

Ricardo was piecing together the sections of the puzzle.

"No doubt he knew of the necklace in America. No doubt he followed it to England."

Hanaud agreed.

"Mrs. Blumenstein's jewels were quite famous in New York."

"But to hide them here!" cried Mr. Clements. "He must have been mad."

"Why?" asked Hanaud. "Can you imagine a safer hiding-place? Who is going to burgle the property-room of Covent Garden? Who is going to look for a priceless string of pearls amongst the stage jewels of an opera house?"

"You did," said Mr. Ricardo.

"I?" replied Hanaud, shrugging his shoulders. "Joan Carew's dreams led me to André Favart. The first time we came here and saw the pearls of the Madonna, I was on the look-out, naturally. I noticed Favart at the back of the stalls. But it was a stroke of luck that I noticed those pearls through my opera glasses."

"At the end of the second act?" cried Ricardo suddenly. "I remember now."

"Yes," replied Hanaud. "But for that second act the pearls would have stayed comfortably here all through the season. Carmen Valeri—a fool as I told you—would have tossed them about in her dressing-room without a notion of their value, and at the end of July, when the murder at the Semiramis Hotel had been forgotten, Favart would have taken them to Amsterdam and made his bargain."

"Shall we go?"

They left the theatre together and walked down to the grill-room of the Semiramis. But as Hanaud looked through the glass door he drew back.

"We will not go in, I think, eh?"

"Why?" asked Ricardo.

Hanaud pointed to a table. Calladine and Joan Carew were seated at it taking their supper.

"Perhaps," said Hanaud with a smile, "perhaps, my friend—what? Who shall say that the rooms in the Adelphi will not be given up?"

They turned away from the hotel. But Hanaud was right, and before the season was over, Mr. Ricardo had to put his hand in his pocket for a wedding present.

The Dancing Girl

Anthony Wynne

Anthony Wynne was the pen-name under which Robert McNair Wilson (1882–1963) wrote detective fiction. McNair Wilson was a Scot who studied at Glasgow Academy and Glasgow University before working as house surgeon at the city's Western Infirmary. An Asquithian Liberal, he contemplated a career in politics and stood for election in the Saffron Walden constituency in Essex at the general election of 1922, and again a year later, but with no success. After that he combined medicine with a literary career and he enjoyed a long stint as medical correspondent of *The Times*. His non-fiction books included *Napoleon the Man, High Finance, The Defeat of Debt*, and *Financial Freedom for Housing*. Under the name Harry Colindale, he published a novel which rejoiced in the title *They Want Their Wages*.

This fascination with matters financial seeped into his detective fiction, notably in *Death of a Banker* (1934), in which we are told that Dr. Eustace Hailey, his series detective, had a "heroic quality" which made him rebel against "the self-righteousness of the great age of Progress." Hailey yearned, as perhaps his creator did, "for the freedom of a vanished age." The Wynne novels combine social comment with intricate mysteries, often featuring a cunningly contrived "impossible crime," but at times the author's use of his fiction as a platform for his pontificating counts against readability. The short form of mystery doesn't permit such self-indulgence, and the tales collected in Wynne's *Sinners Go Secretly* (1927) include some of his best work. This example originally saw the light of day in *Flynn's Magazine* on 23 January 1926.

———

THERE WAS A GAIETY ABOUT THIS DANCING GIRL WHICH was as heady as wine and which was making the fortune of the Jermyn Cabaret.

Doctor Hailey leaned back in his chair and adjusted his eyeglass slowly. She was very pretty. A smile flickered on his lips as he thought of the description given of her by one of his friends; "So pretty that you don't know what to do."

There lay the secret. Lalette, so she called herself, aroused all sorts of emotions so quickly that they tumbled over one another until laughter, the laughter of children suddenly come to a Christmas fair with its bewilderment of attraction, was the only possible means of expression.

He raised his glass to his lips and sipped the exquisite wine, which it contained, very slowly. It was white Clos Vouget, the pale sister of the immortal red Burgundy of that name. Golden points of light shone from its clear depths. He set the glass down again and once more turned to Lalette; in some mysterious fashion she resembled the wine. It might even be possible to call her insipid if one had developed a taste for more exuberant gaiety. Men who drank red wine habitually, he reflected, were ignorant as a rule of the profound simplicity of white, that quality which transcends all the vintners' descriptions.

Lalette ceased to dance and stood on her tip-toes on the polished floor. The ribbons which clothed her hung straight down on her limbs, tremulously still like leaves when no breath of wind is stirring. Their garish mingling of colours intensified the whiteness of her skin and the pure gold of her hair. She gathered a handful of the rose petals which filled the basket on her arm and flung them up in the air so that they fell about her shoulders. Then she looked demure and sang a tiny love song, the last verse of which ran:

> *And when you come to me*
> *Your little feet must tread*
> *On flowers, and there must be*
> *White clouds above your head.*

As she sang, the white clouds were there, somewhere, between the dark floor and the absurd roof with its painted cupids. Doctor Hailey let his eyeglass fall. So had he seen those solemn clouds go sailing across the green face of the Dourto in high summer. The people at the tables forgot their applause for a moment, and that gave Lalette time to laugh and wave the clouds away with a sweep of her hand. She began to dance again, going among the tables with her rose leaves and her laughter like a naughty child escaping, by its short wits, from the dismissal already promised it.

She came in that fashion to the furthest table, under the little stage and close to the place where Doctor Hailey was sitting. A young man was waiting there and he rose as she approached. She turned and bowed to the audience, telling them that so far as they were concerned she had finished. Then, while they tried to win her back again, she gave her basket to an attendant and sat down. Other girls came tripping from the stage. The young man called a waiter, who brought a bottle of champagne very quickly.

Only Lalette would have dared so much. But in her case there were apparently no rules.

The young man, whose face was rather aggressive without being noble, bent towards her, and Doctor Hailey saw that his expression was strained as though he was greatly uneasy about something. Once he turned away from the girl and looked round the cabaret with questioning eyes. He scarcely tasted the supper which he had ordered.

And then a strange thing happened. A man, whom Doctor Hailey recognised with a thrill of incredulity as Lord Rushmere, strode into the room and came swiftly to Lalette's table. He appeared to start when he saw the girl's companion, then he held out his hand:

"My dear Dale."

His tones were friendly. But they exercised nevertheless, a tremendous effect on the young man. He sprang to his feet and sent his chair crashing backwards. He shouted:

"You damned scoundrel!"

Lord Rushmere started and his cold face flushed suddenly.

But he maintained an admirable self-control. He turned to Lalette, ignoring her companion entirely. She rose and laid her fingers on his arm.

"Lalette, you shall not leave me!"

The young man's voice rang out desperately so that all eyes were fixed on them. Then the girl's answer came clear and distinct in every syllable:

"My dear sir, don't be absurd, please."

She turned away. An attendant touched her former companion on the shoulder. He glanced round and was lost. It seemed to the doctor that he shuddered. As the couple moved to another table, he drew his hand, in dazed fashion, across his eyes. Then he stumbled from the table and left the supper room.

Doctor Hailey glanced at Lalette. She was laughing.

He was aware again of the infectiousness of her gaiety. He murmured to himself: "So pretty that you don't know what to do."

"Lady Rushmere, did you say, Jenkins?"

"Yes, sir."

"But she hasn't an appointment."

"No, sir."

Doctor Hailey glanced at his consultation book. The afternoon, until four o'clock, was uncharted.

"Very well," he said, "show her in."

Lady Rushmere entered the room slowly, almost reluctantly, holding out her hand to the doctor as though even that commonplace action cost her an effort. He indicated a chair, and she sank down into it without a word. He crossed the room to the window and drew down one of the blinds. When he turned again she was looking at him.

"As always," she said, "you understand."

His genial face discounted the compliment without rejecting it. He moved back to his chair and sat down.

"This spring sunlight is apt to be a trifle disconcerting," he remarked, "after the months of darkness."

"Especially when one must disclose anxieties and fears. My dear Doctor Hailey, is it possible that you too have heard?"

He realised that she was searching his face as she spoke. Lady Rushmere had been a beautiful girl, and even in middle age her eyes retained their lustre. They were, he reflected, difficult eyes from which to hide anything.

He extracted his snuff-box from his waistcoat pocket and took a pinch with much elegance. Then he adjusted his eyeglass.

"One hears so much," he said evasively, "and believes so little."

"Tell me what you have heard."

Her tones were tense now and vibrant. It was as though she had opened a window of her soul and bade him behold the emptiness, the bitterness, which dwelt within.

"My dear lady, it is not worth repeating."

He moved a trifle uneasily in his chair.

His great shoulders, the broadest in the whole profession of medicine, were raised slightly, as though he would, if he could, dismiss the idle gossip from his memory. But Lady Rushmere was determined.

"You know my husband," she exclaimed suddenly. "You

have known him for years. Do you think that he is going mad?"

She had straightened her body as she spoke so that it appeared to be held at tension. Her hands moved nervously, plucking at her dark gloves. He thought that the semi-mourning she was still wearing for her father became her excellently.

"I confess that I did ask myself that question."

"When you heard the stories?"

The question came sharply.

"No. When I saw him at the Jermyn cabaret two nights ago."

"Ah!"

Lady Rushmere sank back in the chair again and closed her eyes. Her expression had changed suddenly from eagerness to despondency. It was as though he had dealt her a blow. In the silence which followed, the lurch of a taxicab down Harley Street sounded loud and unnatural, almost aggressive.

At last she opened her eyes.

"That has been going on for months now," she said in low tones.

"Since his father's death or before it." She hesitated a moment and then added: "The girl has completely turned his head."

"She is a very attractive girl."

Lady Rushmere's eyes narrowed. Her lips were drawn for a moment on her teeth.

"That," she said, "is the excuse which men always make for men. Men shield each other—like thieves."

She uttered the last word with extreme bitterness so that

Doctor Hailey started. He regarded her closely with his rather dull eyes, and concluded that her husband's married life must have lacked much happiness in spite of her good looks and reputation for good nature. It was his experience that women who spoke ill of men in general, had usually disappointed the hopes or the faith of some particular man. Their abuse of the opposite sex was a sop offered to their own consciences, or perhaps to their vanity. He took another pinch of snuff and then asked:

"Your married life has been unhappy?"

"Very unhappy. Gerald never even tried to understand me. Besides, as you know, he is very rich and I am very poor— and very proud."

She spoke in low tones. But her voice, Doctor Hailey thought, was singularly calm.

"What about the war period? Did not that anxious time bring you closer together?"

"Oh dear no." She caught her breath. "He used to write me long letters from the front about his own doings and yet, will you believe it, my letters to him about my work in hospitals made so little impression on him that he scarcely mentioned them." She sighed. "But there, what is the use of going back to that time? In spite of everything, Doctor Hailey, I love my husband. We women are fools—fools."

Tears gleamed in her eyes. She turned her face away from him. Then she said in matter-of-fact tones:

"I am here to ask you to help me by coming down to Frings tomorrow for the week-end. He will be there, and I can pretend that I have invited you as an ordinary guest. I want you to study him and tell me exactly what conclusion you come to, and whether you think anything at all can be done. Please don't refuse me that great comfort."

The doctor bowed. "Very well," he said. "I shall come."

He reached the old Buckinghamshire house in time for dinner the next evening. As he entered the drawing-room, he restrained an exclamation of astonishment. Standing on the hearth rug, talking to Lord Rushmere, was the young man whom he had seen at supper with Lalette in the Jermyn Street cabaret! The two appeared to be on cordial terms.

Lord Rushmere introduced: "Mr. Michael Dale," in his crisp, clipped tones.

Doctor Hailey could not be sure if Dale recognised him; but he thought that the fellows' eyes gleamed significantly as he held out his hand. He was about to sit down when a fresh thrill or surprise was afforded him. Lady Rushmere entered the room accompanied by Lalette. She came at once to his side and introduced the girl as Miss Yorke. Her manner betrayed not the slightest embarrassment.

Lalette was dressed very quietly in a black frock of the severest cut. She looked, Doctor Hailey thought, more lovely, more spiritual than ever—as if having put away her gaiety she had won in its stead a most serene happiness. He bowed over her hand. When he raised his eyes to her face, he saw that her expression was sad.

Dinner was announced and they went to the dining-room. From the very beginning the meal proved an exceedingly uncomfortable one. Indeed the only members of the party who attempted to enliven it were Dale and Lalette, and their efforts seemed to exasperate rather than to relieve the tension. Dale, the doctor noted, was one of those agreeable fellows who speak always on a note of interrogation. He addressed his witticisms to everybody in the room in the evident hope that they would please everybody.

Lord Rushmere tried to show some interest, but Lady Rushmere preserved a cold and difficult silence. Doctor Hailey glanced at her uneventful face and wondered by what alchemy her husband had induced her to receive the dancing girl. And then he wondered why Dale should have consented to come to Frings and accept the hospitality of the man he had publicly denounced as a scoundrel. He could not answer these questions, and the fact that he could not answer them troubled him. He was recalled from that trouble by Dale's voice. It had become somewhat louder, as though he intended that, on this occasion at least, his wit should not fall on deaf ears.

"My dear Miss Yorke," he was saying, "men are only the counters with which you women play the great game of forfeits with one another."

Dale laughed as he spoke, and the nervous, rather irritating tone of his laughter startled the silence of the old room. Lalette tossed her pretty, golden head; it seemed that she was jogging her wits for a reply.

"Men," Lady Rushmere declared suddenly with vehemence, "are brutes—all of them. Is it not so?"

She addressed herself to Lalette, who flushed painfully.

"I don't think so, Lady Rushmere."

"Ah, because you are young and attractive. The moths love to burn their wings at a bright candle." Her eyes flashed suddenly, and she seemed to catch her breath. "Stolen fruit, I suppose, is always sweet," she exclaimed with unmistakable significance, "but wait till the day comes when you cannot steal any longer."

"My God!"

Lord Rushmere had risen from his seat. His face was pale and his lips trembled. But he was too late to stay the storm. His wife jumped up and confronted him with blazing cheeks; tears gleamed in her big eyes.

"I shall say it," she cried. "I shall! Everywhere, everywhere, humiliation and shame. Oh God, I wish that I were dead!"

She covered her face with her hands. Then she fled to the door of the room. At the door she turned and Doctor Hailey saw that anger was now dominant in her expression. He glanced at her husband and beheld a look of deep anxiety as though that unhappy man knew what was toward.

"I tell you I will not tolerate it any longer. I am going away—away."

They sat mute and helpless under the onslaught. The butler was entering the room with a crystal claret jug on his hand; his mistress saw him, and with a gesture which was swift as the spring of a panther, snatched the vessel from him. She dashed it down on the floor. Next moment she had gone.

Lord Rushmere bent over his plate. The butler filled his glass again. A cruel silence fell on them. Then Lalette rose and went quickly out of the room, and a moment later Dale followed her. Doctor Hailey and his host were left to themselves. Lord Rushmere drew a deep breath.

"It is terrible, is it not?" he asked in low tones.

The doctor raised his glass of Chateau Y'quem to his lips and drank thoughtfully. The vintage, he suspected, was the noble one of 1887. He did not venture to offer any reply.

"As I think you saw the beginning of this wretched episode and have now witnessed the end of it," his host declared, "you may as well hear the explanation also. You were in the cabaret in Jermyn Street on Wednesday night, if I am not mistaken?"

"Yes."

"And heard Dale call me a scoundrel?"

Doctor Hailey inclined his head. He took another sip of wine.

Lord Rushmere sighed deeply.

"The poor fool," he declared, "is wildly infatuated with Lalette Yorke, who I am afraid, does not return his love. When I approached her that night, he jumped to the wrong conclusion, as men in that state of mind are so apt to do."

He paused a moment and then raised his glass to his lips.

"Lalette," he added, "is the daughter of my oldest and dearest friend, Geoffrey Yorke. He died penniless ten years ago and left her, a child of eight, to my care. I have treated her as if she were my own daughter except in one particular direction." His voice grew hard suddenly, and his expression changed. "I have never invited her to this house because, had I done so, abuse and ill treatment would certainly have befallen her."

He became silent again. They heard the ticking of the big clock on the mantelpiece with strange distinctness. Doctor Hailey took a pinch of snuff.

"I see."

"Naturally her wonderful success has been an immense joy to both of us. I should have liked to share that happiness with my wife, but it was not possible. Our relationship, for years now, has been strained to the breaking point, and, as you know, a woman who is childless herself, is unable to bear the sight of her husband in the rôle of foster father. I never so much as mentioned Lalette's name."

He took another sip of wine.

"It was foolish, because naturally, we saw a good deal of one another. Dale's outburst opened my eyes to the extent of the mistake we had made. He is a close personal friend of my wife's, and his brother is my own lawyer. I called at his flat the next morning and told him everything. I told him, in addition, that I was going to explain matters to my wife right away and insist on her inviting Lalette down for the week-end, and I urged him to join the party. I felt that I owed that to the girl as well as to him."

He shook his head sadly.

"You have seen the result."

Doctor Hailey raised his eyeglass and set it carefully in position.

"How did Lady Rushmere receive your explanation?" he asked in slow tones.

"Wonderfully well. So well that I was astonished. She told me that she had heard I was often seen in Lalette's company and that she was profoundly glad to know the true facts of the case. She made not the least difficulty about inviting her down. I actually thought she had believed me for once in her life."

"I do not see how she could very well help believing you."

Lord Rushmere shrugged his shoulders. The gesture declared that his wife's convictions were infinitely elastic.

"It is sufficiently obvious, my dear doctor, is it not," he said, "that that attitude was mere pretence to afford her the opportunity of insulting Lalette? I imagine you were brought down here to witness the scene so that you might take the part of a woman brutally abandoned and betrayed by her husband. My wife, in our fifteen years of married life, has never missed a chance of convincing the world that she is the victim of a faithless cad. Dale, as his conduct showed, was certainly under that impression."

Doctor Hailey let his eyeglass fall. He leaned toward his host.

"Miss Yorke," he asked, "did not tell you that Dale was making love to her?"

"She never told me about her love affairs, and I never questioned her about them."

"So that the fellow may have been jealous of you for some time?"

"Oh, yes. It is very likely that he has seen us together. I'm afraid there must have been a good deal of gossip. As I have told you, my wife had heard all about it."

The doctor took snuff again. His face wore a puzzled expression.

"In that case he would be almost certain, would he not, to demand from the girl an explanation of her intimacy with you? And she would be compelled to satisfy him to some extent?"

Lord Rushmere contracted his brow.

"I don't quite follow you," he said dubiously.

"I mean that it is scarcely credible that Dale really believed you to be the scoundrel he called you?"

Doctor Hailey's voice was low, but he emphasised every word.

"But what possible reason could he have for calling me a scoundrel if he didn't believe that the name fitted me? Dale is an old friend, the brother of a very old friend. He is a friend, too, to whom I owe a good deal."

Lord Rushmere leaned back in his chair.

"As it happens, he was motoring with my father in Scotland last autumn, when the poor old man had his fatal seizure. His kindness at that time made a deep impression on me."

They went to the smoking room and Doctor Hailey settled himself in an armchair. His eyes were vacant, a sign that his mind was active. Lord Rushmere poured himself out a whisky and soda, working the syphon in sharp jerks.

"It is obvious," he said, "that the sooner this wretched party is broken up the better. I mean to take Lalette back to town tomorrow morning."

As he spoke, the door of the room opened and the butler approached Doctor Hailey.

"Her ladyship," he announced, "would be glad if you could see her for a few minutes."

Lady Rushmere's maid was waiting in the corridor. She escorted the doctor to her mistress's bedroom. A dim lamp was burning in the room, and by its light he saw his patient lying, with half-closed eyes, apparently in a state of great exhaustion. She held out her hand to him as he entered the room.

"Will you forgive me, my dear friend?"

Her voice was low and gentle. It was evident that the storm had blown itself out. Doctor Hailey sat down on a chair placed ready beside the bed.

"I have been talking to Lord Rushmere," he said in quiet

tones. "If I may say so, I think that you have been living under a complete misunderstanding."

He had scarcely spoken before he saw the dark eyes flash with new anger. Lady Rushmere raised herself on her elbow.

"That story about his ward!" she sneered bitterly.

"Quite so. I formed the impression that it was a true story."

She drew a sharp breath and the colour rushed to her cheeks.

"Oh, you men," she cried, "how easily you deceive one another. Do you suppose for a moment that, if the story had been true, Michael—Mr. Dale—would have behaved as he did in the cabaret?"

She sank back again on the pillows and closed her eyes. Doctor Hailey asked:

"But surely it is possible that Dale was unaware of her true position in relation to your husband?"

"It was he who told me that they were constantly seen together." Again she raised herself a little: "Do you really think that any lover would refrain from asking about such a relationship? What girl, too, would dare to refuse an answer?"

Doctor Hailey did not reply. These were the very questions which had been uppermost in his own mind during his talk with Lord Rushmere. His patient remained silent for a moment and then added:

"As it happens, she has confessed everything."

"You knew that, and yet you consented to ask her down here?"

The doctor's voice was scarcely raised above a whisper. He thought that he detected a movement of uneasiness as he spoke.

"I did not know until Michael told me an hour before dinner."

She closed her eyes again. Doctor Hailey rose and stood beside the bed.

"I cannot think," he said, "why Dale should have consented to come to this house with that knowledge in his mind."

Again Lady Rushmere moved uneasily.

"He came because I asked him to come. Yesterday I sent him a telegram."

Doctor Hailey had it on the point of his tongue to say that Lord Rushmere's invitation had preceded this one by a considerable period. But he restrained himself. Lady Rushmere seemed to have become very tired again and disinclined to talk. He excused himself and went back to the smoking room.

"Well?" his host asked as he entered.

"Your wife is exhausted, my dear sir."

"She told you I had deceived you, is it not so?"

The doctor nodded. He did not offer any further information. Lord Rushmere invited him to have a drink and filled a tumbler for him.

"In the circumstances," he declared, "I think that it will be best if I do not return here for some time. Do you agree?"

"Yes. I agree."

They talked for a few minutes on indifferent subjects, and then Doctor Hailey went to bed. But he found himself unable to sleep. Always the same questions presented themselves to his mind: If Dale knew that Lord Rushmere was in fact Lalette's lover, why had he accepted the man's invitation and come to Frings as a friend? One does not denounce a man as a scoundrel one day to take his hospitality the next.

On the other hand, if Dale believed the story that had been told him, why should he go out of his way to pretend to Lady Rushmere that it was untrue? He could discover no answer to these conundrums and was about to try to dismiss them finally from his mind when he heard a swift footfall in the corridor outside of his door.

The footsteps passed and the silence of the old house descended again. Then there came to him the unmistakable sound of a window being opened. It was a faint sound, as though great care was being exercised in the carrying out of the operation. He lay still a moment and then jumped out of bed and went to the window. But the night was too dark to enable him to see anything. It was also bitterly cold, even for March, and he shivered as he stood. Impelled by he knew not what impulse, he pulled on his dressing-gown and socks and went out into the corridor. The house was profoundly silent. He moved slowly along the staircase and looked down into the wide hall. But again the darkness defeated him. After a moment he descended the stair.

As he did so a chill draught again warned him that the window, the opening of which he had heard, was still open. He followed the direction of the draught and came to the window. There was no sound anywhere.

The window was at the back of the hall facing the offices. It had been opened just wide enough to allow of egress from the house. He was about to climb out when he saw a faint gleam of light issuing from beneath a door on the opposite side of the yard. He strained his ears, but the silence yielded none of its secret. He hoisted himself on to the sill, an operation not very congenial to his build and disposition, and listened again. This time he distinctly heard a thudding, as of a muffled hammer, a stroke repeated several times in quick succession. He lowered himself to the yard and moved away a little distance from the window. At the same moment the spark of light under the door was extinguished. There was the sound of a heavy gate being moved. Then the same quick footsteps he had heard outside of his room came towards him across the yard. Next moment the beam of an electric torch shone on the open window, and was reflected therefrom to the face of the man carrying it.

It was Dale.

Doctor Hailey took a swift step forward and confronted the fellow.

At the sound of his footfall Dale shrank back with an exclamation of dismay. But an instant later he seemed to recover himself. He flashed his torch in the doctor's face.

"Doctor Hailey!" he cried in sheer bewilderment.

"Yes. I fancied I heard the sound of a window being opened and came down to reconnoitre. I had just climbed out here when I heard your steps."

Dale drew a sigh, the relief of which was unmistakable. His tones became immediately friendly.

"The fact is," he explained, "that I remembered, after I had gone to bed, that I hadn't covered up the radiator of my car. I was afraid the water might freeze in this sudden frost."

He stood back as he spoke for the doctor to enter the house, keeping the beam of light focused on the window meanwhile. When they had both entered he closed the sash carefully and replaced the bolt.

"I thought I should make less noise going this way than by the front door," he added. "That has so many bolts and bars."

They ascended the stair and came to the door of Doctor Hailey's bedroom. Dale muttered a hasty good-night and moved away along the corridor. The doctor went to bed and fell asleep immediately.

When he came downstairs next morning Lord Rushmere was on the point of leaving for London. He was standing with Lalette before the big fire in the dining-room and his face wore an expression of deep despondency. His car, a handsome blue saloon, was at the front door.

"You will forgive me, doctor," he apologised, "for this unceremonious leave-taking, but in the circumstances—"

He broke off and left the room to give some orders to his servants. Doctor Hailey and Lalette were alone. He turned to the girl with his gentle smile:

"Will you satisfy the curiosity of a student of the mind on one small point?" he asked her.

"Oh, yes." Her eyes were still full of the unhappiness he had seen in them on the previous evening; her hands, he noticed, twitched nervously.

"Did Mr. Dale ever ask you about your friendship with Lord Rushmere?"

She started slightly and then shook her head.

"It is strange," she declared, "that you should ask that, because Lord Rushmere has asked me the same question himself this morning. Mr. Dale never once spoke of our friendship."

"Did he know about it?"

"Oh, yes. I told him myself."

"What! But in that case why should he have made the scene in the cabaret?"

Doctor Hailey's voice held a note of excitement.

"I can't think why, unless he disbelieved me. I couldn't understand it at the time." She added after a moment, "Mr. Dale is not a very close friend of mine, you see."

"You are going to London now with Lord Rushmere?"

"Oh, yes, as soon as possible. I came down here by train, but there are no trains on Sunday till the afternoon, and I refuse to stay."

Lord Rushmere returned to the room and announced that the car was ready. Doctor Hailey accompanied them to the front door. He stood beside the car while a servant arranged the rugs about Lalette's feet.

"Have you turned on the heater, George?" Lord Rushmere asked him.

"No, my lord."

"Hailey, like a good fellow, open that back door beside you and turn the handle you will see on the floor just under the seat."

The doctor did as he was requested. The servant finished his task, Lord Rushmere waved his hand.

"Well, good-bye."

"Good-bye."

The big blue car glided away down the long avenue, the panels gleaming splendidly in the clear sunlight. Doctor Hailey turned back to the house. As he did so he cried out in amazement, staring at his right hand with eyes in which, already, an expression of horror had appeared.

There was a reddish smear, like rust, across two of his finger tips. He turned to the servant at his side.

"Tell me, quick, did you notice any stains on the upholstery of the car when you cleaned it, this morning?"

The man stared. "No, sir. But there was a stain on the door-handle—like a blood stain."

"Good Lord!"

The doctor sprang into the houses almost colliding with Dale as he did so. He rushed to the window by which that young man had gone out the night before and drew out the bolt. At sight of it he exclaimed again. He flung it open and leaped out, coming almost at a bound to the door of the garage. His servant was washing his own big Daimler car just outside of the door.

"Start her up," he shouted. "Start her up, for God's sake."

The astonished chauffeur did as he was told. His master sprang to the wheel and directed the servant to get inside with him. The car began to move. At that moment Dale ran round the side of the house and jumped on the footboard. He placed a hand, some of the fingers of which were bandaged, on the side of the car.

"What the devil is wrong?" he cried. "Where are you going?"

"You murderous swine."

Doctor Hailey's strong arm shot out and his fist crashed into the face that was thrust towards him. Dale went reeling back and fell full length on the tiles of the yard. At the same instant a woman's cry, shrill, piteous, rang out from somewhere above them. The great car bounded towards the avenue and went sweeping forth between the long lines of the leafless beech trees.

Doctor Hailey's expression was blank now; his eyes were quite cold and his lips were set. His driver, who sat beside him, saw that he was giving full throttle and that, already, the speedometer had leaped up beyond thirty. They took the curve into the main road in a fashion which caused that usually daring young man to hold his breath.

The needle indicated forty...fifty...fifty-five miles an hour. The great car sobbed on the hard, frostbitten road. Doctor Hailey's expression grew tranquil. His mind began to gather the pieces of evidence which he had collected and to arrange them in an orderly pattern—the fact that Lord Rushmere was a millionaire whereas his wife was penniless; the description given him of the death of Lord Rushmere's father—a multi-millionaire—while motoring in Scotland with Michael Dale; the obvious affection in which Lady Rushmere held that unpleasant young man. These were the outer ring of material circumstances; surrounded by them, as it were, lay the scene in the Jermyn Street cabaret and the scene in the dining-room at Frings, Dale's midnight visit to the garage, his bandaged fingers, injured no doubt at his task, the bloodstains on the handle of the heater in the saloon—the fact that this heater derived its warmth from the poisonous gases of the car's exhaust pipe.

They swept round another bend and there was disclosed a long stretch of road. The doctor's eyes challenged the distance as a brave man challenges his fate. But the road was empty. Dale's brother was Lord Rushmere's lawyer. So that if—as was probable in the highest degree—Lord Rushmere had made a will in Lalette's favour, Dale might very well know about it. He would know in that case, that it would be useless to kill the man and leave the girl alive—worse than useless.

But how to entice man and girl together to a place convenient for their simultaneous undoing?

Another corner—another vista of road.

If Lord Rushmere and Lalette perished together Lady Rushmere would probably inherit everything. Her lover might set his hands on a million.

He cried out suddenly and indicated, with a swift gesture, a dark speck far ahead of them.

"The blue saloon!"

He turned to his man.

"How fast do you suppose they are travelling?"

"As fast as she'll do, sir. Good God!"

The man jumped in his seat. The blue saloon had swerved across the road. Doctor Hailey drew his breath sharply. But the car righted itself again and went sweeping onward.

So it followed that Dale had begun making love to Lalette in order to work up to the cabaret scene and so compel Lord Rushmere to bring the girl to Frings. (A very pretty piece of mind study that, which, without doubt, owed something of its sureness of touch to Lady Rushmere's inspiration.) It followed, too, that the scene in the dining-room had been designed to force the victims to ride away together at the earliest possible hour, in the bitter cold, when a heater would prove a godsend.

"I'm going to pass her," Doctor Hailey spoke through clenched teeth. "It is the only hope of stopping them."

"Oh, sir, look how she's swerving."

The doctor's lips were tightly pressed together. He swung the big car and drew closer to his quarry. Then a cry broke from his lips.

The blue saloon had plunged again. It reeled fearfully and seemed to throw itself up against the embankment of the road like a terrified horse. Next instant it went crashing out of their view.

The trial of Michael Dale at Edinburgh for the murder of Lord Rushmere's father in his motor car in Scotland is still fresh in the public mind. The car employed on that occasion was a landaulette and the Crown, it will be recalled, advanced the theory that Dale, after opening a joint in the heater, and thus causing poisonous gases and fumes to escape into the closed vehicle so soon as it began to move, had used the speaking-tube to obtain for himself a supply of fresh air. The evidence of the chauffeur showed that the young man had occupied the side of the car in which the tube was situated.

His motive was obvious enough when the letters which had passed between him and Lady Rushmere were read in court. He meant to murder father and son in succession and so secure their wealth by marriage.

The public, however, did not learn all the facts of the story. The circumstances attending the suicide of Lady Rushmere after the plot had miscarried were but lightly touched on at the trial. Nor was the name of Lalette Yorke brought into the case except in a passing reference to her own and Lord Rushmere's wonderful recoveries from the double effect of the lethal gases in the saloon and the shock of the accident occasioned by their influence—recoveries due, without any doubt, to the promptness of the measures taken to afford rescue and restoration.

In View of the Audience

Marguerite Steen

Born in Liverpool and educated in Kendal, Marguerite Steen (1894–1975) abandoned a career in teaching to try her luck on the stage. In 1921, she joined a company run by Fred Terry and his wife, Julia Neilson (who had starred on the stage as Lady Blakeney, wife of the Scarlet Pimpernel), and toured with them for three years. Her friend Ellen Terry encouraged her to write a novel which was published in 1927 and launched a long and prolific writing career. Steen was for many years the companion of the artist Sir William Nicholson.

Steen wrote a handful of plays, as well as many novels and biographies of Nicholson, Hugh Walpole, and the Terry family. Her novels include such titles as *Matador* and *Who Would Have Daughters?* and she was elected a Fellow of the Royal Society of Literature in 1951. One of her stranger claims to fame was that the *Coronation Street* actress Pat Phoenix, a major celebrity in the 1960s, took her stage name from Steen's novel *Phoenix Rising*. Steen is not generally thought of as a crime writer, but this story, which first appeared in the *Strand Magazine* in June 1934, is a good example of her talent for storytelling.

———

GEORGE BREWSTER PICKED UP HIS HAT, GLOVES, walking-stick, a seven-and-sixpenny thriller and, finally, himself from the floor of the first-class compartment, assembled the units with as much dignity as he could muster, decided that dignity, in the circumstances, was a little ridiculous, and ended by grinning at the solitary witness of the pantomime turn which he, involuntarily, had provided.

"A near thing," he admitted, regarding with sympathy the remains of what had been, a few seconds previously, a goodish hat, and now, owing to his own ill-timed impetuosity, more nearly resembled a grey felt pancake than anything he could remember having seen before.

"Ah, yes—awfully near!" gasped the little man, who sat at the further end of the compartment. To look at him, one might have imagined that it was he, rather than George Brewster, who had just succeeded, at imminent risk to life and limb, in boarding the train as the end carriages swung past the platform. His smooth, straw-coloured face was overlaid with pallor, and he blinked his eyelids so rapidly that it was not until some time had passed that Brewster had the opportunity of noticing that the eyes themselves were rather remarkable, of a surprisingly light turquoise blue.

"Excuse me," murmured the little man, a few moments later. "Would you mind—so very much—if we had the windows *both* up for a minute or two? We're just coming to the tunnel."

"Pleasure," mumbled George Brewster, dropping his paper to comply with the timid request. "Afraid I gave you rather a shock," he roared, above the tunnel thunder of the train.

"Oh, not at all," came the protestant squeak of the other's voice. They did not attempt to pursue the conversation further until the train ran again into open country; when, to Brewster's surprise, the little man ventured, diffidently:

"I suppose—that is to say—would you care for me to lend you a brush? The floors of these carriages are not kept as they ought to be—by any manner of means."

"Good lord, no, they aren't, are they?" said Brewster, perceiving for the first time the abominable smear of dust down the crease of his trousers. "I'd be very much obliged—if you've got such a thing handy."

His companion opened a dressing bag and produced a brush, which Brewster proceeded to put to its proper use.

"By the way," he said, carelessly, while so employed, "have you any idea what time this train gets into Crewe?"

"Crewe?" repeated the little man, with a puzzled stare. "Did you say Crewe? Dear me, I'm very sorry; I'm afraid this isn't the Crewe train at all. How very unfortunate!"

Swaying with the train, Brewster gaped speechlessly.

"The first stop," explained the little man, punctiliously, "is at a place called Coalford, in the Midlands. It's rather an odd run, this one," he went on in a conversational voice. "In fact, one might call it an example of the pleasing whimsy which now and again takes possession even of the railway companies! One can hardly understand why a place like Coalford should have a non-stop special of its own. We leave the main line at Stafford—"

"Good lord, man," gasped George Brewster, weakly, "are you certain? The Crewe train always starts from that platform."

"Not now," corrected the other. "Dear, dear me, I'm so sorry about it!" He seemed to adopt the whole affair as a matter of personal oversight. "Really," he continued with deep concern, "you could hardly be coming to a more unfortunate place than Coalford! There's no main-line train for three hours after this gets in—"

"I suppose I can get a car," interrupted Brewster, scowlingly.

"You may," said the little man, doubtfully, "or you may not. I, personally, should be very sorry to entrust myself to any of Coalford's means of locomotion for a long-distance journey. I'm terribly afraid—you see, Coalford is a dreadfully primitive place. In fact, it's quite a frightful place. A sort of little down-and-out industrial town. I've just bought a theatre there," he concluded, startlingly.

In spite of his anger and perturbation, Brewster could not help being arrested by the final words. They completed his conviction that his travelling companion, although pleasant, was slightly mad. It was annoying to be shut up with a mad person for an hour and a half—it must be at least that before they got into the Midlands. He said, huffily:

"Sounds rather a venture, doesn't it? I didn't think any provincial theatres were flourishing at present; and if the place is as you describe—!"

"It was very cheap," confessed his companion, naïvely. "And I've got an idea of turning it into a picture-house. I think if we could manage to get hold of one or two really good films—one of Maureen Maguire's, for instance—"

The frown on George Brewster's forehead smoothed

itself away, and the irritation from his mind. His whole soul expanded with a ridiculous brotherliness towards the man whom, a few seconds before, he had regarded as an unmitigated bore. It is an incontrovertible fact that the average person regards any purveyor of unpleasant news with a feeling of unjust resentment, and in this respect George Brewster was very average. But, in common with ninety per cent of the audiences who had seen the Magnificent All-British Super-Drama, *Piccadilly Princess*, he was convinced that he was in love with the heroine, Maureen Maguire; and the mention of the lady of his heart, the totally unexpected opportunity it afforded of discoursing upon a topic near his soul, completely banished his former unworthy thoughts of his companion.

"You certainly ought to make money with Maureen Maguire," he agreed, eagerly. "Now, tell me: have you ever noticed—"

"I like drama," put in the little man, dreamily.

"She's got the whole lot of them whacked for drama!" beamed George Brewster. "Shearer, Garbo, Dietrich—"

"I wasn't thinking of screen drama, I'm afraid," was the disappointing response. "The drama of real life: that's the thing for me. I'm afraid I don't think a great deal of film drama: in fact, I'm not interested in films, as films, at all."

"Your point of view is interesting," said George Brewster, a trifle stiffly, for he resented being arrested in full flight upon a topic on which he felt he could do himself justice. "You know, it's curious," he could not help adding, "but I should never have connected you with the theatre in any way—acting, or management."

"I never looked well in an astrachan collar," smiled the

little man, wanly. "And cigars make me sick." He paused to extract a card from his note-case, which he handed to George Brewster. "Not," he added, with an air of modest disclaimer, "that it will convey anything to you."

George made the polite noises one uses to disguise the fact that a name actually does convey nothing at all. "Henry Morpeth" was engraved upon the card, and an address that one connects vaguely with the region about Portman Square. He volunteered the information that his own name was Brewster—George Brewster; which was received by his companion with a courteous inclination of the head.

"No, I suppose I don't look much like a manager," said Mr. Morpeth, regretfully. "Although," he added, "I once wrote a play. Still, that doesn't make one a manager, does it?"

Brewster agreed it didn't. By now he was quite convinced that Henry Morpeth, if not positively crazy, was definitely feeble-minded. To humour him, he asked, on the kindly contemptuous note that one adopts towards the breed:

"Ever have your play produced?"

"Oh, yes," said Mr. Morpeth, gently. "Maureen Maguire played in it. That would be—let me see—twenty years ago."

George Brewster nearly shot out of his seat: an involuntary betrayal of his feelings which was not lost upon Mr. Morpeth.

"Wonderful woman," he murmured, the smile playing once more across his pale, somewhat foolish-looking face. "One of the immortals, I should say—really—what? Naturally, I was very much in love with her. She was about eighteen at the time; I a trifle older—well, maybe nine or ten years older. Romantic, you know, like all young men in those days."

A kind of depression had fallen upon George Brewster;

he made the simultaneous discovery that his feet were cold and that he was thirsty. He was, also, furious with himself for having been such a muttonheaded idiot as to get on the wrong train and ready to gnash his teeth at the prospect of spending three hours in such a place as Henry Morpeth had described.

"Perhaps," said Mr. Morpeth, diffidently, "if you have nothing better to do—that is, if you really can't find a means of getting away from Coalford until the main-line connection comes in—you might care to look at my newly acquired property with me?"

Brewster grunted conventional thanks and dug his hands in his pockets. He began, under his breath, in a mournful, valedictory fashion, to whistle the first bars of the theme-song from *Piccadilly Princess.*

"Of course," continued Mr. Morpeth, "it may be no good at all. Quite useless. Only fit to be pulled down. Deterioration, you know, and all that. Dry rot. Rats. What?"

Involuntarily, Brewster ceased his whistling and stared.

"Do you mean to say you've bought a theatre—in a place like Coalford—without the slightest idea what condition it is in?" He began, against his will, to find something interesting in what looked like large-scale idiocy.

"It really was *very* cheap," deprecated Mr. Morpeth. "I happened to hear it was for sale—and I had a little money by me—so I instructed my solicitors to buy. You see, they couldn't ask very much for a property that had been lying empty getting on for twenty years; could they?"

"I should say not," snorted Mr. Brewster, his commercial instinct rising in outrage in the presence of such foolishness.

"No," said Mr. Morpeth, thoughtfully. "It's really very

queer. You never know which way a thing like that will strike the public. You know what people are: how they'll go and stare for hours at the outside of a house where a crime's been committed. It might, of course, have been the making of the place. Instead—for some reason or other—they simply sheered off. Funny, isn't it?"

"Something queer took place in the theatre?" suggested Brewster, as the other broke off.

"Oh, yes. Really. Devilish queer," murmured the little man, softly; he wiped away the vapour with his cuff, and stared through the window at a rain-sodden landscape. "Horrid weather we're having, for the time of year, don't you think?"

A very odd feeling began to creep over George Brewster. He was not an imaginative young man, neither was he given to apprehensions; yet the rhythmical beat of the wheels over the metals suddenly seemed, to his startled fancy, to be charged with some kind of mysterious purpose, faintly sinister, that crystallised in the innocuous person of his travelling companion.

He leaned back in his corner and scowled forensically at the profile of Henry Morpeth. Any less suggestive personality could hardly be imagined; a small, quiet, conventional-looking man, with a middle-class timorousness in the parting of his hair. The last person on earth, one would have said, to indulge any impulse, prudent or imprudent; cautious, humble, self-effacing, of comfortable but not excessive means. Possibly a retired Government official; his age might be anywhere between thirty-five and fifty-five. His face was smooth and unlined, but the skin itself had a look almost of antiquity. A furious curiosity took possession of George Brewster, which he controlled in his next remark.

"So you're thinking of turning it into a picture-house?"

"Well, yes, rather; if it isn't too dilapidated to do anything with at all. You see, it struck me it would be amusing to fetch Maureen Maguire back into the place where I first met her—twenty years ago."

Again the cold, uncomfortable twinge passed through George Brewster. Apart from the shock experienced by a young man when he learns that the charmer whom he has regarded as being in the heyday of her youth and beauty is approaching her fortieth year, there was something—some hidden shade of meaning that seemed to slide beneath his companion's mild words.

"I suppose, Mr. Brewster, you never by any chance happened to write a play?" The little man's voice was apologetic, as though he felt that he was, merely by making the suggestion, attributing a wholly unjustifiable indiscretion to his unknown companion.

"Well, no," said Brewster. "What sort of a play was it?" he added, with an effort; he did not really want to know, but Morpeth was making so obvious an effort to be agreeable, one could not but meet him half way.

"Oh, it was really a very bad play," he confessed, hastily. "Very bad indeed. It was supposed to be a thriller. It was, in fact, a sort of pot-pourri of all the thrillers I had ever read. I was, in fact, I still am, very fond of thrillers; a taste, I venture to think, you share with me?" he added, with a questioning glance at the book which lay between them.

"I must say I enjoy a good detective yarn as much as anything," admitted Brewster, uneasily, without knowing why.

"Only, of course, nothing that happens in books is ever

quite so interesting as real life," qualified Mr. Morpeth. "To begin with, the mystery, if there is a mystery, is always solved. Now—perhaps you won't agree with me—the best mysteries are those for which there is no possible solution."

Brewster frowned; he had an orderly and business-like mind; he detested leaving a thing unfinished. He disagreed, verbally, with Mr. Morpeth.

"Well, perhaps I'm wrong," said the latter, obligingly. "But I confess to a great weakness for the unsolved mystery. It always—how shall I put it?—*gratified* my sense of—well, I dare say it sounds ridiculous, but if I might call it my artistic sense?—that the affair at the Coalford Theatre Royal was never cleared up: in spite of the fact that everybody in the audience saw it take place—just as clearly as I can see you now." He gave a little apologetic cough—his whole life seemed to be tuned to a key of apology—and concluded, "But no doubt I'm boring you. All rather before your time— what? Let's see—we shall be in in a quarter of an hour or so. Singularly unattractive scenery, what?"

A sordid panorama, common to the coal-mining districts, lay about them; beneath the filthy haze of smoke stretched a squalid network of mean streets, and clusters of chimneys poked their ugly black fingers up at the sky of yellowish grey, from which descended a drizzle that laid a slimy polish upon roofs and pavements. A little down-and-out industrial town, Mr. Morpeth called it; Brewster agreed with the description. Even from the train one could perceive the ugly languor of poverty in the movements of figures about the streets.

The thought that, but for this chance meeting, he would have been condemned to three hours' solitude in such a place, sent a shudder down Brewster's spine. He could imagine what the station, or the hotels, would be like.

He was now positive that Morpeth was raving mad to purchase a theatre in such a town. Something called the Coliseum raised its leprous façade above the railway line: it carried a few tattered posters of old-fashioned films; its upper windows were black with grime, its woodwork had obviously had no acquaintance with the paint-brush for many years. Apparently, Coalford could not support one picture-house, let alone two.

Brewster turned a look of recrimination upon his companion, and was startled by the curious change which had come over the aspect of Mr. Henry Morpeth. His thin, colourless face was twitching with excitement; smiles came and went about his nervously moving lips; his turquoise-blue eyes glittered with light.

"I used to live here, you know," he babbled, "years ago. I was living here when I wrote my play—the one Maureen Maguire acted in. It was a frightfully important thing for me. Of course, no one knew how important it was—except for Maureen and Caryll." He gave a little laugh. "How it would surprise—both of them! If they knew I'd bought the theatre."

When they were out upon the sticky, mud-printed platform, and Brewster had sent a necessary wire or two, Morpeth turned to him eagerly.

"Do you mind walking? It is only a step or two, and we can share my umbrella."

Henry Morpeth walked with the quick, short steps of a man with a definite object before him: holding his head down, hunching his shoulders, driving his spare body between the dull crowds of the pavements with such sure effect that presently Brewster was left behind him—plodding along, with coat-collar turned up, rain trickling from his hat-brim, and a murderous feeling in his heart. What a devilish hole! It actually made one feel poor oneself, he was reflecting, when he saw Morpeth beckoning him from the corner of a murky-looking alley which took them out of the main traffic stream into one of those unspeakably dreary backwaters wherein, usually, are situated stage-doors.

"I have the key," muttered Henry Morpeth in his undertone of excitement. He fumbled with a latch, the door itself creaked open, and they passed into a darkness which drove chill to the very marrow of George Brewster's bones.

"Mind how you come," said Morpeth's voice out of the darkness. "You'll soon be used to it—your eyes, I mean. There *are* some windows, somewhere; I suppose they're covered up with dirt. Look out!—here's the door on to the stage; it's come partly off its hinges. Dear, dear, how tiresome! It's all right, I'm holding it up for you. Go straight ahead. Now you're on the stage itself."

Gradually darkness was dissolving into twilight round George Brewster; he saw himself standing in the middle of a vast, empty space, with another space, blacker, on his left. And, almost simultaneously, he got the impression that of all places in the world there is none more evilly eerie than an empty, deserted theatre. A rat whisked across at an angle and vanished between the edges of some flats stacked in the scene-dock at the back of the stage. The boards he stood upon crackled with rottenness; things like immense, obscene cobwebs—he supposed they had once been scenery—hung down from above. And over all was the fearful, penetrating cold. It was a beast of a place. He loathed it.

"Look out for those trapdoors," Henry Morpeth was saying in a voice louder and sharper than the one he had previously used. "I should think the hinges are gone: you don't want to take an unexpected trip into the mezzanine, do you?"

"I don't want to take a trip anywhere," snapped Brewster. "I'm sorry, Morpeth—and it's no business of mine; but someone made the biggest mug in creation of you. The only thing this is fit for is burning. It's—it's—" He was going to add "haunted," but was ashamed of the word. As though he had spoken it, Morpeth answered quietly:

"You feel it's ghostly, don't you? That's what they complained of, I believe; I mean the companies who came, afterwards, to play here. Of course, you're standing, as a matter of fact, on just about the place where the murder happened."

George Brewster ached all over with the effort he made not to take a sideways leap from the spot where he was standing. Instead, he achieved a laugh, which went echoing horridly out into the empty auditorium.

"So there was a murder, was there? I must say I think your taste's a bit morbid."

"In full view of the audience," said the voice of Morpeth behind his shoulder. "And nobody moved a muscle. You see, quite naturally, they thought it was part of the play."

"Oh, hell!" said Brewster, feeling his nerves cracking up. "I suppose you've brought me here to tell me about it. Can't we find a place a bit less—a bit more agreeable, for your story?"

"Just through there," said Morpeth, pointing obligingly to a dark pit of a doorway, "there's the dressing-room where they found Peters—that was the ASM—I don't know if you're accustomed to these theatrical terms, but ASM stands for assistant stage-manager—bound and gagged after the murder took place. He died, incidentally, as well—of suffocation. I always think that was a mistake; I mean it wasn't intended. The person who committed the murder trussed Peters up closer than he intended—no one had anything against Peters. I don't doubt there'll be a chair in his dressing-room; we can go in there, if you like."

"Thanks very much," said Brewster, shortly. "I think perhaps this will do after all."

"Well, I'll go and get the chairs," said Morpeth, calmly, and vanished into what resembled the mouth of the Black Hole of Calcutta, leaving Brewster alone upon the dim stage. He would have given all he possessed, at that moment, to turn round and walk straight out of the theatre. The few minutes which elapsed before Morpeth's return were an eternity filled with the most detestable and humiliating fears. Nor were these entirely banished by the return of his companion: for once again Brewster became aware of that underlying queerness that ran like an undercurrent of darkness beneath Morpeth's mild demeanour. Morpeth sat down and linked his hands about his knees.

"It takes rather an effort of the imagination," he offered, peering at Brewster, "to see Maureen Maguire on this stage, now?"

"She wouldn't like the rats," mumbled Brewster, seeing out of the corner of his eye a particularly large, aggressive specimen.

"She didn't then," said Morpeth, quickly. "Caryll used to

put them in her dressing-room, so as to scare her, while they were rehearsing."

"Unpleasant fellow, evidently, this Caryll," observed Brewster.

"Oh, very!" agreed Morpeth, casually. "He was murdered, of course."

"Look here," said Brewster, suddenly "although this allusive style of yours is very—what's it?—provocative, hadn't you better get down to brass tacks and tell me the whole tale, straight through?"

"It's an odd thing," returned Morpeth, with his look of rather foolish surprise. "That's a thing I've always had the greatest difficulty in doing. Other things snatch at my attention. I could never, for instance, write a novel; and perhaps that's why I couldn't write a decent play. However, I'll do my best.

"You see, Caryll bought my play. I'd written it, of course, for Maureen Maguire, because I'd seen her in some other show—a melodrama, I think it was—and I suppose I'd fallen for that little tragic way of hers: it reminded me rather of a wood-anemone that has been beaten down by rain. Excuse me, won't you? That sort of thing will strike you as old-fashioned, but I find the greatest difficulty in moving with the times.

"Caryll bought my play—I think he gave me five pounds for it. Not excessive; but as things turned out—I mean to say, when I found out what a rotten, lying, yellow cheat Caryll was, I thought I was pretty lucky to have got a fiver out of him." For some reason, the very coolness of the tone in which Morpeth affixed these opprobrious epithets to the name of Caryll sent a shiver down Brewster's back.

"Then they came down here to rehearse, with a little company of sorts; I say of sorts because you couldn't expect a troupe of Beerbohm Trees or Tempests for the money Caryll was paying. Maureen was his leading lady, and she got two pounds a week—except when he talked her out of it. Those were the times she was adoring him. There were other times she hated him; and always she had a terror of him that made one a little—well, sick to watch them together. Caryll had a gift for playing on her terror."

"I suppose she could have found another manager," put in Brewster, gruffly.

"She wasn't famous then, you know," said Morpeth, mildly. "And I know she was keeping somebody. The women, who were jealous of her, said it was a child; and the men swore it was her old mother. I never bothered about it much. You see, I loved Maureen; I would quite cheerfully have cut my own throat if it would have given her any pleasure—or saved her from Caryll. He was the kind of thing lady novelists describe, I believe, as a 'hulking brute,' and I—well, you see me. I don't think I ever topped the scale much above nine stone. Besides, if I'd interfered he would only have taken it out of Maureen, so I was as polite to him as I knew how, although he spent the greater part of rehearsals in telling me the play was— what's the modern word?—lousy. *Not* a pretty word; but Caryll's language was worse. It used to make me feel quite sick, sometimes, when Maureen was there, looking like a wood-an—looking like she always did: so sweet and gentle, and pitiful for me and for all of them, when Caryll knocked them about at rehearsals.

"Of course, it was a frightfully bad play. I should say the

only reason for Caryll's buying it was that I was unknown, and therefore easy to pluck, and that it had a showy part for him. Though he loathed being killed in the second act. That shows you how much I knew about play-writing; I killed the hero in the second act. It was altered, of course; Caryll got stabbed and the audience thought he was dead, and then he turned up in a hospital bed at the beginning of Act Three—an extra bit I had to write in, as well as Caryll's part for the rest of the play.

"The supposed 'murder,' I must say, was absolutely tran-spontine; it took place in a blue light, and Caryll was supposed to be stabbed from behind by a man with a sort of hood over his face. The fellow who did this was Peters, the ASM, because the villain, who should have done it, had a quick change just then. You see how it was? Not a word was spoken, and the man wore a mask, so anyone who happened to be about the same height and build as the villain could rush on and do it; the business only took a few seconds; then the curtain came down. I rather fancied that bit, myself; thought it was neat.

"Of course, after rehearsals started I didn't think of anything very much except Maureen. I suppose she was a good actress; I haven't the slightest idea. All I can tell you is that her slightest movement, a quiver of her lip, the droop of her little shoulders, simply drove all the blood away from my heart and I could have fainted. Rather exaggerated—what? I assure you that's how it was with me—and not only with me, but with one or two of the others as well.

"I suppose I was very young and green in those days, and Caryll saw it and got a lot of fun out of me.

"Someone said he was a good lover. Maureen didn't look

like it. One day he'd be all over her, making love and mauling her in public until no one knew where to look; and the next day he'd call her every foul name you can think of, in front of the whole company—and twice he struck her.

"I dare say you think we were a poor lot to stand for that. I, as I've said, was about nine stone to Caryll's fifteen; and the rest were dependent upon him for their bread-and-butter. It's odd how that soaks the natural nobility out of men.

"Sometimes the air was so thick with hate you could feel it shiver; and Caryll would come down through the shivering air—great blond beast, six feet or more in height—smiling, and be filthily rude to Maureen in front of everyone; and then he'd turn round and grin at the company, as much as to say, 'You see who's master of this theatre—and this woman!'

"You mustn't let me start on about Caryll!" screamed Morpeth, suddenly. "It's past—that madness! It must never, never come back again!"

"Shut up!" bellowed Brewster, shaken out of his uncertain self-control by Morpeth's outburst, which went ringing round the emptiness like a shrieking ghost. Quite suddenly, Morpeth was still: deadly still, as though Brewster's words had stunned him. Then, once again, he gave his soft, infinitely strange laugh.

"We must be getting on," said Morpeth, softly. "Have you noticed how dark it's growing? It will soon be time for you to catch your train.

"Well, to cut a long story short—the play was somehow pushed and banged into some kind of shape which Caryll said would do for the public, and we were billed to produce on a Monday night; you know the way it's done in the provinces.

Of course, I recognised by now what tripe it was, and my one consolation was that it was being done in a place like Coalford, where no one would ever hear about it—although Caryll, in one of his 'big' moods, had blustered about getting down some of the London managers to see him in the new part. I don't suppose he knew any of the London managers, even by sight.

"On that day, of all days, Caryll chose to treat us all to a first-rate display of his diabolism. He called a morning rehearsal and had the whole crowd in pulp. It was the only occasion on which I—or, I believe, any of them—had seen Maureen go to pieces. She stopped suddenly, covered her face with her hands, and screamed out: 'Don't! You mustn't! I absolutely can't do a thing if you treat me like this!'

"You can't imagine what the effect of Maureen's break-down was upon the rest of the crowd. I didn't then—I don't now—know anything about play-producing, but even I knew from that moment that the play was done for. The whole lot of them became simply blethering idiots. Maureen rushed off the stage, and after a minute Caryll, black as ink, followed her."

Morpeth's face was a white rectangle in the gloom; the sockets of his eyes seemed to Brewster to have developed into two dark chasms, like the eye-sockets of a skull; and his hands were twisting between his knees. In the silence there was a creak and a slither; Brewster could feel his heart thudding against his breast-bone.

"He thrashed her," continued Morpeth, in a thin, distant voice. "Let me say for Peters that he threw himself at the dressing-room door, but Caryll had locked it. Peters was not much bigger than I; it was brave of him.

"I'd bought a few flowers for Maureen, and when I came down to the theatre at night I took them to her dressing-room. I'd meant to have them handed, in the conventional way, across the footlights, but I thought if she had them first they might comfort her—give her a little courage. I had not meant to say anything else to her, but I suddenly found myself begging her to leave Caryll; to marry me. It was ridiculous, because I was only, then, earning a few shillings a week. But I forgot all that. She was wearing a thin kind of scarf across the shoulders of the evening gown she wore in the first act, and I knew why it was there. She shook her head very gently, and I remembered about the person—whoever it was—she had to keep. And she said, 'Dear Henry. I promise you I will do my very best with your play tonight.'

"I met Peters in the passage: as we passed each other he caught hold of my arm and whispered, 'By God, I'll *murder* Caryll some day!' Odd, wasn't it? Of course, I never mentioned that to anybody. But I remember when I went into a room where several of the men were dressing, thinking that the same look was in each man's eyes. No one said much; there was a lot of drinking, among the few who could afford it. But there was the *murder* thought, as big and black as a thundercloud, behind the stage that night.

"All the seats were cheap, and the house was soon packed. I was too nervous, at the beginning, to go in front; I hung about the wings and the dressing-rooms, watching for Caryll. I was determined, if he did anything to Maureen then, that I'd go for him—whatever the effect was on the play.

"But he came down presently, beaming, considerably drunk, and clapped me on the back, as if I were his best friend. I could have done it then...

"The first act went through all right, apparently. Coalford isn't critical. Caryll swaggered and posed and gave them what they considered value for their money. I simply couldn't watch Maureen.

"They came off stage together; I was standing just behind a flat, and two or three of the others were with me. We all heard him say to Maureen, 'If you can't support me better than that in the next act, I'll give you hell!' Those were his exact words. We all heard them. And the black cloud—the murder thought—seemed to drop lower upon us all. We felt it; we saw it in each other's eyes. One of the men muttered to me—well, never mind what he said.

"You know now, of course, what happened? When at the end of the second act the curtain came down (to a good deal of applause) and the stage hands started to rush forward to change the set, Caryll didn't get up. Before they got to him they could see what had happened, from the stage-cloth.

"The property dagger with which the 'murder' was always committed was found on Peters's dressing-bench. There was a door, centre-back, through which the murderer, whoever he was, had made his escape. There was never anyone by that door; the 'hands' were down at the sides, waiting for their signal, which Peters was supposed to give them when he ran round. When he didn't appear, they simply did what they were accustomed to doing. The 'murderer' wore ordinary evening dress: anyone in evening dress could have done it, with Peter's hood, or bag, with the eyeholes cut in it, over his face.

"The whole cast had a complete alibi; no one was on the stage at that moment, except Caryll and, usually, Peters; the others were changing into day clothes, for the next act. The stage hands, and the SM himself, had the obvious alibi of their working suits. And, of course, there was pandemonium behind, as soon as it was found out; anyone could have slipped through the pass door, or even out into the street, because it was found out afterwards the stage doorkeeper had been indulging his usual weakness in the neighbouring pub."

Brewster moved uneasily. The story left him with a sneaking apprehension of something moving in the shadows that might any moment launch itself upon his own defenceless shoulders.

Morpeth had risen, and was tiptoeing with an odd movement about the stage. His movements had something of the effect of a macabre dance, they had a kind of rhythm, he was waving his hands.

"The oddest thing," he said, in his thin, light voice, "was that the weapon was never found with which the crime was committed! They found out what it was—or what they thought it was—afterwards; a large chisel was found to be missing from the carpenter's bench—just through there. The wound was at the base of Caryll's skull—not in the shoulder, where Peters had always planted it at rehearsal. Of course, the murderer knew that the chisel, however sharp, wouldn't go through the cloth and the underclothing—unless, at any rate, it had been driven by a very big and heavy man. Now, how could a large thing, bloodstained, as the chisel must have been, be disposed of, hurriedly, as the murderer must have disposed of it? Every inch of the mezzanine was searched, to see if it had gone down one of the traps when they jerked the stage-cloth up. Nowhere. Odd, isn't it?"

"I've had enough of this," said Brewster, suddenly. "Thanks very much for your story—you can keep your theatre! I doubt if, as a movie-house, it will shake off the—shake off the—"

"Oh, wait just a moment!" said Morpeth, coming up to him and pawing him softly—an action which filled Brewster with an indescribable feeling of repulsion. "Can't you see what a fascination the place has got for me? All these years it has never lost its fascination. I've only to look at this stage and I can see Maureen drifting across it—as she did at rehearsals. Look—can't you see? There she goes—there!—with her timid smile and that little droop of the shoulder—"

"Pull yourself together!" said Brewster abruptly, and shook the little man by the shoulder. "If you take my advice you'll re-sell the place—or throw it away!"

With a high, eerie laugh, Morpeth threw off the detaining hand and again flitted across the stage.

"It was here, just here, where I am standing, that Caryll was murdered. Up here"—he moved a few paces upstage—"was the door, centre-back, through which the murderer escaped. Everyone was watching; the men on the curtain—down there, where the screen will hang—the screen on which Maureen will appear—were waiting for their signal from the stage manager, who had to count ten from the time when Caryll fell, and then ring down.

"The murderer came out through this door—here, like this. Straight opposite the scene dock."

He flitted, still with his odd, dancing movements, up towards the stack of flats, which had been leaning, for heaven knows how many years, against the wall of the dock. The dust lay upon them, an inch deep of grey powder; the lower edges had been torn and nibbled away by the theatre rats.

Morpeth flung a glance across his shoulder at Brewster, before dropping on his knees. A blade of horrible certainty drove into Brewster's mind. There was a scuffle; a whole stream of rats darted out, and a spider with a body the size of a walnut came trundling down the rake of the stage. Only the lower part of Morpeth's legs were visible; an acute nausea seized upon Brewster as he imagined the depths into which Morpeth's body was exploring.

Now he was wriggling backwards. As he finally emerged cobwebs were clarted upon his shoulders and his hair, where they formed a hideous crown, hanging pendant to his eyebrows. In his hand he held something...

"I thought," said Morpeth, softly, insanely, "it would still be there!"

Blood Sacrifice

Dorothy L. Sayers

A theatrical streak ran through the complex personality of Dorothy Leigh Sayers (1893–1957), an outstanding detective novelist who also enjoyed great success with plays written for radio and the stage. One of her biographers, James Brabazon, described listening to a talk she gave in 1943 on the subject of the theatre: "she sold us her vision of the theatre as the place that offered the things that a church ought to offer, but rarely did. Inside a stage door, she said, you found comradeship, charity and most of all a sense of common dedication to a common purpose."

Sayers's final mystery featuring Lord Peter Wimsey, *Busman's Honeymoon*, began life as a play, co-written with Muriel St. Clare Byrne, who taught at the Royal Academy of Dramatic Art in London. Sayers attended rehearsals and travelled round with the production company as the play was performed around the country; it became a West End hit, and she turned it into her final novel. Among her other work for the stage, *The Zeal of Thy House*, written for the Canterbury Festival, made an especially strong impression. Her radio drama *The Man Born to Be King* courted controversy but proved highly popular. "Blood Sacrifice" was originally written for an interesting and unusual book, *Six against the Yard* (1936), in which six members of the Detection Club wrote stories about "perfect murders," the perfection of which was then critiqued by a retired Scotland Yard superintendent, G. W. Cornish.

———

IF THINGS WENT ON AT THIS RATE, JOHN SCALES WOULD be a very rich man. Already he was a man to be envied, as any ignoramus might guess who passed the King's Theatre after eight o'clock. Old Florrie, who had sat for so many years on the corner with her little tray of matches, could have given more than a guess, for what she didn't know about the King's was hardly worth knowing. When she had ceased to adorn its boards (thanks to a dreadful accident with a careless match and some gauze draperies, that had left her with a scarred face and a withered arm), she had taken her stand near the theatre for old sake's sake, and she watched over its fortunes, still, like a mother. She knew, none better, how much money it held when it was playing to capacity, what its salary list was like, how much of its earnings went in permanent charges, and what the author's share of the box-office receipts was likely to amount to. Besides, everybody who went in or out by the stage door came and had a word with Florrie. She shared good times and bad at the King's. She had lamented over lean days caused by slumps and talkie competition, shaken her head over perilous excursions into highbrow tragedy, waxed tearful and indignant over the disastrous period (now happily past) of the Scorer-Bitterby management, which had ended in a scandal, rejoiced when the energetic Mr. Garrick Drury, launching out into management after his tremendous triumph in the name-part of *The Wistful Harlequin*, had taken the old house over, reconditioned it inside and out (incidentally squeezing two more rows into the reconstructed pit), and voiced his optimistic determination to break the run of ill-luck; and since then she had watched its steady soaring into prosperity on the well-tried wings of old-fashioned adventure and romance.

Mr. Garrick Drury (Somerset House knew him as Obadiah Potts, but he was none the less good-looking for that) was an actor-manager of the sort Florrie understood; he followed his calling in the good old way, building his successes about his own glamorous personality, talking no nonsense about new schools of dramatic thought, and paying only lip-service to "team-work." He had had the luck to embark on his managerial career at a moment when the public had grown tired of gloomy Slav tragedies of repressed husbands, and human documents about drink and diseases, and was (in its own incoherent way) clamouring for a good romantic story to cry about, with a romantic hero suffering torments of self-sacrifice through two and three-quarter acts and getting the girl in the last ten minutes. Mr. Drury (forty-two in the day-light, thirty-five in the lamplight, and twenty-five or what you will in a blond wig and the spotlight) was well fitted by nature to acquire girls in this sacrificial manner, and had learnt the trick of so lacing nineteenth-century sentiment with twentieth-century nonchalance that the mixture went to the heads equally of Joan who worked in the office and Aunt Mabel up from the country.

And since Mr. Drury, leaping nightly from his Rolls saloon with that nervous and youthful alacrity that had been his most engaging asset for the past twenty years, always had time to bestow at least a smile and a friendly word on old Florrie, he affected her head and heart as much as anybody else's. Nobody was more delighted than Florrie to know that he had again found a winner in *Bitter Laurel*, now sweeping on to its hundredth performance. Night by night she saluted with a satisfied chuckle each board as it appeared: "Pit Full," "Gallery Full," "Dress Circle Full," "Upper Circle Full," "Stalls Full," "Standing Room Only," "House Full." Set to run for ever it was, and the faces that went in by the stage door looked merry and prosperous, as Florrie liked to see them.

As for the young man who had provided the raw material out of which Mr. Drury had built up this glittering monument of success, if he wasn't pleased, thought Florrie, he ought to be. Not that, in the ordinary way, one thought much about the author of a play—unless, of course, it was Shakespeare, who was different; compared with the cast, he was of small importance, and rarely seen. But Mr. Drury had one day arrived arm-in-arm with a sulky-looking and ill-dressed youth, whom he had introduced to Florrie, saying in his fine, generous way: "Here, John, you must know Florrie. She's our mascot—we couldn't get on without her. Florrie, this is Mr. Scales, whose new play's going to make all our fortunes." Mr. Drury was never mistaken about plays; he had the golden touch. Certainly, in the last three months, Mr. Scales, though still sulky-looking, had become much better dressed.

On this particular night—Saturday, April 15th, when *Bitter Laurel* was giving its ninety-sixth performance to a full house after a packed matinée—Mr. Scales and Mr. Drury arrived together, in evening dress and, Florrie noted with concern, rather late. Mr. Drury would have to hurry, and it was tiresome of Mr. Scales to detain him, as he did, by arguing and expostulating upon the threshold. Not that Mr. Drury seemed put out. He was smiling (his smile, one-sided and slightly elfin in quality, was famous), and at last he said, with his hand (Mr. Drury's expressive hands were renowned) affectionately upon Mr. Scales' shoulder, "Sorry, old boy, can't stop now. Curtain must go up, you know. Come round and see me after the show—I'll have those fellows there." Then he vanished, still smiling the elfin smile and waving the expressive hand; and Mr. Scales, after hesitating a moment, had turned away and came down past Florrie's corner. He seemed to be still sulky and rather preoccupied, but, looking up, caught sight of Florrie and grinned at her. There was nothing elfin about Mr. Scales's smile, but it improved his face very much.

"Well, Florrie," said Mr. Scales, "we seem to be doing pretty well, financially speaking, don't we?"

Florrie eagerly agreed. "But there," she observed, "we're getting used to that. Mr. Drury's a wonderful man. It doesn't matter what he's in; they all come to see him. Of course," she added, remembering that this might not sound very kind, "he's very clever at picking the right play."

"Oh, yes," said Mr. Scales. "The play. I suppose the play has something to do with it. Not much, but something. Have you seen the play, Florrie?"

Yes, indeed, Florrie had. Mr. Drury was so kind, he always

remembered to give Florrie a pass early on in the run, even if the house was ever so full.

"What did you think of it?" inquired Mr. Scales.

"I thought it was lovely," said Florrie. "I cried ever so. When he came back with only one arm and found his fiancée gone to the bad at a cocktail party—"

"Just so," said Mr. Scales.

"And the scene on the Embankment—lovely, I thought that was, when he rolls up his old army coat and says to the bobby: 'I will rest on my laurels'—that was a beautiful curtain line you gave him there, Mr. Scales. And the way he put it over—"

"Yes, rather," said Mr. Scales. "There's nobody like Drury for putting over that kind of line."

"And when she came back to him and he wouldn't have her any more and then Lady Sylvia took him up and fell in love with him—"

"Yes, yes," said Mr. Scales. "You found that part moving?"

"Romantic," said Florrie. "And the scene between the two girls—that was splendid. All worked-up, it made you feel. And then in the end, when he took the one he really loved after all—"

"Sure-fire, isn't it?" said Mr. Scales. "Goes straight to the heart. I'm glad you think so, Florrie. Because, of course, quite apart from anything else, it's very good box-office."

"I believe you," said Florrie. "Your first play, isn't it? You're lucky to have it taken by Mr. Drury."

"Yes," said Mr. Scales, "I owe him a lot. Everybody says so, so it must be true. There are two fat gentlemen in astrachan coats coming along tonight to settle about the film rights. I'm a made man, Florrie, and that's always pleasant, particularly after five or six years of living hand-to-mouth. No fun in not having enough to eat, is there?"

"That there isn't," said Florrie, who knew all about it. "I'm ever so glad your luck's turned at last, dearie."

"Thank you," said Mr. Scales. "Have something to drink the health of the play." He fumbled in his breast-pocket. "Here you are. A green one and a brown one. Thirty bob. Thirty pieces of silver. Spend it on something you fancy, Florrie. It's the price of blood."

"What a thing to say!" exclaimed Florrie. "But you writing gentlemen will have a bit of a joke. And I know poor Mr. Milling, who wrote the book for *Pussycat, Pussycat* and *The Lipstick Girl* always used to say he sweated blood over every one of 'em."

A nice young gentleman, thought Florrie, as Mr. Scales passed on, but queer and, perhaps, a little bit difficult in his temper, for them that had to live with him. He had spoken very nicely about Mr. Drury, but there had been a moment when she had fancied that he was (as they said) registering sarcasm. And she didn't quite like that joke about the thirty pieces of silver—that was New Testament, and New Testament (unlike Old) was blasphemous. It was like the difference between saying: "Oh, God!" (which nobody minded) and "Oh, Christ!" (which Florrie had never held with). Still, people said all kinds of things nowadays, and thirty bob was thirty bob; it was very kind of Mr. Scales.

Mr. John Scales, slouching along Shaftesbury Avenue and wondering how he was going to put in the next three hours or so, encountered a friend just turning out of Wardour Street. The friend was a tall, thin young man, with a shabby overcoat and a face, under a dilapidated soft hat, like a hungry hawk's. There was a girl with him.

"Hullo, Molly!" said Scales. "Hullo, Sheridan!"

"Hullo!" said Sheridan. "Look who's here! The great man himself. London's rising dramatist. Sweet Scales of Old Drury."

"Cut it out," said Scales.

"Your show seems to be booming," went on Sheridan. "Congratulations. On the boom, I mean."

"God!" said Scales, "have you seen it? I did send you tickets."

"You did—it was kind of you to think of us amid your busy life. We saw the show. In these bargain-basement days, you've managed to sell your soul in a pretty good market."

"See here, Sheridan—it wasn't my fault. I'm just as sick as you are. Sicker. But like a fool I signed the contract without a controlling clause, and by the time Drury and his producer had finished mucking the script about—"

"He didn't sell himself," said the girl, "he was took advantage of, your worship."

"Pity," said Sheridan. "It was a good play—but he done her wrong. But," he added, glancing at Scales, "I take it you drink the champagne that she sends you. You're looking prosperous."

"Well," said Scales, "what do you expect me to do? Return the cheque with thanks?"

"Good Lord, no," said Sheridan. "It's all right. Nobody's grudging you your luck."

"It's something, after all," said Scales defensively, "to get one's foot in at all. One can't always look a gift horse in the mouth."

"No," said Sheridan. "Good Lord, I know that. Only I'm afraid that you'll find this thing hang round your neck a bit if you want to go back to your own line. You know what the public is—it likes to get what it expects. Once you've made a name for sob-stuff, you're labelled for good or bad."

"I know. Hell. Can't do anything about it, though. Come and have a drink."

But the others had an appointment to keep, and passed on their way. The encounter was typical. Damnation, thought Scales, savagely, turning in to the Criterion bar, wasn't it enough to have had your decent play cut about and turned into the sort of thing that made you retch to listen to it, without your friends supposing you had acquiesced in the mutilation for the sake of making money?

He had been a little worried when he knew that George Philpotts (kindly, officious George, who always knew everybody) had sent *Bitter Laurel* to Drury. The very last management he himself would have selected; but also the very last management that would be likely to take so cynical and disillusioned a play. Miraculously, however, Drury had expressed himself as "dead keen" about it. There had been an interview with Drury, and Drury, damn his expressive eyes, had—yes, one had to admit it—Drury had "put himself across" with great success. He had been flattering, he had been charming. Scales had succumbed, as night by night pit and stalls and dress circle succumbed, to the gracious manner and the elfin smile. "A grand piece—grand situations,"

Garrick Drury had said. "Of course, here and there it will need a little tidying up in production." Scales said modestly that he expected that—he knew very little about writing for the stage—he was a novelist—he was quite ready to agree to alterations, provided, naturally, nothing was done to upset the artistic unity of the thing. Mr. Garrick Drury was pained by the suggestion. As an artist himself, he should, of course, allow nothing inartistic to be done. Scales, overcome by Drury's manner, and by a flood of technicalities about sets and lighting and costing and casting poured out upon him by the producer, who was present at the interview, signed a contract giving the author a very handsome share of the royalties, and hardly noticed that he had left the management with full power to make any "reasonable" alterations to fit the play for production.

It was only gradually, in the course of rehearsal, that he discovered what was being done to his play. It was not merely that Mr. Drury had succeeded in importing into the lines given to him as the war-shattered hero, a succulent emotionalism which was very far from the dramatist's idea of that embittered and damaged character. So much, one had expected. But the plot had slowly disintegrated and reshaped itself into something revoltingly different. Originally, for example, the girl Judith (the one who had "gone to the bad at a cocktail party") had not spurned the one-armed soldier (Mr. Drury). Far from it. She had welcomed him and several other heroes home with indiscriminate, not to say promiscuous, enthusiasm. And the hero, instead of behaving (as Mr. Drury saw to it that he did in the acted version) in a highly sacrificial manner, had gone deliberately and cynically to the bad in his turn. Nor had "Lady Sylvia," who rescued him from the Embankment, been (as Mr. Drury's second leading lady now represented her to be) a handsome and passionate girl deeply in love with the hero, but a nauseous rich elderly woman with a fancy for a gigolo, whose attentions the hero (now thoroughly deteriorated as a result of war and post-war experience) accepted without shame or remorse in exchange for the luxuries of life. And finally, when Judith, thoroughly shocked and brought to her senses by these developments, had tried to recapture him, the hero (as originally depicted) had so far lost all sense of decency as to prefer—though with a bitter sense of failure and frustration—to stick to Lady Sylvia, as the line of least resistance, and had ended, on Armistice Day, by tearing away the public trophies of laurel and poppy from the Cenotaph and being ignominiously removed by the police after a drunken and furious harangue in denunciation of war. Not a pleasant play, as originally written, and certainly in shocking taste; but an honest piece of work so far as it went. But Mr. Drury had pointed out that "his" public would never stand the original Lady Sylvia or the final degradation of the hero. There must be slight alterations—nothing inartistic, of course, but alterations, to make the thing more moving, more uplifting, more, in fact, true to human nature.

Because, Mr. Drury pointed out, if there was one thing you could rely on, it was the essential decency of human nature, and its immediate response to generous sentiments. His experience, he said, had proved it to him.

Scales had not given way without a struggle. He had fought hard over every line. But there was the contract. And in the end, he had actually written the new scenes and lines himself, not because he wanted to, but because at any rate his own lines would be less intolerable than the united efforts of cast and producer to write them for themselves. So that he could not even say that he had washed his hands of the whole beastly thing. Like his own (original) hero, he had taken the line of least resistance. Mr. Drury had been exceedingly grateful to him and delighted to feel that author and management were working so well together in their common interest.

"I know how you feel," he would say, "about altering your artistic work. Any artist feels the same. But I've had twenty years' experience of the stage, and it counts, you know, it counts. You don't think I'm right—my dear boy, I should feel just the same in your place. I'm terribly grateful for all this splendid work you're putting in, and I know you won't regret it. Don't worry. All young authors come up against the same difficulty. It's just a question of experience."

Hopeless, Scales, in desperation, had enlisted the services of an agent, who pointed out that it was now too late to get the contract altered. "But," said the agent, "it's quite an honest contract, as these things go. Drury's management has always had a very good name. We shall keep an eye on these subsidiary rights for you—you can leave that to us. I know it's a nuisance having to alter things here and there, but it *is* your first play, and you're lucky to have got in with Drury. He's very shrewd about what will appeal to a West End audience. When once he's established you, you'll be in a much better position to dictate terms."

Yes, of course, thought Scales—to dictate to Drury, or to anybody else who might want that type of play. But in a worse position than ever to get anybody to look at his serious work. And the worst of it was that the agent, as well as the actor-manager, seemed to think that his concern for his own spiritual integrity didn't count, didn't matter—that he would be quite genuinely consoled by his royalties.

At the end of the first week, Garrick Drury practically said as much. His own experience had been justified by the receipts. "When all's said and done," he remarked, "the box-office is the real test. I don't say that in a commercial spirit. I'd always be ready to put on a play I believed in—as an artist—even if I lost money by it. But when the box-office is happy, it means the public is happy. The box-office is the pulse of the public. Get that and you know you've got the heart of the audience."

He couldn't see. Nobody could see. John Scales's own friends couldn't see; they merely thought he had sold himself. And as the play settled down to run remorselessly on, like a stream of treacle, John Scales realised that there would be no end to it. It was useless to hope that the public would revolt at the insincerity of the play. They probably saw through it all right, just as the critics had done. What stood in the way of the play's deserved collapse was the glamorous figure of Garrick Drury. "This broken-backed play," said the *Sunday Echo*, "is only held together by the magnificent acting of Mr. Garrick Drury." "Saccharine as it is," said the *Looker-On*, "*Bitter Laurel* provides a personal triumph for Mr. Garrick Drury." "Nothing in the play is consistent," said the *Dial*, "except the assured skill of Mr. Garrick Drury, who— "Mr. John Scales," said the *Daily Messenger*, "has constructed his situations with great skill to display Mr. Garrick Drury in all his attitudes, and that is a sure recipe for success. We prophesy a long run for *Bitter Laurel*." A true prophecy, or so it seemed.

And there was no stopping it. If only Mr. Drury would fall ill or die or lose his looks or his voice or his popularity, the beastly play might be buried and forgotten. There were circumstances under which the rights would revert to the author. But Mr. Drury lived and flourished and charmed the public, and the run went on, and after that there were the touring rights (controlled by Mr. Drury) and film rights (largely controlled by Mr. Drury) and probably radio rights, and God only knew what else. And all Mr. Scales could do was to pocket the wages of sin and curse Mr. Drury, who had (so pleasantly) ruined his work, destroyed his reputation, alienated his friends, exposed him to the contempt of the critics and forced him to betray his own soul.

If there was one living man in London whom John Scales would have liked to see removed from the face of the earth, it was Garrick Drury, to whom (as he was daily obliged to admit to all and sundry) he owed so much. Yet Drury was a really charming fellow. There were times when that inexhaustible charm got so much on the author's nerves that he could readily have slain Mr. Drury for his charm alone.

Yet, when the moment came, on that night of the 15th–16th April, the thing was not premeditated. Not in any real sense. It just happened. Or did it? That was a thing that even John Scales could not have said for certain. He may have felt a moral conviction, but that is not the same thing as a legal conviction. The doctor may have had his suspicions, but if so, they were not directed against John Scales. And whether they were right or wrong, nobody could say that it had made any difference; the real slayer may have been the driver of the car, or the intervening hand of Providence, sprinkling the tarmac with April showers. Or it may have been Garrick Drury, so courteously and charmingly accompanying John Scales in quest of a taxi, instead of getting straight into his own car and being whirled away in the opposite direction.

In any case, it was nearly one in the morning of Sunday when they got the film people off the premises, after a long and much-interrupted argument, during which Scales found himself, as usual, agreeing to a number of things he did not approve, but could see no way to prevent.

"My dear John," said Mr. Garrick Drury, pulling off his dressing-gown (he always conducted business interviews in a dressing-gown, if possible, feeling, with some truth, that its flowing outline suited him), "my dear John, I know exactly how you feel—Walter!—but it needs experience to deal with these people, and you can trust me not to allow anything inartistic—oh, thank you, Walter. I'm extremely sorry to have kept you so late."

Walter Hopkins was Mr. Drury's personal dresser and faithful adherent. He had not the smallest objection to being kept up all night, or all the next morning for that matter. He was passionately devoted to Mr. Drury, who always rewarded his services with a kind word and the smile. He now helped Mr. Drury into his coat and overcoat and handed him his hat with a gratified murmur. The dressing-room was still exceedingly untidy, but he could not help that; towards the end of the conversation the negotiations had become so very delicate that even the devoted Walter had had to be dismissed to lurk in an adjacent room.

"Never mind about all this," went on Mr. Drury, indicating a litter of greasepaint, towels, glasses, siphons, ash-trays, tea-cups (Mr. Drury's aunts had looked in), manuscripts (two optimistic authors had been given audience), mascots (five female admirers had brought Mickey Mice), flowers (handed in at the stage-door) and assorted fan-mail, strewn over the furniture. "Just stick my things together and lock up the whisky. I'll see Mr. Scales to his taxi—you're sure I can't drop you anywhere, John?—Oh! and bring the flowers to the car—and I'd better look through that play of young what's his name's—Ruggles, Buggles, you know who I mean—perfectly useless, of course, but I promised dear old Fanny—chuck the rest into the cupboard—and I'll pick you up in five minutes."

The night-watchman let them out; he was an infirm and aged man with a face like a rabbit, and Scales wondered what he would do if he met with a burglar or an outbreak of fire in the course of his rounds.

"Hullo!" said Garrick Drury, "it's started to rain. But there's a rank just down the Avenue. Now look here, John, old man, don't you worry about this, because—Look out!"

It all happened in a flash. A small car, coming just a trifle too fast up the greasy street, braked to avoid a prowling cat, skidded, swung round at right angles, and mounted the pavement. The two men leapt for safety—Scales rather clumsily, tripping and sprawling in the gutter. Drury, who was on the inside, made a quick backward spring, neat as an acrobat's, just not far enough. The bumper caught him behind the knee and flung him shoulder-first through the plate-glass window of a milliner's shop.

When Scales had scrambled to his feet, the car was halfway through the window, with its driver, a girl, knocked senseless over the wheel; a policeman and two taxi-drivers were running towards them from the middle of the street; and Drury, very white and his face bleeding, was extricating himself from the splintered glass, with his left arm clutched in his right hand.

"Oh, my God!" said Drury. He staggered up against the car, and between his fingers the bright blood spurted like a fountain.

Scales, shaken and bewildered by his fall, was for the moment unable to grasp what had happened; but the policeman had his wits about him.

"Never mind the lady," he said, urgently, to the taxi-men. "This gent's cut an artery. Bleed to death if we ain't quick." His large, competent fingers grasped the actor's arm, found the right spot, and put firm pressure on the severed blood-vessel. The dreadful spurting ceased. "All right, sir? Lucky you 'ad the presence of mind to ketch 'old of yourself." He eased the actor down on to the running-board, without relaxing his grip.

"I got a 'andkercher," suggested one of the taxi-men.

"That's right," said the policeman. "'Itch it round 'is arm above the place and pull it as tight as you can. That'll 'elp. Nasty cut it is, right to the bone, by the looks of it."

Scales looked at the shop-window and the pavement, and shuddered. It might have been a slaughter-house.

"Thanks very much," said Drury to the policeman and the taxi-man. He summoned up the ghost of the smile and fainted.

"Better take him into the theatre," said Scales. "The stage-door's open. Only a step or two up the passage. It's Mr. Drury, the actor," he added, to explain this suggestion. "I'll run along and tell them."

The policeman nodded. Scales hurried up the passage and met Walter just emerging from the stage-door.

"Accident!" said Scales, breathless. "Mr. Drury—cut an artery—they're bringing him here."

Walter, with a cry, flung down the flowers he was carrying and darted out. Drury was being supported up the passage by the two drivers. The policeman walked beside him, still keeping a strong thumb on his arm. They brought him in, stumbling over the heaps of narcissus and daffodil; the crushed blossoms smelt like funeral flowers.

"There's a couch in his dressing-room," said Scales. His mind had suddenly become abnormally clear. "It's on the ground floor. Round here to the right and across the stage."

"Oh, dear, oh, dear!" said Walter. "Oh, Mr. Drury! He won't die—he can't die! All that dreadful blood!"

"Now, keep your 'ead," admonished the policeman. "Can't you ring up a doctor and make yourself useful?"

Walter and the night-watchman made a concerted rush for the telephone, leaving Scales to guide the party across the deserted stage, black and ghostly in the light of one dim bulb high over the proscenium arch. Their way was marked by heavy red splashes on the dusty boards. As though the very sound of those boards beneath their tread had wakened the actor's instinct, Drury opened one eye.

"What's happened to those lights?"...Then, with returning consciousness, "Oh, it's the curtain line... Dying, Egypt, dying...final appearance, eh?"

"Rot, old man," said Scales hastily. "You're not dying yet by a long chalk."

One of the taxi-drivers—an elderly man—stumbled and panted. "Sorry," said Drury, "to be such a weight...can't help you much...find it easier...take your grip further down..."

The smile was twisted, but his wits and experience were back on the job. This was not the first or the hundredth time he had been "carried out" from the stage of the King's. His bearers took his gasping instructions and successfully negotiated the corner of the set. Scales, hovering in attendance, was unreasonably irritated. Of course, Drury was behaving beautifully. Courage, presence of mind, consideration for others—all the right theatrical gestures. Couldn't the fellow be natural, even at death's door?

Here, Scales was unjust. It was natural to Drury to be theatrical in a crisis, as it is to nine people out of ten. He was, as a matter of fact, providing the best possible justification for his own theories about human nature. They got him to the dressing-room, laid him on the couch, and were thanked.

"My wife," said Drury, "...in Sussex. Don't startle her... she's had 'flu...heart not strong."

"All right, all right," said Scales. He found a towel and drew some water into a bowl. Walter came running in.

"Dr. Debenham's out...away for the week-end... Blake's telephoning another one...suppose they're all away...whatever shall we do?...they oughtn't to *let* doctors go away like this."

"We'll try the police-surgeon," said the constable. "Here, you, come and 'old your thumb where I've got mine. Can't trust that there bandage. Squeeze 'ard, mind, and don't let go. And don't faint," he added sharply. He turned to the taxi-men. "You better go and see what's 'appened to the young lady. I blew me whistle, so you did oughter find the other constable there. You (to Scales) will 'ave to stay here—I'll be wanting your evidence about the accident."

"Yes, yes," said Scales, busy with the towel.

"My face," said Drury, putting up a restless hand. "Has it got the eye?"

"No, it's only a scalp-wound. Don't get excited."

"Sure? Better dead than disfigured. Don't want to end like Florrie. Poor old Florrie. Give her my love... Cheer up, Walter... Rotten curtain, isn't it?... Get yourself a drink... You're certain the eye's all right?... You weren't hurt, were you, old man?... Hell of a nuisance for you, too...stop the run..."

Scales, in the act of pouring out whisky for himself and Walter (who looked nearly as ready to collapse as his employer), started and nearly dropped the bottle. Stop the run—yes, it would stop the run. An hour ago he had been praying for a miracle to stop the run. And the miracle had happened. And if Drury hadn't had the wits to stop the bleeding—if he had waited only one minute more—the run would have stopped and the film would have stopped, and the whole cursed play would have stopped dead for good and all. He swallowed down the neat spirit with a jerk, and handed the second glass to Walter. It was as though he had made the thing happen by wishing for it. By wishing a little harder— Nonsense!... But the doctor didn't come and, though Walter was holding on like grim death (*grim death!*) to the cut artery, the blood from the smaller vessels was soaking and seeping through the cloth and the bandages...there was still the chance, still the likelihood, still the *hope*—

This would never do. Scales dashed out into the passage and across the stage to the night-watchman's box. The policeman was still telephoning. Drury's chauffeur, haggard and alarmed, stood, cap in hand, talking to the taxi-men. The girl, it appeared, had been taken to hospital with concussion. The divisional police-surgeon had gone to an urgent case. The nearest hospital had no surgeon free at the moment. The policeman was trying the police-surgeon belonging to the next division. Scales went back.

The next half-hour was a nightmare. The patient, hovering between consciousness and unconsciousness, was still worrying about his face, about his arm, about the play. And the red stain on the couch spread and spread...

Then, with a bustle, a short, stout man came in, carrying a bag. He took a look at the patient, tested his pulse, asked a few questions, shook his head, muttering something about loss of blood and loss of time and weakness. The policeman, somewhere in the background, mentioned that the ambulance had arrived.

"Nonsense," said the doctor. "Can't possibly move him. Got to deal with it here and now." With a few brisk words of commendation, he dislodged Walter from his post. He worked quickly, cutting away the sodden sleeve, applying a proper tourniquet, administering some kind of stimulant, again assuring the patient that his eye was not damaged and that he was suffering from nothing but shock and loss of blood.

"You won't take my arm off?" said Drury, suddenly visited with a new alarm. "I'm an actor—I can't—I won't—you can't do it without telling me—you—"

"No, no, no," said the doctor. "Now we've stopped the bleeding. But you must lie still or you might start it again."

"Shall I have the use of it?" The expressive eyes searched the doctor's face. "Sorry. But a stiff arm's as bad as no arm to me. Do your best...or I shall never play again... Except in

Bitter Laurel... John, old man... funny, isn't it? Funny it's this arm... Have to live on your play for the rest of my days... the only, only play..."

"Good God!" cried Scales, involuntarily.

"Now, I must have this room clear," said the doctor, with authority. "Officer, get these people out and send me in those ambulance men."

"Come along," said the policeman. "And I'll take your statement now, sir—"

"Not me!" protested Walter Hopkins, "I can't leave Mr. Drury. I can't. Let me stay. I'll help. I'll do anything—"

"The best way you can help," said the doctor, not unkindly, but with determination, "is by giving me room to work. Now, please—"

Somehow they got Walter, struggling and hysterical, into the dressing-room across the passage. Here he sat, gathered together on the edge of a chair, starting at every sound from outside, while the constable interrogated and dismissed the two taxi-men. Then Scales found himself giving a statement, in the midst of which the doctor put his head in to say:

"I want some of you to stand by. It may be necessary to make a blood transfusion. We must get that arm stitched, but his pulse is very weak and I don't know how he'll stand it. I don't suppose any of you know which blood-group you belong to?"

"I'll do it!" cried Walter, eagerly. "Please, sir, let it be me! I'd give all the blood in my body for Mr. Drury. I've been with him fifteen years, Doctor—"

"Now, now," said the doctor.

"I'd sacrifice my life for Mr. Drury—"

"Yes, I daresay," said the doctor with a resigned look at the constable, "but there's no question of that. Where do people get these ideas? Out of the papers, I suppose. Nobody's being asked to sacrifice any lives. We only want a pint or so of blood—trifling affair for a healthy man. It won't make the slightest difference to you—do you good, I shouldn't wonder. My dear sir, don't excite yourself so much. I know you're willing—very naturally—but if you haven't the right kind of blood, you're no good to me."

"I'm very strong," said Walter, palpitating. "Never had a day's illness."

"It's nothing to do with your general health," said the doctor, a little impatiently. "It's a thing you're born with. I gather there is no relation of the patient's handy?... What? Wife, sister, and son in Sussex—well, that's rather a long way off. I'll test the two ambulance men first, but unfortunately the patient isn't a universal recipient, so we may not get the right grouping first go-off. I'd like one or two others handy in case. Good thing I brought everything with me. Always do in an accident case. Never know what you may need, and time's everything."

He darted out, leaving behind him an atmosphere of mystery and haste. The policeman shook his head and pocketed his notebook.

"Dunno as blood-offerings is part of my dooty," he observed. "I did oughter get back to me beat. But I'll 'ave to give that there car the once-over and see what my chum 'as to say about it. I'll look in again when I done that, and if they wants me, they'll know where to find me. Now, then, what do *you* want?"

"Press," said a man at the door, succinctly. "Somebody phoned to say Mr. Drury was badly hurt. That true? Very sorry to hear it. Ah! Good evening, Mr. Scales. This is all very distressing. I wonder, can you tell me...?"

Scales found himself helplessly caught up in the wheels of the Press—giving an account of the accident—saying all the right things about Drury—what Drury had done for him—what Drury had done for the play—quoting Drury's words—expatiating on Drury's courage, presence of mind and thought for others—manufacturing a halo round Drury—mentioning the strange (and to the newspaper man, gratifying) coincidence that the arm actually wounded was the arm wounded in the play—hoping that Roger Brand, the understudy, would be able to carry on till Mr. Drury was sufficiently recovered to play again—feeling his hatred for Drury rise up in him like a flood with every word he uttered—and finally insisting, with a passion and emphasis that he could not explain to himself, on his own immense personal gratitude and friendship towards Drury and his desperate anxiety to see him restored to health. He felt as though, by saying this over and over again, he might stifle something—something—some frightful thing within him that was asserting itself against his will. The reporter said that Mr. Scales had his deepest sympathy...

"Mr.—ha, hum—" said the doctor, popping his head in again.

"Excuse me," said Scales, quickly. He made for the door; but Walter was there before him, agitatedly offering his life-blood by the gallon. Scales thought he could see the pressman's ears prick up like a dog's. A blood-transfusion, of course, was always jam for a headline. But the doctor made short work of the reporter.

"No time for *you*," he said, brusquely, pulling Scales and Walter out and slamming the door. "Yes—I want another test. Hope one of you's the right sort. If not," he added, with a sort of grim satisfaction, "we'll try bleeding the tripe-hound. Learn him not to make a fuss." He led the way back into Drury's dressing-room where the big screen which usually shrouded the washstand had been pulled round to conceal the couch. A space had been cleared on the table, and a number of articles laid out upon it; bottles, pipettes, needles, a porcelain slab oddly marked and stained, and a small drum of the sort used for protecting sterilised instruments. Standing near the washbasin, one of the ambulance men was boiling a saucepan on a gas-ring.

"Now then," said the doctor. He spoke in a low tone, perfectly clear, but calculated not to carry beyond the screen. "Don't make more noise than you can help. I'll have to do it here—no gas-ring in the other room, and I don't want to leave the patient. Never mind—it won't take a minute to make the tests. I can do you both together. Here, you—I want this slab cleaned—no, never mind, here's a clean plate; that'll do—it needn't be surgically sterile." He wiped the plate carefully with a towel and set it on the table between the two men. Scales recognised the pattern of pink roses; it had often held sandwiches while he and Drury, endlessly talking, had hammered out new dialogue for *Bitter Laurel* over a quick lunch. "You understand"—the doctor looked from one to the other and addressed himself to Walter, as though feeling that the unfortunate man might burst unless some notice was taken of him soon—"that your blood—everybody's blood—belongs to one or other of four different groups." He opened the drum and picked out a needle. "There's no necessity to go into details; the point is that, for a transfusion to be successful, the donor's blood must combine in a particular way with the patient's. Now, this will only be a prick—you'll scarcely feel it." He took Walter by the ear and jabbed the needle into the lobe. "If the donor's blood belongs to an unsuitable group, it causes agglutination of the red cells, and the operation is worse than useless." He drew off a few drops of blood into a pipette. Walter watched and listened, seeming to understand very little, but soothed by the calm, professional voice. The doctor transferred two separate droplets of diluted blood to the plate, making a little ring about each with a grease pencil. "There is one type of person"—here he captured Scales and repeated the operation upon his ear with a fresh needle and pipette—"Group 4, we call them, who are universal donors; their blood suits anybody. Or, of course, if one of you belongs to the patient's own blood-group, that would do nicely. Unfortunately, he's a Group 3, and that's rather rare. So far, we've been unlucky." He placed two drops of Scales's blood on the other side of the plate, drawing a pencil-mark from edge to edge to separate the two pairs of specimens, set the plate neatly between the two donors, so that each stood guard over his own property, and turned again to Walter:

"Let's see, what's your name?"

As though in answer, there was a movement behind the screen. Something fell with a crash, and the ambulance man put out a scared face saying urgently: "Doctor!" At the same moment came Drury's voice: "Walter—tell Walter—!"

trailing into silence. Walter and the doctor dived for the screen together, Scales catching Walter as he pushed past him. The second ambulance man put down what he was doing and ran to assist. There was a moment of bustle and expostulation, and the doctor said: "Come, now, give him a chance." Walter came back to his place at the table. His mouth looked as though he were going to cry.

"They won't let me see him. He asked for me."

"He mustn't exert himself," you know, said Scales, mechanically.

The patient was muttering to himself and the doctor seemed to be trying to quiet him. Scales and Walter Hopkins stood waiting helplessly, with the plate between them. Four little drops of blood—absurd, thought Scales, that they should be of so much importance, when you remembered that horrible welter in the street, on the couch. On the table stood a small wooden rack, containing ampoules. He read the labels: "Stock Serum No. II." "Stock Serum No. III"; the words conveyed nothing to him; he noticed, stupidly, that one of the little pink roses on the border of the plate had been smudged in the firing—that Walter's hands were trembling as he supported himself upon the table.

Then the doctor reappeared, whispering to the ambulance men: "Do try to keep him quiet." Walter looked anxiously at him. "All right, so far," said the doctor. "Now then, where were we? What did you say your name was?" He labelled the specimens on Walter's side of the plate with the initials "W.H."

"Mine's John Scales," said Scales. The doctor wrote down the initials of London's popular playwright as indifferently as though they had been those of a rate-collector and took from the rack the ampoule of Serum II. Breaking it, he added a little of the contents, first to a drop of the "J.S." blood and, next, to a drop of "W.H." blood, scribbling the figure II beside each specimen. To each of the remaining drops he added, in the same way, a little of Serum III. Blood and serum met and mingled; to Scales, all four of the little red blotches looked exactly alike. He was disappointed; he had vaguely expected something more dramatic.

"It'll take a minute or two," said the doctor, gently rocking the plate. "If the blood of either of you mixes with both sera without clumping the red corpuscles, then that donor is a universal donor, and will do. Or, if it clumps with Serum II and remains clear with Serum III, then the donor belongs to the patient's own blood group and will do excellently for him. But if it clumps with both sera or with Serum III only, then it will do for the patient in quite another sense." He set the plate down and began to fish in his pocket.

One of the ambulance men looked round the screen again. "I can't find his pulse," he announced helplessly, "and he's looking very queer." The doctor clicked his tongue in a worried way against his teeth and vanished. There were movements, and a clinking of glass.

Scales gazed down at the plate. Was there any difference to be seen? Was one of the little blotches on Walter's side beginning to curdle and separate into grains as though some one had sprinkled it with cayenne pepper? He was not sure. On his own side of the plate, the drops looked exactly alike. Again he read the labels; again he noted the pink rose that had been smudged in the firing—the pink rose—funny about the pink rose—but what was funny about it? Certainly, one of Walter's drops was beginning to look different. A hard ring was forming about its edge, and the tiny, peppery grains were growing darker and more distinct.

"He'll do now," said the doctor, returning, "but we don't want to lose any time. Let's hope—"

He bent over the plate again. It was the drop labelled III that had the queer, grainy look—was that the right way or the wrong way round? Scales could not remember. The doctor was examining the specimens closely, with the help of a pencil microscope… Then he straightened his back with a small sigh of relief.

"Group 4," he announced; "we're all right now."

"Which of us?" thought Scales (though he was pretty sure of the answer). He was still obscurely puzzled by the pink rose.

"Yes," went on the doctor, "no sign of agglutination. I think we can risk that without a direct match-up against the patient's blood. It would take twenty minutes and we can't spare the time." He turned to Scales. "You're the man we want."

Walter gave an anguished cry.

"Not me?"

"Hush!" said the doctor authoritatively. "No, I'm afraid we can't let it be you. Now, you"—he turned to Scales again—"are a universal donor; very useful person to have about. Heart quite healthy, I suppose? Feels all right. You look fit enough, and thank goodness, you're not fat. Get your coat off, will you, and turn up your sleeve. Ah, yes. Nice stout-looking vein. Splendid. Now, you won't take any harm—you may feel a little faint perhaps, but you'll be right as rain in an hour or so."

"Yes," agreed Scales. He was still looking at the plate. The smudged rose was on his right. Surely it had always been on his right. Or had it started on his left? When? Before the blood-drops had been put on? Or after? How could it have altered its position? When the doctor was handling the plate? Or could Walter have caught the plate with his sleeve and swivelled it round when he made his mad rush for the screen? If so, was that before the specimens had been labelled? After, surely. No, before—*after* they were taken and *before* they were labelled. And that would mean...

The doctor was opening the drum again; taking out bandages, forceps, a glass flask...

That would mean that his own blood and Walter's had changed places before the serum was added, and if so...

... scissors, towels, a kind of syringe...

If there was the smallest doubt, one ought to draw attention to it and have the specimens tested again. But perhaps either of their bloods would have done equally well; in that case, the doctor would naturally give the preference to John Scales, rather than to poor Walter, shivering there like a leaf. Clump with II, clear with III; clump with III, clear with II— he couldn't remember which way it went...

"No, I'm sorry," repeated the doctor. He escorted Walter firmly to the door and came back. "Poor chap—he can't make out why his blood won't do. Hopeless, of course. Just as well give the man prussic acid at once."

...The pink rose...

"Doctor—" began Scales.

And then, suddenly, Drury's voice came from behind the screen, speaking the line that had been written to be spoken with a harsh and ugly cynicism, but giving it as he had given it now on the stage for nearly a hundred performances:

"*All right, all right, don't worry—I'll rest on my laurels.*"

The hated, heart-breaking voice—the professional actor's voice—sweet as sugar plums—liquid and mellow like an intoxicated flute.

Damn him! thought Scales, feeling the rubber band tighten above his elbow, I hope he dies. Never to hear that damned awful voice again. I'd give anything. I'd give…

He watched his arm swell and mottle red and blue under the pressure of the band. The doctor gave him an injection of something. Scales said nothing. He was thinking:

Give anything. I would give my life. I would give my blood. I have *only* to give my blood—and say nothing. The plate *was* turned round… No, I don't know that. It's the doctor's business to make sure… I can't speak now… He'll wonder why I didn't speak before… Author sacrifices blood to save benefactor… Roses to right of him, roses to left of him… roses, roses all the way… I will rest on my laurels.

The needle now—plump into the vein. His own blood flowing, rising in the glass flask…somebody bringing a bowl of warm water with a faint steam rising off it…

…His life for his friend…right as rain in an hour or two…blood-brothers… The blood is the life…as well give him prussic acid at once…to poison a man with one's own blood…new idea for a murder… Murder…

"Don't jerk about," said the doctor.

…and what a motive!… Murder to save one's artistic soul…who'd believe that?…and losing money by it…your money or your life his life for his friend…his friend for his life…life or death, and not to know which one was giving… not *really* know…not know at all, *really*…too late now…

absurd to say anything now…nobody *saw* the plate turned round…and who would ever imagine…?

"That'll do," said the doctor. He loosened the rubber band, dabbed a pad of wool over the puncture and pulled out the needle, all, it seemed to Scales, in one movement. He plopped the flask into a little stand over the bowl of water and dressed the arm with iodine. "How do you feel? A trifle faint? Go and lie down in the other room for a minute or two."

Scales opened his mouth to speak, and was suddenly assailed by a queer, sick qualm. He plunged for the door. As he went, he saw the doctor carry the flask behind the screen.

Damn that reporter! He was still hanging round. Meat and drink to the papers, this kind of thing. Heroic sacrifice by grateful author. Good story. Better story still if the heroic author were to catch him by the arm, pour into his ear the unbelievable truth—were to say: "I hated him, I hated him, I tell you—I've poisoned him—my blood's poison—serpent's blood, dragon's blood—"

And what would the doctor say? If this really had gone wrong, would he suspect? What *could* he suspect? He hadn't seen the plate move. Nobody had. He might suspect himself of negligence, but he wouldn't be likely to shout *that* from the housetops. And he *had* been negligent—pompous, fat, chattering fool. Why didn't he mark the specimens earlier? Why didn't he match-up the blood with Drury's? Why did he need to chatter so much and explain things? Tell people how easy it was to murder a benefactor?

Scales wished he knew what was happening. Walter was hovering outside in the passage. Walter was jealous—he had looked on enviously, grudgingly, as Scales came stumbling in from the operation. If only Walter knew what Scales had been doing, he might well look… It occurred to Scales that he had played a shabby trick on Walter—cheated him—Walter, who had wanted so much to sacrifice his right, his true, his life-giving blood…

Twenty minutes…nearly half an hour… How soon would they know whether it was all right or all wrong? "As well give him prussic acid," the doctor had said. That suggested something pretty drastic. Prussic acid was quick—you died as if struck.

Scales got up, pushed Walter and the pressman aside, and crossed the passage. In Drury's room the screen had been pushed back. Scales, peeping through the door, could see Drury's face, white and glistening with sweat. The doctor bent over the patient, holding his wrist. He looked distressed—almost alarmed. Suddenly he turned, caught sight of Scales and came over to him. He seemed to take minutes to cross the room.

"I'm sorry," said the doctor. "I'm very much afraid—you did your best—we all did our best."

"No good?" Scales whispered back. His tongue and palate were like sawdust.

"One never can be certain with these things," said the doctor. "I'm very much afraid he's going." He paused and his eyes were faintly puzzled. "So much haemorrhage," he muttered as though explaining the trouble to himself. "Shock—cardiac strain—excitable"—and, in a worried voice—"he complained almost at once of pain in the back." He added, with more assurance: "It's always a bit of a gamble, you see, when the operation is left so late—and sometimes there is a particular idiosyncrasy. I should have preferred a direct test; but it's not satisfactory if the patient dies while you wait to make sure."

With a wry smile he turned back to the couch, and Scales followed him. If Drury could have acted death as he was acting it now!... Scales could not rid himself of the notion that he *was* acting—that the shine upon the skin was greasepaint, and the rough, painful breathing, the stereotyped stage gasp. If truth could be so stagey, then the stage must be disconcertingly like truth.

Something sobbed at his elbow. Walter had crept into the room, and this time the doctor made way for him.

"Oh, Mr. Drury!" said Walter.

Drury's blue lips moved. He opened his eyes: the dilated pupils made them look black and enormous.

"Where's Brand?"

The doctor turned interrogatively to the other two men. "His son?"

"His understudy," whispered Scales. Walter said: "He'll be here in a minute, Mr. Drury."

"They're waiting," said Drury. He drew a difficult breath and spoke in his old voice:

"Brand! Fetch Brand! The curtain must go up!"

Garrick Drury's death was very "good theatre."

Nobody, thought Scales, could ever know. He could never really know himself. Drury might have died, anyhow, of shock. Even if the blood had been right he might have died. One couldn't be certain, now, that the blood hadn't been right; it might have been all imagination about the smudged pink rose. Or—one might be sure, deep in one's own mind. But nobody could prove it. Or—could the doctor? There would have to be an inquest, of course. Would they make a post-mortem? Could they prove that the blood was wrong? If so, the doctor had his ready explanation—"particular idiosyncrasy" and lack of time to make further tests. He *must* give that explanation, or accuse himself of negligence.

Because nobody could prove that the plate had been moved. Walter and the doctor had not seen it—if they had, they would have spoken. Nor could it be proved that he, Scales, had seen it—he was not even certain himself, except in the hidden chambers of the heart. And he, who lost so much by Drury's death—to suppose that *he* could have seen and not spoken was fantastic. There are things beyond the power even of a coroner to imagine or of a coroner's jury to believe.

The Wrong Make-Up

Brandon Fleming

Brandon Fleming (1889–1970) was a playwright and screen-writer whose work ventured from time to time into criminal territory. He is perhaps most likely to be remembered for co-writing the 1925 "farcical melodrama" *None but the Brave.* His co-author was Bernard Merivale, whose other collaborators included Arnold Ridley, later renowned as Private Godfrey in the BBC TV series *Dad's Army.* Four years earlier, Fleming had enjoyed some success with a solo effort for the stage, *The Eleventh Commandment*, which was later filmed.

Fleming wrote the script for a 1933 crime film *Mayfair Girl* and such "quota quickies" of the Thirties as *Great Stuff, Forging Ahead*, and *The Flaw* (a mystery movie which origin-ated as a short story and was remade in 1955 with John Bentley and Donald Houston in the lead roles). "The Wrong Make-Up" is another of his short stories, and it first appeared in the *Strand Magazine* in 1941.

On the night of January 10 the Mall Theatre contributed a sensation to theatrical history. Ten minutes after the opening of the third act of the play—just past its hundredth performance—the curtain was suddenly rung down. The manager appeared in front of it, and informed the packed house that owing to the serious illness of Sir John Furnival during the interval it would be impossible to continue the performance.

Almost before the audience had left the theatre the news had gone round that Furnival had been found dead in his dressing-room just before he had been due on the stage. Then came the hint of murder. And after that a whisper of something vaguely, grotesquely horrible...

The facts, briefly, were these. At the end of the second act, Furnival had gone up the short flight of steps to his dressing-room, which was the nearest one to the stage. There was an interval of fifteen minutes before the commencement of the last act, and Furnival himself did not appear in it for nearly another quarter of an hour. He had, therefore, about half an hour from the fall of the curtain on the second act to his entrance in the third. During that time he had not only to change his clothes but also his make-up, as there was a time lapse between the acts which necessitated a complete alteration in his appearance.

Usually he had plenty of time to spare to see any callers or to deal with letters and business if necessary. On this particular night, however, about five minutes after he had reached his room, his dresser, Bendle, had come out, wearing his hat and coat, and told the stage-doorkeeper that Sir John had sent him out on an errand and was dressing himself. Bendle had seemed a good deal annoyed at being sent out, as it was a cold and wet night.

As it happened, there were no callers for Furnival; but a friend of his had rung up on the telephone just after the beginning of the last act. Tyler, the stage-doorkeeper, had rung through to the dressing-room to ask if the call should be put through, and had been surprised at the length of time it had taken Furnival to answer. When at last he did come to the telephone he had seemed very angry and agitated, and refused to speak to anyone. His voice had been very loud, and there had been a strange unnatural sound about it. Tyler supposed that something had annoyed him—a by no means infrequent occurrence—and had thought no more about it.

The call-boy, Jackson, had knocked at the dressing-room door, and given the usual preliminary calls. But when he gave the final personal call for Furnival, to which he had to receive an answer, there was no response. He knocked and called again. Still there was no reply, nor could he hear any sound whatever in the room. He opened the door and looked in.

Furnival was sitting in front of his dressing-table at the far end of the room, with his back to the door. The boy repeated the call, but there was no movement or answer. He went forward alarmed, thinking that Furnival was ill. But Furnival was dead.

He was leaning back in his chair, the mark of a heavy blow on his right temple, his wide-open eyes fixed in a dreadful stare at the mirror in front of him. But the thing that terrified

Jackson, even more than the actual discovery of the dead man, was that he was looking down into a strange and horrible face; a face that bore no resemblance whatever to the Sir John Furnival he knew, either as himself or as the character he impersonated in the play; a face disfigured by such a hideous, unmeaning, inhuman make-up, in which he could not possibly have gone on the stage in that play or any other, that the boy just turned and bolted out of the room, screaming for help.

The stage manager rushed round. A few minutes later the curtain was rung down. The police and a doctor were sent for. Until they came, the door was locked on the dead figure, sagging back in the chair before the looking-glass, in its old greasepaint-stained dressing-gown, the horrible, meaningless make-up on its face, that could have been for no play ever written.

There was a growing crowd in the narrow street at the back of the theatre when Detective-Inspector Fay and Sergeant Barker pushed their way through to the stage-door. In the main passage, on to which most of the dressing-rooms opened, members of the cast were standing about in excited groups. Outside Furnival's room, Bendle, the dresser, was protesting angrily against the stage manager's refusal to admit him until the police arrived. From the open door of the only other dressing-room on that level a girl stood staring across the square landing. Inspector Fay glanced at her only for a moment, but in that glance he saw that she was very lovely and very frightened.

"Good heavens!" said Bendle. "Look at his face!"

For fully a minute no other word was spoken. They stood

looking down at the dead actor in the chair. He had apparently been struck a savage blow on the forehead with some heavy, sharp instrument. So much was plain. But the rest...

"What could he have been doing?" the stage manager whispered. "He must have intended to go on in the last act. He hadn't missed a single performance since the play started. And yet, just before he was killed he must have been sitting there playing the fool with his make-up like that within a few minutes of being called on the stage. Unless..." he paused a moment, "it seems too monstrous to suggest...unless the murderer, after killing him, took the risk of staying in the room...to make a mockery of his dead face..."

Inspector Fay turned away and looked round the room. It was large and luxuriously furnished. His eyes found the telephone instrument on a bracket behind a couch at the other end. He walked over to it.

This was the instrument from which Tyler had heard Furnival's voice, loud and angry, with the strange unnatural quality he had spoken of. He was positive it had been Furnival's voice, and no other. There seemed to be no doubt whatever about that.

Inspector Fay walked back from the telephone far more slowly than he had walked to it. On the way back he took a great deal of interest in the floor. Twice he stooped down...

Tyler was certain that no stranger had entered or left the stage-door during the evening. He was prepared to swear to that. The stage manager was equally sure that no one had passed through the pass-door from the stage to the front of the house.

Inspector Fay accepted both statements without question.

"Now, Mr. Bendle, just one or two points. I think you said when we first came in that you had been acting as Sir John's valet and dresser for a good many years. Fifteen, wasn't it?"

"Nearer sixteen."

"Nearer sixteen. That's pretty good. So of course you knew him very well. When he came up here after the end of the second act did he seem to be quite himself?"

A quick glance passed between the dresser and the stage manager.

"Much as usual," said Bendle. "There'd been a bit of something earlier on. Mr. Grafton'll tell you about that."

"There was rather an unpleasant incident at the end of the first act," the stage manager explained, "between Sir John and Miss Margaret Archer. Miss Archer plays the leading woman's part—"

The inspector stopped him.

"Was it Miss Archer who was standing at the door of the room opposite when we came in?"

"Yes. I'm sure it was not really anything serious—"

"We'll come to it in a minute," said the inspector. "Was it usual, Mr. Bendle, for Sir John to send you out on errands between the acts and dress himself?"

"No, it wasn't."

"What was the errand he sent you out on tonight?"

Hostility crept into Bendle's attitude. His eyes narrowed.

"To deliver a letter."

"Whom was it addressed to, and where did you take it?"

"It was a private errand," returned Bendle surlily.

"Very likely," said Inspector Fay. "Whom was it addressed to, and where did you take it?"

The dresser stared at him defiantly.

"I'm not going to tell. It was the guv'nor's private business."

"Come, Bendle," said the inspector, "you know better than that. Nothing is private in an affair like this. We've got to know things. You'll have to answer sooner or later. You'd better save trouble by doing it now."

"I should tell the inspector, Bendle," advised the stage manager. "He has the right to ask questions. You'll only make things more difficult by refusing. It's quite plain you can't have had any hand in the trouble."

"I was out on the guv'nor's business," repeated Bendle obstinately. "And that's all I've got to say."

The inspector looked at him steadily.

"I wonder if you'd have any objection, Bendle," he said quietly, "to turning out your pockets?"

The man drew back quickly. For an instant, fear flashed across his face. His hands clenched tightly.

"I won't do it," he said hoarsely. "You can't make me. You've nothing to touch me on. I'm not going to be treated like that by you or anyone else."

Inspector Fay shrugged his shoulders.

"All right, Bendle. Don't be upset. It was just a suggestion." He turned to the sergeant, who was standing behind him. "Barker," he said pleasantly, "pop out into another room with Mr. Bendle and keep him company for a few minutes. Perhaps he might be able to give you a hint or two about that queer make-up. It's the most important thing in the case."

For a moment the dresser's face was livid.

"What d'you mean?" he demanded truculently. "I wasn't here. How could I know anything about it?"

"That's what I'm wondering," said Inspector Fay.

Then Tyler brought in the divisional surgeon.

There was no doubt that Furnival had been detested by every-one in the theatre. No one had a good word for him, from the top to the bottom. He was selfish, arrogant, an overbearing egotist, without the slightest consideration for anyone but him-self. But he was a great artist, a man of tremendous personality. Whatever he might have been in other ways, there could be no question that he was a fine actor. And that night, curiously enough, he had been treating the crowded audience to the great-est performance he had ever given of one of the most difficult and successful parts of his career. He had held them spellbound. And yet, unknown to the hundreds who had applauded him, strange things had happened behind the dividing curtain.

Inspector Fay left the doctor to his examination, and crossed the landing to the open door of Margaret Archer's room. He found a young man with her, a tall, good-looking fellow, of about twenty-eight or so. Both were still in their stage clothes.

Margaret Archer looked at the inspector gravely. She had recovered herself, and there was hardly anything remaining of the fear that had been in her face when he had seen her first.

"I expected you'd want to see me," she said, "so I didn't begin to change." She turned to the young man. "This is Mr. Jack Vane." There was just the slightest hesitation. "We are engaged to be married."

"Miss Archer," said Inspector Fay, "I understand that when you came off the stage with Sir John Furnival at the end of the first act tonight, you struck him in the face in the presence of a good many of the cast?"

She shivered a little.

"Yes," she said, "I did. Some time ago he started making disagreeable whispers to me during the play. I warned him what I would do if he didn't stop. And tonight…I had to do it."

The inspector nodded.

"I am sure you acted under great provocation. Mr. Vane, I think, was not present when the incident took place?"

"I was not," said the young man definitely. "If I had been—"

She stopped him.

"Jack—please don't."

Vane put his arm round her.

"It's no use trying to hide anything, sweetheart," he said firmly. "So far as I'm concerned I'm going to be quite frank. For some months, Inspector, Furnival had been making himself objectionable to Miss Archer. She showed as plainly as she could that she didn't want to have anything to do with him, but he went on pestering her. I interfered several times."

"So I've heard, Mr. Vane," the inspector said. "I heard also that you had uttered threats."

"I may have, and they were quite justified. She was beginning to find it unbearable. He was making her almost afraid to go on the stage."

The girl's hands closed tightly on his.

"I suppose I was nervy tonight," she confessed. "This play always frightens me a little. It used to even when we were rehearsing. I couldn't do my part properly if it didn't. Every scene I played with him…I used to feel it was real…terrifyingly real."

"You ought not to be playing in it," Vane told her. "It's the wrong sort of show for you. Your nerves aren't strong enough, especially when you had to play such scenes with a man like Furnival."

She drew away from him, pausing a moment.

"Of course it's stupid to let a thing get hold of one…but he frightened me. Every time he spoke to me or looked at me on the stage, I felt I couldn't get away. I was helpless. I just said my lines mechanically. He was supposed to half-hypnotise me in the play, and I believe he did…" Another convulsive shudder ran through her. She made a strong effort to keep her voice under control. "Tonight I *had* to do something to resist him. I made myself do it. I knew that if I didn't…he'd break me."

"You can see how it was, Inspector," Vane said. "Furnival would have had me sacked from the cast long ago, only Miss Archer declared positively that she would leave if I did, and they couldn't afford to lose her. There's no one could play the part as she does."

Inspector Fay smiled.

"I'm sure of that. When did you hear of this 'incident' at the end of the first act, Mr. Vane?"

"Not until the second act had begun. If I'd heard about it before, I should have gone down to Furnival's room straight away."

The next question came slowly and deliberately.

"Instead of which, you waited until the end of the second act?"

"Yes."

The terror came back into Margaret Archer's face. She clung to him.

"Jack, for God's sake—"

He kissed her. "Don't you worry, darling. I'm going to tell exactly what happened. It's the only thing to do."

"Go on," said Inspector Fay.

"I have a fairly quick change myself for the third act, so I got that done first. Then I went to Furnival's room. I was so angry, I didn't knock at the door. I just walked right in."

"Was Bendle, the dresser, there?"

"No. Furnival was alone."

"What was he doing when you went in?"

"Sitting in front of his dressing-table."

"Making himself up?"

"Yes."

"Go on," said the inspector again.

"He turned on me and asked what the devil I meant by coming into his room. I told him I'd heard what had happened, that Miss Archer was engaged to me, and if he ever annoyed her again in any way, I'd give him a hiding."

"How did he take the news of Miss Archer's engagement?"

"He was furious. I repeated my warning, and went down to the stage for my cue."

Inspector Fay paused. The young man had given his account in a perfectly frank, straightforward way.

"Did anyone see you go into the room, or come out?"

Vane shook his head. "There was no one about. The third act had begun, and practically everybody was on the stage."

"So it's not possible to know definitely whether you were in the room before or after Tyler rang through and heard Sir John's voice on the 'phone?"

"I'm afraid not. All I can say is that no 'phone call came through while I was there."

The inspector looked at him closely.

"You see the value of the point, Mr. Vane?"

"Of course I do," Vane retorted. "If I could prove that Tyler had heard Furnival's voice on the 'phone after I had gone out of the room, it would show that he was alive when I left him, and clear me from suspicion."

"Exactly. Can you prove it?"

"No, I can't," said Vane decidedly. "All I can do is to give you my word that I don't know a thing about Furnival's death. I never laid a finger on him, and he was alive when I went out. I've no proof. I can only tell you it was so. Whether you believe me or not is your affair."

"Now, Mr. Vane," said Inspector Fay, "about that very strange make-up."

"I don't know anything about that."

"You said that when you went into the room, Sir John was sitting in front of his table making himself up for the third act?"

"Yes."

"How far had he got?"

Vane considered a moment.

"I should say his face was about half done."

"As much as that?"

"Yes, quite."

"Did he go on making himself up while you were there?"

"No. He was much too angry."

"Was there anything queer or unusual about his make-up, so far as he had gone at that time?"

"Nothing," Vane declared. "It was quite all right."

"You're sure of that?" the inspector insisted.

"Perfectly."

"Have you been in the room since he was found dead?"

"Yes. We all crowded in after the alarm was given."

"You saw his face again then?"

"I did. It was horrible."

"Can you make any suggestion," continued the inspector, "as to how or why, after you had left the room, that half-finished normal make-up should have become changed to what you saw the second time?"

"I can't think of any reason," Vane replied. "It seems an incredible thing for him to have done himself, or for anyone else to have done to him when he was dead. If I had killed him I certainly shouldn't have stayed in the room to play about with his make-up when he was liable to be called at any moment."

"You don't think," the inspector suggested, "that the announcement of Miss Archer's engagement to you could suddenly have sent him off his head?"

"I am absolutely certain it couldn't. He wasn't that sort. He would have been much more likely to have made up his mind to get her away from me by hook or crook. I don't like talking about him like that after he's dead, but it can't be helped. I can't believe he did that to his own face. I am sure that while he was alive, he intended to go on in the third act. He was very conscientious in that way. He wouldn't have let the play down for any private reasons whatsoever. I'm convinced of that."

Margaret Archer went to Inspector Fay and put a hand on his arm.

"I want to tell you something," she said slowly. "I've been told I'm psychic. I don't know. I've never tried to test it. But when I went into the room with the others... I was conscious of something that I'm sure no one else felt. It's very hard to describe. It came to me so strongly. I felt I was on the scene of a great fight. I don't mean a physical fight... And when I looked at his face...somehow it didn't appear hideous to me. I seemed to see something beyond...something rather wonderful...like the face of a man who'd died in a great cause..."

Her voice trembled. She broke off.

"Please don't laugh at me," she said. "I suppose it sounds silly."

There was no sign of laughter on the inspector's face.

"Miss Archer, it isn't at all silly. In fact, it's very much the opposite. You've got nearer to the truth—"

There was the sound of a sudden commotion—a loud voice shouting. Inspector Fay hurried out on to the landing. On the stairs a man was struggling to free himself from the expert grip of Sergeant Barker. It was Bendle. Tyler was behind them. The sergeant brought matters to a climax by lifting Bendle bodily up the last half-dozen steps, and depositing him at the top.

"Tried to force his way out of the room, sir. Said he wouldn't wait any longer. Stand still, will you?"

"Don't be a fool, Bendle," said the inspector curtly. "You are only making things worse—"

He stopped, and turned quickly. The stage manager came out of the room opposite. He had a folded slip of paper in his hand.

"Inspector, the doctor asked me to give you this."

Inspector Fay unfolded the note, and read it. He looked back with a slight smile at Vane and Margaret standing together in the doorway behind him.

"What's that?" asked Vane sharply.

The inspector refolded the note, and put it into his pocket.

"Your vindication, Mr. Vane. But I may say you were not really under suspicion at any time. The doctor has just sent me the answer to a question I asked him." He turned back to the others. "Now then, Bendle. I asked you a little time ago to turn out your pockets. You refused. Do you still refuse?"

"Yes, I do. I'll see you damned first."

"Then I'm going to do it myself."

"You've no right to."

"Perhaps not. You've still the chance to do it for me. Which is it to be?"

For a moment the dresser stood glaring at him helplessly. Then he put his hand to an inner pocket, brought out a small sealed packet, and threw it across to him.

"That's what you want! Take it, and be damned to you!"

The inspector caught it.

"Thanks, Bendle. You might as well have done it at first. I'm not going to ask you where you got it yet. That will have to be dealt with later, and I should advise you to be frank about it." He put the packet away into his own pocket. "Now I think I can tell you what happened in Sir John's room tonight."

"There are two people here," said Inspector Fay, "who are in a way responsible for Sir John Furnival's death. One is Tyler."

The stage-doorkeeper started.

"Me? What do you mean? I never went near him. I was at the door the whole time."

"I know that," agreed the inspector, "and I can assure you it won't trouble your conscience. The other one is Bendle— and I'm not going to say anything about his conscience at the moment."

The dresser was silent. His face had changed to a sickly paleness. He stared down at the floor. The inspector turned his back on him.

"Sir John was a brave man. He died because he *was* brave. If he had been a man of less strength of will and determination, he would have been alive now. Whatever his faults we must allow him that. But one of the faults was that he was a drug addict.

"For many years I was attached to the special branch for dealing with the drug traffic, and I had to study the effects of the different drugs, and how to detect their use. Sir John's eyes caused me to ask the doctor a question, which he has been able to answer after making a test. The dead man had been in the habit of taking a certain drug—I am not going to mention its name. I do not know whether Bendle's part was merely to act as a messenger, or whether he had any larger share in procuring the drug. That will have to be the subject of investigation. The important thing is that this particular drug produces two separate effects. One is on the heart, and is very dangerous because it can remain unsuspected until some sudden shock reveals it. The other is that taken in increasing doses over a long period it has the property of inducing attacks of blindness."

There were startled exclamations all round him.

"Blindness!" Vane exclaimed. "By Jove, yes—that accounts for it!"

"As I see it," said Inspector Fay, "what happened was this: Sir John came up to his room after the first act very much upset by the incident with Miss Archer. In order to compose himself for the next act he took a large dose of the drug, which happened to be all he had left. Is that right, Bendle?"

The dresser nodded sullenly.

"During the next interval he sent Bendle out to the place from which he obtained the drug for a further supply, and sat down in front of his glass to make himself up for the third act. Then in came Mr. Vane, and the effect of the interview was to leave Sir John beside himself with rage. This sudden acute mental disturbance, on the top of the large dose of the drug he had taken, brought on the first attack. He was struck blind."

The inspector paused. Margaret Archer swayed a little, and put a hand on the back of a chair to steady herself. There were tears in her eyes.

"It must have been a dreadful shock to him," the inspector went on, "but, as I said, he was a brave man. He made up his mind to finish the performance without letting anyone know. He had played the part more than a hundred times. He knew every inch of the way from that room to the stage, and no doubt could have visualised the scenes quite well enough to have carried on without betraying himself. The great difficulty, the worst risk he had to take, was with his make-up. It was only half done. He had to finish it. If he could fix in his mind's eye the position of the different sticks of grease paint and other things on the table in front of him as they were when his sight was cut off, he could do it. He took the risk—but, as you know, he failed.

"While he was doing this, Tyler rang through on the

'phone. He was surprised that Sir John took so long in answering, but the reasons are obvious. He did not want to get up from the table and break up his mental picture of it until he had finished; but he could not ignore the call, particularly if it was an important one, without bringing about inquiry. Then he had to grope his way to the telephone instrument. No wonder his voice sounded strange and unnatural."

The door of the room opposite opened again, and the doctor came out. He beckoned to Inspector Fay.

"You were quite right. He must have tripped up over the edge of the rug on his way back from the telephone, and caught his forehead on the projecting foot of the table. The grease paint you found on it proves that. He just managed to stagger up and get to his chair, but his heart was so bad with that infernal stuff that it gave out under the double shock."

1944

The Case of the Ventriloquist's Doll

Ernest Dudley

Many of the contributors to this volume were enthusiastic actors. This was certainly the case with Vivian Ernest Coltman-Allen (1908–2006), who became better known under the name Ernest Dudley. Aged seventeen, he left home to become an actor, joining a company which performed Shakespeare in small Irish towns. He met Jane Grahame, who for several years played one of the Lost Boys in *Peter Pan*, and they married in 1930. For a time he performed in the West End, alongside the likes of Fay Compton and Charles Laughton, while he and his wife took the leads in the first British touring production of Noël Coward's *Private Lives*. He became friendly with Fred Astaire, but increasingly gravitated towards journalism and other forms of writing, including radio scripts.

His enduring love of the theatre was illustrated by the publication of a book about Lillie Langtry in 1958, but by that time he was most closely associated with detective fiction and in particular with Doctor Morelle, a character originally created for the BBC radio programme *Monday Night at Eight*. Morelle was originally played by Dennis Arundell, while his secretary, Miss Frayle, was a part written with Jane Grahame in mind. This story was included in his collection *Meet Doctor Morelle Again*, published in 1944.

———

"KINDLY HAND ME THAT RETORT, MISS FRAYLE," SAID Doctor Morelle as he bent over some chemicals which he was distilling over a bunsen-burner in his laboratory. "Also the crucible lid."

She grasped both the required articles in each hand, and moved across to him. Then, quite suddenly, she caught her breath, her eyes screwing up and her lips quivering. Her shoulders began to shake in an uncontrollable spasm.

"Quick, Doctor," she managed to gasp. "Take them! Quickly. Oh!" He jerked round rapidly, eyeing her with baleful displeasure, and relieved her of the retort and the crucible lid. Frenziedly she clapped her hands over her mouth and nose and ran from the laboratory as though she had a sudden premonition it would blow sky-high any moment. She heard the doctor's sardonic laughter following her as she retreated.

She slammed the laboratory door, and leaned supportingly against the door handle. She gasped for breath. Relief came over her features, then puzzlement. Again, she breathed deeply. At last the paroxysm quivered on the brink of its climax.

"A-Ah-A-tis-SHOO!" she sneezed violently. She smiled breathlessly. That was a near thing! If she had sneezed when she was holding the chemical apparatus, she would undoubtedly have smashed it. Also, if she had sneezed in the laboratory she would have been the target for a farrago of sarcastic abuse from the Doctor. She sneezed again—it was a refined squeak this time rather than an explosive detonation. With tears in her eyes she laughed to herself. Here she was, sneezing her head off—and there in the laboratory was the Doctor pursuing his research for a final and efficacious remedy for the common cold. There was irony for you!

As though by auto-suggestion, she had contracted the cold the very day Doctor Morelle had announced his intention of experimenting with the distillation of some new drugs which might prove to be a cure for colds.[1]

"It is singularly inconsiderate of you, my dear Miss Frayle," he had told her testily, "to contract a chill while our research is still only at the formative stage. If you had postponed the attack for two weeks you might have been useful at our final experiments."

"I don't think I'd care to be used as a guinea-pig!" she retorted.

"How odd," he had observed. "I should have imagined that you would have raised no objections."

"I think that remark's a little unworthy of you, Doctor," she had retorted indignantly, but unfortunately had been constrained to rush out of the study to sneeze before he could reply, and so she was never to know whether, for once, she had effectively succeeded in crushing him.

She broke off these speculations when she heard an

---

1 The outcome of biochemical research in other directions more profound and obscure; whether the Doctor achieved any concrete results in the comparatively mundane mystery of the common cold has not yet been announced.

imperative ring at the front door. She ran to open it. A dark, bulky figure loomed through the doorway and, without even glancing at her, made as if to move past her.

"Whom do you wish to see?"

"Doctor Morelle, of course, who else?" The huge man spoke in an authoritative manner. She ran after him, noticing in greater detail his appearance after the first shock of his peremptory entrance. The man would be about fifty, over six feet tall. He was wearing a heavy, dark overcoat with a massive fur collar. A large-brimmed, black hat was on his wide head, and from under the hat she could see red hair curling long down his neck.

"Have you an appointment?" she demanded.

The impressive-looking stranger did not even deign to turn his head as he said:

"I do not need an appointment," and he continued striding along the hall.

"Does the Doctor know you?" she asked anxiously.

"Everybody knows me," was the terse reply. "The whole world! The Doctor will be honoured to see me."

Miss Frayle had by now caught up with him. She was frantically trying to evolve some strategy. Only a few weeks previously she had permitted two gate-crashers in the house at the time when the Doctor was investigating the Wolf Spiders Case. His terse admonitions for her gross carelessness were still fresh in her mind. She tried hard not to be impressed and abashed by this dynamic caller. Desperately, she attempted to classify him. He was either someone very important—or a lunatic! And if he were a person of some importance, he ought to know better. Frantically she grasped at the man's arm as he began opening doors in his search for the Doctor. He was already about to fling open the door of the laboratory.

"No—you don't!" she cried. She pushed herself in front of him, and barred his way, stretching her arms across the door. She felt rather like the heroine in a melodramatic film, and she would have said: "Over my dead body!" if she could have made it sound convincing.

"Stand aside!" he ordered. "My time is valuable!"

"I won't stand aside!" She felt that she was going to sneeze again. Would—would she then be compelled to release her hold on the door? "If only you'd make an appointment—"

"Appointment!" The man twisted his lips scornfully. "*I* do not have to make an appointment—I *arrive!*"

"Yes, so I see, but—" she squeaked helplessly and she thought: "If he does see Doctor Morelle, he'll be the only man in the whole world who's a match for him." The pair of them would be a good team in a contest of bombast, conceit, self-satisfaction and downright rudeness.

"You do not seem to realise who I am!" the man said tersely. "I am—"

At that moment the laboratory door opened.

"Oh, dear!" gasped Miss Frayle. Doctor Morelle looked over her shoulder at the tall, massive intruder. There was an indignant tightness about his features.

"Whomsoever you may be," he retorted icily, "*I* happen to be Doctor Morelle."

A condescending smile of welcome came over the other man's features. The Doctor returned it with a freezing glare. Then he studiously turned away from the man and addressed Miss Frayle.

"What does this disturbance mean?" he demanded.

"I'm sorry, I tried to stop him. But he pushed his way in. He walked right in without a word, started opening doors—"

The man held a silencing hand to Miss Frayle. He bowed gravely to the Doctor, removing his hat with a sweeping gesture.

"I am Voxio," he declared resonantly. He made the declaration with an air of finality, as though the fact would explain the most eccentric behaviour.

"Voxio!" repeated Doctor Morelle distastefully. "So far as I am concerned the name might be that of some patent medicine for the alleviation of laryngitis."

The intruder's dark eyes flashed, but it seemed as though the man's haughtiness dwindled and the corners of his flexible lips drooped. Behind his veneer of bombast, there appeared to be genuine distress. He drew himself up, and he seemed to tower over Miss Frayle and the Doctor.

"I am not a medicine, but an artist! Voxio, the Ventriloquist," he intoned impressively. "You must listen to me. I am here to beg you to restore to me my little boy." Suddenly the big man began to sob. His distress and tears seemed almost ludicrous because of the colossal size of the man. "My little boy has been kidnapped," he went on dramatically. Then in a down-to-earth tone, he added: "He's been stolen by some dirty, thieving rat!"

"Oh, you poor man," burst out Miss Frayle, with her effervescent sympathy which never failed to find expression. "How worried you must be! No wonder you rushed in here as though you were out of your mind." She turned to the Doctor, her eyes pleading behind their lenses.

He did not even glance at her. It was as though she had

not spoken. With raised eyebrows the Doctor addressed the ventriloquist.

"I presume you are referring to the theft last night of the effigy with which you give your performance," he observed enigmatically. "The occurrence is reported in this morning's *Telegram*."

The ventriloquist nodded with grief-stricken vigour. He pulled agitatedly at the fur round his collar.

"Yes, yes, Doctor. I happened to meet the theatrical correspondent of the paper later. As a personal favour I let him have the—what's the phrase for it?—the *exclusive* story. I never take the paper myself—too highbrow. What does it say?"

Doctor Morelle reached for that morning's *Telegram* which lay on a rack near the laboratory door.

"I was reading it only half an hour ago." He scanned the column. "This is the item, I believe." Voxio took the paper from him and read in trumpet-like tones: "'Exclusive to the *Telegram*. After the conclusion of his performance at the Rotunda Music Hall last night, Voxio the Ventriloquist's doll disappeared. It is believed—'"

"Oh, your *doll*," broke in Miss Frayle. "I thought you meant your son had been kidnapped."

"Doll!" echoed Voxio with vibrant scorn. "My Joey is more than a doll. He is more human than you, young lady—or your Doctor. He *is* a son to me. Doesn't he work for me, keep me from starving? Doesn't he sleep beside me? Doesn't he—?" He became incoherent in his expressions of devotion. "But never mind," he went on at last, "you wouldn't understand. What you might understand is that he must be found in time for my show tonight. You must find him, Doctor."

Doctor Morelle backed into his laboratory, half closing the door.

"Really, Mr. Voxio," he said definitely, "I hardly think I can undertake—"

Voxio waved aside his excuse. "I have heard of you, Doctor," he stated. "You are a brilliant investigator."

Doctor Morelle coughed and half smiled self-effacingly.

"Well, I—" he began.

"Almost as brilliant as I am a ventriloquist," added Voxio, smiling widely as though he had conferred on the Doctor the greatest compliment in the world. "Come, I have a car waiting. We will go to the theatre and there you can pick up the clues. I implore you to find my Joey before tonight. Please, please, Doctor Morelle."

The Doctor paused ponderously. Finally he nodded his head briskly.

"I will elucidate this mystery for you," he stated, "if you will promise to give me a certain undertaking."

"Anything! Anything!" Voxio repeated, sweeping an arm expansively. "Money, recommendations, even a free box for the second house on Saturday night! Just name it."

"Next time you happen to contract a common cold, I would deem it a favour if you would kindly attend my laboratory where I may be afforded the opportunity of administering to you a special drug on which I am now experimenting."

"Willingly," Voxio smilingly agreed. "I'm often getting colds. Have to get over them quickly at my job. Joey and I have to joke about it on the stage." The ventriloquist, to exemplify his statement, launched into a two-voiced ventriloquial patter: "'How did you get that cold, Joey?—I opened the window—You opened the window?—Yes, I opened the window and in-flew-enza.'" Patiently Voxio waited for the laugh, but as Miss Frayle felt another sneezing spasm coming on, she dared not open her lips. The Doctor was not amused. Voxio shrugged his shoulders hopelessly. "Anyway, we have to joke," he finished. "I'll stick to my bargain, Doctor, and you can experiment any time you like."

In the car, Doctor Morelle insisted that Miss Frayle sit in front beside the driver so that she would not fill the atmosphere with microbes. However, the sliding window was open, and she could hear Voxio giving Doctor Morelle more details about the disappearance of his doll.

"Of course this tragedy would never have happened if my own dresser had not been away sick," he was saying.

"Dresser? I fear I am not cognisant—"

"The fellow who looks after my costumes, lays them out and runs errands."

"In his absence doubtless you are employing a substitute?"

"For this last half of the week. He's nothing but a fool—an idiot!"

Doctor Morelle unwound the window and flung out his Le Sphinx.

"Do you suspect anyone—him, for instance, the substitute—er—dresser?"

"He hasn't the sense!"

"Is he a cretin?"

"I don't know about that. But he's a half-wit." Voxio stroked his chin thoughtfully. "Joey might have been stolen by one of my enemies," he pondered. "As a successful artist, I have plenty—"

"I can understand that," murmured the Doctor softly.

"That may be it," declared Voxio, pursuing his train of thought and missing the sarcasm. "One of my enemies might hope to do a deal with the insurance company. Joey is insured for three thousand pounds."

"Good Gracious!" ejaculated Miss Frayle involuntarily from the front of the car. "What a lot of money!"

"A mere bagatelle," countered Voxio airily. "Joey is worth it and more. He is human, I tell you—more human than—" he looked at Doctor Morelle as he searched for a simile.

"Quite!" The Doctor cut him short. He bent forward to peer out of the taxi window. "Is this the place of entertainment at which we are drawing up?"

"This is the Old Rotunda. Only a number two house," Voxio said condescendingly, "I'm playing it just as a fill-in." He paid the driver and gallantly armed Miss Frayle on to the pavement. "The stage door's round this side—next door to the fish and chip shop. Disgraceful locality!"

In a dusty cubby-hole by the red painted stage door, a dour, grey-headed man, shirt-sleeved, and unshaven, gave them no more than a cursory glance. It might have been Miss Frayle's imagination, but she thought that he glowered at Mr. Voxio.

"Any telephone messages?" Voxio asked aggressively.

"Somebody did telephone about something, left their name and message," the doorkeeper muttered sullenly. "Dunno what it was all about." He yawned. "I've gorn an' forgotten."

"You should write the message down. This is monstrous," Voxio stormed. "I'll report you."

"I dare say you would like to see me lose me job," the man muttered under his breath, "me with a sick wife and two growing kids." He turned his back on Voxio. "Stage folk ain't what they were."

"Silence—impertinent wretch!" Then the ventriloquist turned to the Doctor with a synthetically bland smile, "Come, Doctor—come, Miss Frayle." He strode like a king down the dusty, squalid corridor. "Jealousy! Professional jealousy," he was observing. "A great artist has to suffer such indignities from the lower orders."

Doctor Morelle lit a Le Sphinx, and said:

"I think you would have been better advised to have gone to the police in the first instance."

Already, it seemed, he was regretting that he had undertaken the investigation.

Voxio clicked his tongue in scorn: "The police? Dolts! Thickheaded blunderers! No, *you* are the one who will solve this affair. This way, please. Along here is my dressing-room. I have the star one, of course." He paused as he saw a dark-clad figure disappearing into an office at the end of the corridor.

"Pardon me one moment while I speak to our far-from-genial manager," he said, and strode away muttering: "I really must report that insolent doorman before I forget. Disgraceful!"

"My time is not at your disposal all day!" Doctor Morelle called after him with quick impatience, but Voxio had already entered the manager's office. His indignant, bombastic voice could be heard complaining loudly.

Miss Frayle straightened her spectacles thoughtfully as she waited.

"Did you notice, Doctor, what a nasty look the stage door-keeper gave him, when we came in?" she asked.

"I fear I cannot blame anyone for regarding him with certain disfavour," he commented.

"He has an objectionable way with him, hasn't he?"

"So vain, so aggressive. They are two qualities I abhor."

Miss Frayle sighed and with difficulty refrained from making the obvious comment.

Doctor Morelle exhaled a cloud of smoke. "He would appear to enjoy delusions of grandeur, almost bordering on paranoia," he diagnosed. "Many successful men, I have observed, appear to have almost pathologically inflated egos. Interesting. I wonder if delusions of grandeur help them to success or whether success makes them—"

His psycho-analytical ponderings were interrupted by the return of Voxio.

"The fool of a manager refuses to dismiss the stage door-keeper," he announced. "It's monstrous! Disgraceful!"

Miss Frayle smiled in relief.

Voxio moved towards his dressing-room. "Here we are—in here." He noticed that the door was ajar. "Hello, who left the door open?" He glanced inside. "Albert!" he exclaimed. "What the devil are you doing here?"

Miss Frayle entering the room saw a pale youth fiddling with some jars of make-up on a long table which stood underneath a mottled mirror. The youth started and dropped a jar. He stooped to recover it and almost tripped over himself.

"I jest thought I'd come in an' tidy up a bit like, Mr. Voxio," the youth said in a whining voice.

"But you are supposed to be sick, in bed."

"I know—but I'm not much of a one for sticking in bed—makes me 'ead ache," the youth exclaimed. "Up all last night

I was, coughing. Then this morning reads what 'appened in the *Echo*, so I gets out of bed and comes along in case I could 'elp, see?"

He rubbed a grimy hand over his nose.

"I told the new feller you'd engaged, that you wouldn't be wantin' 'im today, seeing as 'ow I've come back, sir, and I can dress you tonight."

"Very well, Albert. But it's strange—the doorman never said you were here."

"P'raps 'e didn't notice me come in."

"He wouldn't—never notices anything," Voxio declared, "any more than he noticed anyone last night who could have taken Joey."

"Wasn't it a terrible thing to 'appen, Mr. Voxio?" the youth commiserated. "When I reads about it in the *Echo*, I thinks to meself, 'Now 'ow will pore Mr. Voxio manage…'"

"Yes, yes, I can quite imagine how you felt!" The other cut him short. He turned to the Doctor and pointed to a brown case which lay on one end of the table. "This is the case in which Joey is kept. When, after leaving the theatre, I had the intuition all was not well and returned here, the case was as you see it now."

Doctor Morelle walked across to the case and examined it closely. Miss Frayle peered over his shoulder. He said:

"The locks, both of which are of intricate pattern, have not been forced. Well, Miss Frayle, what would you deduce from that significant fact?"

"Someone must have used a key," she declared, with what she thought was commendable promptness.

"Precisely." He permitted himself a faintly derisive smile.

"For once you have found the truth in the obvious—you are improving."

"Thank you, Doctor!"

He inspected some lettering at the base of the container.

"Observe, too," he said softly, "that the receptacle is of foreign manufacture."

"It was specially made for me in Rio de Janeiro," declared Voxio, removing his wide-brimmed hat and propelling it skilfully on to a hook. "Wasn't my South American tour an enormous success, Albert? The crowds! Colossal!"

"Yes, Mr. Voxio," murmured Albert dutifully. "You was a sensation. They'd never seen anyfink like you afore."

"True! True!" The ventriloquist struck an attitude. "Voxio the Great—Voxio, the *Unique*. It might be an idea for a billing. Make a note of it, Albert."

"Very good, Mr. Voxio."

"Your assistant accompanied you on your world tour, I gather?"

"Yes, everywhere," the other replied with a sweep of his arm. "Let's see—how many years have you been with me, Albert?"

"It's going on lor three years. You'd promised arter the first year to give me a rise, but I 'aven't—"

"Tush! This is no time and place to broach such a trivial matter, my lad."

Albert was about to make some protest, but was interrupted by a tap at the door. A shock-headed man of about thirty put his head round and appeared embarrassed when he saw so many people in the dressing-room.

"Oh! Good morning, Mr. Voxio—I just looked in. I'll come back later," he declared in a thin Cockney voice.

"Come in *now*. Close the door, you dolt!" ordered Voxio. "Miss Frayle has a cold." In a stage whisper, Voxio hissed at Doctor Morelle: "This is the other dresser, the fool!"

"I see."

"'Appened to be passing the theatre, I did, and—I thought I'd look in to see 'ow Albert felt, 'im not having been well. I thought 'e might need an 'and," the man twisted his cap in his hands, "and I 'oped I might see you too, Mr. Voxio."

"And why?"

"Well, begging your pardon, sir, and excuse me mentioning it in front of this lady and gentleman, but I—I er—"

"Go on, you fool!"

"I thought you might want to settle up with me for the two days I've been working for you, seeing as 'ow you won't be needing me now Albert's back an' all."

"The matter will be attended to."

"Oh, thanks… Sorry about your trouble, sir, about Joey I mean. You could 'ave knocked me down with a fevver when I 'eard…"

Doctor Morelle eyed the substitute dresser piercingly.

"I understood you were the last to leave the dressing-room last night? In accordance with instructions, you locked the door after you?"

"S'right, sir," the man nodded. "Left the key on me way out. The doll—I mean Joey—was safe and sound in his box then—Mr. Voxio'd tucked him up 'isself."

"I would not let a clumsy idiot like you touch him."

"No, Mr. Voxio," the man said meekly enough. Then, with a bright smile he added: "But look 'ere, instead of messing everyone about, why don't you call the perlice? They'd soon—"

"Shut up!" snapped the ventriloquist. "When I want your advice, I'll ask for it. Now get out."

"I think in point of fact you might take his advice," Doctor Morelle said softly.

"What—what? Do you mean to say that you cannot—"

"As I am not in a position to take the culprit into custody, the presence of the proper authorities would be advisable," the Doctor added.

"Culprit? You mean you know the thief? You know who's taken my Joey?"

"Precisely!" Doctor Morelle swiftly walked to the door and closed it. "In fact I'd go further and state that the thief is now in this room."

"In this room? Here?"

"I speak plainly, do I not?"

"'Ere, 'oo are you accusing?" gasped the Cockney substitute dresser. "I could 'ave the law on you for that."

"So far, I have not specified the thief—" the Doctor retorted calmly.

"Well, if it ain't Albert, ye're accusing me, and I won't 'ave it. Jest 'cause I'm new—and I 'elps Mr. Voxio out of his fix, Albert being ill—"

"Calm yourself, you fool!" Voxio shouted. He glanced in turn at the two dressers. One of them was guilty. Which? Albert was sullen, looking as though he'd begin to whine at any moment. The new man was defiant, indignant.

"Well, who is it, Doctor?" Voxio asked, clenching his hands tightly.

"The young man who bears the name of—Albert," the Doctor declared.

Albert rushed forward, the corners of his mouth working frenziedly. His thin hands caught at Voxio's coat pleadingly.

"I didn't mean to keep it," he babbled. "I'll bring it back to you… I'll find Joey again. I sold it to a man in a café. I've got the money 'ere in me pocket. I'll find the man again and…"

The veins showed on Voxio's forehead. With one large hand he grasped the back of Albert's coat.

"Wretch. Ungrateful swine!" he shrieked. He raised an arm and crashed it down full in Albert's face. With the other hand he gave him a resounding slap across his mouth.

"I'll thrash you to death," he cried. He was like a madman. "You fiend, treating my Joey like that. I'll—I'll—"

He grasped the swaying youth, and fixed his large hands round his thin neck, pressing against his wind-pipe with his wide thumb.

"Do something, Doctor Morelle!" cried Miss Frayle. "He'll murder him. He'll—he'll…" Her shoulders shook in a wild paroxysm. "A-A-Ah-tis-Shoo," she sneezed.

"Desist, Voxio!" the Doctor ordered.

"I'll kill him!"

Doctor Morelle approached the big man from the rear, grasped his left elbow, and twisted quickly, catching the other in a ju-jitsu lock. Albert broke free and fell against the wall, sobbing.

"To preserve you from a murder charge," the Doctor said levelly, "I think it would be advisable if I escorted Albert to the police station myself."

"I'll come quietly," Albert sobbed breathlessly. "Get me away from him! Don't let him come near me. He's—he's a—cruel swine, 'e is. Everyone 'ates 'im. Everyone… I 'ope 'e never gets Joey back, I 'ope. I won't tell where—now—"

Babbling incoherently, Albert followed Doctor Morelle and Miss Frayle from the room, while the ventriloquist sank on to a broken-down settee, and watched them with stupefied eyes. It seemed as though he knew he would never see his beloved doll again, and the blow stunned him.

Later in his study Doctor Morelle lit a Le Sphinx, and took a deep draw at it.

"Strange how a man should lavish every modicum of his consideration and devotion on a doll," he was reflecting, "and yet have none for his fellow creatures."

Miss Frayle straightened the papers on her desk.

"It's Albert I feel sorry for," she declared. "Do you think they'll send him to prison, Doctor?"

"I think not." He tapped the ash from his cigarette. "I shall make it my business to speak for him at the police court proceedings. Since the creature was not engaged in crime previously, he will be indubitably bound over on probation. I will make a point of using my influence with the probation officer to find him more harmonious employment."

"Why—why, Doctor Morelle! That is most awfully kind of you," Miss Frayle uttered in astonishment.

He regarded her quizzically.

"Am I to assume by the surprise in your tone, my *dear* Miss Frayle, that you consider acts of kindness are foreign to my nature?"

"No, Doctor Morelle. Oh, no!" she exclaimed. "It was just that—" she became confused, and decided it would be safer to change the subject quickly. "I think you were awfully clever over that case. How could you possibly deduce Albert had stolen the doll?"

He sank into a chair and gazed ceiling-wards.

"It was quite obvious to me he was the thief," he said calmly, "as he admitted, on the way to the police station, he had contrived to obtain duplicate keys of the effigy's case and the dressing-room. Providing himself with an alibi by his pretence of illness, he had slipped into the theatre that night and removed the effigy. The stage doorkeeper, used to seeing him at the theatre, had not noticed him on the occasion in question—an easily comprehended fact and one which induced me firstly to believe the thief might be someone connected with the music-hall."

"But how did he give himself away?"

"He revealed himself as the culprit when he stated he had read of the theft in his newspaper, the *Echo*, while in bed that morning. Voxio had mentioned it only to the correspondent of the—as he described it—highbrow *Telegram* which printed the affair as an *exclusive* report. In other words, the knowledge of the occurrence was not in the possession of the *Echo* or any other newspaper. Thus, the young man, in seeking to ward off any suspicion and ingratiate himself with his employer by arriving at the theatre, did, in fact, incriminate himself."

Miss Frayle nodded understandingly.

"And, of course, Doctor, it was most unlikely that he ever read the *Telegram*," she observed.

"Quite—a journal of somewhat erudite composition and intellectual aspect."

"Or, 'just a stuffy old paper' would be a concise and apt description, eh, Doctor Morelle?" she suggested mischievously.

"My dear Miss Frayle!" Irritably, he stubbed out his cigarette. "When I am desirous of tuition in colloquial English, I will advise you. Furthermore, I really must request you to—to—"

He broke off quickly. His eyes suddenly went glassy. He appeared to be panting for breath. He stood up, took a quick step forward and paused spasmodically.

"What is it, Doctor?" she asked anxiously. "Don't you feel well? Are you ill? Oh, what is it?"

Doctor Morelle opened his mouth. His eyes closed. His limbs jerked and he moved quickly to the window, flinging it open and thrusting out his head and shoulders. His answer to her question burst on her ears with an explosive report.

"A-Ah-Ah-tis-SHOO!"

1945

The Blind Spot

Barry Perowne

Barry Perowne was the pen-name of Philip Atkey (1908–85), whose uncle, Bertram Atkey, was also a thriller writer and an occasional actor. Curiously, Perowne is today remembered principally for writing about the exploits of a character created by someone else. He admired the "amateur cracksman" A. J. Raffles, whom E. W. Hornung (Arthur Conan Doyle's brother-in-law) introduced to the reading public in 1893. Forty years later, Perowne wrote the first of his "continuation stories" about Raffles. He wrote the adventures with such a deft touch that some people prefer them to the originals.

In addition to novels and short stories, Perowne wrote the screenplay for *Walk a Crooked Path*, a 1969 suspense movie set in a boys' school which benefited from a strong cast including Faith Brook, Peter Copley, Tenniel Evans, and the young Robert Powell. "The Blind Spot" was first published in *Ellery Queen's Mystery Magazine* in November 1945. Described by Otto Penzler, the renowned American editor, publisher, and bookstore owner as "one of the most ingenious stories ever written," it was filmed in 1947.

———

ANNIXTER LOVED THE LITTLE MAN LIKE A BROTHER. He put an arm around the little man's shoulders, partly from affection and partly to prevent himself from falling.

He had been drinking earnestly since seven o'clock the previous evening. It was now nudging midnight, and things were a bit hazy. The lobby was full of the thump of hot music; down two steps, there were a lot of tables, a lot of people, a lot of noise. Annixter had no idea what this place was called, or how he had got here, or when. He had been in so many places since seven o'clock the previous evening.

"In a nutshell," confided Annixter, leaning heavily on the little man, "a woman fetches you a kick in the face, or fate fetches you a kick in the face. Same thing, really—a woman and fate. So what? So you think it's the finish, an' you go out and get plastered. You get good an' plastered," said Annixter, "an' you brood.

"You sit there an' you drink an' you brood—an' in the end you find you've brooded up just about the best idea you ever had in your life! 'At's the way it goes," said Annixter, "an' 'at's my philosophy—the harder you kick a playwright, the better he works!"

He gestured with such vehemence that he would have collapsed if the little man hadn't steadied him. The little man was poker-backed; his grip was firm. His mouth was firm, too—a straight line, almost colourless. He wore hexagonal rimless spectacles, a black hard-felt hat, a neat pepper-and-salt suit. He looked pale and prim beside the flushed, rumpled Annixter.

From her counter, the hat-check girl watched them indifferently.

"Don't you think," the little man said to Annixter, "you ought to go home now? I've been honoured you should tell me the scenario of your play, but—"

"I had to tell someone," said Annixter, "or blow my top! Oh, boy, what a play, what a play! What a murder, eh? That climax—"

The full, dazzling perfection of it struck him again. He stood frowning, considering, swaying a little—then nodded abruptly, groped for the little man's hand, warmly pumphandled it.

"Sorry I can't stick around," said Annixter. "I got work to do."

He crammed his hat on shapelessly, beaded on a slightly elliptical course across the lobby, thrust the double doors open with both hands, lurched out into the night.

It was, to his inflamed imagination, full of lights, winking and tilting across the dark. *Sealed Room* by James Annixter. No. *Room Reserved* by James—No, no. *Blue Room. Room Blue. Room Blue* by James Annixter—

He stepped, oblivious, off the kerb, and a taxi, swinging in toward the place he had just left, skidded with suddenly locked, squealing wheels on the wet road.

Something hit Annixter violently in the chest, and all the lights he had been seeing exploded in his face.

Then there weren't any lights.

> *Mr. James Annixter, the playwright, was knocked down by a taxi late last night when leaving the Casa Havana. After hospital treatment for shock and superficial injuries, he returned to his home.*

The lobby of the Casa Havana was full of the thump of music; down two steps there were a lot of tables, a lot of people, a lot of noise. The hat-check girl looked wonderingly at Annixter—at the plaster on his forehead, the black sling which supported his left arm.

"My," said the hat-check girl, "I certainly didn't expect to see *you* again so soon!"

"You remember me, then?" said Annixter, smiling.

"I ought to," said the hat-check girl. "You cost me a night's sleep! I heard those brakes squeal right after you went out the door that night—and there was a sort of a thud!" She shuddered. "I kept hearing it all night long. I can still hear it now—a week after! Horrible!"

"You're sensitive," said Annixter.

"I got too much imagination," the hat-check girl admitted. "F'rinstance, I just *knew* it was you even before I run to the door and see you lying there. That man you was with was standing just outside. 'My heavens,' I says to him, 'it's your friend!'"

"What did he say?" Annixter asked.

"He says, 'He's not my friend. He's just someone I met.' Funny, eh?"

Annixter moistened his lips.

"How d'you mean," he said carefully, "funny? I *was* just someone he'd met."

"Yes, but—man you been drinking with," said the hat-check girl, "killed before your eyes. Because he must have seen it; he went out right after you. You'd think he'd 'a' been interested, at least. But when the taxi driver starts shouting for witnesses it wasn't his fault, I looks around for that man—an' he's gone!"

Annixter exchanged a glance with Ransome, his producer, who was with him. It was a slightly puzzled, slightly anxious glance. But he smiled, then, at the hat-check girl.

"Not quite 'killed before his eyes,'" said Annixter. "Just shaken up a bit, that's all."

There was no need to explain to her how curious, how eccentric, had been the effect of that "shaking up" upon his mind.

"If you could 'a' seen yourself lying there with the taxi's lights shining on you—"

"Ah, there's that imagination of yours!" said Annixter.

He hesitated for just an instant, then asked the question he had come to ask—the question which had assumed so profound an importance for him.

He asked, "That man I was with—who was he?"

The hat-check girl looked from one to the other. She shook her head.

"I never saw him before," she said, "and I haven't seen him since."

Annixter felt as though she had struck him in the face. He had hoped, hoped desperately, for a different answer; he had counted on it.

Ransome put a hand on his arm, restrainingly.

"Anyway," said Ransome, "as we're here, let's have a drink."

They went down the two steps into the room where the band thumped. A waiter led them to a table, and Ransome gave him an order.

"There was no point in pressing that girl," Ransome said to Annixter. "She doesn't know the man, and that's that. My advice to you, James, is: Don't worry. Get your mind on to something else. Give yourself a chance. After all, it's barely a week since—"

"A week!" Annixter said. "Hell, look what I've done in that week! The whole of the first two acts, and the third act right up to that crucial point—the climax of the whole thing: the solution: the scene that the play stands or falls on! It would have been done, Bill—the whole play, the best thing I ever did in my life—it would have been finished two days ago if it hadn't been for this—" he knuckled his forehead— "this extraordinary blind spot, this damnable little trick of memory!"

"You had a very rough shaking-up—"

"That?" Annixter said contemptuously. He glanced down at the sling on his arm. "I never even felt it; it didn't bother me. I woke up in the ambulance with my play as vivid in my mind as the moment the taxi hit me—more so, maybe, because I was stone cold sober then, and knew what I had. A winner—a thing that just couldn't miss!"

"If you'd rested," Ransome said, "as the doc told you, instead of sitting up in bed there scribbling night and day—"

"I had to get it on paper. Rest?" said Annixter, and laughed harshly. "You don't rest when you've got a thing like that. That's what you live for—if you're a playwright. That *is* living! I've lived eight whole lifetimes, in those eight characters, during the past five days. I've lived so utterly in them, Bill, that it wasn't till I actually came to write that last scene that I realised what I'd lost! Only my whole play, that's all! How was Cynthia stabbed in that windowless room into which she had locked and bolted herself? How did the killer get to her? *How was it done?*

"Hell," Annixter said, "scores of writers, better men than I am, have tried to put that sealed room murder over—and never quite done it convincingly: never quite got away with it: been overelaborate, phony! I had it—heaven help me, *I* had it! Simple, perfect, glaringly obvious when you've once seen it! And it's my whole play—the curtain rises on that sealed room and falls on it! That was my revelation—*how it was done!* That was what I got, by way of playwright's compensation, because a woman I thought I loved kicked me in the face—I brooded up the answer to the sealed room! And a taxi knocked it out of my head!"

He drew a long breath.

"I've spent two days and two nights, Bill, trying to get that idea back—*how it was done!* It won't come. I'm a competent playwright; I know my job; I could finish my play, but it'd be like all those others—not quite right, phony! It wouldn't be *my play!* But there's a little man walking around this city somewhere—a little man with hexagonal glasses—who's got my idea in his head! He's got it because I told it to him. I'm going to find that little man, and get back what belongs to me! I've got to! Don't you see that, Bill? I've *got* to!"

If the gentleman who, at the Casa Havana on the night of January 27th so patiently listened to a playwright's

*outlining of an idea for a drama will communicate
with the Box No. below, he will hear of something to
his advantage.*

A little man who had said, "He's not my friend. He's just someone I met—"

A little man who'd seen an accident but hadn't waited to give evidence—

The hat-check girl had been right. There *was* something a little queer about that.

A little queer?

During the next few days, when the advertisements he'd inserted failed to bring any reply, it began to seem to Annixter very queer indeed.

His arm was out of its sling now, but he couldn't work. Time and again, he sat down before his almost completed manuscript, read it through with close, grim attention, thinking, "It's *bound* to come back this time!"—only to find himself up against that blind spot again, that blank wall, that maddening hiatus in his memory.

He left his work and prowled the streets; he haunted bars and saloons; he rode for miles on 'buses and subway, especially at the rush hours. He saw a million faces, but the face of the little man with hexagonal glasses he did not see.

The thought of him obsessed Annixter. It was infuriating, it was unjust, it was torture to think that a little, ordinary, chance-met citizen was walking blandly around somewhere with the last link of his, the celebrated James Annixter's play— the best thing he'd ever done—locked away in his head. And with no idea of what he had: without the imagination, probably, to appreciate what he had! And certainly with no idea of what it meant to Annixter!

Or *had* he some idea? Was he, perhaps, not quite so ordinary as he'd seemed? Had he seen those advertisements, drawn from them tortuous inferences of his own? Was he holding back with some scheme for shaking Annixter down for a packet?

The more Annixter thought about it, the more he felt that the hat-check girl had been right, that there was something very queer indeed about the way the little man had behaved after the accident.

Annixter's imagination played around the man he was seeking, tried to probe into his mind, conceived reasons for his fading away after the accident, for his failure to reply to the advertisements.

Annixter's was an active and dramatic imagination. The little man who had seemed so ordinary began to take on a sinister shape in Annixter's mind—

But the moment he actually saw the little man again, he realised how absurd that was. It was so absurd that it was laughable. The little man was so respectable; his shoulders were so straight; his pepper-and-salt suit was so neat; his black hard-felt hat was set so squarely on his head—

The doors of the subway train were just closing when Annixter saw him, standing on the platform with a briefcase in one hand, a folded evening paper under his other arm. Light from the train shone on his prim, pale face; his hexagonal spectacles flashed. He turned toward the exit as Annixter lunged for the closing doors of the train, squeezed between them on to the platform.

Craning his head to see above the crowd, Annixter elbowed his way through, ran up the stairs two at a time, put a hand on the little man's shoulder.

"Just a minute," Annixter said. "I've been looking for you."

The little man checked instantly, at the touch of Annixter's hand. Then he turned his head and looked at Annixter. His eyes were pale behind the hexagonal, rimless glasses—a pale grey. His mouth was a straight line, almost colourless.

Annixter loved the little man like a brother. Merely finding the little man was a relief so great that it was like the lifting of a black cloud from his spirits. He patted the little man's shoulder affectionately.

"I've got to talk to you," said Annixter. "It won't take a minute. Let's go somewhere."

The little man said, "I can't imagine what you want to talk to me about."

He moved slightly to one side, to let a woman pass. The crowd from the train had thinned, but there were still people going up and down the stairs. The little man looked, politely inquiring, at Annixter.

Annixter said, "Of course you can't, it's so damned silly! But it's about that play—"

"Play?"

Annixter felt a faint anxiety.

"Look," he said, "I was drunk that night—I was very, very drunk! But looking back, my impression is that you were dead sober. You were, weren't you?"

"I've never been drunk in my life."

"Thank heaven for that!" said Annixter. "Then you won't have any difficulty in remembering the little point I want you to remember." He grinned, shook his head. "You had me going there, for a minute. I thought—"

"I don't know what you thought," the little man said. "But I'm quite sure you're mistaking me for somebody else. I haven't any idea what you're talking about. I never saw you before in my life. I'm sorry. Good night."

He turned and started up the stairs. Annixter stared after him. He couldn't believe his ears. He stared blankly after the little man for an instant, then a rush of anger and suspicion swept away his bewilderment. He raced up the stairs, caught the little man by the arm.

"Just a minute," said Annixter. "I may have been drunk, but—"

"That," the little man said, "seems evident. Do you mind taking your hand off me?"

Annixter controlled himself. "I'm sorry," he said. "Let me get this right, though. You say you've never seen me before. Then you weren't at the Casa Havana on the 27th— somewhere between ten o'clock and midnight? You didn't have a drink or two with me, and listen to an idea for a play that had just come into my mind?"

The little man looked steadily at Annixter.

"I've told you," the little man said. "I've never set eyes on you before."

"You didn't see me get hit by a taxi?" Annixter pursued, tensely. "You didn't say to the hat-check girl, 'He's not my friend. He's just someone I met'?"

"I don't know what you're talking about," the little man said sharply.

He made to turn away, but Annixter gripped his arm again.

"I don't know," Annixter said, between his teeth, "anything

about your private affairs, and I don't want to. You may have had some good reason for wanting to duck giving evidence as a witness of that taxi accident. You may have some good reason for this act you're pulling on me, now. I don't know and I don't care. But it is an act! You *are* the man I told my play to!

"I want you to tell that story back to me as I told it to you; I have my reasons—personal reasons, of concern to me and me only. I want you to tell the story back to me—that's all I want! I don't want to know who you are, or anything about you. *I just want you to tell me that story!*"

"You ask," the little man said, "an impossibility, since I never heard it."

Annixter kept an iron hold on himself.

He said, "Is it money? Is this some sort of a hold-up? Tell me what you want; I'll give it to you. Lord help me, I'd go so far as to give you a share in the play! That'll mean real money. I know, because I know my business. And maybe—maybe," said Annixter, struck by a sudden thought, "*you* know it, too! Eh?"

"You're insane or drunk!" the little man said.

With a sudden movement, he jerked his arm free, raced up the stairs. A train was rumbling in, below. People were hurrying down. He weaved and dodged among them with extraordinary celerity.

He was a small man, light, and Annixter was heavy. By the time he reached the street, there was no sign of the little man. He was gone.

Was the idea, Annixter wondered, to steal his play? By some wild chance did the little man nurture a fantastic ambition to be a dramatist? Had he, perhaps, peddled his precious manuscripts in vain, for years, around the managements? Had Annixter's play appeared to him as a blinding flash of hope in the gathering darkness of frustration and failure: something he had imagined he could safely steal because it had seemed to him the random inspiration of a drunkard who by morning would have forgotten he had ever given birth to anything but a hangover?

That, Annixter thought, would be a laugh! That would be irony—

He took another drink. It was his fifteenth since the little man with the hexagonal glasses had given him the slip, and Annixter was beginning to reach the stage where he lost count of how many places he had had drinks in tonight. It was also the stage, though, where he was beginning to feel better, where his mind was beginning to work.

He could imagine just how the little man must have felt as the quality of the play he was being told, with hiccups, gradually had dawned upon him.

"This is mine!" the little man would have thought. "I've got to have this. He's drunk, he's soused, he's bottled—he'll have forgotten every word of it by the morning! Go on! Go on, mister! Keep talking!"

That, was a laugh, too—the idea that Annixter would have forgotten his play by the morning. Other things Annixter forgot, unimportant things; but never in his life had he forgotten the minutest detail that was to his purpose as a playwright. Never!

Except once, because a taxi had knocked him down.

Annixter took another drink. He needed it. He was on

his own now. There wasn't any little man with hexagonal glasses to fill in that blind spot for him. The little man was gone. He was gone as though he'd never been. To hell with him! Annixter had to fill in that blind spot himself. He *had* to do it—somehow!

He had another drink. He had quite a lot more drinks. The bar was crowded and noisy, but he didn't notice the noise—till someone came up and slapped him on the shoulder. It was Ransome.

Annixter stood up, leaning with his knuckles on the table.

"Look, Bill," Annixter said, "how about this? Man forgets an idea, see? He wants to get it back—gotta get it back! Idea comes from inside, works outwards—right? So he starts on the outside, works back inward. How's that?"

He swayed, peering at Ransome.

"Better have a little drink," said Ransome. "I'd need to think that out."

"I," said Annixter, "*have* thought it out!" He crammed his hat shapelessly on to his head. "Be seeing you, Bill. I got work to do!"

He started, on a slightly tacking course, for the door—and his apartment.

It was Joseph, his "man," who opened the door of his apartment to him, some twenty minutes later. Joseph opened the door while Annixter's latchkey was still describing vexed circles around the lock.

"Good evening, sir," said Joseph.

Annixter stared at him. "I didn't tell you to stay in tonight."

"I hadn't any real reason for going out, sir," Joseph explained. He helped Annixter off with his coat. "I rather enjoy a quiet evening in, once in a while."

"You got to get out of here," said Annixter.

"Thank you, sir," said Joseph. "I'll go and throw a few things into a bag."

Annixter went into his big living-room-study, poured himself a drink.

The manuscript of his play lay on the desk. Annixter, swaying a little, glass in hand, stood frowning down at the untidy stack of yellow paper, but he didn't begin to read. He waited until he heard the outer door click shut behind Joseph, then he gathered up his manuscript, the decanter and a glass, and the cigarette box. Thus laden, he went into the hall, walked across it to the door of Joseph's room.

There was a bolt on the inside of this door, and the room was the only one in the apartment which had no window—both facts which made the room the only one suitable to Annixter's purpose.

With his free hand, he switched on the light.

It was a plain little room, but Annixter noticed, with a faint grin, that the bedspread and the cushion in the worn basket-chair were both blue. Appropriate, he thought—a good omen. *Room Blue* by James Annixter—

Joseph had evidently been lying on the bed, reading the evening paper; the paper lay on the rumpled quilt, and the pillow was dented. Beside the head of the bed, opposite the door, was a small table littered with shoe-brushes and dusters.

Annixter swept this paraphernalia on to the floor. He put his stack of manuscript, the decanter and glass and cigarette box on the table, and went across and bolted the door. He pulled the basket-chair up to the table, sat down, lighted a cigarette.

He leaned back in the chair, smoking, letting his mind ease into the atmosphere he wanted—the mental atmosphere of Cynthia, the woman in his play, the woman who was afraid, so afraid that she had locked and bolted herself into a windowless room, a sealed room.

"This is how she sat," Annixter told himself, "just as I'm sitting now: in a room with no windows, the door locked and bolted. Yet he got at her. He got at her with a knife—in a room with no windows, the door remaining locked and bolted on the inside. *How was it done?*"

There was a way in which it could be done. He, Annixter, had thought of that way; he had conceived it, invented it— and forgotten it. His idea had produced the circumstances. Now, deliberately, he had reproduced the circumstances, that he might think back to the idea. He had put his person in the position of the victim, that his mind might grapple with the problem of the murderer.

It was very quiet: not a sound in the room, the whole apartment.

For a long time, Annixter sat unmoving. He sat unmoving until the intensity of his concentration began to waver. Then he relaxed. He pressed the palms of his hands to his forehead for a moment, then reached for the decanter. He splashed himself a strong drink. He had almost recovered what he sought; he had felt it close, had been on the very verge of it.

"Easy," he warned himself, "take it easy. Rest. Relax. Try again in a minute."

He looked around for something to divert his mind, picked up the paper from Joseph's bed.

At the first words that caught his eye, his heart stopped.

The woman, in whose body were found three knife wounds, any of which might have been fatal, was in a windowless room, the only door to which was locked and bolted on the inside. These elaborate precautions appear to have been habitual with her, and no doubt she went in continual fear of her life, as the police know her to have been a persistent and pitiless blackmailer.

Apart from the unique problem set by the circumstance of the sealed room is the problem of how the crime could have gone undiscovered for so long a period, the doctor's estimate from the condition of the body as some twelve to fourteen days.

Twelve to fourteen days—

Annixter read back over the remainder of the story; then let the paper fall to the floor. The pulse was heavy in his head. His face was grey. Twelve to fourteen days? He could put it closer than that. *It was exactly thirteen nights ago that he had sat in the Casa Havana and told a little man with hexagonal glasses how to kill a woman in a sealed room!*

Annixter sat very still for a minute. Then he poured himself a drink. It was a big one, and he needed it. He felt a strange sense of wonder, of awe.

They had been in the same boat, he and the little man— thirteen nights ago. They had both been kicked in the face by a woman. One, as a result, had conceived a murder play. The other had made the play reality!

"And I actually, tonight, offered him a share!" Annixter thought. "I talked about 'real' money!"

That was a laugh. All the money in the universe wouldn't have made that little man admit that he had seen Annixter before—that Annixter had told him the plot of a play about how to kill a woman in a sealed room! Why, he, Annixter, was the one person in the world who could denounce that little man! Even if he couldn't tell them, because he had forgotten, just *how* he had told the little man the murder was to be committed, he could still put the police on the little man's track. He could describe him, so that they could trace him. And once on his track, the police would ferret out links, almost inevitably, with the dead woman.

A queer thought—that he, Annixter, was probably the only menace, the only danger, to the little prim, pale man with the hexagonal spectacles. The only menace—as, of course, the little man must know very well.

He must have been very frightened when he had read that the playwright who had been knocked down outside the Casa Havana had only received "superficial injuries." He must have been still more frightened when Annixter's advertisements had begun to appear. *What must he have felt tonight, when Annixter's hand had fallen on his shoulder?*

A curious idea occurred, now, to Annixter. It was from tonight, precisely from tonight, that he was a danger to that little man. He was, because of the inferences the little man must infallibly draw, a deadly danger as from the moment the discovery of the murder in the sealed room was published. That discovery had been published tonight, and the little man had had a paper under his arm—

Annixter's was a lively and resourceful imagination.

It was, of course, just in the cards that, when he'd lost the little man's trail at the subway station, the little man might have turned back, picked up *his*, Annixter's trail.

And Annixter had sent Joseph out. He was, it dawned slowly upon Annixter, alone in the apartment—alone in a windowless room, with the door locked and bolted on the inside, at his back.

Annixter felt a sudden, icy and wild panic.

He half rose, but it was too late.

It was too late, because at that moment the knife slid, thin and keen and delicate, into his back, fatally, between the ribs.

Annixter's head bowed slowly forward until his cheek rested on the manuscript of his play. He made only one sound—a queer sound, indistinct, yet identifiable as a kind of laughter.

The fact was, Annixter had just remembered.

I Can Find My Way Out

Ngaio Marsh

The New Zealander Ngaio Marsh (1895–1982) was, along with Allingham and Sayers, one of the "Queens of Crime." Her Golden Age detective fiction, like theirs, has enjoyed sustained popularity. Yet she never made any secret of the fact that her first love was the theatre, and in her biography of Marsh, Margaret Lewis points out that her devotion to the stage was originally influenced by her parents, both of whom were enthusiastic amateur actors; they first met while acting together in a production in Christchurch. Ngaio says that, even as a child she "loved to hear all the theatre-talk, the long discussions on visiting actors, on plays and on the great ones of the past. When I was big enough to be taken occasionally to the play my joy was almost unendurable." She became a key figure in the "Golden Age of New Zealand drama," which experts define as the ten years starting with 1943, the year in which she was responsible for a version of *Hamlet* in modern dress performed by members of the Canterbury University College Drama Society and hailed as a major triumph.

As one might expect, Marsh's love and knowledge of the theatre often provides interesting background material in her detective fiction. *Death at the Dolphin* (1966, known in the U.S. as *Killer Dolphin*), for instance, is an Edgar-nominated mystery featuring a glove once owned by Hamnet Shakespeare, the only son of William Shakespeare, who died at age 11. The glove is on display at the newly renovated Dolphin Theatre, whose director Peregrine Jay proved to be such an appealing character that Marsh brought him back in her final novel, *Light Thickens* (1982). This story first appeared in 1946 and has been described by the crime genre scholar Douglas Greene, editor of a collection of her infrequent short stories, as containing "her bow to one of the most famous detectival plot devices, murder in a locked room."

———

AT HALF PAST SIX ON THE NIGHT IN QUESTION, ANTHONY Gill, unable to eat, keep still, think, speak, or act coherently, walked from his rooms to the Jupiter Theatre. He knew that there would be nobody backstage, that there was nothing for him to do in the theatre, that he ought to stay quietly in his rooms and presently dress, dine, and arrive at, say, a quarter to eight. But it was as if something shoved him into his clothes, thrust him into the street and compelled him to hurry through the West End to the Jupiter. His mind was overlaid with a thin film of inertia. Odd lines from the play occurred to him, but without any particular significance. He found himself busily reiterating a completely irrelevant sentence: "She has a way of laughing that would make a man's heart turn over."

Piccadilly, Shaftesbury Avenue. "Here I go," he thought, turning into Hawke Street, "towards my play. It's one hour and twenty-nine minutes away. A step a second. It's rushing towards me. Tony's first play. Poor young Tony Gill. Never mind. Try again."

The Jupiter. Neon lights: I CAN FIND MY WAY OUT—*by Anthony Gill*. And in the entrance the bills and photographs. *Coralie Bourne with H. J. Bannington, Barry George and Canning Cumberland.*

Canning Cumberland. The film across his mind split and there was the Thing itself and he would have to think about it. How bad would Canning Cumberland be if he came down drunk? Brilliantly bad, they said. He would bring out all the tricks. Clever actor stuff, scoring off everybody, making a fool of the dramatic balance. "In Mr. Canning Cumberland's hands indifferent dialogue and unconvincing situations seemed almost real." What can you do with a drunken actor?

He stood in the entrance feeling his heart pound and his inside deflate and sicken.

Because, of course, it was a bad play. He was at this moment and for the first time really convinced of it. It was terrible. Only one virtue in it and that was not his doing. It had been suggested to him by Coralie Bourne: "I don't think the play you have sent me will do as it is but it has occurred to me—" It was a brilliant idea. He had rewritten the play round it and almost immediately and quite innocently he had begun to think of it as his own although he had said shyly to Coralie Bourne: "You should appear as joint author." She had quickly, over emphatically, refused. "It was nothing at all," she said. "If you're to become a dramatist you will learn to get ideas from everywhere. A single situation is nothing. Think of Shakespeare," she added lightly. "Entire plots! Don't be silly." She had said later, and still with the same hurried, nervous air: "Don't go talking to everyone about it. They will think there is more, instead of less, than meets the eye in my small suggestion. Please promise." He promised, thinking he'd made an error in taste when he suggested that Coralie Bourne, so famous an actress, should appear as joint author with an unknown youth. And how right she was, he thought, because, of course, it's going to be a ghastly flop. She'll be sorry she consented to play in it.

Standing in front of the theatre he contemplated nightmare possibilities. What did audiences do when a first play flopped? Did they clap a little, enough to let the curtain rise and quickly fall again on a discomforted group of players? How scanty must the applause be for them to let him off his own appearance? And they were to go on to the Chelsea Arts Ball. A hideous prospect. Thinking he would give anything in the world if he could stop his play, he turned into the foyer. There were lights in the offices and he paused, irresolute, before a board of photographs. Among them, much smaller than the leading players, was Dendra Gay with the eyes looking straight into his. *She had a way of laughing that would make a man's heart turn over.* "Well," he thought, "so I'm in love with her." He turned away from the photograph. A man came out of the office. "Mr. Gill? Telegrams for you."

Anthony took them and as he went out he heard the man call after him: "Very good luck for tonight, sir."

There were queues of people waiting in the side street for the early doors.

At six thirty Coralie Bourne dialled Canning Cumberland's number and waited.

She heard his voice. "It's me," she said.

"O God! darling, I've been thinking about you." He spoke rapidly, too loudly. "Coral, I've been thinking about Ben. You oughtn't to have given that situation to the boy."

"We've been over it a dozen times, Cann. Why not give it to Tony? Ben will never know." She waited and then said nervously, "Ben's gone, Cann. We'll never see him again."

"I've got a Thing about it. After all, he's your husband."

"No, Cann, no."

"Suppose he turns up. It'd be like him to turn up."

"He won't turn up."

She heard him laugh. "I'm sick of all this," she thought suddenly. "I've had it once too often. I can't stand any more... Cann," she said into the telephone. But he had hung up.

At twenty to seven, Barry George looked at himself in his bathroom mirror. "I've got a better appearance," he thought, "than Cann Cumberland. My head's a good shape, my eyes are bigger and my jaw line's cleaner. I never let a show down. I don't drink. I'm a better actor." He turned his head a little, slewing his eyes to watch the effect. "In the big scene," he thought, "I'm the star. He's the feed. That's the way it's been produced and that's what the author wants. I ought to get the notices."

Past notices came up in his memory. He saw the print, the size of the paragraphs; a long paragraph about Canning Cumberland, a line tacked on the end of it. "Is it unkind to add that Mr. Barry George trotted in the wake of Mr.

Cumberland's virtuosity with an air of breathless dependability?" And again: "It is a little hard on Mr. Barry George that he should be obliged to act as foil to this brilliant performance." Worst of all: "Mr. Barry George succeeded in looking tolerably unlike a stooge, an achievement that evidently exhausted his resources."

"Monstrous!" he said loudly to his own image, watching the fine glow of indignation in the eyes. Alcohol, he told himself, did two things to Cann Cumberland. He raised his finger. Nice, expressive hand. An actor's hand. Alcohol destroyed Cumberland's artistic integrity. It also invested him with devilish cunning. Drunk, he would burst the seams of a play, destroy its balance, ruin its form and himself emerge blazing with a showmanship that the audience mistook for genius. "While I," he said aloud, "merely pay my author the compliment of faithful interpretation. Psha!"

He returned to his bedroom, completed his dressing, and pulled his hat to the right angle. Once more he thrust his face close to the mirror and looked searchingly at its image. "By God!" he told himself, "he's done it once too often, old boy. Tonight we'll even the score, won't we? By God, we will."

Partly satisfied, and partly ashamed, for the scene, after all, had smacked a little of ham, he took his stick in one hand and a case holding his costume for the Arts Ball in the other, and went down to the theatre.

At ten minutes to seven, H. J. Bannington passed through the gallery queue on his way to the stage door alley, raising his hat and saying: "Thanks so much," to the gratified ladies who let him through. He heard them murmur his name. He walked briskly along the alley, greeted the stage-doorkeeper, passed under a dingy lamp, through an entry and so to the stage. Only working lights were up. The walls of an interior set rose dimly into shadow. Bob Reynolds, the stage manager, came out through the prompt entrance. "Hello, old boy," he said, "I've changed the dressing rooms. You're third on the right: they've moved your things in. Suit you?"

"Better, at least, than a black-hole the size of a WC but without its appointments," HJ said acidly. "I suppose the great Mr. Cumberland still has the star room?"

"Well, yes, old boy."

"And who pray, is next to him? In the room with the other gas fire?"

"We've put Barry George there, old boy. You know what he's like."

"Only too well, old boy, and the public, I fear, is beginning to find out." HJ turned into the dressing room passage.

The stage manager returned to the set where he encountered his assistant. "What's biting *him*?" asked the assistant.

"He wanted a dressing room with a fire."

"Only natural," said the ASM nastily. "He started life reading gas meters."

On the right and left of the passage, nearest the stage end, were two doors, each with its star in tarnished paint. The door on the left was open. HJ looked in and was greeted with the smell of greasepaint, powder, wet white, and flowers. A gas fire droned comfortably. Coralie Bourne's dresser was spreading out towels. "Good evening, Katie, my jewel," said HJ. "La Belle not down yet?"

"We're on our way," she said.

HJ hummed stylishly: "*Bella filia del amore*," and returned to the passage. The star room on the right was closed, but he could hear Cumberland's dresser moving about inside. He went on to the next door, paused, read the card, "Mr. Barry George," warbled a high derisive note, turned in at the third door and switched on the light.

Definitely not a second lead's room. No fire. A washbasin, however, and opposite mirrors. A stack of telegrams had been placed on the dressing table. Still singing he reached for them, disclosing a number of bills that had been tactfully laid underneath and a letter, addressed in a flamboyant script.

His voice might have been mechanically produced and arbitrarily switched off, so abruptly did his song end in the middle of a roulade. He let the telegrams fall on the table, took up the letter and tore it open. His face, wretchedly pale, was reflected and endlessly re-reflected in the mirrors.

At nine o'clock the telephone rang. Roderick Alleyn answered it. "This is Sloane 84405. No, you're on the wrong number. *No*." He hung up and returned to his wife and guest. "That's the fifth time in two hours."

"Do let's ask for a new number."

"We might get next door to something worse."

The telephone rang again. "This is not 84406," Alleyn warned it. "No, I cannot take three large trunks to Victoria Station. No, I am not the Instant All Night Delivery. No."

"They're 84406," Mrs. Alleyn explained to Lord Michael Lamprey. "I suppose it's just faulty dialling, but you can't imagine how angry everyone gets. Why do you want to be a policeman?"

"It's a dull hard job, you know—" Alleyn began.

"Oh," Lord Mike said, stretching his legs and looking critically at his shoes, "I don't for a moment imagine I'll leap immediately into false whiskers and plainclothes. No, no. But I'm revoltingly healthy, sir. Strong as a horse. And I don't think I'm as stupid as you might feel inclined to imagine—"

The telephone rang.

"I say, do let me answer it," Mike suggested and did so.

"Hullo?" he said winningly. He listened, smiling at his hostess. "I'm afraid—" he began. "Here, wait a bit—Yes, but—" His expression became blank and complacent. "May I," he said presently, "repeat your order, sir? Can't be too sure, can we? Call at 11 Harrow Gardens, Sloane Square, for one suitcase to be delivered immediately at the Jupiter Theatre to Mr. Anthony Gill. Very good, sir. Thank you, sir. Collect. Quite."

He replaced the receiver and beamed at the Alleyns.

"What the devil have you been up to?" Alleyn said.

"He just simply wouldn't listen to reason. I tried to tell him."

"But it may be urgent," Mrs. Alleyn ejaculated.

"It couldn't be more urgent, really. It's a suitcase for Tony Gill at the Jupiter."

"Well, then—"

"I was at Eton with the chap," said Mike reminiscently. "He's four years older than I am, so of course he was madly important while I was less than the dust. This'll larn him."

"I think you'd better put that order through at once," said Alleyn firmly.

"I rather thought of executing it myself, do you know,

sir. It'd be a frightfully neat way of gate-crashing the show, wouldn't it? I did try to get a ticket but the house was sold out."

"If you're going to deliver this case, you'd better get a bend on."

"It's clearly an occasion for dressing up though, isn't it? I say," said Mike modestly, "would you think it most frightful cheek if I—well I'd promise to come back and return everything. I mean—"

"Are you suggesting that my clothes look more like a vanman's than yours?"

"I thought you'd have things—"

"For Heaven's sake, Rory," said Mrs. Alleyn, "dress him up and let him go. The great thing is to get that wretched man's suitcase to him."

"I know," said Mike earnestly. "It's most frightfully sweet of you. That's how I feel about it."

Alleyn took him away and shoved him into an old and begrimed raincoat, a cloth cap, and a muffler. "You wouldn't deceive a village idiot in a total eclipse," he said, "but out you go."

He watched Mike drive away and returned to his wife.

"What'll happen?" she asked.

"Knowing Mike, I should say he will end up in the front stalls and go on to supper with the leading lady. She, by the way, is Coralie Bourne. Very lovely and twenty years his senior so he'll probably fall in love with her." Alleyn reached for his tobacco jar and paused. "I wonder what's happened to her husband," he said.

"Who was he?"

"An extraordinary chap. Benjamin Vlasnoff. Violent temper. Looked like a bandit. Wrote two very good plays and got run in three times for common assault. She tried to divorce him but it didn't go through. I think he afterwards lit off to Russia." Alleyn yawned. "I believe she had a hell of a time with him," he said.

"All Night Delivery," said Mike in a hoarse voice, touching his cap. "Suitcase. One."

"Here you are," said the woman who had answered the door. "Carry it carefully, now, it's not locked and the catch springs out."

"Fanks," said Mike. "Much obliged. Chilly, ain't it?"

He took the suitcase out to the car.

It was a fresh spring night. Sloane Square was threaded with mist and all the lamps had halos round them. It was the kind of night when individual sounds separate themselves from the conglomerate voice of London; hollow sirens spoke imperatively down on the river and a bugle rang out over in Chelsea Barracks; a night, Mike thought, for adventure.

He opened the rear door of the car and heaved the case in. The catch flew open, the lid dropped back and the contents fell out. "Damn!" said Mike and switched on the inside light.

Lying on the floor of the car was a false beard.

It was flaming red and bushy and was mounted on a chin-piece. With it was incorporated a stiffened moustache. There were wire hooks to attach the whole thing behind the ears. Mike laid it carefully on the seat. Next he picked up a wide black hat, then a vast overcoat with a fur collar, finally a pair of black gloves.

Mike whistled meditatively and thrust his hands into the pockets of Alleyn's mackintosh. His right hand fingers closed on a card. He pulled it out. "Chief Detective-Inspector Alleyn," he read, "CID. New Scotland Yard."

"Honestly," thought Mike exultantly, "this is a gift."

Ten minutes later a car pulled into the kerb at the nearest parking place to the Jupiter Theatre. From it emerged a figure carrying a suitcase. It strode rapidly along Hawke Street and turned into the stage door alley. As it passed under the dirty lamp it paused, and thus murkily lit, resembled an illustration from some Edwardian spy story. The face was completely shadowed, a black cavern from which there projected a square of scarlet beard, which was the only note of colour.

The doorkeeper who was taking the air with a member of stage staff, moved forward, peering at the stranger.

"Was you wanting something?"

"I'm taking this case in for Mr. Gill."

"He's in front. You can leave it with me."

"I'm so sorry," said the voice behind the beard, "but I promised I'd leave it backstage myself."

"So you will be leaving it. Sorry, sir, but no one's admitted be'ind without a card."

"A card? Very well. Here is a card."

He held it out in his black-gloved hand. The stage door-keeper, unwillingly removing his gaze from the beard, took the card and examined it under the light. "Coo!" he said, "what's up, governor?"

"No matter. Say nothing of this."

The figure waved its hand and passed through the door.

"'Ere!" said the doorkeeper excitedly to the stage hand, "take a slant at this. That's a plainclothes flattie, that was."

"*Plain* clothes!" said the stage hand. "Them!"

"'E's disguised," said the doorkeeper. "That's what it is. 'E's disguised 'isself."

"'E's bloody well lorst 'isself be'ind them whiskers if you arst me."

Out on the stage someone was saying in a pitched and beautifully articulate voice: *"I've always loathed the view from these windows. However if that's the sort of thing you admire. Turn off the lights, damn you. Look at it."*

"Watch it, now, watch it," whispered a voice so close to Mike that he jumped.

"OK," said a second voice somewhere above his head. The lights on the set turned blue.

"Kill that working light."

"Working light gone."

Curtains in the set were wrenched aside and a window flung open. An actor appeared, leaning out quite close to Mike, seeming to look into his face and saying very distinctly: "God: it's frightful!" Mike backed away towards a passage, lit only from an open door. A great volume of sound broke out beyond the stage. "House lights," said the sharp voice. Mike turned into the passage. As he did so, someone came through the door. He found himself face to face with Coralie Bourne, beautifully dressed and heavily painted.

For a moment she stood quite still; then she made a curious gesture with her right hand, gave a small breathy sound, and fell forward at his feet.

Anthony was tearing his programme into long strips and dropping them on the floor of the OP box. On his right hand, above and below, was the audience; sometimes laughing, sometimes still, sometimes as one corporate being, raising its hands and striking them together. As now; when down on the stage, Canning Cumberland, using a strange voice, and inspired by some inward devil, flung back the window and said: "God: it's frightful!"

"Wrong! Wrong!" Anthony cried inwardly, hating Cumberland, hating Barry George because he let one speech of three words override him, hating the audience because they liked it. The curtain descended with a long sigh on the second act and a sound like heavy rain filled the theatre, swelled prodigiously and continued after the house lights welled up.

"They seem," said a voice behind him, "to be liking your play."

It was Gosset, who owned the Jupiter and had backed the show. Anthony turned on him stammering: "He's destroying it. It should be the other man's scene. He's stealing."

"My boy," said Gosset, "he's an actor."

"He's drunk. It's intolerable."

He felt Gosset's hand on his shoulder.

"People are watching us. You're on show. This is a big thing for you; a first play, and going enormously. Come and have a drink, old boy. I want to introduce you—"

Anthony got up and Gosset, with his arm across his shoulders, flashing smiles, patting him, led him to the back of the box.

"I'm sorry," Anthony said. "I can't. Please let me off. I'm going backstage."

"Much better not, old son." The hand tightened on his

shoulder. "Listen, old son—" But Anthony had freed himself and slipped through the pass door from the box to the stage.

At the foot of the breakneck stairs Dendra Gay stood waiting. "I thought you'd come," she said.

Anthony said: "He's drunk. He's murdering the play."

"It's only one scene, Tony. He finishes early in the next act. It's going colossally."

"But don't you understand—"

"I do. You *know* I do. But you're a success, Tony darling! You can hear it and smell it and feel it in your bones."

"Dendra—" he said uncertainly.

Someone came up and shook his hand and went on shaking it. Flats were being laced together with a slap of rope on canvas. A chandelier ascended into darkness. "Lights," said the stage manager, and the set was flooded with them. A distant voice began chanting. "Last act, please. Last act."

"Miss Bourne all right?" the stage manager suddenly demanded.

"She'll be all right. She's not on for ten minutes," said a woman's voice.

"What's the matter with Miss Bourne?" Anthony asked.

"Tony, I must go and so must you. Tony, it's going to be grand. *Please* think so. *Please*."

"Dendra—" Tony began, but she had gone.

Beyond the curtain, horns and flutes announced the last act.

"Clear please."

The stage hands came off.

"House lights."

"House lights gone."

"Stand by."

And while Anthony still hesitated in the OP corner, the curtain rose. Canning Cumberland and H. J. Bannington opened the last act.

As Mike knelt by Coralie Bourne he heard someone enter the passage behind him. He turned and saw, silhouetted against the lighted stage, the actor who had looked at him through a window in the set. The silhouette seemed to repeat the gesture Coralie Bourne had used, and to flatten itself against the wall.

A woman in an apron came out of the open door.

"I say—here!" Mike said.

Three things happened almost simultaneously. The woman cried out and knelt beside him. The man disappeared through a door on the right.

The woman, holding Coralie Bourne in her arms, said violently: "Why have you come back?" Then the passage lights came on.

Mike said: "Look here, I'm most frightfully sorry," and took off the broad black hat. The dresser gaped at him, Coralie Bourne made a crescendo sound in her throat and opened her eyes.

"Katie?" she said.

"It's all right, my lamb. It's not him, dear. You're all right." The dresser jerked her head at Mike: "Get out of it," she said.

"Yes, of course, I'm most frightfully—" He backed out of the passage, colliding with a youth who said: "Five minutes, please."

The dresser called out: "Tell them she's not well. Tell them to hold the curtain."

"No," said Coralie Bourne strongly. "I'm all right, Katie. Don't say anything. Katie, what was it?"

They disappeared into the room on the left.

Mike stood in the shadow of a stack of scenic flats by the entry into the passage. There was great activity on the stage. He caught a glimpse of Anthony Gill on the far side talking to a girl. The call boy was speaking to the stage manager who now shouted into space: "Miss Bourne all right?"

The dresser came into the passage and called: "She'll be all right. She's not on for ten minutes."

The youth began chanting: "Last act, please."

The stage manager gave a series of orders. A man with an eyeglass and a florid beard came from further down the passage and stood outside the set, bracing his figure and giving little tweaks to his clothes. There was a sound of horns and flutes. Canning Cumberland emerged from the room on the right, and on his way to the stage, passed close to Mike, leaving a strong smell of alcohol behind him. The curtain rose.

Behind his shelter, Mike stealthily removed his beard and stuffed it into the pocket of his overcoat.

A group of stage hands stood nearby. One of them said in a hoarse whisper: "'E's squiffy."

"Garn, 'e's going good."

"So 'e may be going good. And for why? *Becos* 'e's squiffy."

Ten minutes passed. Mike thought: "This affair has definitely not gone according to plan." He listened. Some kind of tension seemed to be building up on the stage. Canning Cumberland's voice rose on a loud but blurred note.

A door in the set opened. "Don't bother to come," Cumberland said. "Good-bye. I can find my way out." The door slammed. Cumberland was standing near Mike. Then, very close, there was a loud explosion. The scenic flats vibrated. Mike's flesh leapt on his bones and Cumberland went into his dressing rooms. Mike heard the key turn in the door. The smell of alcohol mingled with the smell of gunpowder. A stage hand moved to a trestle table and laid a pistol on it. The actor with the eyeglass made an exit. He spoke for a moment to the stage manager, passed Mike and disappeared in the passage.

Smells. There were all sorts of smells. Subconsciously, still listening to the play, he began to sort them out. Glue. Canvas. Greasepaint. The call boy tapped on the doors. "Mr. George, please. Miss Bourne, please." They came out, Coralie Bourne with her dresser. Mike heard her turn a door handle and say something. An indistinguishable voice answered her. Then she and her dresser passed him. The others spoke to her and she nodded and then seemed to withdraw into herself, waiting with her head bent, ready to make her entrance. Presently she drew back, walked swiftly to the door in the set, flung it open and swept on, followed a minute later by Barry George.

Smells. Dust, stale paint, cloth. Gas. Increasingly, the smell of gas.

The group of stage hands moved away behind the set to the side of the stage. Mike edged out of cover. He could see the prompt corner. The stage manager stood there with folded arms, watching the action. Behind him were grouped the players who were not on. Two dressers stood apart, watching. The light from the set caught their faces. Coralie Bourne's voice sent phrases flying like birds into the auditorium.

Mike began peering at the floor. Had he kicked some gas fitting adrift? The call boy passed him, stared at him over his shoulder and went down the passage, tapping. "Five minutes to the curtain, please. Five minutes."

The actor with the elderly make-up followed the call boy out. "God, what a stink of gas," he whispered.

"Chronic, ain't it?" said the call boy. They stared at Mike and then crossed to the waiting group. The man said something to the stage manager who tipped his head up, sniffing. He made an impatient gesture and turned back to the prompt box, reaching over the prompter's head. A bell rang somewhere up in the flies and Mike saw a stage hand climb to the curtain platform.

The little group near the prompt corner was agitated. They looked back towards the passage entrance. The call boy nodded and came running back. He knocked on the first door on the right. "*Mr. Cumberland! Mr. Cumberland!* You're on for the call." He rattled the door handle. "*Mr. Cumberland! You're on.*"

Mike ran into the passage. The call boy coughed retchingly and jerked his hand at the door. "Gas!"

"Break it in."

"I'll get Mr. Reynolds."

He was gone. It was a narrow passage. From halfway across the opposite room Mike took a run, head down, shoulder forward, at the door. It gave a little and a sickening increase in the smell caught him in the lungs. A vast storm of noise had broken out and as he took another run he thought: "It's hailing outside."

"Just a minute if *you* please, sir."

It was a stage hand. He'd got a hammer and screwdriver.

He wedged the point of the screwdriver between the lock and the doorpost, drove it home and wrenched. The screws squeaked, the wood splintered and gas poured into the passage. "No winders," coughed the stage hand.

Mike wound Alleyn's scarf over his mouth and nose. Half-forgotten instructions from anti-gas drill occurred to him. The room looked queer but he could see the man slumped down in the chair quite clearly. He stooped low and ran in.

He was knocking against things as he backed out, lugging the dead weight. His arms tingled. A high insistent voice hummed in his brain. He floated a short distance and came to earth on a concrete floor among several pairs of legs. A long way off, someone said loudly: "I can only thank you for being so kind to what I know, too well, is a very imperfect play." Then the sound of hail began again. There was a heavenly stream of clear air flowing into his mouth and nostrils. "I could eat it," he thought and sat up.

The telephone rang. "Suppose," Mrs. Alleyn suggested, "that this time you ignore it."

"It might be the Yard," Alleyn said, and answered it.

"Is that Chief Detective-Inspector Alleyn's flat? I'm speaking from the Jupiter Theatre. I've rung up to say that the Chief Inspector is here and that he's had a slight mishap. He's all right, but I think it might be as well for someone to drive him home. No need to worry."

"What sort of mishap?" Alleyn asked.

"Er-well-er, he's been a bit gassed."

"*Gassed!* All right. Thanks, I'll come."

"*What* a bore for you, darling," said Mrs. Alleyn. "What sort of case is it? Suicide?"

"Masquerading within the meaning of the act, by the sound of it. Mike's in trouble."

"What trouble, for Heaven's sake?"

"Got himself gassed. He's all right. Good night, darling. Don't wait up."

When he reached the theatre, the front of the house was in darkness. He made his way down the side alley to the stage door where he was held up.

"Yard," he said, and produced his official card.

"'Ere," said the stage doorkeeper, "'ow many more of you?"

"The man inside was working for me," said Alleyn and walked in. The doorkeeper followed, protesting.

To the right of the entrance was a large scenic dock from which the double doors had been rolled back. Here Mike was sitting in an armchair, very white about the lips. Three men and two women, all with painted faces, stood near him and behind them a group of stage hands with Reynolds, the stage manager, and, apart from these, three men in evening dress. The men looked woodenly shocked. The women had been weeping.

"I'm most frightfully sorry, sir," Mike said. "I've tried to explain. This," he added generally, "is Inspector Alleyn."

"I can't understand all this," said the oldest of the men in evening dress irritably. He turned on the doorkeeper. "You said—"

"I seen 'is card—"

"I know," said Mike, "but you see—"

"This is Lord Michael Lamprey," Alleyn said. "A recruit to the Police Department. What's happened here?"

"Doctor Rankin, would you—"

The second of the men in evening dress came forward. "All right, Gosset. It's a bad business, Inspector. I've just been saying the police would have to be informed. If you'll come with me—"

Alleyn followed him through a door onto the stage proper. It was dimly lit. A trestle table had been set up in the centre and on it, covered with a sheet, was an unmistakable shape. The smell of gas, strong everywhere, hung heavily about the table.

"Who is it?"

"Canning Cumberland. He'd locked the door of his dressing room. There's a gas fire. Your young friend dragged him out, very pluckily, but it was no go. I was in front. Gosset, the manager, had asked me to supper. It's a perfectly clear case of suicide as you'll see."

"I'd better look at the room. Anybody been in?"

"God, no. It was a job to clear it. They turned the gas off at the main. There's no window. They had to open the double doors at the back of the stage and a small outside door at the end of the passage. It may be possible to get in now."

He led the way to the dressing room passage. "Pretty thick, still," he said. "It's the first room on the right. They burst the lock. You'd better keep down near the floor."

The powerful lights over the mirror were on and the room still had its look of occupation. The gas fire was against the left hand wall. Alleyn squatted down by it. The tap was still turned on, its face lying parallel with the floor. The top of the heater, the tap itself, and the carpet near it, were covered with a creamish powder. On the end of the dressing table shelf nearest to the stove was a box of this powder. Further along the shelf, greasepaints were set out in a row beneath the mirror. Then came a wash basin and in front of this an overturned chair. Alleyn could see the track of heels, across the pile of the carpet, to the door immediately opposite. Beside the wash basin was a quart bottle of whisky, three parts empty, and a tumbler. Alleyn had had about enough and returned to the passage.

"Perfectly clear," the hovering doctor said again, "Isn't it?"

"I'll see the other rooms, I think."

The one next to Cumberland's was like his in reverse, but smaller. The heater was back to back with Cumberland's. The dressing shelf was set out with much the same assortment of greasepaints. The tap of this heater, too, was turned on. It was of precisely the same make as the other and Alleyn, less embarrassed here by fumes, was able to make a longer examination. It was a common enough type of gas fire. The lead-in was from a pipe through a flexible metallic tube with a rubber connection. There were two taps, one in the pipe and one at the junction of the tube with the heater itself. Alleyn disconnected the tube and examined the connection. It was perfectly sound, a close fit and stained red at the end. Alleyn noticed a wiry thread of some reddish stuff resembling packing that still clung to it. The nozzle and tap were brass, the tap pulling over when it was turned on, to lie in a parallel plane with the floor. No powder had been scattered about here.

He glanced round the room, returned to the door, and read the card: "Mr. Barry George."

The doctor followed him into the rooms opposite these, on the left-hand side of the passage. They were a repetition in design of the two he had already seen but were hung with women's clothes and had a more elaborate assortment of greasepaint and cosmetics.

There was a mass of flowers in the star room. Alleyn read the cards. One in particular caught his eye: "From Anthony Gill to say a most inadequate 'thank you' for the great idea." A vase of red roses stood before the mirror: "To your greatest triumph, Coralie darling. C C." In Miss Gay's room there were only two bouquets, one from the management and one "From Anthony, with love."

Again in each room he pulled off the lead-in to the heater and looked at the connection.

"All right, aren't they?" said the doctor.

"Quite all right. Tight fit. Good solid grey rubber."

"Well, then—"

Next on the left was an unused room, and opposite it, "Mr. H. J. Bannington." Neither of these rooms had gas fires. Mr. Bannington's dressing table was littered with the usual array of greasepaint, the materials for his beard, a number of telegrams and letters, and several bills.

"About the body," the doctor began.

"We'll get a mortuary van from the Yard."

"But—Surely in a case of suicide—"

"I don't think this is suicide."

"But, good God!—D'you mean there's been an accident?"

"No accident," said Alleyn.

At midnight, the dressing room lights in the Jupiter Theatre were brilliant, and men were busy there with the tools of their trade. A constable stood at the stage door and a van waited in the yard. The front of the house was dimly lit and there, among the shrouded stalls, sat Coralie Bourne, Basil Gosset, H. J. Bannington, Dendra Gay, Anthony Gill, Reynolds, Katie the dresser, and the call boy. A constable sat behind them and another stood by the doors into the foyer. They stared across the backs of seats at the fire curtain. Spirals of smoke rose from their cigarettes and about their feet were discarded programmes. "Basil Gosset PRESENTS I CAN FIND MY WAY OUT by Anthony Gill."

In the manager's office Alleyn said: "You're sure of your facts, Mike?"

"Yes, sir. Honestly. I was right up against the entrance into the passage. They didn't see me because I was in the shadow. It was very dark offstage."

"You'll have to swear to it."

"I know."

"Good. All right, Thompson. Miss Gay and Mr. Gosset may go home. Ask Miss Bourne to come in."

When Sergeant Thompson had gone Mike said: "I haven't had a chance to say I know I've made a perfect fool of myself. Using your card and everything."

"Irresponsible gaiety doesn't go down very well in the service, Mike. You behaved like a clown."

"I *am* a fool," said Mike wretchedly.

The red beard was lying in front of Alleyn on Gosset's desk. He picked it up and held it out. "Put it on," he said.

"She might do another faint."

"I think not. Now the hat: yes—yes, I see. Come in."

Sergeant Thompson showed Coralie Bourne in and then sat at the end of the desk with his notebook.

Tears had traced their course through the powder on her face, carrying black cosmetic with them and leaving the greasepaint shining like snail tracks. She stood near the doorway looking dully at Michael. "Is he back in England?" she said. "Did he tell you to do this?" She made an impatient movement. "Do take it off," she said, "it's a very bad beard. If Cann had only looked—" Her lips trembled. "Who told you to do it?"

"Nobody," Mike stammered, pocketing the beard. "I mean—As a matter of fact, Tony Gill—"

"*Tony?* But *he* didn't know. Tony wouldn't do it. Unless—"

"Unless?" Alleyn said.

She said frowning: "Tony didn't want Cann to play the part that way. He was furious."

"He says it was his dress for the Chelsea Arts Ball," Mike mumbled. "I brought it here. I just thought I'd put it on—it was idiotic, I know—for fun. I'd no idea you and Mr. Cumberland would mind."

"Ask Mr. Gill to come in," Alleyn said.

Anthony was white and seemed bewildered and helpless. "I've told Mike," he said. "It was my dress for the ball. They sent it round from the costume hiring place this afternoon but I forgot it. Dendra reminded me and rang up the Delivery people—or Mike, as it turns out—in the interval."

"Why," Alleyn asked, "did you choose that particular disguise?"

"I didn't. I didn't know what to wear and I was too rattled to think. They said they were hiring things for themselves and would get something for me. They said we'd all be characters out of a Russian melodrama."

"Who said this?"

"Well—well, it was Barry George, actually."

"*Barry*," Coralie Bourne said. "*It was Barry.*"

"I don't understand," Anthony said. "Why should a fancy dress upset everybody?"

"It happened," Alleyn said, "to be a replica of the dress usually worn by Miss Bourne's husband who also had a red beard. That was it, wasn't it, Miss Bourne? I remember seeing him—"

"Oh, yes," she said, "you would. He was known to the police." Suddenly she broke down completely. She was in an armchair near the desk but out of the range of its shaded lamp. She twisted and writhed, beating her hand against the padded arm of the chair. Sergeant Thompson sat with his head bent and his hand over his notes. Mike, after an agonised glance at Alleyn, turned his back. Anthony Gill leant over her: "Don't," he said violently. "Don't! For God's sake, stop."

She twisted away from him and, gripping the edge of the desk, began to speak to Alleyn; little by little gaining mastery of herself. "I want to tell you. I want you to understand. Listen." Her husband had been fantastically cruel, she said. "It was a kind of slavery." But when she sued for divorce he brought evidence of adultery with Cumberland. They had thought he knew nothing. "There was an abominable scene. He told us he was going away. He said he'd keep track of us and if I tried again for divorce, he'd come home. He was very friendly with Barry in those days." He had left behind him the first draft of a play he had meant to write for her and Cumberland. It had a wonderful scene for them. "And now you will never have it," he had said, "because there is no other playwright who could make this play for you but I." He was, she said, a melodramatic man but he was never ridiculous. He returned to the Ukraine where he was born and they had heard no more of him. In a little while she would have been able to presume death. But years of waiting did not agree with Canning Cumberland. He drank consistently and at his worst used to imagine her husband was about to return. "He was really terrified of Ben," she said. "He seemed like a creature in a nightmare."

Anthony Gill said: "This play—was it—?"

"Yes. There was an extraordinary similarity between your play and his. I saw at once that Ben's central scene would enormously strengthen your piece. Cann didn't want me to give it to you. Barry knew. He said: 'Why not?' He wanted Cann's part and was furious when he didn't get it. So you see, when he suggested you should dress and make-up like Ben—" She turned to Alleyn. "You see?"

"What did Cumberland do when he saw you?" Alleyn asked Mike.

"He made a queer movement with his hands as if—well, as if he expected me to go for him. Then he just bolted into his room."

"He thought Ben had come back," she said.

"Were you alone at any time after you fainted?" Alleyn asked.

"I? No. No, I wasn't. Katie took me into my dressing room and stayed with me until I went on for the last scene."

"One other question. Can you, by any chance, remember if the heater in your room behaved at all oddly?"

She looked wearily at him. "Yes, it did give a sort of plop, I think. It made me jump. I was nervy."

"You went straight from your room to the stage?"

"Yes. With Katie. I wanted to go to Cann. I tried the door when we came out. It was locked. He said: 'Don't come in.' I said: 'It's all right. It wasn't Ben,' and went on to the stage."

"I heard Miss Bourne," Mike said.

"He must have made up his mind by then. He was terribly drunk when he played his last scene." She pushed her hair back from her forehead. "May I go?" she asked Alleyn.

"I've sent for a taxi. Mr. Gill, will you see if it's there? In the meantime, Miss Bourne, would you like to wait in the foyer?"

"May I take Katie home with me?"

"Certainly. Thompson will find her. Is there anyone else we can get?"

"No, thank you. Just old Katie."

Alleyn opened the door for her and watched her walk into the foyer. "Check up with the dresser, Thompson," he murmured, "and get Mr. H. J. Bannington."

He saw Coralie Bourne sit on the lower step of the dress-circle stairway and lean her head against the wall. Nearby, on a gilt easel, a huge photograph of Canning Cumberland smiled handsomely at her.

H. J. Bannington looked pretty ghastly. He had rubbed his hand across his face and smeared his make-up. Florid red paint from his lips had stained the crêpe hair that had been gummed on and shaped into a beard. His monocle was still in his left eye and gave him an extraordinarily rakish look. "See here," he complained, "I've about *had* this party. When do we go home?"

Alleyn uttered placatory phrases and got him to sit down. He checked over HJ's movements after Cumberland left the stage and found that his account tallied with Mike's. He asked if HJ had visited any of the other dressing rooms and was told acidly that HJ knew his place in the company. "I remained in my unheated and squalid kennel, thank you very much."

"Do you know if Mr. Barry George followed your example?"

"Couldn't say, old boy. He didn't come near *me*."

"Have you any theories at all about this unhappy business, Mr. Bannington?"

"Do you mean, why did Cann do it? Well, speak no ill of the dead, but I'd have thought it was pretty obvious he was morbid-drunk. Tight as an owl when we finished the second act. Ask the great Mr. Barry George. Cann took the big scene away from Barry with both hands and left him looking pathetic. All wrong artistically, but that's how Cann was in his cups." HJ's wicked little eyes narrowed. "The great Mr. George," he said, "must be feeling very unpleasant by now. You might say he'd got a suicide on his mind, mightn't you? Or don't you know about that?"

"It was not suicide."

The glass dropped from HJ's eye. "God," he said. "God. I told Bob Reynolds! I told him the whole plant wanted overhauling."

"The gas plant, you mean?"

"Certainly. I was in the gas business years ago. Might say I'm in it still with a difference, ha-ha!"

"Ha-ha!" Alleyn agreed politely. He leaned forward. "Look here," he said: "We can't dig up a gas man at this time of night and may very likely need an expert opinion. You can help us."

"Well, old boy, I was rather pining for a spot of shut-eye. But, of course—"

"I shan't keep you very long."

"God, I hope not!" said HJ earnestly.

Barry George had been made up pale for the last act. Colourless lips and shadows under his cheek bones and eyes had skilfully underlined his character as a repatriated but broken prisoner-of-war. Now, in the glare of the office lamp, he looked like a grossly exaggerated figure of mourning. He began at once to tell Alleyn how grieved and horrified he was. Everybody, he said, had their faults, and poor old Cann was no exception but wasn't it terrible to think what could happen to a man who let himself go downhill? He, Barry George, was abnormally sensitive and he didn't think he'd ever really get over the awful shock this had been to him. What, he wondered, could be at the bottom of it? Why had poor old Cann decided to end it all?

"Miss Bourne's theory," Alleyn began. Mr. George laughed. "Coralie?" he said. "So she's got a theory! Oh, well. Never mind."

"Her theory is this. Cumberland saw a man whom he mistook for her husband and, having a morbid dread of his return, drank the greater part of a bottle of whisky and gassed himself. The clothes and beard that deceived him had, I understand, been ordered by you for Mr. Anthony Gill."

This statement produced startling results. Barry George broke into a spate of expostulation and apology. There had been no thought in his mind of resurrecting poor old Ben, who was no doubt dead but had been, mind you, in many ways one of the best. They were all to go to the Ball as exaggerated characters from melodrama. Not for the world—he gesticulated and protested. A line of sweat broke out along the margin of his hair. "I don't know what you're getting at," he shouted. "What are you suggesting?"

"I'm suggesting, among other things, that Cumberland was murdered."

"You're mad! He'd locked himself in. They had to break down the door. There's no window. You're crazy!"

"Don't," Alleyn said wearily, "let us have any nonsense about sealed rooms. Now, Mr. George, you knew Benjamin Vlasnoff pretty well. Are you going to tell us that when you suggested Mr. Gill should wear a coat with a fur collar, a black sombrero, black gloves, and a red beard, it never occurred to you that his appearance might be a shock to Miss Bourne and to Cumberland?"

"I wasn't the only one," he blustered. "HJ knew. And if it had scared him off, *she* wouldn't have been so sorry. She'd had about enough of him. Anyway, if this is murder, the costume's got nothing to do with it."

"That," Alleyn said, getting up, "is what we hope to find out."

In Barry George's room, Detective Sergeant Bailey, a fingerprint expert, stood by the gas heater. Sergeant Gibson, a police photographer, and a uniformed constable were near the door. In the centre of the room stood Barry George, looking from one man to another and picking at his lips.

"I don't know why he wants me to watch all this," he said. "I'm exhausted. I'm emotionally used up. What's he doing? Where is he?"

Alleyn was next door in Cumberland's dressing room, with HJ, Mike and Sergeant Thompson. It was pretty clear now of fumes and the gas fire was burning comfortably. Sergeant Thompson sprawled in the armchair near the heater, his head sunk and his eyes shut.

"This is the theory, Mr. Bannington," Alleyn said. "You and Cumberland have made your final exits; Miss Bourne and Mr. George and Miss Gay are all on the stage. Lord Michael is standing just outside the entrance to the passage. The dressers and stage staff are watching the play from the side. Cumberland has locked himself in this room. There he is, dead drunk and sound asleep. The gas fire is burning, full pressure. Earlier in the evening he powdered himself and a thick layer of the powder lies undisturbed on the tap. Now."

He tapped on the wall.

The fire blew out with a sharp explosion. This was followed by the hiss of escaping gas. Alleyn turned the taps off. "You see," he said, "I've left an excellent print on the powdered surface. Now, come next door."

Next door, Barry George appealed to him stammering: "But I didn't know. I don't know anything about it. I don't *know*."

"Just show Mr. Bannington, will you, Bailey?"

Bailey knelt down. The lead-in was disconnected from the tap on the heater. He turned on the tap in the pipe and blew down the tube.

"An air lock, you see. It works perfectly."

HJ was staring at Barry George. "But I don't know about gas, HJ, HJ, tell them—"

"One moment." Alleyn removed the towels that had been spread over the dressing shelf, revealing a sheet of clean paper on which lay the rubber push-on connection.

"Will you take this lens, Bannington, and look at it. You'll see that it's stained a florid red. It's a very slight stain but it's unmistakably greasepaint. And just above the stain you'll see a wiry hair. Rather like some sort of packing material, but it's not that. It's crêpe hair, isn't it?"

The lens wavered above the paper.

"Let me hold it for you," Alleyn said. He put his hand over HJ's shoulder and, with a swift movement, plucked a tuft from his false moustache and dropped it on the paper. "Identical, you see, ginger. It seems to be stuck to the connection with spirit gum."

The lens fell. HJ twisted round, faced Alleyn for a second, and then struck him full in the face. He was a small man but it took three of them to hold him.

"In a way, sir, it's handy when they have a smack at you," said Detective Sergeant Thompson half an hour later. "You can pull them in nice and straightforward without any 'will you come to the station and make a statement' business."

"Quite," said Alleyn, nursing his jaw.

Mike said: "He must have gone to the room after Barry George and Miss Bourne were called."

"That's it. He had to be quick. The call boy would be round in a minute and he had to be back in his own room."

"But look here—what about motive?"

"That, my good Mike, is precisely why, at half past one in the morning, we're still in this miserable theatre. You're getting a view of the duller aspect of homicide. Want to go home?"

"No. Give me another job."

"Very well. About ten feet from the prompt entrance, there's a sort of garbage tin. Go through it."

At seventeen minutes to two, when the dressing rooms and passage had been combed clean and Alleyn had called a spell, Mike came to him with filthy hands. "*Eureka*," he said, "I hope."

They all went into Bannington's room. Alleyn spread out on the dressing table the fragments of paper that Mike had given him.

"They'd been pushed down to the bottom of the tin," Mike said.

Alleyn moved the fragments about. Thompson whistled through his teeth. Bailey and Gibson mumbled together.

"There you are," Alleyn said at last.

They collected round him. The letter that HJ Bannington had opened at this same table six hours and forty five minutes earlier, was pieced together like a jigsaw puzzle.

Dear H J,

Having seen the monthly statement of my account, I called at my bank this morning and was shown a cheque that is undoubtedly a forgery. Your histri- onic versatility, my dear H J, is only equalled by your audacity as a calligraphist. But fame has its disadvantages. The teller has recognised you. I propose to take action.

"Unsigned," said Bailey.

"Look at the card on the red roses in Miss Bourne's room signed CC. It's a very distinctive hand." Alleyn turned to Mike. "Do you still want to be a policeman?"

"Yes."

"Lord help you. Come and talk to me at the office tomorrow."

"Thank you, sir."

They went out, leaving a constable on duty. It was a cold morning. Mike looked up at the façade of the Jupiter. He could just make out the shape of the neon sign: I CAN FIND MY WAY OUT *by Anthony Gill.*

1948

The Lady Who Laughed

Roy Vickers

William Edward Vickers (1889–1965) is remembered today under the name Roy Vickers; he also wrote under such pen-names as David Durham, Sefton Kyle, and John Spencer. His first novel, *The Mystery of the Scented Death*, was published in 1921, and by the time *The Radingham Mystery* appeared seven years later, his publishers Herbert Jenkins were suffi-ciently confident of his appeal to the readers to issue publicity postcards describing him as "The Master of the Unusual" and claiming that "No living writer can handle a complicated plot more ingeniously than Roy Vickers."

Vickers was a prolific novelist, but he owes his repu-tation primarily to his short stories about Scotland Yard's Department of Dead Ends. In an introduction to an anthol-ogy of his fiction published in the year of his death, he wrote that: "The Department keeps an eye open for any unusual occurrence to any of the persons who were once in the orbit of an unsolved murder. The Department does not grope for points missed in the investigation. Its clues come freshly into existence as the splinter from the broken pattern is picked up by Detective-Inspector Rason." This story first appeared in *Ellery Queen's Mystery Magazine* in February 1948.

———

To those under thirty, the name of Lucien Spengrave probably suggests nothing but one of those 'famous crimes' which are periodically retold. Actually, Spengrave himself was famous; his crime only so by virtue of the round-about way in which it was uncovered by Scotland Yard.

You may have heard that he was a successful comedian. He was a unique comedian. He played only one role—that of a circus clown. But he had never played it in a circus. For the last ten years of his life he played it in his own West End theatre—in which the cheap seats were half and the expensive seats double the prevailing prices.

His jokes and stage business—as eminent historians of the theatre and the circus have pointed out—were literally hundreds of years old. For instance, that almost incredibly crude act in which the clown helps the Ringmaster's attendants roll up a carpet, trips, and gets himself rolled up in the carpet. They say that, in a real circus, young children will still laugh at it. Spengrave played that act to the most sophisticated audiences in the world. From all classes he drew belly-laughs and tears—from that same carpet that can be traced back to eleventh-century Bohemia.

The clue to the mystery—as opposed to evidence of the murder—lay in the personality of the man who could evolve such a technique. When June, Spengrave's wife, disappeared so dramatically and was later found dead, the armchair detective might well have beaten the practical man by betting blindly on Spengrave's genius in manipulating the deadly obvious.

She disappeared during a cocktail party on the lawn of their riverside house at Wheatbourne on the last Thursday of August, 1936. Spengrave never played during August, though he had to practise in his gymnasium five days a week, muscular control being as essential to him as to a pianist.

There were some twenty guests, all being June's friends. She had complained that he was never "matey" with her friends—he was, indeed, rather ponderous in private life and a poor mixer; so he said he would give the guests a light version of the lecture he periodically delivered to Universities—the lecture that had brought him three honorary degrees.

The guests felt themselves highly privileged. From the gymnasium, whose double doors gave on to the garden, six of the male guests brought the classic carpet; others, the tray with the goblet screwed down and the masks for the two-headed dog. There was brisk competition for the honour of being selected as stooges to roll the carpet for Spengrave's demonstration.

"The Clown is traditionally a sub-human, struggling to reach the level of humanity. The Clown never consciously plays the fool. He is desperately anxious to help the normal men roll the carpet in the normal way. Observe my shoulders as I approach the men at the carpet."

Thus he dissected the carpet act. The two-headed dog act followed. The garden sloped down to the river in three little levelled lawns. June led her guests to the second lawn, clear of the carpet.

For some six minutes he traced the act from its origin at the court of King Henry VIII, then turned to the tray and goblet.

"In this act we see anxiety expressed exclusively with the feet. I shall need more space for this. The upper lawn is wide enough, I think. Oh, the carpet is in the way!"

"Shall we roll it up again and put it back in the gym, Mr. Spengrave?"

The speaker was Fred Periss, a youngish, handsome man. Spengrave turned and looked at him as if the offer were surprising. Then:

"Yes, please," said Spengrave.

There was a scramble to deal with the carpet, in which some of the girls joined. It would be something to talk about afterwards—that they had once helped the great Spengrave with the very carpet that was used on the stage.

When they had all come back from the gymnasium, Spengrave resumed his lecture.

"The Clown is proud because he has been entrusted with the dignified duty of carrying wine to the lady. To reduce this to its basic values, I shall want June to stooge for me, if she will." He called: "June, dear!"

To keep the great man waiting—even if it was his wife who was doing it—was an outrage.

"June!" they shouted. "June, where are you? June!"

The time when they were calling her was reconstructed and checked as being about six-fifty. At six-thirty she had been well in evidence, quietly magnificent in a dress of green crêpe, a trifle self-conscious over her duties as hostess.

Her disappearance spoilt the lecture. The party began to break up. The honoured stooges returned the tray and goblet, and the masks for the two-headed dog act, to the gymnasium. By seven-fifteen the last guest had gone.

At eight, Spengrave toyed with a lonely dinner. At eight-thirty he rang the Reading police. The Inspector came at once with a sergeant. The routine investigation revealed that there were no signs whatever of Mrs. Spengrave having prepared for her departure. The possibility of her having thrown herself into the river, unobserved, was explored and dismissed.

An hour later, because Spengrave was so distinguished, the Chief Constable appeared in person.

"There's one question I must ask in your own interest, Mr. Spengrave—"

"Has my wife bolted with a lover?" cut in Spengrave. "No. If there had been a lover in the offing—she would thoroughly have enjoyed telling me."

The Chief was sufficiently convinced. His eye strayed to a large photograph of a woman with a strange, cold beauty.

"Is that Mrs. Spengrave?" As her husband nodded: "I have never had the pleasure of meeting her. But I've seen her somewhere."

"Perhaps in one of the many pictures of her in the Academy years ago. She used to be an artist's model. Also, she appeared in one of my acts for four years—before we were married."

"That's where I saw her! In *The Lady Who Wouldn't Laugh*."

"Correct! She ought to be easy to find."

"If nothing happens by midday tomorrow we'll fix a broadcast appeal," said the Chief, and departed.

Close upon midnight on Friday the police rang. There had been an answer from Edinburgh, of a loss of memory case, which bore some slight resemblance to the description of Mrs. Spengrave.

"I'll go by air taxi early tomorrow," said Spengrave. "I'm rehearsing my company all next week, and I don't want to lose more time than I can help."

Before leaving, after a very early breakfast, he told his housekeeper:

"The men should be here this morning from the theatre to overhaul my things and take some of them back. If they aren't here by eleven, 'phone the theatre and tell the manager I want to know why. When they come, make things easy for them, will you, and give them all they want."

All that the men wanted was the loan of a vacuum cleaner.

When they unrolled the classic carpet, they found the dead body of June Spengrave.

———

Lucien Spengrave had begun as an artist. At the Slade School, where he learnt his technique, he kept his individuality in check. When he began painting he attracted a great deal of attention but very few cheques.

As a person he enjoyed a kind of oblique popularity. "Funny thing, but I can't help rather liking Spengrave." His life was blameless, yet men tended to apologise for liking him. There was the hint of a reason in the background, unexpressed because no one knew how to express it.

There was nothing odd about him physically except that, if you were to see him for the first time sitting down, you might think that he was a large, tall man, whereas he just escaped being short. That was because he had a large, long, lean face, suggesting a scholarly monk; the mouth was long and thin-lipped, but in the eyes—wide and unusually blue— the prevailing expression was that of gentleness.

When Kenfield became a Minister, he commissioned Spengrave to paint him, but refused to accept the portrait, on the ground that it was not like him. Carron James, whose plays were about to earn him a knighthood, gave Spengrave a hundred guineas for the portrait.

"I'm buying it, Spengrave, because it's an excellent bit o' work. Also because I have always hated Kenfield. Gosh, he must have felt that portrait like a whip across the face! It enables me to see him as a poor, ineffectual devil like myself. And I don't hate him any more. D'you see what I mean?"

"No," said Spengrave. "But your cheque is a godsend."

"Is it! It oughtn't to be, to a man of your talent." Carron James couldn't help rather liking the fellow. "If you're hard up, why not try a sideline in caricature? I'll give you an intro- duction if you like."

With a topical caricature of the Prime Minister under his arm, Spengrave kept an appointment with the editor of a leading Opposition paper. The editor looked at the caricature. He chuckled, but the chuckle died in his throat.

"I like that! But I can't publish it. If you care to sell it to me personally I'll give you a tenner for it."

"You can have it for nothing," said Spengrave, "if you will tell me why you won't publish it, though you obviously like it."

"Your picture is true. But it tells an unbearable truth. It's— cruel! It even pulls *me* into a kind of nervous sympathy with *him*."

"Thank you," said Spengrave. "The drawing is yours. I'll send you a receipt. Good-bye!"

"Hi! I'm not going to charge you a tenner for saying that!"

"I am content with our bargain if you are," returned Spengrave and left.

Spengrave walked back to his studio; wishing he could have accepted the tenner without wounding his self-respect. Things were getting very low. In three months he would be starting the round of the pawnshops. He looked at himself in one of the long mirrors.

"You thought you were being topical and damned witty. And you were only being cruel and killing your market. *Clown!*"

He snatched brush and palette and began to paint a portrait of himself—became absorbed, barely conscious that the clown-theme was predominating until, four hours later, he had finished.

He stood back, looking at his self-portrait.

"The best thing I've done!" He giggled weakly and the tears ran down his cheeks. "But it tells an unbearable truth. It's cruel!"

He began to pace the studio, uncertainly, like a drunkard.

"Carron James said much the same thing. That means I must have a streak of cruelty in me without knowing it. But the others know it. However civil people are, they never accept me as one of themselves.

"I want to be like other men. I want to eat and drink without thought and be clean and have proper clothes. I want a woman to love me terrifically and be glad to have children with me. *I want to be like other men!*"

Melancholia drove him to self-pity, but intelligence warned him that if he wanted something he must fight for it. He returned to the portrait.

"If I turn the cruelty on to myself, the others will be— 'pulled into a kind of nervous sympathy' with me. That's what he said. And then I can make them laugh or cry."

Thus he found the formula which carried him to stardom in three months and kept him there for the rest of his life.

———

For five years he was the star turn in the music halls, touring all the capitals that could fill a large house at good prices. Always he played the circus clown in difficulties. He used the fact that a white-faced clown is not particularly funny to a modern audience—he exposed the clown's unfunniness with a stark brutality that shocked his audience into sympathy with the clown—a twist in the story brought release and the belly-laugh. That put the audience in his pocket. He could play on all the basic emotions. The grey-white, idiot face of the clown could flash into a disconcerting sensitiveness that gave a new tang to poltroonery.

With the coming of the talkies and the decay of the music hall, he took a theatre for himself, filling out with straight musical and dramatic acts of a high class.

He met June in the course of a visit to one of his artist friends. She was tall and blonde with regular features and regular lines, handsome rather than beautiful. Her curves were artistically correct rather than voluptuous. His glance was wholly professional.

"Let me know when you've finished with that girl," he said in an undertone.

"I've finished now, if you've got work for her—I owe her for three sittings. June, come and meet Mr. Spengrave."

Like many an artist's model, June was respectable to the point of prudery, educated in genteel snobbery but in hardly anything else. She was conscientious and unmercenary at this stage of her life, and would work loyally for anyone who would affect to treat her as a lady.

Her lucky physicality gave her the appearance of a solemn young queen disguised as a housemaid. Spengrave himself designed for her a dress, of red corduroy velvet, which emancipated the regal from the domestic.

On Spengrave's stage she was required to behave exactly as she behaved in a studio—sit stock still, not utter a word and look handsomely expressionless—The Lady Who Wouldn't Laugh.

On the first night, she virtually killed the act. For when the twist came in the story, bringing the release, June laughed too.

"*Don't laugh, you dreadful little fool!*" he hissed with such venom that she had no difficulty in obeying. He more or less gagged his way out of the debacle, but the act was not a success that night.

Afterwards, she came tearfully to his dressing-room.

"I'm very sorry indeed, Mr. Spengrave. No wonder you were so angry! But it was suddenly all so funny!"

"My fault for not rehearsing you enough! Be here tomorrow at ten, and we'll go over it again."

He was not quite sure of her after the morning rehearsal. He gave her lunch in his suite at the top of the theatre, and afterwards asked her if she felt confident.

"I'm still worried about that bit where you fall in the carpet the second time—the funny time, Mr. Spengrave!"

"Hm! I know you're trying hard. Perhaps too hard. Sit in that armchair and relax all you can. Now, don't make any effort. Just let your will gently slide into your mind and tell it you mustn't laugh. Repeat this after me… The carpet isn't funny… The goblet and tray isn't funny… Nothing that he does is funny… I will never laugh again."

He left her, went to his bedroom to rest. A couple of hours later when he returned to the living-room she was still there.

"*Ooh!* I must have had a nap!" she exclaimed. She added: "It's all right now, Mr. Spengrave. I'll never laugh again."

———

The Lady Who Wouldn't Laugh became one of the most popular acts. It stayed in the bill for four years—and was only taken off when June contracted pneumonia. He could fairly easily have replaced her, but she had been loyal and efficient and regular, and he felt that as a decent employer he owed her some consideration.

As a decent employer, he went to see her at the nursing home when she was convalescent, bringing her the usual gift of grapes. In four years, with other members of the company, she had toured Europe and America with him; yet he had had hardly any personal conversation with her, knew nothing about her.

He exerted himself to draw her out, discovered that, when she forgot to be genteel, she was a simple, likeable person. He suspected that she had few friends and at his next visit asked her whether this were true.

"Oh, I don't know, Mr. Spengrave! I get on well enough with most people, though I do keep myself to myself. Of course, there are always men of the wrong sort, but they don't appeal to me. I'll own up I've got the idea that ordinary people think me a bit queer. It makes you feel lonely, sometimes, if you know what I mean."

Spengrave knew what she meant—knew it a hundred times better than she did. In those hours of self-revelation when he had painted his own portrait he had found a formula for commercial success; but he had found nothing else.

At his next call at the nursing home he asked her to marry him.

"*Ooh!* Mr. Spengrave!" She was staggered. "Well, of course, I will, if you're sure you want to!"

After a while, she said:

"It'll take a bit of getting used to. You see, I've always thought of you as not being like other men."

He caught his breath as if she had stabbed him.

"Ever since you were so kind to me that first time when I let you down by laughing, I've put you in a class apart. I thought you superior to all the men and women I've ever met. And I still think it. So, nach'rally, it makes me a bit shy of you."

"Oh, my darling!" He kissed her with love and overwhelming gratitude. "And I am shy of you, June—because you think that of me. We'll help each other."

So they did, for three years—with very different effects on their very different natures. June, who had been a conscientious stooge, became a conscientious wife, striving solemnly to serve him and to please him. She discovered that he liked her to look always as nice as possible, so she studied dress. When he did not require her presence she regarded her time as her own, and developed along her own lines. In a sense, she loved him—did not suspect that, in no sense, was she in love with him.

In an undreamed affluence, dormant traits in her character became active. She began to preen herself as the wife of a wealthy celebrity cultivated by High-ups, who were seeking neither money nor publicity nor introductions. Such people were outside her orbit, but at the local river-sailing club and the tennis club she was somebody.

She gathered a large circle of friends. Although she patronised them a little, they liked her. That she never laughed at their quips they took as her reminder that she was the wife of the world's greatest clown. One youngish man, Fred Periss, tall and dark, handsome as a stage Guardsman, was particularly attracted to her.

Spengrave for his part was aware of partial failure, for which he blamed himself with secret humiliation. In the essentials of their life together she obeyed him as punctiliously as she had formerly obeyed a call to rehearsal. But there was a barrier he had never passed. If she did not stand in awe of him, she certainly held him in a kind of respectfulness that numbed spontaneity. Like a damp cloud the conviction settled on him that he was not regarded by his wife as other men were regarded by their wives.

He had not the leisure to go visiting with her. His appearances at her parties were perfunctory. He was glad for her sake that she had made so many friends, though he found them noisy and dull-witted.

One afternoon in the first week in August, when he was dozing in the drawing-room, he was startled by an unfamiliar sound. He sat bolt upright, fully awake. The sound came again, from the garden.

It was the sound of June laughing.

In his spine was an eerie tingling as a thought formed itself against his will.

"I've never heard her laugh—since that night she killed the act."

He ran into the garden, could not see her. He turned the corner by the laurel bushes and saw her in the arms of Fred Periss. She was not struggling.

"*Fred!* Oh, why did you have to do that!" she cried in distress.

"Why pretend? You didn't hate it, darling, did you!"

"That makes it all the worse. I shall have to tell Lucien now. It wasn't worth troubling him before."

Spengrave slipped back to his chair in the drawing-room and picked up a book. Within a few minutes she came. She had smoothed her hair and shaken out her frock, where Periss had rumpled it.

"Lucien, Fred Periss kissed me just now. Not a party kiss— the real sort, I think it was. I expect it was partly my fault."

"We needn't lose our heads. Better ask him in here."

"He's gone. Are you angry with me?"

Spengrave was thinking. He himself could crush her up and kiss her. But he could not draw from her that lovely rippling laugh—full of fun and games. Other men, of course, could make their wives laugh like that.

"I'm not angry with you, June. It isn't the sort of thing one can be angry about. Are you in love with him?"

She meditated her answer, tried honestly to clear her thought and failed.

"*Ooh!* I don't understand love."

She meant it, but it was obviously untrue. She would very soon discover that she did understand love. Perhaps, thought Spengrave, there was still time for him.

"Then let's forget it, dear."

"I'm so glad you aren't angry, Lucien. And I think I can forget it all right. I'll try hard to think of other things."

"Try thinking of me!" he said, rising nimbly from his chair.

Again came the delicious rippling sound that was her rediscovered laughter. Vibrant with happiness he put his arms round her. "You laugh because at last you're happy?" he asked.

"I laughed because you looked so funny, jumping out of that chair—like a jack-in-the-box."

It spoilt the kiss, ruined his moment. He was not disconsolate. There were kisses to come—"the real sort," if he could thrust himself into her imagination.

She said she would like to go on the river before dinner. He brought the punt alongside, called to her when he was ready, steadied the boat with one foot on the landing stage. He watched her approaching, watched her with reawakened desire—and again she laughed.

"Standing like that with that funny look on your face, you reminded me of something," she explained. "Can't think what it was!"

"Somebody's pet poodle begging for its dinner?" he suggested.

"No, it wasn't that." She had taken his question seriously. "I wish I could remember."

In himself was a deep inner disturbance which he shrank

from defining. Presently she was babbling about giving a cocktail party.

"When will it be, dear?"

"On the last Thursday of the month. It would be so nice if you could spare an hour or so. They would appreciate it so!"

He would give her anything, do anything for her, if only she would regard him as other men were regarded by their wives. And perhaps she would.

"Darling, I'll be there the whole time and I'll do everything I can to make your party a riproaring success." When she had finished exclaiming, he went on: "I always feel I'm a bit of a wet blanket at parties. I just haven't got the trick of sitting around and swapping backchat about sport and that sort of thing. How would they like it if I were to give them the lecture I gave at Oxford last year? We could get the props out on the lawn."

They would adore it, she assured him. She knew that, though much of it might be above their heads, they would be flattered by his condescension.

Over dinner she was companionable, more light-hearted, more spirited than he had ever known her to be. She was expanding, he thought, opening like a rose in the sunshine of their new understanding. He held fast to that conception throughout the evening.

That night she laughed—she said—at his dressing-gown. It was a black silk dressing-gown, by no means new, which she had often seen before. Uncertain of himself and her, he sat on the edge of her bed and talked of anything that came into his head—became aware that she was unconscious of any strain.

"There's plenty of time before the party, June. Would you

like us to go away for a fortnight somewhere? We might pop over to Switzerland."

"Well, if it's for me I'm in no hurry to go away." She added: "I love it here."

"So do I!" He touched her hand, gripped it. "It's our home, yours and mine. Not a bad old place, is it! And it would be just fine if we happened to have a family. Wouldn't it, June?"

She did not answer. Her face was hard and drawn, and he feared lest she had read into his words a reproach that she had not yet borne a child.

"June, darling!" He bent over her, touched her hair with his lips. "I only meant—"

From the back of her nostrils came the absurd noise made by a schoolboy trying not to laugh in class.

As he sprang away, she burst into open laughter. He stood at a distance from the bed, staring down at her. When she looked up at him, the laughter started afresh. He waited, standing very still, until she stopped from exhaustion.

"Perhaps you will tell me why you laugh at me, though I think I know."

"I couldn't help it!" she gasped. "You, perched on the side of the bed with that dressing-gown, saying—all that!— you were so *funny!*" She spluttered with the aftermath of laughter.

He strode in silence to the door.

"Oh, Lucien, it's not fair to be offended and angry with me! You *are* funny—or you wouldn't be you—especially when you're saying something serious. You can't expect me to behave as if you were like other men."

"Yes. I thought that was why," he said, and left her room.

Her reasoning was slovenly, for she had forgotten that she had not thought him funny in his personal life until today. The man who intended to be her lover had already awakened her to full womanhood—had enabled her to see that she was in very truth married to a clown.

He went downstairs to his study, which adjoined the gymnasium, poured himself a stiff brandy. Presently, rummaging in a cabinet, he took out the portrait of himself which he had painted long ago in his Bloomsbury studio.

"The best thing I've done!" The words echoed down the years. "And it tells an unbearable truth. It's cruel!"

But its cruelty was not as unbearable as the cruelty of that laughter which was as a flaming sword holding him from his human heritage—a mirror into which he must gaze and see himself "not like other men".

He turned again to the self-portrait, remembered his despair.

"Last time, I cashed in on my own misery. Can I do it a second time? Work. Thank heavens she didn't want to go for that holiday! I can work instead of thinking."

With nervous eagerness he grabbed a pencil and a folder. He flopped into his armchair and began to work up some notes he had made for a new scene—a change-ring on the classic carpet act, employing a girl stooge.

He drove up to London next day, put in a couple of hours' desk work at the theatre, which he was re-opening in the second week in September. There was a letter from the mother of June's successor saying the girl had had measles, but expected to be well enough to rehearse in a fortnight.

A week later, June, passing by the open garden doors of the gymnasium, saw him leaning ill-temperedly against the wall.

"Do you want anything, Lucien?"

"Mabel is sick. I wanted to rehearse myself rather than her. Hangs me up."

"Well, what's wrong with me?" She came in from the garden. "What's the job?"

"Nothing you'd fancy, my dear. The girl gets rolled in the carpet instead of the clown."

"All right. Only, it'll ruin this dress." She slipped it off.

"The carpet will scratch your shoulders. Here!" He helped her into a dressing-gown—it happened to be the black silk dressing-gown.

"I shall split the seams," she warned. "I'm bigger than you."

The words made him feel as if he were a dwarf, which added a spur to rehearsal.

"When I unroll you, sit up and stare at me; hold the stare while I do my business. You'll want two coils of the carpet, or else you'll show. Better do it yourself, or I may hurt you. Lie down, your middle as near dead centre as you can. You can pull one coil over you. Then use all your weight to complete another coil."

For two hours she helped him uncomplainingly, while the idea came to her that it would be rather a lark if he would consent to doing the act at her party, with herself as the stooge. She was a little anxious lest that lecture on the theory of the clown, which appealed to the dons of Oxford, might be above the heads of her friends. She, at any rate, would give them a good laugh when she popped out of the carpet. She knew that the carpet was used in the lecture.

When she asked him, he showed no enthusiasm. But she

pointed out how easily she could steal away while he was holding their attention.

"What about your frock, though. You'll be varnished up for the party, won't you?"

"I was thinking—I could nip up to my room and slip on the frock I used in our old act. No one has worn it since I dropped out. It's still in the property wardrobe—if you'll bring it down for me tomorrow. It's velvet corduroy, and the carpet won't do it any harm—being red, it'll make a fine splash of colour."

"I might keep you there two or three minutes. You could breathe all right, couldn't you?"

"Yes—it's a bit stuffy. And when I called out to you when you kept me waiting just now, you couldn't hear me. Anyway, I shan't mind."

"Hm! I must be careful not to suffocate Mabel. She'll have to lie in it for upwards of ten minutes."

When he was at the theatre the following morning, there was no dresser present. He himself collected the key from the caretaker, found the number on the list and took the velvet corduroy frock from one of the fireproof cupboards and put it in June's suitcase.

"She has the mind of a child," he reflected as he drove home. Her child mind labelled him a very clever man, strong, kind, good, rich, influential. But her adult woman's instinct thought him funny.

———

With the impetus given by the stage hands, the corpse of June Spengrave rolled clear of the carpet. When they had recovered from the momentary shock, the men correctly shut the gymnasium and mounted guard, while one rang the police.

The Inspector was shortly followed by the Chief Constable. He caused a telephone message, sympathetically worded, to be sent to the airfield at Edinburgh. By the time Spengrave arrived, after stopping at the mortuary in Reading to identify the body, the Chief had possessed himself of the main facts. It was assumed that June had died of asphyxia, though the later medical report established that the immediate cause of death was shock.

Spengrave's account of the incidents of the party did not differ in any essential detail from that already obtained from some of the guests.

"When you asked the men of the party to roll up the carpet and take it back to the gym, Mr. Spengrave, I gather that they all went at the job, and some of the women joined in. D'you think it possible that poor Mrs. Spengrave may have joined in the scramble, that she may have fallen down and been rolled up without anybody noticing—in fact, just as the thing happens in the circus?"

"You ask if I think it possible. Theoretically, anything is possible. I think it very grossly improbable. There were at least six men rolling. If she fell flat on the carpet, the faces of at least three of them would have been within a few feet of her. They must have seen her."

"Then she must have been inside the first coil or two of the carpet when the men started to roll it?"

"Obviously!" agreed Spengrave.

"The doctor is already able to say that there are no signs of violence on the body. No one knocked her out and partly rolled her in the carpet. Therefore—a hostess suddenly slips away from her guests, rolls herself in the carpet—so that her guests may unconsciously assist her to commit suicide?"

Spengrave looked tired and indifferent, as if all this were none of his business.

"She was not happy with me, as I hinted to you yesterday. But she was not melancholic. The last person to think of suicide."

Spengrave, thought the Chief, was no humbug. He was not pretending to be grief-stricken. But he was being very wooden, showed no desire to help.

"Against the theory of her having rolled herself up," continued the Chief, "is the fact that she had had some stage experience under yourself. She was familiar with that carpet, knew how heavy it was, must have known she was doing a very dangerous thing."

Spengrave snapped his fingers excitedly.

"That's a glimmer in the dark!" he exclaimed. "She was familiar with that carpet, you said. Hold that thought, while I add something. That carpet was rolled up the wrong way— namely from right to left, standing with your back to the river. I noticed it, but did not want to ask the guests to unroll it and start again. Now are you guessing what I've guessed?"

This was what the Chief had been waiting for.

"She assumed it would be rolled up from the other end," said the Chief, "and that therefore *she* would be *unrolled*." As Spengrave nodded encouragingly: "But why—when there was no need to be there at all?"

"To give her guests a laugh—and to guy my lecture. She had," he added, "the mind of a child."

Thus Spengrave, for all his subtlety, had suggested a cause of death other than murder—always an unwise course when there is any chance of murder being suspected.

At the inquest Spengrave gave substantially the same answers as he had given to the Chief. The Chief Constable did not waste time studying him while he was giving evidence. Actors never betray themselves with involuntary movements of body, hands or face. The jury returned a verdict of death by misadventure. The Chief, without any publicity, consulted Scotland Yard.

Chief Inspector Karslake was very dubious.

"If it's murder at all, where is the overt act?" he asked. "The guests did the actual killing. And Spengrave didn't even incite them to it."

"If you were to induce a drunkard to lie down on a railway track and then watched him being killed I could hang you, Mr. Karslake, without proving that you had incited the engine driver," said the Chief Constable.

"But the lady wasn't drunk," objected Karslake. "And Spengrave didn't—"

"Yes, he did. Look here!" The Chief spread out a chart of the garden, with all distances noted in feet and inches. "The woman was last seen at six-thirty-five, when Spengrave finished his demonstration with the carpet. Between six-forty and about six-forty-seven, the guests were all—*here*—their eyes glued to Spengrave, who was lecturing about the double-headed dog." He carried his pencil upwards and to the right. "Spengrave alone can see the carpet—he has a clear view. He would have seen his wife—must have seen her—go to that carpet."

"You've certainly got something there," admitted Karslake.

"Spengrave told them he doubted whether he had enough room on the lower lawn for the tray-and-goblet business. One of the men—Periss—asked him if they should roll up the carpet at once and take it back to the gym. Spengrave said 'Yes, please'. That's incitement." The Chief went on:

"As Spengrave is standing pat, it won't matter if he knows we're on his track. He thinks that, whatever we suspect, we can't get any evidence."

"So do I!" said Karslake gloomily. "But we'll try."

Karslake tried so hard that he came within an ace of committing homicide himself. He had his junior rolled in Spengrave's carpet, observed that at the fourth coiling the weight of the carpet bore down the fringes so that air was excluded. The unfortunate junior had observed the same phenomenon some minutes before Karslake.

"That Chief Constable was simply passing the buck!" said Karslake after a month of fruitless investigation. "How can we prove that Spengrave induced her to get into the carpet, and that he wasn't looking at his notes or something when she did it? I'm sick of the sight of those dossiers. Shove 'em along to Dead Ends and forget 'em!"

Spengrave sold his house by the river, warehoused his expensive furniture, and resumed residence in the suite at the top of the theatre. The act of the girl in the carpet was never put on.

———

The Department of Dead Ends, by its nature, could not function until a new light was thrown on a case by some tangential occurrence, some chance echo, even if it were only a chance remark. When this happened and a prosecution followed, Chief Inspector Karslake always called it Detective Inspector Rason's "luck."

"I've got a niece too," protested Karslake. "And I hope I'm at least as good an uncle as you are. But my niece has never yet happened to babble out the dope on a case that's been dead meat for over a year. So I still say it's luck."

This, in a police car shortly before midday in October, 1937—some fourteen months after the death of June Spengrave. They laboured the matter of Rason's niece because they were both secretly ill at ease—for they were on their way to Spengrave's theatre, to ask him some questions they were confident he could not answer—which is a strange state of mind for a detective. But Spengrave was a distinguished man, whom nearly everybody could not help liking.

"She didn't give me any dope—she gave me backchat," retorted Rason. "I told her she didn't need a new frock, because she had a lovely one already. And she said if she went to a garden party in August in her corduroy velvet, people would be laughing over it when she was an old woman. I happened to remember the words 'corduroy velvet' in the dossier—and a garden party too! I've put in more than two months' work on that bit o' corduroy velvet, and you call it luck—*sir!*"

"You don't have to 'sir' me till we get back," chuckled Karslake. "This is your case, my boy, and welcome!"

The car stopped at the theatre. Rason thrust his card through the window of the box office. In due course an attendant presented himself.

"Mr. Spengrave is sorry he will have to keep you waiting for a few minutes. Will you follow me, please."

They were led through unsuspected corridors to the back of the stage and thence, up a single flight of stairs, to Spengrave's dressing-room. It was a very large room with more than the usual number of mirrors. Above the mirrors was a frieze, depicting the Clown throughout the ages. In one wide corner was a writing table. There were two divans. The detectives took one each.

"Haven't had much to do with the stage!" remarked Karslake. "What's the good of putting all those telephones over the wash basin?—to say nothing of there being a bathroom behind this curtain."

"They use the dressing-room as an office and a parlour as well." Rason's eye travelled along the frieze, to the court jester, to the hunchback pelted by the mediaeval audience, to the buffoon-god of Greek comedy, to the Sacaea of ancient Babylon where the King of the Revels, still wearing his mock crown, is sacrificed to the goddess Ishtar.

"Good Lord, they've all got Spengrave's face!" ejaculated Rason. He caught Karslake's eye and added defiantly: "I'm going to put the cards on the table with this bloke."

For some minutes they sat in silence. Then the door opened. Both men gasped. Both were momentarily as confused as schoolboys.

"I'm sorry I had to keep you waiting, gentlemen."

Spengrave was in make-up. They stared at the grey-white, idiot face of the Clown, the splash of carmine, harsh and hideous at close quarters, the bald wig, the conical cap.

"Perhaps we—perhaps you would rather we waited while you change, Mr. Spengrave?" faltered Rason.

"Quite unnecessary! You don't imagine that I'm going to make jokes and fall over carpets." The voice coming out of that preposterous face was both irritable and authoritative. "I've just been having stills taken of a new act. Sit down, please. What can I do for you?"

"We've come on a very serious matter, Mr. Spengrave. We have to put to you certain questions arising out of your wife's death. If you refuse to answer, or if your answers are unsatisfactory, we shall have to ask you to come along with us."

As Spengrave swung a swivel chair from his dressing-table the mirrors caught him in cross-reflection, so that Rason was compelled to contemplate the Clown face multiplied to infinity, staring into his.

"Go ahead, Inspector!"

"Can you describe the dress your wife was wearing at that party?"

"No. I've no eye for women's dress and no memory."

"That's unusual in one of your profession, especially as you yourself were once a pictorial artist." Rason was opening an attache case. He took out a mill board, on which was a painting of a woman's dress of green crepe.

"Is this the dress she was wearing?"

Spengrave looked at the painting. No expression was perceptible through the clown make-up.

"It may have been," he said. "I think it is."

"Quite right! It is! Five of the women who were your guests that day have identified it." Rason added: "I obtained a judge's order to examine your furniture at the repository. *That dress was in the wardrobe of the deceased.* By the way, both the men and women guests remarked that they had not been allowed to see the poor lady after death."

"That was nothing to do with me—the local police were in charge," rasped Spengrave. "In any case it was unnecessary. I identified the body myself."

"Yes, of course. After you had flown down from Edinburgh. The major examination had not then taken place. The body was almost exactly as it had been found in the gymnasium." Rason leant forward and tapped the picture of the green crepe dress. "Did you see that dress on the dead body of your wife, Mr. Spengrave?"

"I can't remember."

"You can't remember!" echoed Rason. "Do you mean that you may or may not have seen that dress on the body?" As Spengrave assented, Rason produced a police photograph of the corpse taken in the gymnasium.

"That is the dress you saw in the mortuary. You can't see the colour, but the line of that dress is quite different. And here it is in colour."

Rason thrust at him a second mill board, a little crumpled and faded, on which was a painting of a red dress in velvet corduroy.

"Do you recognise that red velvet corduroy dress, Mr. Spengrave?"

"No," snapped Spengrave. "I've told you I've no memory for women's dress."

"But you've a memory for your own work, haven't you? You designed that dress yourself. You painted the picture you have in your hand. It's the dress she wore in her act with you—The Lady Who Wouldn't Laugh."

"By Jove, you're right!" exclaimed Spengrave, as if surprised.

"On August 18th last year," continued Rason, "you signed the book, in the keeping of your caretaker, for the key of the robe-room, or whatever you call it. You entered the robe-room with a suitcase. On August 21st, your chief dresser sent you a chit reporting that that dress was missing. You wrote on the chit 'O.K.,' and initialled it. Why did your wife want that property dress, Mr. Spengrave?"

"I now remember the incidents you describe." Spengrave spoke in the same authoritative, irritable voice. "But I don't remember why my wife wanted that dress."

"Let me suggest why you wanted her to have it, and you tell me if I'm wrong," pressed Rason. "You created an act in which a girl is rolled in that carpet of yours. You asked your wife to play the girl and said you'd put on the act for the party. You fixed it so that she could slip into that carpet without anyone seeing her but you. And you fixed it so that someone should suggest rolling that carpet up. When Mr. Periss offered to do it you said, 'Yes, please,' thereby procuring the death of your wife. And that means murder."

"You asked me to tell you if you were wrong," chuckled Spengrave. "You are."

"Maybe I've slipped up on a few details," said Rason. "But do you deny that you created an act in which a girl is rolled up—"

"I deny it absolutely," thundered Spengrave. "It would be an utterly futile act."

"At the repository, I found nothing in your desk—it was practically empty," said Rason. "But under the cushion of the armchair that used to be in your study I found a manuscript in your handwriting. Here's a typed copy. I don't altogether understand stage directions. But there's one bit where it says: 'Clown kicks coil of carpet (laugh). Clown struggles with carpet. Fails. Walks away (laugh). Returns. Unrolls carpet. Girl sits up—'"

"All right!" Spengrave stood up. The figure of the clown facing destruction was not even tragic, only bizarre. "It will take me twenty minutes to change. Do you mind waiting in the foyer?"

"Sorry, Mr. Spengrave." Again Rason's eye travelled along the frieze—to the altar of Ishtar, where the Clown is slain. "We shall have to stay with you."

But, as is well known, Spengrave succeeded in shooting himself while he was changing, with the gun which he kept in a drawer for precisely that contingency.

1950

The Thirteenth Knife

Bernard J. Farmer

Bernard James Farmer was born in Maidstone, Kent in 1902, and trained as an engineer. At age twenty-one, he set off for Canada, but an injury sustained while he was working on an engineering project there led to his being laid up in hospital; during his convalescence, he wrote a short story for the *Saturday Evening Post*; it won an award and set him on a fresh course as a writer, publishing a variety of short stories in magazines. In 1934, he returned to England; two years later he published a novel based on his experiences in Canada, *Go West, Young Man*. After the Second World War he joined the "J" branch of the Metropolitan Police Force and in later years he worked as a journalist, novelist, and short story writer. A keen bibliophile, he published *The Gentle Art of Book Collecting* in 1950 and is credited with producing the first bibliography of the writings of Winston Churchill.

Farmer published his first detective novel, *Death at the Cascades*, in 1953. This introduced a police constable called Wigan, who reappeared after a gap of three years in *Death of a*

Bookseller. This mystery, crammed with book lore, became the one hundredth book to appear in the British Library Crime Classics series in 2022. Farmer continued to write about Wigan, but declining health meant that his last published work appeared in 1960; he died four years later. "The Thirteenth Knife" is set, like so many of Farmer's early stories, in Canada. I am grateful to Jamie Sturgeon for directing my attention to the publication of the story in the *Gloucester Citizen* on 6 January 1950.

———

THERE WAS IN MONTREAL A NIGHT CLUB CALLED THE Cafe Rouge to which many tourists used to go. They went to dance, to dine; but most of all to watch the famous cabaret. And the greatest act in this cabaret was that of Simone, the knife-thrower.

"Messieurs et Mesdames"—Old Madame Motte, proprietor of the cafe had lungs of brass—"I now present to you the beautiful Mademoiselle Simone, who will outline a living target with knives. She will throw thirteen knives—"

Patrons always perked up interest at this. Some of them shuddered. To throw thirteen knives—it was tempting Providence. It was bound to be unlucky!

"And the thirteenth knife," concluded Madame on a high note, "will be the most dangerous knife of all. It will touch the head. It will cut through the hair of the living target, so close will it pass. I must ask for absolute silence; for a slight movement, a jerk of the head, may mean—death."

Needless to say, all were silent; and so far Jean La Morse, the name of the living target, had escaped injury, for he possessed the nerve to stand completely still. He had confidence in Simone. To him she was the most skilful knife-thrower in the world—she had been trained from a little girl by a master of the art—and more important still: she loved him. And what woman will be careless with the life of the man she loves?

If anyone ever came between them... But Jean would not think of this. Because she was so beautiful she was often besieged by admirers who wished to invite her to their tables for supper; and though for the good of the establishment (Madame Motte wished to sell the champagne) she would sometimes accept, Simone remained true to her lover.

Already he had saved sufficient to make a down-payment on one of a row of neat villas being built on the outskirts of the city. Soon he hoped to buy furniture. And when the nest was ready, then he would make Simone his wife.

But an evening came when an admirer of Simone's was more than usually determined. At the first meeting he made a proposal of marriage. Jean learned this later, and the name of the man, Monsieur Canew.

"But of course you refused him," said Jean to Simone.

"Of course. He is not, I think, a man who is used to being refused anything he desires."

Jean looked from the lovely face of Simone to a big gross figure about to leave the cafe. He was being escorted with all possible pomp by Madame and the head waiter. Jean had seen the vast car which awaited Monsieur Canew's pleasure: and a waiter, fingering a ten-dollar tip, had told of Monsieur Canew's great wealth and importance.

"So he wants a wife," muttered Jean. "Ten thousand devils, why must he pick on you?"

"I gave him no encouragement but for Madame's sake one must be polite. He ordered bottle after bottle of champagne..."

"You must not sup with him again," said Jean; and when next evening a waiter brought a message from Monsieur Canew to Mademoiselle Simone asking her to supper, Jean went himself to Monsieur Canew's table and said:

"Pardon, M'sieu. Mademoiselle Simone is my fiancee. It is right you should know."

The other stared at him.

"Women sometimes change their minds."

Jean could have struck him, but he had the good name of the establishment to think of. "That will not happen," he said hoarsely. "And Mademoiselle Simone regrets that she cannot take supper with you."

The big man replaced in his mouth the cigar he was smoking. Jean, gazing at him, waiting for him to speak, noted the coarse lips and thought: "Simone is right. He is used to being denied nothing. He owns the earth—at least in his own estimation!"

Deliberately Monsieur Canew expelled a cloud of smoke in Jean's face. Jean trembled with rage but he controlled himself. Madame—she was always on the side of the patrons, and he had the greatest possible reason for not losing a good job now. Another job suited to him would not be so easy to find. He turned and strode to his dressing room to change into the tight-fitting black clothes he wore for his act.

Monsieur Canew crooked his finger slightly, and his waiter came hurrying.

"M'sieu desires?"

"I will tell you," said the big man.

At length the performance of the thirteen knives was announced, Madame Motte adding as usual: "I must ask for the most complete silence. The slightest movement, a jerk of the head, may mean—death."

Jean took his stand against a white-painted board erected at one end of the room. Above him a spotlight of great power was turned on, heightening the dramatic effect.

Simone came from her dressing room, tall and lovely, wearing a dress of shimmering gold. She walked to a table placed at the farthest point possible from Jean, arranged the knives to be picked up two at a time, then waited, a glittering knife in each hand, holding them, as a professional knife-thrower does, by the tip.

The drummer of the band gave a roll, ending with a sharp tap. The conductor stood with his baton raised, commanding silence. Patrons, crowded round the sides of the room to give floor space down the middle, were still. A waiter, on his way to the kitchen entrance with a tray, turned and stood still. All was still.

"They don't take any chances," whispered someone.

"Or they've got nothing to learn about showmanship."

"Hush."

The conductor nodded to Simone. Jean stood like an image.

One, two—three, four—five, six—seven, eight... She sent the knives in pairs, throwing them high so that a terrifying pause ensued before they fell on the target, outlining Jean's figure, starting from the feet. It was an extraordinary exhibition of skill.

Nine, ten. His arms, tight to his side, were touched.

Eleven, twelve; his shoulders.

Thirteen. There was a terrible crash.

The audience jumped. A woman screamed. Heads jerked towards the kitchen entrance. The waiter standing near had dropped his tray loaded with bottles and glasses.

Then in a split-second heads jerked back to Jean. The thirteenth knife has reached its target. It had cut through his thick black hair, so close was it to his head. But he was not harmed, for he had not moved: no—not by a fraction of an inch!

Monsieur Canew, at the table of honour near Jean, stared at him as if he could hardly believe his eyes. For the timing of the crash had been perfect: just after the knife left Simone's hand. The young man who had looked at him with strained intentness, who had trembled so with rage, must have more cold inhuman nerve than seemed possible.

To make further attempt to murder him might land one in trouble. Monsieur Canew, who had built up his fortune by breaking the law only when it was reasonably safe to do so, decided not to risk it. As for Simone—he snapped his fingers. The waiter who had dropped the tray went to his table. The big man said one word: "L'addition"—the bill, paid it, and walked out.

"Calm, everybody, please—" Madame Motte's strident voice filled the room. "It was an accident. No one is hurt…"

Simone and Jean continued their act as if nothing had happened. Jean, after releasing himself from the outline of knives, threw playing-cards across the board for Simone to transfix.

Later, the waiter who had dropped the tray spoke to Simone: "You can guess who instructed me. I will give you half the thousand-dollar bribe I received. It is but fair. So the thirteenth knife has brought you luck."

"Yes," she answered, "and Jean. We can now have our home together."

The waiter smiled. "That is so. And the risk was not great. I did not tell M'sieu Canew everything. I did not tell him that Madame's words about complete silence are part of the show. And Jean must have deceived him when he spoke to him at the table. He can read the lips so well. Who is to know that he is stone-deaf?"

Drink for an Actor

John Appleby

John Appleby (1912–73) is perhaps the most obscure of all the contributors to this volume. I'm indebted to Jamie Sturgeon for drawing my attention to his work and for providing me with some information about his life. Appleby was born in Worcester and graduated in English from Leeds University, where he edited a magazine called *The Gryphon*. He became a reporter and worked in the News Division of the BBC. During the Second World War, he served in the Foreign Office and he travelled widely in the years prior to his death in Salisbury, Rhodesia.

J. I. M. Stewart, known to detective fiction fans by his pen-name Michael Innes, is generally associated with Oxford University, where he studied and lectured for many years. In the 1930s, however, Stewart spent several years teaching at Leeds University, and it seems that he knew John Appleby there. When he came to write his first Michael Innes detective novel, the name he chose for his Scotland Yard detective was—John Appleby. This is quite a claim to fame so far as the original Appleby is concerned, for his own detective fiction is now long-forgotten. This story first appeared in the *Evening Standard* on 4 September 1950.

———

THE CURTAIN WENT UP ON THE THIRD ACT AND revealed Mervyn Corinth pacing his study restlessly, the red of his smoking jacket a vivid glow against the dark furniture.

At the door of the study to the right a bulky figure appeared, muffled in a dark overcoat. Corinth swung round.

"Have you got it?" The bulky man spoke in a hoarse whisper.

Corinth's nervousness dropped from him like a cloak. He said easily, "My dear fellow, don't I always get what I want?"

He moved to the little square table at the rear of the stage, opened a drawer and pulled out a letter. Suspiciously the other crossed and took it. A slow smile came over his face.

"I thought you would be pleased," said Corinth. On the table was a decanter and on each side of it a balloon brandy glass, already charged. He took the nearer one and indicated the other. "A drink, I suggest, to mark our success."

They drank together and put down their glasses. Then Corinth behaved in a peculiar way, which in a matter of seconds became quite horrible. The other looked down at him in stupefaction. In the play Mervyn Corinth was not supposed to die.

In the manager's office Inspector Bristow flicked through the statements in front of him with a sigh.

"Plenty to go on, George."

Detective Sergeant Redding said, "Plenty, sir."

"Cyanide, for instance. None in the other glass and none in the decanter. Now who could have done that?"

"According to Miss Coate, quite a number of people."

"I think we might see her again, George."

Sheila Coate, the assistant stage manager, was slight, pretty in a demure way, and scared. Bristow said politely, "Will you tell us again what happens at the end of act two?"

Twisting her fingers she said breathlessly, "We strike the set—take down the scenery of the summerhouse and set up the study."

"Is that a long job?"

"Four or five minutes. The stagehands are experts. We've been running 50 nights now."

"And who sees to the bits and pieces, if you know what I mean—for instance, the brandy?"

She smiled timidly. "It's not brandy, of course, but brown sugar water. I see to that, as part of the property plot."

"Property plot?"

"The bits and pieces. I check before each act that the cast are carrying cigarettes or a handkerchief or a gun—whatever the action of the play calls for. It's the same with the set—cushions, or a lampshade, or drinks."

"Was there any departure from routine last night?"

"No." She pondered. "Towards the end of act two the table was in the wings. I put a glass on each side, poured out, and left the decanter in the middle. Then I put the letter in the drawer. When the curtain fell I carried it all on to the stage to its position." She looked at him anxiously. "Actually, as furniture, the table ought to be moved by a stagehand, but we find this way quicker."

"I won't tell the union," said the Inspector gravely. "Was anyone near the table before you took it on to the stage?"

"At the end of act two, three people come offstage at the side past the table. They are quite used to seeing it ready. And the stagehands were about all the time."

So, anyone could have monkeyed with the drink. Bristow asked, "Which three?"

"Mr. Corinth, Mr. Judd—Mr. Judd was on with him when—"

"Yes. And the other?"

"Miss Dailey, the lead. They all rushed past as they always do, because they have to make a quick change."

"Thank you."

They saw Judd next, a stoutish man of near middle age.

"You needn't answer this, Mr. Judd, but in your opinion was Mr. Corinth well-liked?"

"Liked? Don't make me laugh." He pulled himself up and went on warily. "I got on with him well enough. But he was a temperamental devil, like so many of them when they shoot to the top."

"He shot to the top, did he?"

"Since he came back from the war. A couple of films and a stage hit put him right on top of the heap. This play was helping, too. Some people can take it, some can't." He shrugged, and was dismissed.

Gloria Dailey had the lacquered look of one whose every public appearance may lead to a photograph in a shiny magazine. She was cool and composed and bored.

But in response to the inspector's cautious probing she became contemptuously forthright.

"I could give you half a dozen addresses of girls who are glad," she said. "Not that I will. Mervyn was that sort of swine. I almost fell for his line myself once, but I tumbled to him. If there's nothing else…" She uncrossed her elegant legs.

The stagehands had nothing useful to add, except to confirm Miss Coate's account of the drill backstage. Inspector Bristow sighed wearily.

In his office three days later he mulled over the results of patient police research.

"Corinth," he observed, "appears to have been all we were told and a bit more."

"Partly reaction from the war, sir," said Redding, who went in for psychology. "After five years in a German prison camp you want to throw your weight about a little. And he was able to. They were paying him the earth, and he doesn't seem to have had a bean."

"Anyone eliminated yet?"

"Not a one."

Gloomily Bristow agreed. He considered Judd. Judd, it was known, had at one time been unswervingly devoted to Gloria Dailey, and in a queenly way she had been gracious. But then Corinth came along and expertly swept her away from him.

Not that the new romance had lasted long. Evidently Miss

Dailey had been fibbing when she suggested the break came from her side, because it was established that it was Corinth who had shown her the gate. Charmingly, but firmly. In theatrical circles, which combine irrepressible gossip with a certain shrewdness, this was held to be a rash thing to do.

Especially when the new favourite was a timid mouse like Sheila Coate.

But little Miss Coate went the way of the others. Reason enough for action, if she was given to brooding.

"Some people," said Bristow mildly, "lead uncommonly untidy lives." He turned to another aspect of the case. "Why the hell can't we get a lead on the cyanide?"

"We're still checking," said Redding, "but so far there's not a trace."

"It isn't," said Bristow fretfully, "as though you could pick up prussic acid like a packet of crisps. Getting the stuff is apt to make you conspicuous. You can't hide the fact when you've got it."

"I don't know, sir," Redding grinned. "Goering did."

"Goering?" the inspector sat up suddenly. "Goering," he repeated softly. "He had a phial of prussic acid, hadn't he? Himmler too. It was standard equipment when the Nazis saw how the war was going."

The sergeant looked puzzled. "You mean Corinth may have committed suicide? I don't see that, sir."

"Not suicide. Far from that." Bristow explained, and the other listened in silence. When his chief had finished he said grimly, "I'll follow it up right away."

They sent for Judd two days later. He arrived sweating and sat uneasily at the other side of the table.

Bristow said, "Did you know that Mr. Corinth was a prisoner of war in Germany?"

"Everybody knew that, though he didn't talk about it."

"He didn't like it."

"I can't say I blame him."

"In fact, he hated it. So when the Nazis offered him a job he jumped at the chance. He took another name and broadcast for them."

Judd was startled. "How did you know that?"

"We've dug up some recordings. The point is, did you know it?"

"I certainly didn't. You astound me."

Bristow said gently: "I think you did. In spite of his high salary Corinth was perpetually broke. You were blackmailing him."

"You're talking nonsense." The voice was shrill.

"We've examined his banking account. The cheques are made out to 'bearer,' of course. But would you object, sir, if we looked at yours?"

Judd's hands fluttered. "You're investigating his death, aren't you? All right. If I were blackmailing him, why on earth should I want to kill him?"

Bristow glanced at his sergeant. "All ready?" The other nodded. "We'd like you to come to the theatre, Mr. Judd. I don't think you'll be bored."

The auditorium was in sheeted gloom, but stage lights showed the set as it remained when the curtain had come down so hurriedly. In the wings stood Gloria Dailey, tapping her foot impatiently, while Miss Coate hovered in uncertainty. Greetings were brief and taut.

"I wanted you to be here, all three," said the inspector, "because as you no doubt realise, all of you had an opportunity of tampering with the drink. Miss Coate, will you take the table from the stage to the exact position where it was before that?"

It was not heavy, and she carried it without effort into the wings.

"Now, please prepare it as you did the other night."

She looked round helplessly. "The glasses have gone. And the decanter."

The sergeant had made provision for this. He produced a couple of dirty teacups.

"We'll imagine the decanter," said Bristow. "Just carry on." He took an envelope from his pocket. "This will do for the letter."

Facing the unseen auditorium Miss Coate went through the motions. She slipped the letter in the drawer, placed a cup on either side of the table and poured into each an imaginary drink.

"Is that how you were accustomed to seeing it, Mr. Judd?"

He looked closely. "That's right. When we came off it was like that—a glass each side and the decanter in the middle."

"Miss Dailey?"

"As he says. I nearly fell over the damn thing every time I came off."

"Thank you. And now, Miss Coate, the curtain has come down. The players have dashed off to make their change."

She picked up the table and carefully carried it in front of her on to the stage, turned it and set it down in its place. Redding gave a soft whistle.

"You see, Mr. Judd?" said Bristow. But Judd, realisation and horror dawning, had slumped in a dead faint.

When he came round: "Corinth was sick of it," the inspector said. "Judd was sucking him dry and he had to be got rid of. The notion of killing him on stage no doubt had a strong appeal to a nature like his. And on the practical side, it was the only set-up which could throw suspicion equally on a number of people.

"He had the means to do it. Like so many of the Nazi stooges at the end of the war, Corinth carried a phial for emergencies. He never had to use it, but he kept it.

"And every night when he rushed off the stage at the end of act two, those two glasses were staring him in the face: his own this side, Judd's that.

"What he never saw was the table carried on to the stage. When Miss Coate arranged it she was facing the direction of the audience. But when she put it down, her *back* was to them.

"It had to be, so that the drawer with the letter faced front."

"And Corinth..." said Judd weakly.

"He knocked back the glass he intended for you."

Redding said thoughtfully: "So it *was* suicide. In a way."

"I think," said the inspector, "we'll let the legal boys sort that one out."

Credit to William Shakespeare

Julian Symons

Julian Symons (1912–94) was a versatile and gifted writer who began as a promising poet in the 1930s and ultimately became noted as a crime novelist and historian and critic of the genre. He wrote a number of plays for radio and television, and although I have not been able to trace any writing by him for the stage, the recurrence of masks as an ingredient and theme of his stories suggests an interest in play-acting as well as disguise and impersonation.

Symons's history of the crime genre, *Bloody Murder*, aka *Mortal Consequences*, was highly influential, although some enthusiasts of Golden Age detective fiction complained—and a number of them continue to complain—that he was unfair and disdainful towards the conventional whodunit. Patrick Cosgrove, reviewing the book in *The Spectator*, argued that it represented a "sustained and bitter, if unacknowledged, attack on the classical detective story." Symons pointed out in a letter of rebuttal that he had expressed admiration for various authors of traditional mysteries, including Agatha

Christie, Ellery Queen, and John Dickson Carr: "I think I have simply praised the wrong writers." Interestingly, many of his short stories—admittedly written for financial reasons—were in the traditional vein, featuring the private investigator Francis Quarles and often turning on a single, neat trick. "Credit to William Shakespeare" was first published in the *Evening Standard* on 13 December 1950.

———

"It won't do," said acidulous dramatic critic Edgar Burin to private detective Francis Quarles. "The fact is that this young producer's too clever by half. You can't play about with a masterpiece like *Hamlet*." Burin wrinkled his thin nose in distaste as the curtain rose on the Fifth Act.

This *Hamlet* first night was notable because the production was by a young man still in his twenties named Jack Golding, who had already obtained a reputation for eccentric but ingenious work. It was also notable because of the casting. Golding had chosen for his Hamlet a star of light comedy named Giles Shoreham. His Laertes, John Farrimond, had been given his part on the strength of Golding's intuition, since he had played only one walking-on part in the West End. Olivia Marston as the Queen and Roger Peters as the King were acknowledged Shakespearean actors, but their choice was remarkable in another sense. For the name of Olivia Marston, an impressive personality on the stage and a notorious one off it, had been linked by well-informed gossip with those of Peters, Farrimond, and even with Jack Golding himself. Those were rumours. It was certain, however, that

Olivia, a tall handsome woman in her forties, had been married a few weeks ago to Giles Shoreham who was fifteen years her junior.

This agreeably scandalous background was known to most of the first-night audience, who watched eagerly for signs of tension among the leading players. So far, however, they had been disappointed of anything more exciting than a tendency on the part of Giles Shoreham to fluff his lines. By the Fifth Act the audience had settled to the view that this was, after all, only another performance of *Hamlet*, marked by abrupt changes of mood from scene to scene, and by the producer's insistence on stressing the relationship between Hamlet and the Queen.

So the curtain rose on the Fifth Act. Golding had taken unusual liberties with the text, and Burin sucked in his breath with disapproval at the omission of the Second Gravedigger at the beginning of this scene. Giles Shoreham, slight and elegant, was playing now with eloquence and increased confidence. Then came the funeral procession for Ophelia and Hamlet's struggle with Laertes in Ophelia's grave. Here one or two members of the audience sat forward, thinking they discovered an unusual air of reality as Shoreham and Farrimond struggled together, while Roger Peters as the King restrained them and Olivia Marston looked on.

Shoreham, Quarles thought, had gained impressiveness as the play went on. With Osric now he was splendidly ironical, and in the opening of the duel scene he seemed to dominate the stage for all his slightness of stature compared with Farrimond's height and breadth of shoulder. This scene was played faster than usual, and Quarles vaguely noted cuts in the speeches before the duel began. There was Laertes choosing his poisoned foil, there was the poisoned cup brought in and placed on a side table. Then foils were flashing, Hamlet achieved a hit, took the cup to drink and put it down without doing so, with the speech "I'll play this bout first; set it by awhile." Then another hit, and the Queen came over to wipe Hamlet's brow, picked up the cup and drank. Laertes wounded Hamlet with his poisoned foil, and Hamlet snatched it from him and wounded Laertes. The Queen, with a cry, sank down as she was returning to the throne, and at once there was a bustle around her.

Osric and two attendants ran to her. The King moved upstage in her direction. "How does the Queen?" Hamlet asked, and the King made the appropriate reply, "She swoons to see them bleed." There was a pause. Should not the Queen reply? Quarles searched his memory while Burin grunted impatiently by his side. Hamlet repeated "How does the Queen?" and knelt down by her side. The pause this time was longer. Then Hamlet looked up, on his face an unforgettable expression of mingled anguish and irresolution. His lips moved, but he seemed unable to speak. When the words came they seemed almost ludicrous after the Shakespearean speech they had heard. "A doctor," he cried. "Is there a doctor?"

The other players looked at him in consternation. The curtain came down with a rush. Five minutes later Roger Peters appeared before it and told the curious audience that Miss Marston had met with a serious accident.

When Burin and Quarles came on to the stage the players were standing together in small, silent groups. Only Giles

Shoreham sat apart in his red court suit, head in hands. A man bending over Olivia Marston straightened up and greeted Quarles, who recognised him as the well-known pathologist, Sir Charles Palquist.

"She's dead," Palquist said, and his face was grave. "She took cyanide, and there's no doubt she drank it from that cup. Somebody knocked the cup over and it's empty now, but the smell of almonds is still plain enough."

"Now I wonder who did that?" Quarles said. But his meditation on that point was checked by the arrival of his old friend, brisk, grizzled Inspector Leeds. The Inspector had a wonderful capacity for marshalling facts. Like a dog snapping at the heels of so many sheep he now extracted a story from each of the actors on the stage, while Quarles stood by and listened.

When the Inspector had finished this was the result. The cup from which Olivia Marston had taken her fatal drink was filled with red wine and water. The cup had been standing ready in the wings for some time, and it would have been quite easy for anybody on the stage, or indeed anybody in the whole company, to drop poison into it unobserved.

As for what had happened on the stage the duel scene had been played absolutely to the script up to the point where Peters as the King said "She swoons to see them bleed." The Queen should then have replied to him, and her failure to do so was the reason for the very obvious pause that had occurred. Shoreham, as Hamlet, then improvised by repeating his question "How does the Queen?" and went on his knees to look at her, thinking that she felt unwell. But when he saw her face, half-turned to the floor, suffused and contorted, he knew that something was seriously wrong. Shoreham was then faced with a terrible problem. Clasping his hands nervously, white-faced, he said to the Inspector:

"I could have got up and gone on as though nothing had happened—after all, in the play the Queen was dead—and within ten minutes the play would have been over. That way we should have completed the performance." Shoreham's large eyes looked pleadingly round at the other members of the cast. "But I couldn't do it. I couldn't leave her lying there, I just couldn't."

"Since the poor lady was dead it didn't make any difference," said the Inspector in his nutmeg-grater voice. "Now, this lady became Mrs. Shoreham a few weeks ago, I believe? And she was, I imagine, a pretty wealthy woman?"

Giles Shoreham's head jerked up. "Do you mean to insinuate—?"

"I'm not insinuating, sir, merely stating a fact."

Quarles coughed. "I think, Inspector, that there may be other motives at work here." He took the Inspector aside and told him of the rumours that linked the names of Farrimond, Peters and Golding with Olivia Marston. The Inspector's face lengthened as he listened.

"But that means any of those three might have had reason to kill her."

"If they felt passionately enough about her—yes. Which would you pick?"

The Inspector's glance passed from Farrimond, big and sulky, to the assured, dignified, grey-haired Peters and on to the young producer Jack Golding, who looked odd in his lounge suit and thick horn-rimmed spectacles among this collection of Elizabethans. "I'm hanged if I know. It's like a three-card trick."

"May I ask one or two questions?" The Inspector assented. Quarles stepped forward. "A small point perhaps, gentlemen, but one I should like to clear up. The cup was found on its side with the liquid drained out of it. Who knocked it over?" There was silence. With something threatening behind his urbanity Quarles said: "Very well. Let us have individual denials. Mr. Shoreham?" Shoreham shook his head. "Mr. Farrimond?"

"Didn't touch the thing."

"Mr. Peters?"

"No."

"Any of you other gentlemen who were on the stage? Or did anyone see it done?" There was a murmur of denial. "Most interesting. Miss Marston replaced the cup on the table and then some unknown agency knocked it on to its side."

The Inspector was becoming impatient. "Can't see what you're getting at, Quarles. Do you mean she didn't drink out of it?"

Quarles shook his head. "Oh no, she drank from it, poor woman. Mr. Shoreham, did you know that you had some rivals in your wife's affections? And did she ever hint that any one of them was particularly angry when she decided to marry you?"

A wintry suggestion of a smile crossed Shoreham's pale face. "She once said she'd treated everybody badly except me and that one of these days she'd get into trouble. I thought she was joking."

"Mr. Golding." The producer started. "I am not a Shakespearean scholar, but I seem to have noticed more cuts in this *Hamlet* than are usually made."

"No," said Golding. The thickness of his spectacles effectively masked his expression. "*Hamlet* is very rarely played in full. I haven't made more cuts than usual, I've simply made different ones."

"In this particular scene, for instance, you've cut the passage early on where the King drinks and sends somebody across to Hamlet with the cup."

"That's right. It seems to me an unnecessary complication."

"What about the rest of the scene? Any cuts in that?"

"None at all. After what you saw we adhere to the standard printed version, speaking generally the second quarto."

Quarles bent his whole great body forward and said emphatically, "Doesn't that suggest something to you, Mr. Golding? Remember that the cup was knocked over and emptied. Do you understand?"

On Golding's face there was suddenly amazed comprehension. "I understand."

The Inspector had been listening with increasing irritation. "That's more than I do, then. What's all this got to do with the murder? Why the devil was that cup emptied?"

"*Because the murderer thought he would have to drink from it.* Remember what happens after the Queen dies, crying that her drink was poisoned. Laertes tells Hamlet that he has been the victim of treachery. Hamlet stabs the King. And what happens then, Mr. Peters?"

Roger Peters, truly kingly in his robes, was smiling. "Hamlet puts the poisoned cup to the King's mouth and forces him to drink."

"Correct. In fact Shoreham stopped the play before that point was reached. But the murderer couldn't be sure that

Shoreham's instinct as an actor wouldn't impel him to go on and say nothing. And then what would have happened? The King would also have had to drink from the poisoned cup. You couldn't risk that, could you, Mr. Peters?"

Peters's hand was at his mouth. "No. You are a clever man, Mr. Quarles."

"So there was only one person who would have had any motive for knocking over that cup."

"Only one person. But you are a little late, Mr. Quarles. I had two capsules. I swallowed the second thirty seconds ago. I don't think, anyway, that I would have wanted to live without Olivia." Peters's body seemed to crumple suddenly. Farrimond caught him as he fell.

"Well," said Burin, the dramatic critic, afterwards, "you had no evidence, Quarles, but that was a pretty piece of deduction."

"I was merely the interpreter," Quarles said mock-modestly. "The credit for spinning the plot and then unravelling it goes to someone much more famous."

"Who's that?"

"William Shakespeare."

1958

After the Event

Christianna Brand

Christianna Brand (1907–88) was by no means prolific as a detective writer, but the quality of her stories has assured her of a place in the history of the genre as a talented exponent of the classical mystery puzzle. She published her first novel just as the Golden Age of detective fiction was coming to an end. *Death in High Heels* (1941) introduced Inspector Charlesworth, who returned after an absence of thirty-eight years in *The Rose of Darkness* (1979). Much more recently, the novel was adapted for the stage by Richard Harris, a leading TV scriptwriter and playwright, and has been performed in theatres around Britain.

In the mid-1950s, Brand wrote a mystery play, "The Spotted Cat," which included in the cast her most popular detective, Inspector Cockrill. The play was never performed and although she considered turning it into a novel, "The Spotted Cat" did not see the light of day until Tony Medawar included it as the title story of a "Lost Classic" published by the American specialist press Crippen & Landru in 2002.

Brand's novels *Green for Danger* and *Death of Jezebel* are now enjoying a new life as British Library Crime Classics. This story first appeared in *Ellery Queen's Mystery Magazine* in 1958 under the title "Rabbit out of Hat."

———

"Yes, I think I may claim," said the Grand Old Man (of Detection) complacently, "that in all my career I never failed to solve a murder case. In the end," he added, hurriedly, having caught Inspector Cockrill's beady eye.

Inspector Cockrill had for the past hour found himself in the position of the small boy at a party who knows how the conjurer does his tricks. He suggested: "The *Othello* case?" and sat back and twiddled his thumbs.

"As in the *Othello* case," said the Great Detective, as though he had not been interrupted at all. "Which, as I say, I solved. In the end," he added again, looking defiantly at Inspector Cockrill.

"But too late?" suggested Cockie regretfully.

The great one bowed. "In as far as certain evidence had, shall we say?—faded—yes: too late. For the rest, I unmasked the murderer: I built up a water-tight case against him: and I duly saw him triumphantly brought to trial. In other words, I think I may fairly say—that I solved the case."

"Only, the jury failed to convict," said Inspector Cockrill.

He waved it aside with magnificence. A detail. "As it happened, yes; they failed to convict."

"And quite right too," said Cockie; he was having a splendid time.

"People round me were remarking, that second time I saw him play Othello," said the Great Detective, "that James Dragon had aged twenty years in as many days. And so he may well have done; for in the past three weeks he had played, night after night, to packed audiences—night after night strangling his new Desdemona, in the knowledge that his own wife had been so strangled but a few days before; and that every man Jack in the audience believed it was he who had strangled her—believed he was a murderer."

"Which, however, he was not," said Inspector Cockrill, and his bright elderly eyes shone with malicious glee.

"Which he was—and was not," said the old man heavily. He was something of an actor himself but he had not hitherto encountered the modern craze for audience-participation and he was not enjoying it at all. "If I might now be permitted to continue without interruption...?"

"Some of you may have seen James Dragon on the stage," said the old man, "though the company all migrated to Hollywood in the end. But none of you will have seen him as Othello— after that season. Dragon Productions dropped it from their repertoire. They were a great theatrical family—still are, come to that, though James and Leila, his sister, are the only ones left nowadays; and as for poor James—getting very *passé*, very *passé* indeed," said the Great Detective pityingly, shaking his senile head.

"But at the time of the murder, he was in his prime; not yet thirty and at the top of his form. And he was splendid. I see him now as I saw him that night, the very night she died—towering over her as she lay on the great stage bed, tricked out in his tremendous costume of black and gold, with the padded chest and shoulders concealing his slenderness and the great padded, jewel-studded sleeves like cantaloupe melons, raised above his head: bringing them down, slowly, slowly, until suddenly he swooped like a hawk and closed his dark-stained hands on her white throat. And I hear again Emilia's heart-break cry in the lovely Dragon family voice: 'Oh, thou hast killed the sweetest innocent, That e'er did lift up eye…'"

But she had not been an innocent—James Dragon's Desdemona, Glenda Croy, who was in fact his wife. She had been a thoroughly nasty piece of work. An aspiring young actress, she had blackmailed him into marriage for the sake of her career; and that had been all of a piece with her conduct throughout. A great theatrical family was extremely sensitive to blackmail even in those more easy-going days of the late nineteen-twenties; and in the first rush of the Dragons' spectacular rise to fame, there had been one or two unfortunate episodes, one of them even culminating in a—very short—prison sentence: which, however, had effectively been hushed up. By the time of the murder, the Dragons were a byword for a sort of magnificent untouchability. Glenda Croy, without ever unearthing more than a grubby little scandal here and there, could yet be the means of dragging them all back into the mud again.

James Dragon had been, in the classic manner, born—at the turn of the century—backstage of a provincial theatre: had lustily wailed from his property basket while Romeo whispered through the mazes of Juliet's ball-dance, "Just before curtain-up. Both doing splendidly. It's a boy!" had been carried on at the age of three weeks, and at the age of ten formed with his sister such a precious pair of prodigies that the parents gave up their own promising careers to devote themselves to the management of their children's affairs. By the time he married, Dragon Productions had three touring companies always on the road and a regular London Shakespeare season, with James Dragon and Leila, his sister, playing the leads. Till he married a wife.

From the day of his marriage, Glenda took over the leads. They fought against it, all of them, the family, the whole company, James himself: but Glenda used her blackmail with subtlety, little hints here, little threats there, and they were none of them proof against it—James Dragon was their "draw," with him they all stood or fell. So Leila stepped back and accepted second leads and for the good of them all, Arthur Dragon, the father, who produced for the company as well as being its manager did his honest best with the new recruit: and so got her through her Juliet (to a frankly mature Romeo), her Lady Macbeth, her Desdemona; and at the time of her death was breaking his heart rehearsing her Rosalind, preparatory to the company's first American tour.

Rosalind was Leila Dragon's pet part. "But, Dad, she's hopeless, we *can't* have her prancing her way across America grinning like a coy hyena: do speak to James again..."

"James can't do anything, my dear."

"Surely by this time... It's three years now, we were all so certain it wouldn't last a year."

"She knows where her bread is buttered," said the lady's father-in-law, sourly.

"But now, having played with *us*—she could strike out on her own?"

"Why should she want to? With us, she's safe—and she automatically plays our leads."

"If only she'd fall for some man…"

"She won't do that; she's far too canny," said Arthur Dragon. "That would be playing into our hands. And she's interested in nothing but getting on; she doesn't bother with men." And, oddly enough, after a pass or two, men did not bother with her.

A row blew up over the Rosalind part, which rose to its climax before the curtain went up on *Venice. A Street*, on the night that Glenda Croy died. It rumbled through odd moments offstage, and through the intervals, spilled over into hissed asides between Will Shakespeare's lines, and culminated in a threat spat out with the venom of a viper as she lay on the bed, with the great arms raised above her, ready to pounce and close hands about her throat. Something about "gaol." Something about "prisoners." Something about the American tour.

It was an angry and a badly frightened man who faced her, twenty minutes later, in her dressing-room. "What did you mean, Glenda, by what you said on-stage?—during the death scene. Gaolbirds, prisoners—what did you mean, what was it you said?"

She had thrown on a dressing-gown at his knock and now sat calmly on the divan, peeling off her stage stockings. "I meant that I am playing Rosalind in America. Or the company is not going to America."

"I don't see the connection," he said.

"You will," said Glenda.

"But, Glenda, be sensible, Rosalind just isn't your part."

"No," said Glenda. "It's dear Leila's part. But I am playing Rosalind—or the company is not going to America."

"Don't *you* want to go to America?"

"I can go any day I like. You can't. Without me, Dragon Productions stay home."

"I have accepted the American offer," he said steadily. "I am taking the company out. Come if you like—playing Celia."

She took off one stocking and tossed it over her shoulder, bent to slide the other down, over a round white knee. "No one is welcomed into America who has been a gaolbird," she said.

"Oh—that's it?" he said. "Well, if you mean me…" But he wavered. "There was a bit of nonsense… Good God, it was years ago… And anyway, it was all rubbish, a bit of bravado, we were all wild and silly in those days before the war…"

"Explain all that to the Americans," she said.

"I've no doubt I'd be able to," he said, still steadily. "If they ever found out, which I doubt they ever would." But his mind swung round on itself. "This is a new—mischief—of yours, Glenda. How did you find it out?"

"I came across a newspaper cutting." She gave a sort of involuntary glance back over her shoulder; it told him without words spoken that the paper was here in the room. He caught at her wrist. "Give that cutting to me!"

She did not even struggle to free her hand; just sat looking up at him with her insolent little smile. She was sure of herself. "Help yourself. It's in my handbag. But the information's still at the newspaper office, you know—and here in my head, facts, dates, all the rest of it. Plus any little embellishments I may care to add." He relaxed his grip and she freed her hand without effort and sat gently massaging the wrist. "It's wonderful," she said, "what lies people will believe, if you base them on a hard core of truth."

He called her a filthy name and, standing there, blind with his mounting disgust and fury, added filth to filth. She struck out at him then like a wild cat, slapping him violently across the face with the flat of her hand. At the sharp sting of the slap, his control gave way. He raised his arms above his head and brought them down—slowly, slowly with a menace infinitely terrible: and closed his hands about her throat and shook her like a rag doll—and flung her back on to the bed and started across the room in search of the paper. It was in her handbag as she had said. He took it and stuffed it into his pocket and went back and stood triumphantly over her.

And saw that she was dead.

"I had gone, as it happened, to a restaurant just across the street from the theatre," said the Great Detective; "and they got me there. She was lying on the couch, her arms flung over her head, the backs of her hands with their pointed nails brushing the floor; much as I had seen her, earlier in the evening, lying in a pretence of death. But she no longer wore Desdemona's elaborate robes, she wore only the rather solid undies of those days, cami-knickers and a petticoat, under a silk dressing-gown. She seemed to have put up very little struggle: though there was a red mark round her right wrist and a faint pink stain across the palm of her hand.

"Most of the company and the technicians I left for the moment to my assistants, and they proved later to have nothing of interest to tell us. The stage doorkeeper, however, an ancient retired actor, testified to having seen 'shadows against her lighted windows. Mr. James was in there with her. They were going through the strangling scene. Then the light went out: that's all I know.'

"'How did you know it was Mr. Dragon in there?'

"'Well, they were rehearsing the strangling scene,' the doorkeeper repeated, reasonably.

"'Now, however, you realise that she really was being strangled?'

"'Well, yes.' He looked troubled. The Dragon family in their affluence were good to old theatricals like himself.

"'Very well. Can you now say that you know it was Mr. Dragon?'

"'I thought it was. You see, he was speaking the lines.'

"'You mean, you heard his voice? You heard what he was saying?'

"'A word here and there. He raised his voice—just as he does on those lines in the production: the death lines, you know...' He looked hopeful. 'So it *was* just a run-through.'

"They were all sitting in what, I suppose, would be the Green-room: James Dragon himself, his father who, besides producing, played the small part of Othello's servant, the Clown; his mother who was wardrobe mistress, etcetera and had some little walking-on part, Leila Dragon who played Emilia, and three actors (who, for a wonder, weren't members of the family), playing respectively, Iago, Cassio and Cassio's mistress, Bianca. I think," said the Great Detective, beaming round the circle of eagerly listening faces, "that it will be less muddling to refer to them by their stage names."

"Do you really?" asked Inspector Cockrill: incredulous.

"Do I really what?"

"Think it will be less muddling?" said Cockie: and twiddled his thumbs again.

The great man ignored him. "They were in stage make-up, still, and in stage costume: and they sat about or stood, in attitudes of horror, grief, dismay or despair, which seemed to me very much like stage attitudes too.

"They gave me their story—I use the expression advisedly as you will see—of the past half-hour.

"The leading-lady's dressing-room at the Dragon Theatre juts out from the main building, so angled, as it happens, that the windows can be seen from the Green-room, as they can from the doorkeeper's cubby. As I talked, I myself could see my men moving about in there, silhouettes against the drawn blinds.

"They had been gathered, they said, the seven of them, here in the Green-room, for twenty minutes after the curtain came down—Othello, Othello's servant the Clown, Emilia and Mrs. Dragon (the family) plus Iago, Cassio and a young girl playing Bianca; all discussing 'something.' During the time, they said, nobody had left the room. Their eyes shifted to James Dragon and shifted away again.

"He seemed to feel the need to say something, anything to distract attention from that involuntary, shifting glance. He blurted out: 'And if you want to know what we were discussing, we were discussing my wife.'

"'She had been Carrying On,' said Mrs. Dragon in a voice of theatrical doom.

"'She had for some time been carrying on a love affair, as my mother says. We were afraid the affair would develop, would get out of hand, that she wouldn't want to come away on our American tour and it would upset our arrangements. We were taking out *As You Like It*. She was to have played Rosalind.'

"'And then?'

"'We heard footsteps along the corridor. Someone knocked at her door. We thought nothing of it till one of us glanced up and saw the shadows on her blind. There was a man with her in there. We supposed it was the lover.'

"'Who was this lover?' I asked. If such a man existed, I had better send out after him, on the offchance.

"But none of them, they said, knew who he was. 'She was too clever for that,' said Mrs. Dragon in her tragedy voice.

"'How could he have got into the theatre? The stage door-man didn't see him.'

"They did not know. No doubt there might have been some earlier arrangement between them...

"And not the only 'arrangement' that had been come to that night. They began a sort of point counterpoint recital which I could have sworn had been rehearsed. *Iago* (or it may have been Cassio): 'Then we saw that they were quarrelling...' *Emilia*: 'To our great satisfaction!' *Clown*: 'That would have solved all our problems, you see.' *Othello:* 'Not all our problems. It would not have solved mine.' *Emilia*, quoting: 'Was this fair paper, this most goodly book, Made to write "whore" upon...?' *Mrs. Dragon*: 'Leila, James, be careful' (sotto voce, and glancing at me). *Clown*, hastily as though to cover up: 'And then, sir, he seemed to pounce down upon her as far as, from the distorted shadows, we could see. A moment later he moved across the room and then suddenly the lights went out and we heard the sound of a window violently thrown up. My son, James, came to his senses first. He rushed out and we saw the lights come on again. We followed him. He was bending over her…'

"'She was dead,' said James; and struck an attitude against the Green-room mantelpiece, his dark-stained face heavy with grief, resting his forehead on his dark-stained hand. People said later, as I've told you, that he aged twenty years in as many days; I remember thinking at the time in fact he had aged twenty years in as many minutes: and that that was *not* an act.

"A window had been found swinging open, giving on to a narrow lane behind the theatre. I did not need to ask how the lover was supposed to have made his get-away. 'And all this time,' I said, 'none of you left the Green-room?'

"'No one,' they repeated: and this time were careful not to glance at James.

"You must appreciate," said the Great Detective, pouring himself another glass of port, "that I did not then know all I have explained to you. If I was to believe what I was told, I knew only this: that the door-keeper had seen a man strangling the woman, repeating the words of the Othello death-scene—which, however, amount largely to calling the lady a strumpet; that apparently the lady was a strumpet, in as far as she had been entertaining a lover; and that six people, of whom three were merely members of his company, agreed that they had seen the murder committed while James Dragon was sitting innocently in the room with them. I had to take the story of the lover at its face value: I could not then know,

as I knew later, that Glenda Croy had avoided such entan-
glements. But it raised, nevertheless, certain questions in my
mind." It was his custom to pause at this moment, smiling
benignly round on his audience, and invite them to guess
what those questions had been.

No one seemed very ready with suggestions. He was relaxing complacently in his chair, as also was his custom for no
one ever did offer suggestions, when, having civilly waited
for the laymen to speak first, Inspector Cockrill raised his
unwelcome voice. "You reflected no doubt that the lover was
really rather too good to be true. A 'murderer,' seen by seven
highly interested parties and by nobody else: whose existence,
however, could never be disproved; and who was so designed
as to throw no shadow of guilt on to any real man."

"It is always easy to be wise after the event," said the old
man huffily. Even that, however, Inspector Cockrill audibly
took leave to doubt. Their host asked somewhat hastily what
the great man had done next. The great man replied gloomily
that since his fellow guest, Inspector Cockrill, seemed so full
of ideas, perhaps he had better say what *he* would have done.

"Sent for the door-keeper and checked the stories together,"
said Cockie promptly.

This was (to his present chagrin) precisely what the Great
Detective had done. The stories, however, had proved to
coincide pretty exactly, to the moment when the light had
gone out. "Then I heard footsteps from the direction of the
Green-room, sir. About twenty minutes later, you arrived.
That's the first I knew she was dead."

So: what to do next?

"To ask oneself," said Inspector Cockrill, though the

question had been clearly rhetorical, "why there had been fifteen minutes' delay in sending for the police."

"Why should you think there had been fifteen minutes' delay?"

"The man said it was twenty minutes before you arrived. But you told us earlier, you were just across the street."

"No doubt," said the old man, crossly, "as you have guessed my question, you would like to—"

"Answer it," finished Inspector Cockrill. "Yes, certainly. The answer is: because the cast wanted time to change back into stage costume. We know they had changed out of it, or at least begun to change…"

"*I* knew it: the ladies were not properly laced up, Iago had on an everyday shirt under his doublet—they had all obviously hurriedly redressed and as hurriedly re-made up. But how could you…?"

"We could deduce it. Glenda Croy had had time to get back into her underclothes. The rest of them said they had been in the Green-room discussing the threat of her 'affair'. But the affair had been going on for some time, it couldn't have been suddenly so pressing that they need discuss it before they even got out of their stage-costume—which is, I take it, by instinct and training the first thing an actor does after curtain-fall. And besides, you *knew* that Othello, at least, had changed and changed back."

"I knew?"

"You believed it was Othello—that's to say James Dragon—who had been in the room with her. And the door-man had virtually told you that at that time he was not wearing his stage costume."

"I fear then that till this moment," said the great man, heavily sarcastic, "the door-man's statement to that effect has escaped me."

"Well, but…" Cockie was astonished. "You asked him how, having seen his silhouette on the window-blinds, he had 'known' it was James Dragon. And he answered, after reflection, that he knew by his voice and by what he was saying. He did not say," said Cockie, sweetly reasonable, "what otherwise, surely, he would have said before all else: 'I knew by the shape on the window-blind of the raised arms in those huge, padded, cantaloupe-melon sleeves.'"

There was a horrid little silence. The host started the port on its round again with a positive whizz, the guests pressed walnuts upon one another with abandon (hoarding the nut-crackers, however, to themselves); and, after all, it was a shame to be pulling the white rabbits all at once out of the conjurer's top hat, before he had come to them—if he ever got there! Inspector Cockrill tuned his voice to a winning respect. "So then, do tell us, sir—what next did you do?"

What the great man had done, standing there in the Green-room muttering to himself, had been to conduct a hurried review of the relevant times, in his own mind. "Ten-thirty, the curtain falls. Ten-fifty, having changed from their stage dress, they do or do not meet in here for a council of war. At any rate, by eleven o'clock the woman is dead: and then there is a council of war indeed… Ten minutes, perhaps, for frantic discussion, five or ten minutes' grace before they must all be in costume again, ready to receive the police…" But *why*? His eyes roved over them: the silks and velvets, the rounded bosoms thrust up by laced bodices, low cut:

the tight-stretched hose, the jewelled doublets, the melon sleeves…

The sleeves. He remembered the laxly curved hands hanging over the head of the divan, the pointed nails. There had been no evidence of a struggle, but one never knew. He said slowly: "May I ask now why all of you have replaced your stage dress and make-up?"

Was there, somewhere in the room, a sharp intake of breath? Perhaps: but for the most part they retained their stagey calm. Emilia and Iago, point counterpoint, again explained. They had all been halfway, as it were, between stage dress and day dress; it had been somehow simpler to scramble back into costume when the alarm arose… Apart from the effect of an act rehearsed, it rang with casual truth. "Except that you told me that 'when the alarm arose' you were all here in the Green-room, having a discussion."

"Yes, but only half-changed, changing as we talked," said Cassio, quickly. Stage people, he added, were not frightfully fussy about the conventional modesties.

"Very well. You will, however, oblige me by reverting to day dress now. But before you all do so…" He put his head out into the corridor and a couple of men moved in unobtrusively and stood just inside the door. "Mr. James Dragon—would you please remove those sleeves and let me see your wrists?"

It was the girl, Bianca, who cried out—on a note of terror: "No!"

"Hush, be quiet," said James Dragon: commandingly but soothingly.

"But James… But James, he thinks… It isn't true," she

cried out frantically, "it was the other man, we saw him in there, Mr. Dragon was in here with us…"

"Then Mr. Dragon will have no objection to showing me his arms."

"But why?" she cried out, violently. "How could his arms be…? He had that costume on, he did have it on, he was wearing it at the very moment he…" There was a sharp hiss from someone in the room and she stopped, appalled, her hand across her mouth. But she rushed on. "He hasn't changed, he's had on that costume, those sleeves, all the time: nothing could have happened to his wrists. Haven't you, James?—hasn't he, everyone?—we know, we all saw him, he was wearing it when he came back…"

There was that hiss of thrilled horror again: but Leila Dragon said, quickly, "When he came back from finding the body, she means," and went across and took the girl roughly by the arm. The girl opened her mouth and gave one piercing scream like the whistle of a train; and suddenly, losing control of herself, Leila Dragon slapped her once and once again across the face.

The effect was extraordinary. The scream broke short, petered out into a sort of yelp of terrified astonishment. Mrs. Dragon cried out sharply, "Oh, no!" and James Dragon said, "Leila, you *fool*!" They all stood staring, utterly in dismay. And Leila Dragon blurted out: "I'm sorry. I didn't mean to. It was because she screamed. It was—a sort of reaction, instinctive, a sort of reaction to hysteria…" She seemed to plead with them. It was curious that she seemed to plead with them, and not with the girl.

James Dragon broke through the ice-wall of their dismay.

He said uncertainly: "It's just that... We don't want to make—well, enemies of people," and the girl broke out wildly: "How dare you touch me? How dare you?"

It was as though an act which for a moment had broken down, reduced the cast to gagging, now received a cue from prompt corner and got going again. Leila Dragon said, "You were hysterical, you were losing control."

"How dare you?" screamed the girl. Her pretty face was waspish with spiteful rage. "All I've done is to try to protect him, like the rest of you..."

"Be quiet," said Mrs. Dragon, in The Voice.

"Let her say what she has to say," the detective said. She was silent. "Come now. 'He was wearing it when he came back'—the Othello costume. '*When he came back*.' From finding the body, Miss Leila Dragon now says. But he didn't 'come back'. You all followed him to the dressing-room—you said so."

She remained silent, however; and he could deal with her later—time was passing, clues were growing cold. "Very well then, Mr. Dragon, let us get on with it. I want to see your wrists and arms."

"But why me?" said James Dragon, almost petulantly; and once again there was that strange effect of an unreal act being staged for some set purpose: and once again the stark reality of a face grown all in a moment haggard and old beneath the dark stain of the Moor.

"It's not only you. I may come to the rest, in good time."

"But me first?"

"Get on with it, please," he said impatiently.

But when at last, fighting every inch of the way, with an ill grace he slowly divested himself of the great sleeves—there was nothing to be seen: nothing but a brown-stained hand whose colour ended abruptly at the wrist, giving place to forearms startlingly white against the brown—but innocent of scratches or marks of any kind.

"Nor did Iago, I may add in passing, nor did Cassio nor the Clown nor anyone else in the room, have marks of any kind on wrists or arms. So there I was—five minutes wasted and nothing to show for it."

"Well hardly," said Inspector Cockrill, passing walnuts to his neighbour.

"I beg your pardon? Did Mr. Cockrill say something again?"

"I just murmured that there was after all, something to show for it—for the five minutes wasted."

"?"

"Five minutes wasted," said Inspector Cockrill.

Five minutes wasted. Yes. They had been working for it, they were playing for time. Waiting for something. Or postponing something? "And of course, meanwhile, there had been the scene with the girl," said Cockie. "That wasn't a waste of time. That told you a lot. I mean—losing control and screaming out that he had been wearing Othello's costume 'at the very moment...' and, 'when he came back.' 'Losing control'—and yet what she screamed out contained at least one careful lie. Because he hadn't been wearing the costume—that we know for certain." And he added inconsequently that they had to remember all the time that these were acting folk.

But that had not been the end of the scene with the girl. As he perfunctorily examined her arms—for surely no woman had had any part in the murder—she had whispered to him that she wanted to speak to him: outside. And, darting looks of poison at them, holding her hand to her slapped face, she had gone out with him to the corridor. "I stood with her there while she talked," said the old man. "Her face, of course, was heavily made up; and yet under the make-up I could see the weal where Leila Dragon had slapped her. She was not hysterical now, she was cool and clear; but she was afraid and for the first time it seemed to be not at all an act, she seemed to be genuinely afraid, and afraid at what she was about to say to me. But she said it. It was a—solution: a suggestion of how the crime had been done; though she unsaid nothing that she had already said. I went back into the Green-room. They were all standing about, white-faced, looking at her as she followed me in; and with them, also, there seemed to be an air of genuine horror, genuine dread, as though the need for histrionics had passed. Leila Dragon was holding the wrist of her right hand in her left. I said to James Dragon: 'I think at this stage it would be best if you would come down to the station with me, for further questioning…'

"I expected an uproar and there was an uproar. More waste of time. But now, you see," said the old man, looking cunningly round the table, "I knew—didn't I? Waiting for something? Or postponing something? Now, you see, I knew."

"At any rate, you took him down to the station?" said Cockie, sickened by all this gratuitous mystificating. "On the strength of what the girl had suggested?"

"What that was is, of course, quite clear to you?"

"Well, of course," said Cockie.

"Of course, of course," said the old man angrily. He

shrugged. "At any rate—it served as an excuse. It meant that I could take him, and probably hold him there, on a reasonable suspicion: it did him out of the alibi, you see. So off he went, at last, with a couple of my men; and, after a moment, I followed. But before I went, I collected something—something from his dressing-room." Another of his moments had come; but this time he addressed himself only to Inspector Cockrill. "No doubt what that was is also clear to you?"

"Well, a pot of theatrical cleansing cream, I suppose," said Inspector Cockrill; almost apologetically.

The old man, as has been said, was something of an actor himself. He affected to give up. "As you know it so well, Inspector, you had better explain to our audience and save me my breath." He gave to the words "our audience" an ironic significance quite shattering in its effect; and hugged to himself a secret white rabbit to be sprung, to the undoing of this tiresome little man, when all seemed over, out of a secret top hat.

Inspector Cockrill in his turn affected surprise, affected diffidence, affected reluctant acceptance. "Oh, well, all right." He embarked upon it in his grumbling voice. "It was the slap across the girl, Bianca's, face. Our friend, no doubt, will tell you that he paid very little attention to whatever it was she said to him in the corridor." (A little more attention, he privately reflected, would have been to advantage; but still…) "He was looking, instead, at the weal on her face: glancing in through the door, perhaps, to where Leila Dragon sat unconsciously clasping her stinging right hand with her left. He was thinking of another hand he had recently seen, with a pink mark across the palm. He knew now, as he says.

He knew why they had been so appalled when, forgetting herself, she had slapped the girl's face: because it might suggest to his mind that there had been another such incident that night. He knew. He knew what they all had been waiting for, why they had been marking time. He knew why they had scrambled back into stage costume, they had done it so that there might be no particularity if James Dragon appeared in the dark make-up of Othello the Moor. They were waiting till under the stain, another stain should fade—the mark of Glenda Croy's hand across her murderer's cheek." He looked into the Great Detective's face. "I think that's the way your mind worked?"

The great one bowed. "Very neatly thought out. Very creditable." He shrugged. "Yes, that's how it was. So we took him down to the station and without more delay we cleaned the dark paint off his face. And under the stain—what do you think we found?"

"Nothing," said Inspector Cockrill.

"Exactly," said the old man, crossly.

"You can't have found anything; because, after all, he was free to play Othello for the next three weeks," said Cockie, simply. "You couldn't detain him—there was nothing to detain him on. The girl's story wasn't enough to stand alone, without the mark of the slap: and now, if it had ever been there, it had faded. Their delaying tactics had worked. You had to let him go."

"For the time being," said the old man. The rabbit had poked its ears above the rim of the hat and he poked them down again. "You no doubt will equally recall that at the end of three weeks, James Dragon was arrested and duly came up for trial?" Hand over hat, keeping the rabbit down, he gave his adversary a jab. "What do you suggest, sir, happened in the meantime?—to bring that change about."

Inspector Cockrill considered, his splendid head bowed over a couple of walnuts which he was trying to crack together. "I can only suggest that what happened, sir, was that you went to the theatre."

"To the theatre?"

"Well, to The Theatre," said Cockie. "To the Dragon Theatre. And there, for the second time, saw James Dragon play Othello."

"A great performance. A great performance," said the old man, uneasily. The rabbit had poked his whole head over the brim of the hat and was winking at the audience.

"Was it?" said Cockie. "The first time you saw him—yes. But that second time? I mean, you were telling us that people all around you were saying how much he had aged." But he stopped. "I beg your pardon, sir: I keep forgetting that this is your story."

It had been the old man's story—for years it had been his best story, the pet white rabbit out of the conjurer's mystery hat; and now it was spoilt by the horrid little boy who knew how the tricks were done. "That's all there is to it," he said sulkily. "She made this threat about exposing the prison sentence—as we learned later on. They all went back to their dressing-rooms and changed into everyday things. James Dragon, as soon as he was dressed, went round to his wife's room. Five minutes later, he assembled his principals in the Green-room: Glenda Croy was dead and he bore across his face the mark where she had hit him, just before she died.

"They were all in it together; with James Dragon, the company stood or fell. They agreed to protect him. They knew that from where he sat the door-keeper might well have seen the shadow-show on her dressing-room blinds, perhaps even the blow across the face. They knew that James Dragon must come under immediate suspicion; they knew that at all costs they must prevent anyone from seeing the mark of the blow. They could not estimate how long it would take for the mark to fade.

"You know what they did. They scrambled back into costume again, they made up their faces—and beneath the thick greasepaint they buried the fatal mark. I arrived. There was nothing for it now but to play for time.

"They played for time. They built up the story of the lover—who, in fact, eventually bore the burden of guilt, for as you know, no one was ever convicted: and he could never be disproved. But still only a few minutes had passed and now I was asking them to change back into day dress. James created a further delay in refusing to have his arms examined. Another few moments gone by. They gave the signal to the girl to go into her pre-arranged act."

He thought back across the long years. "It was a very good act: she's done well since but I don't suppose she ever excelled the act she put on that night. But she was battling against hopeless odds, poor girl. You see—I did know one thing by then; didn't I?"

"You knew they were playing for time," said Inspector Cockrill. "Or why should James Dragon have refused to show you his arms? There was nothing incriminating about his arms."

"Exactly: and so—I was wary of her. But she put up a good performance. It was easier for her, because of course by now she was really afraid: they were all afraid—afraid lest this desperate last step they were taking in their delaying action should prove to have been a step too far: lest they found their 'solution' was so good that they could not go back on it."

"This solution, however, of course you had already considered and dismissed?"

"Mr. Cockrill, no doubt, will be delighted to tell you what the solution was."

"If you like," said Mr. Cockrill. "But it *could* be only the one 'solution,' couldn't it? especially as you said that she stuck to what she'd earlier said. She'd given him an alibi—they'd all given him an alibi—for the time up to the moment the light went out. She dragged you out into the corridor and she said…"

"She said?"

"Well, nothing new," said Cockie. "She just—repeated, only with a special significance, something that someone else had said."

"The Clown, yes."

"When he was describing what they were supposed to have seen against the lighted blinds. He said that they saw the man pounce down upon the woman: that the light went out and they heard the noise of the window being thrown up. That James, his son, rushed out and that when they followed, he was bending over her. I suppose the girl repeated with direful significance: '*He was bending over her.*'"

"A ridiculous implication, of course."

"Of course," said Inspector Cockrill, readily. "If, which I

suppose was her proposition, the pounce had been a pounce of love, followed by an extinction of the lights, it seemed hardly likely that the gentleman concerned would immediately leave the lady and bound out of the nearest window—since she was reputedly complacent. But supposing that he had, supposing that the infuriated husband, rushing in and finding her thus deserted, had bent over and impulsively strangled her where, disappointed, she reclined—it is even less likely that his own father would have been the first to draw your attention to the fact. Why mention, 'he was bending over her'?"

"Precisely, excellent," said the old man: kindly patronisation was the only card left in the conjurer's hand.

"Her story had the desired effect, however?"

"It created further delay, before I demanded that they remove their make-up. It was beyond their dreams that I should create even more, myself, by taking James Dragon to the police station."

"You were justified," said Cockie, indulging in a little kindly patronisation on his own account. "Believing what you did. And having received that broad hint—which they certainly had never intended to give you—when Leila Dragon lost her head and slapped Bianca's face…"

"And then sat unconsciously holding her stinging hand."

"So you'd almost decided to have him charged. But it would be most convenient to do the whole thing tidily down at the station, cleaning him up and all…"

"We weren't a set of actor-fellows down there," said the old man defensively, though no one had accused him of anything. "We cleaned away the greasepaint enough to see that there was no mark of the blow. But I dare say we left him to do the rest—and I dare say he saw to it that a lot remained about the forehead and eyes... I remember thinking that he looked old and haggard, but under the circumstances that would not be surprising. And when at last I got back to the theatre, no doubt the same thing went on with 'Arthur' Dragon; perhaps I registered that he looked young for his years—but I have forgotten that." He sighed. "By then, of course, anyway, it was too late. The mark was gone." He sighed again. "A man of thirty with a red mark to conceal: and a man of fifty. The family likeness, the famous voice, both actors, both familiar with Othello, since the father had produced it: and both with perhaps the most effective disguises that fate could possibly have designed for them..."

"The Moor of Venice," said Inspector Cockrill.

"And—a Clown," said the Great Detective. The white rabbit leapt out of the hat and bowed right and left to the audience.

"Whether, as I say, he continued to play his son's part—on the stage as well as off," said the Great Detective, "I shall never know. But I think he did. I think they would hardly dare to change back before my very eyes. I think that, backed up by a loyal company, they played Cox and Box with me. I said to you earlier that while his audiences believed their Othello to be in fact a murderer—he was: and he was not. I think that Othello was a murderer; but I think that the wrong man was playing Othello's part."

"And you," said Inspector Cockrill, in a voice hushed with what doubtless was reverence, "went to see him play?"

"And heard someone say that he seemed to have aged twenty years… And so," said the Great Detective, "we brought him to trial, as you know. We had a case all right: the business about the prison sentence, of course, came to light; we did much to discredit the existence of any lover; we had the evidence of the stage door-keeper, the evidence of the company was not disinterested. But alas!—the one tangible clue, the mark of that slap, had long since gone: and there we were. I unmasked him; I built up a case against him: I brought him to trial. The jury failed to convict."

"And quite right too," said Inspector Cockrill.

"And quite right too," agreed the great man graciously. "A British jury is always right. Lack of concrete evidence, lack of unbiased witnesses, lack of demonstrable proof…"

"Lack of a murderer," said Inspector Cockrill.

"Are you suggesting," said the old man, after a little while, "that Arthur Dragon did not impersonate his son? And if so—will you permit me to ask, my dear fellow, who then impersonated who? Leila Dragon, perhaps, took her brother's place? She had personal grudges against Glenda Croy. And she was tall and well-built (the perfect Rosalind—a clue, my dear Inspector, after your own heart!) and he was slight, for a man. And of course she had the famous Dragon voice."

"She also had a 'well-rounded bosom,'" said Inspector Cockrill, "exposed, as you told us, by laced bodice and low-cut gown. She might have taken her brother's part: he can hardly have taken hers." And he asked, struggling with the two walnuts, why anybody should have impersonated anybody, anyway.

"But they were… But they all… But everything they said or

did was designed to draw attention to Othello, was designed to gain time while the mark was fading under the make-up of—"

"Of the Clown," said Inspector Cockrill: and his voice was as sharp as the crack of the walnuts suddenly giving way between his hard brown hands.

"It was indeed," said Inspector Cockrill, "'a frightened and angry man' who rushed round to her dressing-room that night: after his son had told him of the threat hissed out on the stage. 'Something about gaol… Something about prisoners…'" He said to the old man: "You did not make it clear that it was *Arthur* Dragon who had served a prison sentence, all those years ago."

"Didn't I?" said the old man. "Well, it made no difference. James Dragon was their star and their 'draw,' Arthur Dragon was their manager—without either, the company couldn't undertake the tour. But of course it was Arthur: who on earth could have thought otherwise?"

"No one," agreed Cockie. "He said as much to her in the dressing-room. 'If you're referring to me…' and, 'We were all wild and silly in those days before the war…' That was the 1914 war, of course: all this happened thirty years ago. But in the days before the 1914 war, James Dragon would have been a child: he was born at the turn of the century—far too young to be sent to prison, anyway.

"You would keep referring to these people by their stage names," said Cockie. "It was muddling. We came to think of the Clown as the Clown, and not as Arthur Dragon, James Dragon's father—and manager and producer for Dragon

Productions. 'I am taking the company to America... It was not for James Dragon to say that; he was their star, but his father was their manager, it was he who 'took' the company here or there... And, 'You can come if you like—playing Celia.' It was not for James Dragon to say that; it was for Arthur Dragon, their producer, to assign the parts to the company...

"It was the dressing-gown, I think, that started me off on it," said Inspector Cockrill, thoughtfully. "You see—as one of them said, the profession is not fussy about the conventional modesties. Would Glenda Croy's husband really have knocked?—rushing in there, mad with rage and anxiety, would he really have paused to knock politely at his wife's door? And she—would she really have waited to put on a dressing-gown over her ample petticoat, to receive him? For her father-in-law, perhaps, yes: we are speaking of many years ago. But for her husband...? Well, I wouldn't know. But it started me wondering.

"At any rate—he killed her. She could break up their tour, she could throw mud at their great name: and he had everything to lose, an ageing actor who had given up his own career for the company. He killed her; and a devoted family and loyal, and 'not disinterested' company, hatched up a plot to save him from the consequences of what none of them greatly deplored. We made our mistake, I think," said Cockie, handsomely including himself in the mistake, "in supposing that it would be an elaborate plot. It wasn't. These people were actors and not used to writing their own plots: it was in fact an incredibly simple plot. 'Let's all put on our greasepaint again and create as much delay as possible while, under the

Clown make-up, the red mark fades. And the best way to draw attention from the Clown, will be to draw it towards Othello.' No doubt they will have added civilly, 'James—is that all right with you?'

"And so," said Inspector Cockrill, "we come back again to James Dragon. Within the past hour he had had a somewhat difficult time. Within the past hour his company had been gravely threatened and by the treachery of his own wife; within the past hour his wife had been strangled and his father had become a self-confessed murderer… And now he was to act, without rehearsal and without lines, a part which might yet bring him to the Old Bailey and under sentence of death. It was no wonder, perhaps, that when the greasepaint was wiped away from his face that night, our friend thought he seemed to have aged…" If, he added, their friend really had thought so at the time and was not now being wise after the event.

He was able to make this addition because their friend had just got up and, with a murmured excuse, had left the room. In search of a white rabbit, perhaps?

If you've enjoyed *Final Acts*,
you won't want to miss

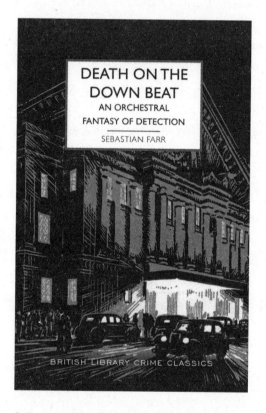

the most recent BRITISH LIBRARY CRIME CLASSIC
published by Poisoned Pen Press,
an imprint of Sourcebooks.

Don't miss these favorite British Library Crime Classics available from Poisoned Pen Press!

*Mysteries written during the
Golden Age of Detective Fiction, beloved by readers and reviewers*

Antidote to Venom
by Freeman Wills Crofts

Bats in the Belfry
by E. C. R. Lorac

*Blood on the Tracks:
Railway Mysteries*
edited by Martin Edwards

Calamity in Kent
by John Rowland

*Christmas Card Crime
and Other Stories*
edited by Martin Edwards

Cornish Coast Murder
by John Bude

Continental Crimes
edited by Martin Edwards

Crimson Snow: Winter Mysteries
edited by Martin Edwards

Death in the Tunnel
by Miles Burton

Death of a Busybody
by George Bellairs

Death on the Riviera
by John Bude

Fell Murder
by E. C. R. Lorac

Incredible Crime
by Lois Austen-Leigh

Miraculous Mysteries
edited by Martin Edwards

Murder at the Manor
edited by Martin Edwards

Murder in the Museum
by John Rowland

Murder of a Lady
by Anthony Wynne

Praise for the
British Library Crime Classics

"Carr is at the top of his game in this taut whodunit... The British Library Crime Classics series has unearthed another worthy golden age puzzle."

—*Publishers Weekly*, STARRED Review,
for *The Lost Gallows*

"A wonderful rediscovery."
—*Booklist*, STARRED Review, for *The Sussex Downs Murder*

"First-rate mystery and an engrossing view into a vanished world."
—*Booklist*, STARRED Review, for *Death of an Airman*

"A cunningly concocted locked-room mystery, a staple of Golden Age detective fiction."
—*Booklist*, STARRED Review, for *Murder of a Lady*

"The book is both utterly of its time and utterly ahead of it."
—*New York Times Book Review* for *The Notting Hill Mystery*

"As with the best of such compilations, readers of classic mysteries will relish discovering unfamiliar authors, along with old favorites such as Arthur Conan Doyle and G.K. Chesterton."
—*Publishers Weekly*, STARRED Review, for *Continental Crimes*

"In this imaginative anthology, Edwards—president of Britain's Detection Club—has gathered together overlooked criminous gems."

—*Washington Post* for *Crimson Snow*

"The degree of suspense Crofts achieves by showing the growing obsession and planning is worthy of Hitchcock. Another first-rate reissue from the British Library Crime Classics series."

—*Booklist*, STARRED Review, for *The 12.30 from Croydon*

"Not only is this a first-rate puzzler, but Crofts's outrage over the financial firm's betrayal of the public trust should resonate with today's readers."

—*Booklist*, STARRED Review, for *Mystery in the Channel*

"This reissue exemplifies the mission of the British Library Crime Classics series in making an outstanding and original mystery accessible to a modern audience."

—*Publishers Weekly*, STARRED Review, for *Excellent Intentions*

"A book to delight every puzzle-suspense enthusiast."

—*New York Times* for *The Colour of Murder*

"Edwards's outstanding third winter-themed anthology showcases 11 uniformly clever and entertaining stories, mostly from lesser known authors, providing further evidence of the editor's expertise...This entry in the British Library Crime Classics series will be a welcome holiday gift for fans of the golden age of detection."

—*Publishers Weekly*, STARRED Review, for *The Christmas Card Crime and Other Stories*

poisonedpenpress.com